DRISCOLL

by

Jolin Malanski

Grosvenor House
Publishing Limited

Jolin Malanski is hereby identified as author of this
work in accordance with Section 77 of the Copyright, Designs
and Patents Act 1988

The book cover picture is copyright to Inmagine Corp LLC

This book is published by
Grosvenor House Publishing Ltd
28-30 High Street, Guildford, Surrey, GU1 3HY.
www.grosvenorhousepublishing.co.uk

A CIP record for this book
is available from the British Library

ISBN 978-1-908447-51-7

For Mum

Dear Bunty & John,

Finally Bessie is back, and an awful lot is about to happen to her, so I hope the book does not prove to be an exhausting read!

With Love & Best Wishes,

Victoria.

Chapter One

The hall looked the same as ever, but felt so very different. Arnold's butler was standing there, and Bessie nodded a greeting as she advanced towards the double doors. On any ordinary day she would knock, but her new-found sense of conviction imbued her with a desire to make a somewhat more dramatic entrance. With fingers poised above the handle, she feared that a bolt of doubt would surge to the fore, denting her resolve at this very last minute, but thankfully it held off, and she waltzed into the dining room.

Arnold was at the head of the table, Thomas to his right, Charles and Harris opposite, and her own place was set. As expected, the first course had already been served.

'You're late,' declared the Master of the house.

'I know,' she replied, wishing to avoid any expression of regret, but then deciding that perhaps something a bit more polite was required. 'My apologies,' she added, and walked forward.

Thomas was staring at her. She could feel it. She could feel the rapid beating of his heart.

'I've come to a decision.'

'We are eating,' growled Arnold.

'But . . .' She was well aware that family-only meals were conducted in silence, but he had already broken that rule himself, and she had thought that today might prove an exception to the rule. 'Surely you want to know?'

'We are eating,' he repeated, and Bessie did the only thing she could – and sat down.

The next hour and a quarter could only be described as torturous. Bessie was left trying to eat, trying to calm herself, searching for some cryptic way to convey the decision to Thomas, and battling an atmosphere that was heavy to say the least.

Charles was giving her the evil eye, clearly outraged that his father had even *considered* proposing to a maid, and not at all enamoured with this idea of having a stepmother his own age. Harris was a nervous wreck, wondering what was going to happen next. Thomas was understandably on edge. While Arnold was cold and in control, confident of her decision, or confident of the joy at her dispatch should it go the wrong way.

But it was not about to go the wrong way. She was ready to accept him – on the surface that is – and then plot with Thomas when to take flight. She was running away with the man that she loved, and the niece she adored, and forgetting everybody else. Leaving the past behind. Leaving Josiah, and the Whitsons, and the mill workers. Her actions had caused havoc, then fixing them had caused even more havoc, and now she was abandoning them all to their fate. It was selfish – and probably stupid with Arnold on their tail, but there was nothing else to be done. As soon as she had asked the question: "Who shall I miss most?" she had known that her choice was only limited to option three – stay with Thomas *and* Ella. She could not lose one, and keep the other. It was as simple as that.

The main course was cleared, dessert served, and Bessie had increasing difficulty in swallowing even a morsel. It was not just the excitement and trepidation, it was the fact that her head was so very hot. She asked for a glass of water, but Arnold stuck to his guns, and refused to utter another sound. She then turned to Thomas, hoping that at least her request might have sent a message to him. Water – Sea – Travelling over the sea – Possibly to the New World – New Life. But as he stared at her, his eyes were vacant and beseeching, and she knew that nothing had made it through.

Taking a sip of wine, she found that it helped, so took a few more. Sober composure was needed for a situation like this, but one glass would not hurt. And it was not as if she was in danger of appearing excessive. Harris had already polished off his third. She wondered why Arnold did not have a word with him about the drinking, but did not wonder for long. Thomas was the heir – although currently out of favour; Charles was the spare; and Harris was kind of . . . pointless. She felt sorry for him. Truly sorry. Especially as he was soon to be here with Arnold and Charles alone.

Just when she was reflecting on how loud a silence could be, Arnold deigned to open his mouth for something other than the input of food, and frightened the life out of her as usual.

'So what is your decision then?'

Bessie twisted her shoulders towards him, and placed both hands upon her lap – fingers crossed, to leave Thomas in no doubt that what she was about to say had no basis in truth whatsoever.

'I want to thank you for the advantages that you have bestowed upon me since coming to Bateford Hall. My promotion to governess, my admittance to the family table, and now your kind offer.'

She paused. There was such a strong impulse imploring her to say: "But I wouldn't let you touch me if

3

you were the last man on earth. My heart belongs to Thomas. We're going to be together – destitute or otherwise. Oh and by the way, you're about to have a Cullen for a daughter-in-law". But common sense prevailed. Leaving him at the altar would hurt so much more. The total and utter humiliation. In front of all those friends and acquaintances. It was just a pity that she would not be around to see it.

'*Well?*' growled Charles.

'I've decided to . . . accept.' She had been preparing to add "gratefully", but that really would be pushing it too far.

The look which spread across Arnold's face was a mixture of smile, smirk, and leer. It had been firmly in evidence at the proposal, but something extra had now been added. If there were any lingering doubts about what she was doing, then that look banished them all. It would be there on their wedding-day, when the guests had left, and the bedroom door closed behind them. She almost shuddered, and before she could draw her eyes away, Thomas had stalked from the room.

Arnold straightened his waistcoat with satisfaction, and Bessie also found herself glad to see Thomas go. He would be up in his room waiting for her, so all she had to do now was excuse herself, and they could begin to make plans. But excusing herself proved to be something of an impossibility. Arnold was in the mood to establish plans of his own.

His fiftieth birthday was coming up on Friday, and the wedding-breakfast would be a double celebration. April the nineteenth 1839. Five days time. The invitations would be sent out tomorrow, and there was no question that everybody would attend. Short notice or not, this was going to set some tongues a-wagging.

Arnold then announced that the church service would be for family members only, which dispirited Bessie for a moment. Nobody would be in the pews to witness her failure to appear. Although of course Arnold would have to present himself at the wedding-breakfast without a bride, and that would be revenge enough. Before he could move on, she quickly explained that her uncle was ill, so nobody from Thurleigh would be able to make it. She tried to appear disappointed, and yet relaxed at the same time – for fear of awkward questions. But none emerged. All that interested Arnold was owning her as soon as possible, and his brother-in-law could step into the breech to give her away.

Charles was then told that he would be chief grooomsman, but this prominent elevation did nothing to lessen the anger. He was furious. In fact you could almost see steam coming out of his ears as Arnold moved onto a detailed discussion of the celebrations, and the preparations required to make them memorable.

Most of it drifted straight over Bessie's head – although not deliberately. She wanted to absorb every detail, share it with Thomas, and reflect on what had been left in their wake, but her brain simply refused to concentrate. Harris even ended up asking if she was alright, which was quite marvellous in front of his father and brother. It was probably the drink that had given him the courage, but she appreciated it nevertheless, and answered in the affirmative – although thankfully Arnold was not convinced:

'No, you're looking rather flushed. I suggest you get some sleep. I won't have you falling ill on Friday.'

'Of course not,' she agreed, and left the room with unladylike speed, desperate to join her real husband-to-be.

Once on the landing, however, she had to resist the urge to rush immediately into his arms. Any impetuous behaviour at this stage could ruin everything, so instead she looked in on Ella, and again felt that unease at the prospect of removing the little girl from this comfortable room in this comfortable house. Where exactly would they be sleeping this time next week? And who would be caring for Ella? Bessie was well aware that they would need two wages to afford a small place, and put food on the table, but hopefully that situation would only be temporary. In exactly fifteen months, Wilf Cullen would be released from prison – all being well – and Marge might soften a little with her husband's return. Luke could also appear by some miracle, and so an extended family might well be established, with plenty of people on hand to help. It would all sort itself out. As long as you had your loved ones around you, and relatively good health, then anything in this world was possible.

Gently closing the nursery door, she entered her own room, stowed the work dress in the safest place she could find, and waited for Arnold to retire. Surely there could not be much more to say? But she was wrong. Ten minutes turned into twenty, and then forty, and Bessie sighed. Why was he determined to be obstructive to the very end? Kicking her shoes off, she propped a pillow against the head-board, and rested her eyes. There was no danger of missing Arnold's ascent – the heavy footsteps, followed by that bang of his bedroom door. He never made any effort to be quiet, and today was no exception. Although Bessie did not hear it. Nor did she hear Harris, nor Charles, nor the hooting of the night. In fact she heard absolutely nothing until the Tawny Owl had returned to his nest, and the dawn chorus had begun.

She opened her eyes, and at first she could not see, but then the bleariness cleared and she thought that she had dozed for only a few minutes – until it hit her that the birds had twittered their way to bed during dinner. So if they were twittering again, that meant only one thing.

Swinging her legs off the mattress, she lurched towards the door. What on earth must Thomas be thinking? How could she have fallen asleep on a night like this? She hurried along the landing, oblivious to the need to creep, and entered his room without warning.

He was not there.

Even though it was dim, she could tell that there was no outline of his head on the pillow. She moved forward and felt the bedding anyway, as if somehow he might be hiding near the bottom, but the sheets were cold and had not been disturbed. He must be in the nursery instead, watching over their niece. She walked back past the other doors, quieter this time, but all she found was Ella sleeping peacefully.

Downstairs! That was it. Thomas was waiting down below, where they could talk so much more freely. Within the minute she was checking the rooms, but still no sign. It did not make any sense. Could he possibly be outside? Packed and ready to go? She returned to his room, but his wardrobe was as full as that day last October, when she had been thrust in there to evade Charles. If only she had understood her feelings back then – because they had been there, deep down. But she had admitted to them eventually, and that was all that really mattered.

She sank onto the side of Thomas' bed, and put his pillow to her face. It was strong and yet soft at the same time – just like he had always been, and lovely and cool too. Her body was shivering, but her head was still hot, and presumably he was the same. The fever of excitement – there was nothing like it. Yes, he was outside, enjoying the refreshing night air, and she would share in it with him.

Racing down the stairs and through the front door, Bessie did two circuits of the house before moving onto the wood.

'Thomas. Thomas!' she cried, nearing their special clearing and twisting her head around in every direction until it was like the oak trees had broken from their roots to dance all around her. Where had he gone? She could not understand it. Had she checked everywhere thoroughly enough?

No! The sofa in the study. She had merely opened the door, nothing more. Careering back through the wood, her bare feet tripping over new spring shoots, she staggered on until standing in front of that sofa. But it was devoid of life. Just like her heart was beginning to feel utterly devoid of hope. He could not possibly have thought. . ? No, surely not. He must have realised what she was doing, that she would come to him in the end.

She set off again down the back stairs. The staff quarters were just as much a part of the house as anywhere else – and they were also very dark. She fell into what was presumably the kitchen table, but did not feel anything as she dropped to the accompanying clatter of plates. It was not until a light shone in her eyes that she attempted to stand up. 'Thomas? Is that you?'

'Miss? Miss!'

'Thomas?'

Duncan stared down at the governess in alarm, and quickly sped towards the cook's door, rapping repeatedly until it opened with a snappy flourish.

'What the blazes is going on?' She was not due to wake up for another hour yet, and when you worked for a living, every hour in bed was very precious indeed.

'It's Miss Arabrook.'

'What about her?' There was already some concern replacing the irritation. She had developed quite a fondness for Elizabeth over the last few weeks.

'She's in the kitchen, and I can't seem to get any sense out of her.'

'What do you mean – sense?' Mrs Evans pushed Duncan back along the corridor, and the answer to her question soon became apparent. Tapping Elizabeth on the face and arms, she then did it again a little harder, but there was no useful response. Nothing except incoherent mumbles from a head that kept lolling to the side.

'Do you think she's got the palsy?' suggested Duncan. 'Or scarlet fever? Her skin looks awfully red.' He stepped back.

'I don't know what she's got, but we need to get her upstairs, back to bed.'

Duncan held off, but Mrs Evans was not about to let any silliness impede her suggestion.

'If she's been struck by the scarlatina, then it's too late to be bothered by it now. Come on.' And Duncan reluctantly obeyed.

They took their own stairs through force of habit, but the narrow spiral was impossible to navigate with three abreast, so Duncan ended up doing all the carrying by himself, while Mrs Evans effectively steered from behind.

'Which room is hers?' he panted when they were almost at the top.

'One at the far end I think,' and soon they were opening the correct door. 'Yes. Those are her shoes. Now put her down on the bed.'

Duncan gratefully did as he was told this time, and immediately retreated.

'Go and raise Mr Bateford. Tell him Miss Arabrook is unwell, and may need a doctor.'

'What? Me?'

'Yes, you! And I'll get a damp cloth.'

'But . . .' Duncan did not need to say any words. The fear of disturbing Arnold Bateford at this hour was etched all over his face.

'Look – just do it, or rouse the butler and get him to do it, but DO IT!'

Duncan shot off, debating which was the lesser of the two evils, but did not debate for very long. Bellamy Jones might be a miserable old coot, but he was better than Bateford.

A couple of hours later, the butler had raised the Master, who had sent for the physician, and they were all standing at Elizabeth's bedside – staring down on a patient who was now quiet and unconscious.

'It doesn't look like the consumption or typhoid,' observed Doctor Stanbury with a certain level of conviction.

'What about influenza?'

'Possible. Has she been out when it's especially bleak recently? Or got herself wet through, and not dried out properly?'

'I don't know. She was away this last weekend.'

'Well it looks to me like the classic symptoms of a chill, but only time will tell.'

'How much time?' demanded Arnold.

'A couple of days I should say. If it's just a chill, and you follow my directions, then the fever ought to break within forty-eight hours.'

'So can she be up and about by Friday?'

'Probably, if she takes things steady.'

'Good. Because we're due to be married.'

'Married?' The doctor had encountered a fair few surprises over the years, but never a declaration quite like that.

'Yes.' Arnold turned to his butler. 'Prepare as instructed. There'll be no delay.' He turned back to the bed, and stared down at Elizabeth. She was tucked under the bedclothes, but that perfectly-formed frame was still visible through the sheets. 'She'll be walking down the aisle on Friday, Doctor Stanbury. You and I will make damn sure of it.'

CHAPTER TWO

By the time Bessie woke properly, it was Wednesday lunchtime, and most of those invited had already sent a response. As Arnold had anticipated, everybody was eager to come and watch the spectacle, but Bessie did not care who was coming. She knew who would not be there, and that was her only preoccupation. Nobody had seen hide nor hair of Thomas since Sunday evening. He had not been back to collect any clothes; he had not sent a message. He had simply vanished into thin air – much to Arnold's disappointment. The Master of Bateford Hall had wanted to see the look on his son's face as he returned from church with Elizabeth as his bride.

Bessie spent most of Wednesday afternoon, and much of the night, wondering how she could have got it all so wrong. No matter how late she had been, she should have kept hanging around outside until dinner was over, and then spoken to Thomas alone before making any declaration. It was not as if Arnold were likely to say: "You're two hours late. The offer's off the table". And if she *had* entered the dining room, it should have been with a much better idea of how to convey her thoughts secretly. Crossed fingers on the lap – how was Thomas supposed to decipher that? Or indeed even notice it in the first place? Then when she announced her decision in the wrong way, she had compounded the stupidity by falling asleep. Yes it was because of the chill, but Thomas did not know that. All he had heard was the sound of her bedroom door closing – and never opening again.

She was sure that he had been in the house at that stage. If he had left before, she would have sensed it. So even then she could have averted disaster if only she had weathered the fever. A fever that had only taken hold because of her insanity in another sphere. Maybe this was her just deserts. She had made so many mindless mistakes over the last two years, rushing in without due care and attention, and was now suffering the consequences as a result. But the same could not be said for the upcoming event on Friday. As far as that was concerned, she had plenty of hours to think.

The wedding was set for noon, and at any point before then, she could run away with Ella. A whole host of options were once more in play, and of course there was always the chance that she might find Thomas. He was out there somewhere. But the question was where? Was he desperate to get as far away from her as possible? With a two-day headstart, he could be at the other end of the country by now, but did he have the money for that? Or the inclination? So many questions, and so few answers.

Arnold paid her a visit on the Thursday morning, and expressed his satisfaction at her recovery. A wedding-dress would be arriving from Anderby's later in the day, and Mrs Muir would make sure that it was brought up.

'What about Ella's dress?' asked Bessie, before quickly correcting herself, and using the name Isabel.

'She will not be at the service,' he replied, smug ripple to his lips. 'She will be waiting here for our return.'

The inference was clear. Should any last-minute doubts arise, Elizabeth would be fleeing from "Ella" as well as from him.

A few more details followed, including confirmation of the time when she would need to be ready. And then he left – formalities complete, and no apparent need for pleasantries in their final conversation before meeting at the altar.

Bessie sat there, staring into space, with a vivid sense of having experienced all this before. In that cell at the courthouse, she had been presented with fresh clothing, and told about her trial the following morning – made fully aware that she should prepare to accept the punishment she deserved. Only instead of prison with its typhus, drunken women, and screaming children, there was Arnold and a bedroom – and in that one regard, the former was not a patch on the latter.

It was several hours before the wedding-dress appeared, and Bessie was still in exactly the same position, trying hard to imagine that this was not really happening to her. Maybe if she kept her feet off the floor, and did not look in the mirror, time might actually stand still, and the day might never arrive. Of course this particular fantasy was smashed to pieces by the sight of Mrs Muir unceremoniously dumping a dress at the end of the bed, and then scanning the scene with disdain.

'You don't like me very much, do you?' observed Bessie, which only aggravated the housekeeper even more.

'I do not like people lounging about when there is no longer any need,' came the impertinent retort, when Ida Muir wanted to scream: "Yes I hate you! I hate the fact that I'm the one who allowed you to come here, and within six months you've gone from maid to governess to mistress of the house. I hate the fact that from tomorrow I'm going to have to bow and scrape at your command, and pretend to like it. And most of all I hate the fact that this chill of yours didn't kill you!"

'Don't worry,' said Bessie calmly. 'I won't be lounging about for much longer. As you well know.'

Mrs Muir adjusted her sleeves, and grudgingly announced: 'If you need any help in the morning, Agatha will be on hand.'

'Isn't she looking after Isabel?'

'Yes, so she'll have to do both.'

'But I don't want her doing both. I want Tess and Constance to be made available.' Bessie stared at the housekeeper, challenging her to refuse.

'You are not entitled to issue me with orders just yet Miss Arabrook.'

'No, but is it wise to upset me only hours before I *do* become so entitled?'

Mrs Muir pursed her lips. So this was how it was going to be, was it? A power-crazed little upstart pushing her weight around. Well not for long. Arnold would see to that.

'As you wish,' she replied through clenched teeth, and comforted herself with a vision of the first Mrs Bateford. Relaxed and radiant, Jane had been the life and soul of any gathering – until Arnold had crushed the life right out of her. That was the future now awaiting Elizabeth Arabrook, and it was going to be a joy to watch every single last minute of it.

'Will there be anything else?' she asked with just a hint of sarcasm.

'Not at the moment,' replied Bessie, and then promptly sighed as the door closed. Provoking all those who had been unpleasant was not a solution of any kind. It was a diversion that she could ill afford. A decision had to be made, and that did not mean delay heaped upon delay as before. It was imperative to make up her mind tonight – indeed *before* nightfall if at all possible.

She really did try to stick to that resolve, but there were three major hurdles which got in the way. Firstly – she still kept thinking that Thomas might appear, and make it all straightforward for her. Secondly – she was tired, and had trouble keeping her eyes open. And thirdly – there was a growing realisation that the decision had already in fact been made.

Maybe it was not stupidity that had brought her to this point, but instead a much greater force. Right from the beginning it had been there. The ease with which she had secured the post of nursemaid; Arnold taking an instant shine to her; her mad escapades with Gil's money; and ultimately that plunge into the canal. It was as if Dame Destiny had known all along that Bessie Cullen's fate was to be at Arnold Bateford's side.

Or perhaps it was to be at Ella's side. Leaving her niece had never really been an option, but now it was definitely not going to happen. Having lost Thomas, there was no way that Bessie was letting go of the one loving person who remained. And supporting the two of them by herself would be hard. In fact nigh on impossible. So was it futile to even explore other nuances and eventualities? Better to simply accept the inevitable? Tomorrow morning she was marrying Arnold Bateford, and tomorrow night she would move from this room into his.

Uttering the words inside her head, she then whispered them out loud, and the nauseous pounding of her body became ever more intense. It was not just what it would entail – although that frightened the life out of her; it was what she would be conceding. She had wanted to hurt her enemy so badly, for so long, and now she was letting herself be hurt instead. And all because she did not have the strength or inclination to do any differently.

Her subconscious kept on deliberating throughout the night, but without any real purpose, and then the time came to put on that dress. She had not picked it up since Mrs Muir had put it down, and now the beauty of its material only made her feel sad. She did not want to look nice; she did not deserve it – and Arnold certainly did not deserve to see it.

Constance knocked at just the right moment to assist with dressing, and then Bessie sent her back down to the kitchen. As she did so, it was hard not to question whether this passive compliance was being driven by the worst of all motives. To spite the likes of Constance, and Charles, and achieve a status that would not otherwise come her way. As Mrs Jennet had once said: 'Follow the purse-strings Bessie, because that way you'll never go hungry, and you'll never die of a broken heart.' Perhaps she was right.

Ella was only next door, but Bessie did not try seeing her. In fact she had not really seen her since leaving last Friday. Agatha had been looking after the toddler for a full seven days, and although that did stir some misguided jealousy, it would be too difficult to change the situation right now. With each passing week, Ella was looking more and more like Luke, a painful reminder of the night that he had left – and of Pauly, the child who had been lost. Even worse, when Ella smiled – which was all the time – the soft gleam in her eyes was an exact match to her favourite uncle. Although sadly his smile was not something that Bessie had seen very often.

'Oh Thomas, where are you?'

Maybe if she kept on saying it, he might hear her from afar. Surely that was possible if you tried really hard. And she did try – gave it absolutely everything – but nothing happened, and when more minutes had ebbed away, she finally had to confront what she had been dreading. It was time to take a look in that full-length mirror.

There was certainly no cause for complaint regarding the dress. It was silk tobine trimmed with satin, and pleated at the waist so that the skirt billowed out in elegant folds down to the floor. Beautiful was the only way to describe it. In fact it was every girl's dream, and a few drops of pride momentarily trickled through her veins. A Cullen from that hovel in the valley had actually made it to this point. If you gave it some thought, it was quite a feat. But it was also totally dreadful as well.

Constance had already put the ribbons in her hair, and now Bessie attached the veil. It provided an extra splash of purity, and she immediately drew the lace back from her face. She did not feel pure, and that was not because of Yates and Garrick. She had lived a lie for so long that she felt mentally corrupted, and now was about to commit the biggest deceit of all, in the house of God. Hopefully he would understand, and hopefully she would not be undone by the litany of lies. Arnold Bateford was set to marry Elizabeth Arabrook – except Elizabeth Arabrook did not exist, and Bessie had a feeling that the next hour could well bring that to light.

Walking forward, she rested her forehead against the glass. What would everybody think if they could see her now? Mother and Father, Luke, Thomas. It was all too terrifying to think about, so she turned to the more important issue. Was she really about to go through with this? She had not yet made a final definitive decision, not reached the point of saying: "Yes, that's it. No going back". It was like she was drifting towards this union in her sleep, full well knowing that she would end up regretting it for a very long time.

'Miss Arabrook?'

It was Duncan on the landing.

'Your carriage is here for you.'

'Thank you. I'll be down in a minute.'

She took one last look in the mirror, before gathering up the train of her dress, and making a move.

'It isn't too late. You can still run away,' said a voice from deep inside.

'With what? You haven't got a penny to your name,' said another, and they proceeded to vie for supremacy as she descended the stairs and reached the hall.

Duncan was there, along with the other staff, but he was the only one to comment on her appearance.

'You look lovely,' he said, and in a tone suggesting that it was because he wanted to, rather than because he thought he ought.

'You're very kind,' she replied, and found herself feeling glad that she was not bidding him farewell forever. He was a good person – like Thomas. One of the few good men.

Mrs Evans was also there, and offered a small smile of agreement.

'Thank you for taking care of me when I was ill,' said Bessie, and the cook's smile widened, but something was about to change, and they both knew it. No longer would they be equals – not in the eyes of society – and although that made absolutely no difference to Bessie, it did make a difference to Mrs Evans.

Agatha had also come down from the nursery – with Ella, and Bessie wondered whether the move had been prompted by a direct instruction from Arnold. Put the right thoughts in her head at the last moment to ensure that all ran smoothly.

The little girl stretched her arms out for a cuddle, and Bessie knelt down, holding on tight, and finding it so hard to let go. 'I love you Ella,' she whispered, and buried her face almost completely in the soft curly hair.

'Mr Bateford will be waiting,' announced the butler, who was clearly obeying his own instruction of seeing that she made it to the church on time.

'Is everybody there?' she asked, holding back the tears, and aware that "everybody" meant Arnold, Charles and Harris – because nobody else was coming.

'Yes, except the Master's brother-in-law, who is waiting for you outside.'

'Right.' Bessie stood up, and slowly moved forward, taking care not to catch her dress in the door, like any bride would do on their special day.

'What a picture,' declared a cheery-looking man as he walked towards her. 'Arnold is indeed a very lucky man.'

'Thank you,' said Bessie automatically. 'It's nice to meet you.'

This man was about to give her away, and yet she did not know him from Adam.

'The pleasure is all mine. I'm Mr Newell, or rather Evan – to my family, and of course that includes you now.'

'Yes,' said Bessie, trying not to sound bleak.

'Are you nervous?'

That was one word for it. 'I suppose a bit, especially without my family here for support.'

'Don't you worry about that. I'll take good care of you right up to the altar, and then it will be time for your husband to take over. In only a matter of minutes now, you'll be Mrs Arnold Bateford. You must be so excited.'

'Please, I'd like you to call me Elizabeth.'

'Oh . . . right . . . yes, of course.'

'Thank you for your assistance. My uncle is too sick to travel today.'

'Which makes me heartily sorry for him, because I consider this to be a great honour.'

Bessie managed a polite nod, but in truth his chirpy enthusiasm was making her thoroughly depressed – after less than a minute.

'My wife Louise is very eager to meet you,' he announced, helping her into the carriage. 'She's Arnold's only sister, but I'm sure you already know that. I must say that we thought he'd probably live out his days as a widower after poor Jane's death, but then you popped up and stole his heart.'

Heart? This had nothing to do with heart. It was about ego and swagger, and the perverse satisfaction of forcing somebody to do something against their will. Heart was the last thing on Arnold's mind.

Evan continued to chatter profusely all the way to Winscott parish church, and the bits which actually managed to register with Bessie left her with a distinctly vivid impression that he could not have encountered Arnold much at all over the years. He did not seem to have even the remotest clue as to how the man operated, and she became increasingly tempted to set the record straight. Presumably it would stem the flow of speech as well if Evan were to hear the bride pulling the bridegroom to pieces only moments before the ceremony. Or maybe not. Maybe Evan knew exactly what his brother-in-law was like, and was simply eulogising as a way of avoiding the blatantly obvious. Either way, it distracted Bessie from what she was trying to think about, and all too quickly they arrived at church.

Leaping out, Evan continued to fulfil his obligations down to the finest detail, and extended his arm as she alighted from the carriage. Then he held open the gate, but instead of passing through it, she asked for a chance to compose herself, and he obligingly stepped back, allowing her to scan the scene.

This was it. In a minute she would have to move, but until then, hope still lived. Surely Thomas was nearby. Surely any moment now he would come running, and she would collapse into his arms. He could not forsake her, he was here, she could feel it. Even the breeze rustling through the trees seemed to be speaking for him, calling her name, begging her not to do it. Should she listen? Or should she follow those purse-strings, and focus on what was best for Ella? The questions began to swirl around her brain again – until Evan gave a small cough to indicate that it was time.

"Oh Thomas, where are you?" she screamed inside, but the trees had gone quiet, and there was nobody in sight. She gave it a few more seconds, pleading, praying, yearning for something to happen, until finally with silent resignation she turned, pulled down the veil, and let herself be led inexorably towards her fate.

An hour later, Bessie was back in the exact same spot – with Arnold by her side. The ceremony had been a brief, solemn affair – beset by surprisingly no hiccups at all – and she had said the right thing at the right time, with only an acceptable period of hesitation. Louise was there too, which had in fact meant a grand total of four witnesses – two in each of the front two pews to provide a sort of balance. Flowers had been completely absent from proceedings, so Bessie had carried a white prayer book down the aisle instead. Appropriate if nothing else, and the vicar had said those all-important words which made such a profound difference. It was quite strange to think that a few sentences spoken by your fellow man could change everything so dramatically.

Once more out in the churchyard, the sun had broken through the clouds to bestow its blessing, and the select band engaged in awkward small talk. Arnold did not want to make an entrance until the last of his guests had arrived at Bateford Hall, so they all dragged their heels for a bit, and then Louise, Evan, Charles and Harris finally departed, leaving Bessie alone with the man who was now her husband. Uncomfortable was an understatement of utterly monumental proportions, but it was nothing compared to what lay ahead. She tried not to think about that, but it was difficult when Arnold was clearly thinking of nothing else.

The carriage took an age to return, but at last Bessie clambered in with relief – until of course Arnold clambered in as well, and they were now alone in an enclosed space. She could not wait to get out and be with other people, but that also changed when they drew up, crossed the threshold, and were met by rapturous applause.

A large gathering of Somerden's great-and-good had lined up in the hall to welcome back the happy couple, and although Bessie knew hardly any of them, she did know three – Stewart Munroe, Sylvia Chaloner, and Gil

Tremaine. It was hard to describe what it felt like to stand before them so conspicuously – as if guilty of a crime, and they were there to pass judgement. For the first time she felt glad that Arnold had invested so much in the dress. People could criticise her as an individual, but they could not find fault with her appearance. And there was one other significant positive as well.

Sylvia was clearly not enamoured with this experience. To have to sit at the same table as a mere governess was an outrage, but to admit her as one of their own – it was enough to make the blood run cold in your veins – and that air of umbrage brought a very definite smile to Bessie's lips. There were going to be many lows as Arnold's wife, so whenever a high came along it was important to make the most of it – and she proceeded to do just that, acting the part of radiant newly-wed with considerable panache.

The celebrations were not a sit-down affair, but more of an informal "help yourself". It was all that Mrs Evans could manage in the time – and would end up cheaper for Arnold. Food and drink were available in both the dining and drawing rooms, and Bessie was grateful for that. To be rendered stationary – with everybody staring – would have been most unpleasant; and mobility also had another advantage – she could flit away from anybody who was proving to be troublesome. Indeed when she came to Sylvia, she did not so much flit away as seek to sidestep her completely. But Gil's social partner was not about to let the impostor pass by just like that.

'You're right,' she declared as if carrying on an existing conversation. 'Class is a very hard thing to define. Can you acquire it through life? Or is it something fundamentally inherent? Personally I believe the latter. You certainly cannot acquire it through the mere receipt of one of these new marriage certificates.'

Bessie stopped. "Should I respond?" Yes. Why not?

'I totally agree with you Mrs Chaloner. I won't magically become middle-class overnight through my marriage to Arnold. Any more than *you* will become aristocratic through your association with Gil.'

'I think you'll find that I already *am* aristocratic.'

'Are you? I'm not quite sure that popular opinion fully supports you in that, so it looks like all your hopes may well be resting on Mr Tremaine, which is a pity since he seems rather . . . shall we say . . . reluctant?'

'You can't talk to me like that,' snarled Sylvia.

'I think I just have,' replied Bessie, and turned away – right into the path of the afore-mentioned male. His left eyebrow went up as his head tilted slightly to one side, and Bessie could not decipher whether he was affronted, amused, or still angry. She chose not to stop and find out.

Everything proceeded without incident after that – until Stewart made a remark about Arnold putting himself to considerable inconvenience with his choice of bride, and Bessie plunged headlong towards her second faux pas of the day by asking why.

'Because he now needs another governess of course. You really should have married a maid Arnold. They're much easier to come by.' He was being deliberately provocative, but not getting very far. Arnold knew that he had what many men in the room wanted, and was content to parade his new wife from one to another like his finest prize cow.

'But *I* can look after Isabel,' argued Bessie, and all of a sudden she seemed to have the ear of half the room.

'That isn't what we do,' said one of the women. 'And you'll soon be preoccupied with other matters anyway, like having children of your own.'

Bessie glanced at Arnold, who had set her with an icy glare. She may be his wife, but that did not give her the right to express opinions, and it never would.

'Well of course,' she agreed with a dismissive shrug. 'If truth be told, I'm only concerned that history might repeat itself, and I'll find my husband developing a decidedly unhealthy interest in my replacement.' She twinkled mischievously, and that generated enough knowing chuckles for the danger to pass.

'Is it alright if Elizabeth shows me up to the nursery?' asked Louise. 'I must see my niece while I'm here.'

Bessie reinforced that request with a look of obedient supplication, and Arnold then gave his permission.

'Don't allow my brother to start dictating everything,' advised Louise as soon as they ascended the stairs. 'If you have a point of view, you must make sure that it is heard.'

"How?" thought Bessie, and clearly the question was written across her face.

'We may be the weaker sex Elizabeth, but we still have certain . . . well . . . resources at our disposal, and I'm sure you will find a way to use them to best effect.' Louise patted her on the arm as if to welcome her into the sisterhood.

'What resources?' asked Bessie, but Louise would only say:

'You'll soon understand,' and then focused her attentions on baby Isabel.

After a few minutes of watching them from the doorway, Bessie left to fetch some milk. It was not really necessary, but she needed to cool down, and there was nowhere cooler than the larder. As anticipated, it had a gloriously numbing impact, and frankly she could have stayed there for the rest of the day, but knew that it would be unwise to annoy her husband with any kind of prolonged absence.

Returning to the hall, she was all set to enter the drawing room when the sound of Arnold's laughter pierced remorselessly through the wood, and she simply could not bring herself to do it. Tonight was bound to be hell whatever she did, so why bother trying to keep on his good side? Not that he had one.

Having listened to the sound for several more seconds, she fled outside in search of solitude. Except that it was not solitude she found – but Gil Tremaine.

'All getting a bit much?' he observed when she came to a halt.

'Yes. Just a bit.' She breathed out slowly, and then swallowed a couple of times. 'Have you managed to recover your money?'

'Take a wild guess.'

'I'm sorry. I know you probably don't want to hear it, but I really am.'

'You're right. I'd much rather hear how you've just managed to walk out of that church as Mrs Arnold Bateford.'

'It's a long story.'

'It can't be that long. I only saw you five days ago.'

'I know, but it's complicated.'

'Complicated?' repeated Gil. 'You accept a proposal from the man who not only sent you to prison, but also sent your father there, and drove your brother from the district. Yes, I should say it's complicated.'

'Please don't talk like that. I know it's awful but I . . .'
She was about to add: "I didn't have any choice", but
that was not strictly true.

'But what?'

'I didn't want any of this to happen. This wasn't my
intention when I came here.'

'Wasn't it?'

'No. Nobody in their right mind would wish to marry
Arnold.'

'Which rather suggests that you *aren't* in your right
mind.'

Bessie lowered her head for a second. 'Sometimes
I really don't think that I am.'

'I suppose it shouldn't come as any great surprise.
Your actions in my house did seem to point to a certain
level of derangement. Although of course it could all
make perfect sense too. You couldn't get your hands
on my money – correction, you couldn't *keep* your
hands on my money – so now you're clinging to Arnold's
instead.'

'This has nothing to do with money!'

'Hasn't it?'

'No!'

'So you haven't been daydreaming about all these fine
gowns, carriage-travel, and what-have-you.'

'Not for a minute. And if you think that being
Arnold's wife means a step up in the world, then you're
wrong. It's a very definite step down!'

'Really? Nursemaid to noblewoman surely has some
advantages – like playing Mistress of the Manor for one.
It's quite clear that you're already enjoying that
particular little aspect.'

Bessie turned away.

'You *are*, aren't you? All that railing at the aristocracy was nothing more than petty jealousy. First chance you get, you can't run down the aisle fast enough.'

'Stop it. Just stop it.'

'Why? You've wanted this for years, and now you've got it – even if it has meant settling for middle-class. You do realise that if you'd wanted to be a proper aristo, you should have married somebody like me. But then again, I would never have offered.'

Bessie turned back with real hurt in her eyes. 'And *I* would never have accepted.'

'God, I come in second to Arnold. I don't think I've ever been so insulted. Although of course I'm not the right age, am I?'

'What?'

'First Munroe, now Arnold – you obviously like them old.'

'From where I'm standing, *you're* old, and I don't like you.'

Gil's jawbone pulsed, and Bessie was suddenly hit by a wave of contrition:

'Look – I know you're upset because I broke into your house, and you have every right. But you must understand that this isn't how I planned it. I just wanted to come here, make him pay, and then leave. But all this other stuff started happening, and there became so many issues at stake, and I didn't know what to do.'

'Oh so you've agonised over it, have you? For what? All of a day? Two?'

Bessie closed her eyes as she announced: 'He asked me last Friday.'

'Well that explains everything!' Gil cast his hands out in an act of complete enlightenment. 'You didn't come for my money because of the workers, it was to escape all this, run off somewhere but keep yourself in the style to which you've become accustomed.'

'No! It was for them, I swear.'

'Forgive me if I appear somewhat dubious.'

'Don't patronise me Gil Tremaine. I may have done a thousand things wrong, but my concern for those families was genuine. I care about them, every last one. They're *my* people.'

'Your people? As if you have any idea who you are any more.'

'I know exactly who I am.'

'No you don't. You just have this ridiculous vision of yourself. Bessie Cullen – Heroine of the Submerged Tenth, battling to secure a brighter future for each and every one of them. The landlocked equivalent of Grace Darling.'

'Grace Who?'

'That woman who rescued people from the sea last year. A single-handed saviour. Surely your inspiration.'

'I don't have an inspiration,' snapped Bessie. 'And I am *not* trying to be a saviour. I just want to help . . .'

'With my money don't forget.'

'Yes with your money, but I wasn't born with a pot of gold at the end of my crib, so I can't use my own, can I? And as for Grace What's-her-name, I didn't hear about her because I was probably incarcerated at the time!'

'Oh yes, there *is* that,' conceded Gil. 'What was it like by the way? You never did say.'

'Because it's none of your business.'

'It's amazing how many times you've considered yourself entitled to say that to me.'

'Well I'll say it again. This is my life and my decision, and absolutely nothing to do with you whatsoever.'

'You're undoubtedly right, but I'll tell you something for free – you've made the worst decision possible.'

'So what if I have? If I live long enough, I'm sure I'll find a way to top it.'

'Oh I'm sure too, have no fear.' He set her with a stern focus, and Bessie could think of nothing else to say except:

'Leave me alone.'

'Alone? That's a good one. As if I've been the one harassing *you* for the best past of eight months. And has it ever crossed that indignant little mind of yours that far from being the victim of an extreme set of circumstances, you are in fact the cause of much of this chaos yourself.'

'Well you needn't worry, because I won't be inflicting chaos on you any more. Indeed if you're really lucky, you might never come across me again.' She gripped the handle of the front door, but was stopped in her tracks by Tremaine's next remark:

'Did you do it because of the child?'

'What?'

'The girl upstairs. Isabel, isn't it?'

'Yes, it's Isabel, and she means a lot to me, but no, I didn't.'

'Are you sure?'

'Yes.'

'So it would be entirely wrong of me to suggest that this Isabel is . . . how can I put this? More closely related to you than you have previously admitted?'

'Yes it would.' Bessie stepped back towards him, and stared really quite fiercely. 'Isabel is not to be discussed, do you hear? She's no concern of yours, nor anybody else's.'

'But I feel she could be hiding some quite fascinating secrets.'

'Stop it!' hissed Bessie, and jerked her hand in anger – forgetting that she was holding onto the milk. A great slosh shot up and landed splat onto Gil's waistcoat. It was woven with images of jousting knights who were charging across his chest on horseback – and now having to wade through a flood. He analysed them for a few seconds before dabbing them off with his cuff.

'Really Mrs Bateford, if you're going to hurl liquid at me, please make it a vintage. Milk does smell so.'

'Do you *ever* take anything seriously?'

'Not if I can help it.'

Bessie emitted a deep guttural noise of contempt, and stalked back to the door – until he caught hold of her arm. 'Let go of me. I'm warning you, I'll . . .'

'What?' Gil raised that eyebrow again.

'I'll pour the rest of this milk right over your head.'

'Ah, now that's the Bessie Cullen we've all come to know and love. Spitting and clawing like a wildcat. While acting indignant at the same time.'

'Yes I'm indignant, and I've clawed Mr Tremaine. I've clawed my way here, and I'll claw my way on from here. Bessie Cullen isn't done yet, and don't you forget it.'

'And what do you have in mind?'

'No idea. Maybe nothing. Maybe I'll simply revel in this life of luxury like you imagine. If you can't beat 'em, join 'em? Isn't that what people say? Well I've just joined 'em!' And with that, she pulled her arm free, and flounced back into the house.

Once more in the nursery, she handed Agatha the milk for Ella – whatever was left of it – pinned up the train of her dress that had begun to feel like a ball and chain, and leaned against the wall.

Nothing stirred her like arguing with that insufferable creature from Carrow Square. Half of what he said was complete nonsense – and he knew it – but he simply liked to see her infuriated. Well she was certainly that. But it did not last. What was the point of claiming to fight on as Bessie Cullen when she was now Bessie Bateford? For the rest of her natural life. And as for any idea of wreaking retribution – it was meaningless. Her previous attempts had ended in abject failure; her ally had now left; and if she did try anything, she was at risk of losing Ella as well.

By the time her subconscious had reminded her of these facts, she was rendered quite subdued, bordering on fearful, and quickly rejoined Arnold – just as he was being asked for the whereabouts of his eldest child. It had taken the best part of three hours for anybody to notice that Thomas was not in attendance, and that seemed to do wonders for Charles' morale. Of course Arnold was unable to answer, so mumbled a few words which did not reflect badly on himself, before moving onto a discussion of how well the mill was doing. He was keen to make clear that in spite of Munroe and those malicious rumours, Bateford enterprises were prospering.

Bessie did not believe it. How could a situation that had been so dire in October, miraculously resolve itself by April? But she had to remember that he had been making a significant saving on the wages, and now the reduction in pay which had been masked by Tremaine money was set to take full effect. And she did not have the foggiest clue what she was going to do about it.

What a mess. What a total, miserable, ghastly mess. It needed sustained deliberation, but she could not think about it now. She could not hear or see anything other than the ticking of the clock. Minutes were racing by, and that meant only one thing. The house would clear, Harris and Charles would disappear, and with it having been such a big day, it would soon be time for bed.

Maybe she could feign some sort of attack? After all, she had been seriously ill only a couple of days ago. Was there any chance that Arnold might be convinced of her need for sleep, and sleep alone? She gave it some thought, and then as the guests began to leave, she gave it even more thought, before dismissing it in a heartbeat. She had spent most of the day with palpitations because of this, and if she found some way to evade it, then she would spend all of tomorrow in the same state. Better to simply get it over and done with.

So rather bizarrely she ended up eager for everybody to go as fast as humanly possible – which of course meant that the exact opposite occurred – and Louise lingered at the Hall long into the evening, with Evan persisting in his chirpiness right to the very end. They were good people, and storm-clouds were indeed gathering overhead, making their return journey an unappealing prospect, but she needed them to move. In fact she needed it more than Arnold, who had become affability itself, and appeared to be in no hurry whatsoever. He was dragging it out, like she should have known he would.

If only she could fly away somewhere nice and safe, like the Whitson cottage, or back to Josiah. There had been no chance to tell him her decision, so he would have read the announcement in the Somerden Register. She could imagine how much he had been thinking about her today, and that he was probably now sitting at the kitchen table with Mrs Jennet, sorrowfully pondering how his Bessie could have made such a hash of things.

The answer to that was easy. Because she was a fool, and she was still being a fool right now. There were thousands of women up and down the country who would be intimate tonight with husbands they no longer loved, or a husband chosen for them, whom they did not even like. Plus there were those women in the prison, selling themselves to anybody, regardless of age, shape, or size – simply for the price of a bottle of gin. It was really not that big an issue. But when something had been churning in your breast for as long as this had, it was hard to rationalise it into anything remotely acceptable.

She tried, really and truly she did, but it continued to loom large and frightful. The worst thing of all was that Arnold would know how she felt, and derive great pleasure from her discomfort. Indeed he would make it obvious, so perhaps she ought to surprise him, and show willingness. That would surely spoil his experience, and her spirits would be lifted as a result. But could she do it? Was she really that good an actress?

Just when she was beginning to hope that the Newells might actually delay their departure until tomorrow, they headed home – wherever that was – and the house became quiet once more. Bessie hovered, unsure of what to do next, until Arnold instructed her to wait in his room.

'But all my things are still . . .'

'Then take what you need for tonight, and the rest will be moved tomorrow.'

'Right.'

Louise had told her not to let Arnold dictate, but he had spent his whole life dictating, and obstruction did not go down too well, so she dutifully entered her bedroom, and tried to concentrate on what she needed. Night-clothes, hairbrush . . . did any of it really matter? Picking up a few things without thinking, she then went into the nursery. Ella was sleeping peacefully, in blissful ignorance as always. It was strange to think that the best part of your life was when you did not even understand that you *were* alive. People gave you food and drink and lots of love, and did not ask for anything in return. Not a single, solitary thing.

She walked across the landing, and found herself doing something that was potentially very foolish indeed – diverting into Thomas' room. She needed to be close to him, just for a moment, and opened the wardrobe so that she could press his favourite jacket against her cheek. It had his smell, such a wonderful smell, and it made her heart ache worse than ever. He was not dead – not as far as she knew – but it felt like grief was tearing her apart. Why was she doing it to herself? Why make this any more harrowing that it had to be? She was her own worst enemy.

Shutting the door angrily, she forced Thomas to the back of her mind, and approached Arnold's room. She had never seen it before, and there was not actually much to see. It had all the items of furniture you would expect, but there was nothing to show that it belonged to a real person. It was also a very big room, which made it seem even less inviting, and the main window looked out over the drive, so the Master could survey his estate.

She pulled the curtain back just as a flash of lightning lit up the sky, and thunder followed a few seconds later. A spring storm. As if the atmosphere needed to be any more charged. But she was glad of it. Watching the fury in the heavens reminded her of the power out there – the fact that her own little world was insignificant. She probably ought to take off her wedding-dress now, but was not sure that she could manage it by herself, and the thought of him finding her in under-garments was abhorrent. So she simply watched and waited, and waited some more, until finally Arnold entered, reeking of cigars.

Closing the door behind him, he then stood there, absorbing the satisfaction of the moment. He had been thinking about this for an awfully long time. Ever since October when he had sworn that Munroe would never get her; ever since he had noticed Thomas wanting her, and removed him as manager so that he could sit in this house and reflect on what was lost. Of course his son's premature exodus had ruined that particular aspect, but Stewart had been witness to it all, and otherwise everything had gone to plan. Two hours left of his birthday, and here was the perfect present ready for unwrapping. Although first he had a present of his own to give.

'Take off the dress,' he ordered, and she was forced to admit that she needed some help, which he provided, breathing down her neck throughout.

Soon the dress was off, and although she was still wearing enough not to feel too exposed, that was soon to change.

'Now do the same with the petticoat.'

She hesitated. Why was he not undressing at the same time? Could he not make this just the slightest bit more bearable?

'Is there a problem?' he added, and the tone of his voice sent defiance coursing through her.

'Not at all,' she replied, and cast off the crinoline with something of a flourish.

'And now the corset.' He walked forward to unlace it, and the feel of him near her was so gut-wrenchingly horrid, but it was not as bad as him standing aloof, staring – as he proceeded to do for a full minute before drawing something out of the wardrobe.

It was a dress – scarlet – just like the one that she had worn to seduce Stewart, with the V-neck bodice revealing far too much. She had sold it in Henningborough, claimed it had been ruined beyond repair, but now here it was, reborn, to haunt her again.

'Put it on.'

Yet another instruction, and this one was the most disturbing of all. What game was he playing? What was he trying to do? But she complied because at least it would mean that she was covered up once more.

'Now close the curtains.'

For the first time she realised that she had been changing right next to where people could see her, but nobody was outside in this weather, and she really did not care anyway. Besides, closing the curtains made her feel like a bird shutting its own cage.

As soon as she had completed the task, she turned around to see that Arnold had pushed the braces off his shoulders, and was slowly undoing the four buttons on the front of his trousers.

'Lie down on the bed.'

His final instruction. Lying flat was the ultimate position of vulnerability, for a woman at least, and he knew it. She began to pull back the eider-down quilt, but he then clarified his desire to see her on *top* of the bedclothes.

Bessie swallowed and tried to control herself. If there was something sharp to hand, she would take it up and kill him with it. There was no question about it. She should have done it when she had a chance, kicked him off the summit of Ulmers Hill as Luke ran for town. Thomas would have inherited, Cynthia would not have been forced to marry Roscoe, Marge would probably have given birth to a healthy baby boy, and Wilf would have remained a free man. She would have gone to the gallows for it, but at least her death would have brought a better life to people, rather than making things infinitely worse, which was all she had done since.

Lifting her feet up off the floor, she lay on her back and it felt like all the people she had ever known were looking down on her from the ceiling, condemning every move that she had ever made. At first it brought sadness, but then resentment took over. She was not the only one who had failed those around her. Thomas had left before making sure of her decision. Gil had helped the workers, but then abruptly changed his mind. Wilf had let his temper overwhelm him. But the face that endured the longest was the one belonging to her brother.

Luke's first experience of intimacy had been in a beautiful wood, with a girl his own age, whom he loved with all his heart. Whereas here she was, in a cold room, with a man old enough to be her father, and about to suffer something that he would make as painful as he possibly could. This ordeal was a direct result of Luke's moment of joy, and she hated him for it, hated him with a passion that gripped at her throat, because she knew that even if he could have foreseen every one of those consequences, he still would not have done any different.

CHAPTER THREE

Next morning found Bessie in a much happier frame of mind. The first night was over. She had survived its humiliation and discomfort, and nothing could ever be as bad again. In fact it had not been quite as bad as originally feared. In her darkest hours, she had envisaged a pain bordering on excruciation, but mercifully that had not actually been the case, and the rain lashing against the windows had provided some very welcome distraction.

The most distressing part had been Arnold's manner. The way he chose to speak to her – or rather chose *not* to speak to her – and the feel of his face so close. She had stared venomously at that face in Somerden courthouse, and now here it was, closer than any man's had ever been. Closer than Thomas, with whom she had once been in love.

She was already forcing herself to use the past tense in his regard. Thomas Bateford was gone, and if he ever came back, it was far too late now. Anyway had he really been the person she imagined him to be? Able to leave his niece just like that. The little girl who needed him. Bessie could not understand how he could do it. But as the days passed, she came to realise that she might as well have done the same.

Following on from those discussions at the wedding-breakfast, Arnold made it perfectly clear that her work as a governess was over. She put in a carefully rehearsed appeal, arguing her desire to embrace new responsibilities as his wife, and to be like a mother to his youngest child. But he would not yield. The nursery was off-limits. No replacement would be hired, so Agatha would be promoted to the position. Bessie was left feeling sick with both fury and frustration. Her own flesh and blood only strides away, and she was forbidden from crossing an invisible divide. Obviously the rebel in her nature meant that she crept in whenever she could, but there was always that risk of being caught, and it never fully went away.

Apart from stealing those few precious moments, Bessie literally had nothing else to fill her time. Yes there was sewing on hand, and she was required to attend breakfast and dinner, but otherwise she had no role and no authority – and more particularly no money. As a member of staff she had handled hundreds of pounds since the Munroe dinner, but now as Lady of the Hall, she could not access so much as a farthing. Even when it came to making something for winter – a scarf, or a pair of mittens, she had to grovel to her husband for permission first. Ultimately he gave it – although only after a lengthy delay, and the yarn she received was enough to keep her occupied for just a short spell before the torment of persistent thought returned. And Arnold made sure that she had plenty to think about.

Every evening after dinner, he would sit and discuss the mill with Charles. Discuss how murmurings of discontent had suddenly started up about the pay-cut that had been in force for nearly six months. How there was no danger of insurrection, because the overseers would see to it that such ideas were crushed. As Charles conceitedly announced, things had gone soft under

Thomas, but now proper order had been restored. She knew exactly what that meant. The likes of Peter Whitson being strapped until he could barely stand up. How she longed for the day when Charles might suffer the same fate.

Unfortunately like so many of her thoughts, this was another that would never bear fruit. She could not help but dream of possible ways to make Arnold squirm – like reporting him to one of those factory inspectors, and hoping to have him shut down, or crippled by a heavy fine. But all the while she knew that he would simply bribe his way out, and even if the plan worked, she still came up against that same intractable problem: The workers would lose their jobs. Starvation pay might be miserable but it was better than no pay at all. So things had to be left in their current state, and she had to listen to the same depressing dialogue night after night – usually while wearing a red dress.

The introduction of Arnold's favourite item during their wedding-night had been an unpleasant and confusing occurrence, but soon the significance became clear. Unlike most middle-class women who presumably chose their own attire, she had no such freedom. Come mid-afternoon, Arnold would select what he wanted her to wear at dinner, and the red dress meant that she should prepare for the performance of obligations afterwards. He wanted her to sit through the entire meal thinking about it, and not have any hope that perhaps he might be too tired, or disinterested.

He was always interested. In fact she wore that dress so often that he was compelled to buy another one – same colour, but different design. This one had a rounded neckline, almost slipping off the shoulder, and a bell-shaped skirt, but she hated it just as much. It even reached the point where she hated her own skin, because of how it felt when he touched it.

Sometimes when he fell asleep, and she was lying awake by his side, she would look across at that bloated belly, and his dribbling mouth, and have great difficulty in controlling herself. How his first wife had tolerated this for twenty-odd years was frankly beyond her. But at least she could hope that her own nightmare might not last quite so long. Surely he would die first and leave her in peace. And perhaps there was a more immediate advantage to his advancing years.

Two weeks into their marriage, and Bessie's bleeding started. It was not only a reprieve, but a wonderful relief. She had been terrified about the prospect of carrying his baby even before accepting the proposal, but now it consumed her every thought. If he were to find out who she was, he would banish her, but the child would belong to him – as Ella did. That would be three children that he had taken from the Cullens, and there was no way that she was letting it happen.

So on a daily basis she employed every old wives' trick in the book to ensure that she remained barren – just in case he was still capable. And she concentrated on her elocution and deportment, to protect her true identity. There was nothing else to do – except burn Josiah's reference of course, but it was not until the beginning of June that she was able to seize her chance.

After six weeks of stagnating with no other purpose than to serve Arnold Bateford, she finally had hope of temporary escape when he announced that he would be away for the day. He did not say where or why, nor did he say what she was to do while he was gone – because he expected her to follow the same numbing ritual as usual. But that would not be the case.

It was a Sunday, and he set off soon after breakfast, leaving her with only Charles and Harris to worry about. The mill did not start work until noon, and she had expected Charles to hang about until close to that hour, but to her surprise he chose to go in early. Presumably he was hoping that Arnold would find out, and appreciate his dedication to the cause.

With him out of the way, only Harris remained, but the third son soon vacated the Hall as well. She had been so absorbed with her own monotony that she had not given any thought to his, but it was clearly taking its toll. He simply could not find anything to fill the hours, and before it had even reached ten o'clock, he had followed Charles to the mill. A lost soul in search of the only company that he had ever known.

Bessie watched until he was out of sight, and then shot into Arnold's study. The drawers in the desk were not locked, and she rummaged through them feverishly. But found nothing. She then went through them again with more care, but still the same result. What had he done with it? It was not in their room – she was fairly sure of that. Had he thrown it away himself? Or did Mrs Muir have it? That last question sprang into her mind out of nowhere, but seemed instantly sensible. The housekeeper was the one who had conducted the interviews – and presiding over her workers was a duty that she took very seriously.

Sitting back in Arnold's chair, Bessie debated how to go about things. Wait – that was the first step, but a most disagreeable one. It felt like she was already wasting the day with waiting, and every minute lost was like a sin, but at last Mrs Muir commenced her round of inspections, and Bessie was able to head down to the kitchen. It was time to question Mrs Evans – subtly if possible – and find out whether Mrs Muir's room held any paperwork.

'Yes. Household accounts, registers, all sorts of things,' said the cook. 'Makes her feel important I think.'

Bessie then explained that she needed to check something, but it would be best if Mrs Muir were not informed, since it would only cause bother. Thankfully Mrs Evans could well understand that point of view, and probed no further.

Within a couple of minutes Bessie was in and out, and back upstairs setting fire to Josiah's reference. It was imperative that she protected him as much as possible, and destruction was the only way. When the flames had eaten up every syllable, she jabbed the ash with a poker to mix it in with the rest. Tess had not yet cleared the grates, but when she did, nothing would appear untoward.

Smiling with satisfaction at a job well done, Bessie then returned to the kitchen to ask for another favour – some vegetables and a flitch of bacon.

'Wrapped up you say?'

'Yes,' confirmed Bessie, and the cook fiddled with her apron-strings. 'It's just like before.'

'But the disappearance of a whole flitch is rather hard to explain Mrs Bateford.'

Bessie kept requesting the use of Elizabeth, but to no avail. 'I know, but you could suggest that it disappeared while your back was turned. Some scamp from the village no doubt.'

Mrs Evans sighed. 'I don't know.'

'It's for a good cause, I promise.'

'What cause?'

'It's best that I don't tell you. *Please*. Just help me out, one more time.'

Mrs Evans closed her eyes in a reluctant act of acceptance, and before she could open them again, Bessie had given her a warm hug.

Ten minutes later, and before Mrs Muir had even finished scrutinising the dining room, Bessie was once again at the bottom of the back stairs – poised for the usual signal. Her wedding-ring had been placed in a drawer, and she was wearing an Arabrook dress. The work dress had met with a fiery demise the day after the nuptials – too dangerous to have it around – but the day dresses remained, and Arnold had not passed comment when she put them in one corner of the wardrobe. They were not to be worn of course. The uniform of a middle-class wife differed very much from that of a nursemaid, but he liked them there as a reminder of what she had come from, and how grateful she ought to be.

In this regard, gratitude was indeed the emotion, because it meant that she had the right look to visit the Whitsons. With the vegetables in a sack over one arm, and bacon under the other, she flashed Mrs Evans a smile of conspiracy before darting out through the rear exit. Making use of all the blind spots, she then reached the wood unseen, and ran helter-skelter into the valley. She would only have an hour before Edie and Peter were called by the factory bell, but sixty minutes was more than enough to make it worth the risk.

Keeping her head down and scurrying in a furtive manner, she was soon knocking on their back door, and being ushered in with words of welcome. They had not known when they would seen her again, and were soon asking what she was doing, where she was living, how she was, but she insisted on hearing about *them* first, and also on giving them a few extra provisions.

'Now I know you hate gifts Seamus, but I can't carry this stuff all the way back to town, so please just take it.' She accompanied her appeal with a pained frown as he removed the bacon from its covering, and stared at it.

'Hate gifts? What on earth makes you think that I'd be such a clod as to hate gifts? You're getting me muddled up with somebody else.' He laughed – the strained laugh of a husband who knew that his wife and children would not go hungry this week, but wished that he was the reason. 'You have to stay and eat some though. That's a must.'

'I wish I could, but I can't be away long. I just wanted you all to know that I'm thinking of you, and that I'm well.'

'But you can stay to hear me read, can't you?' asked Peter. 'I've been practising.'

'Of course I can. I'm not leaving until I've heard at least three passages – and long ones at that.'

His face glowed, and she listened to him with all the pride of a teacher, hoping that one day this knowledge of words would carve out a better life for him.

As soon as he finished, Edie jumped in with some local gossip, and of course top of the list was Arnold's marriage to the governess.

'She's as young as his sons by all accounts, and his first wife not in the ground more than one winter.'

'Indecent. That's the only way of describing it.' Seamus shook his head most disapprovingly. 'And it's all because of the money – there's no doubt about it. Why else would any woman accept a man like Arnold Bateford?'

'It's certainly hard to imagine that it was for love,' agreed Edie. 'Although I must admit to feeling rather sorry for her. It can't be particularly pleasant up there. Not with the likes of him.'

'Aye, she'll be ruing her decision by now. Sure as night follows day.'

Bessie did not contribute to the discussion, but instead sat in hope that it would soon shift onto something else – and when that appeared increasingly unlikely, she found herself longing for the bell. But as soon as its blare reached their ears, she was overwhelmed by guilt. How could she wish for a thing that drained the life out of Peter's face in such an instant? His few hours of respite over, and it would be another seven days before he could revisit that sense of freedom again.

Bidding farewell, Edie hurried up through the valley with her son, while Bessie set off for Ulmers Hill, supposedly taking the short-cut into town, but soon doubling back. It was such a beautiful day – the sort of day when Ella ought to be outside, but Arnold was bound to suspect such a move. He would interrogate Agatha on his return, and it would lead to a host of trouble. Too much trouble for Bessie to handle. So she pushed the suggestion aside, and also ignored the one telling her to see Josiah. Yes it would be wonderful, but almost as soon as she had said a greeting, she would have to say goodbye again, and the prospect of that was enough to dissuade her from embracing it in the first place.

Today would simply have to be spent alone, and not even thoughts of Thomas were going to occupy her. It was his birthday. The second of June. Twenty-two years old. But he was not here, and she refused to ponder yet again where he might be. Giving the mill a wide berth, she ran up into the fields to the west, and kept running until exhaustion forced him out of her mind. Then she flopped down on the ground, and lay there, basking in the sunshine like a star-fish.

Oh it was so marvellous to feel like a child again, like the dust was being shaken from a shabby old rug. Perhaps if she captured this moment so completely, then the worries might stay away forever. Reality might never invade the warm tranquillity. But within minutes, it was not reality but voices which invaded – born on the breeze. She tried to ignore them, but ultimately curiosity got the better of her, and she crossed into the next field, before rising up over a grassy knoll to her left. Then she saw it – a huge crowd of people, all listening in quiet raptures to a man speaking from a makeshift platform. Creeping forward, she joined those at the back, and began to listen too.

'Is there anybody here who has not suffered most grievously as a result of the depression these past few months? But do you think that any of your Masters have suffered the same? The Kings of Industry. Those men in Parliament who are Lords over our lives. Do any of them actually know what it is to go without the basic necessities? Because that is all that we have ever been asking for. Every man has the right to good shelter for his family, and a decent dinner on his plate. And yet these are the things still being denied to us. Generation after generation of you remain trapped in this cycle of hereditary poverty, living on nothing, nothing but hope. Is it not time to live on something else? *We* are the producers of this country's wealth. *We* are the millions, and yet we tolerate an abject misery imposed upon us by the few. It is you and I who endure long hours for low pay, and never complain. Why? Why do we let it happen? Why don't we fight?'

'Fight how?' called a man from the middle of the crowd.

'By signing this Petition today. The Chartist movement was formed specifically to advance the causes of you and I, and its message has reached into every corner and every cottage. Because it demands equality through fairness, through a vote, through a secret ballot, and annual elections. Add your names to this noble cause. Declare: "I am a Chartist, and I will accept nothing but the Charter", and then look forward to the day when at last we shall have a say in the laws which govern us. When at last we shall elect working men to represent our views, and even to rule over us. Some day within our lifetimes one of *you* could rule this great nation of ours. What was once a fantasy can become a truth if we simply believe in it. Our moment in history is here, we are standing on the cusp of a glorious future, and we must seize it. We must seize it, and never let it go!'

The speaker flung out his arms, and spread his legs apart, as if the force of his belief were liable to knock him flat off his feet. And Bessie felt the power as if it was that very first time, in Mrs Langley's kitchen, reading pamphlets with Josiah. The crusade for change needed support from every man, woman and child – and she had been desperate to answer the call – until Bateford had deflected her with his campaign of venom. Now she was a Bateford too, but once that spirit ran through your veins, it never entirely went away, and this man had just lit the touch-paper of revival. She cheered louder than anybody around her, and was about to scream herself hoarse, but it became apparent that there were other sounds among the crowd. Murmurings of disagreement; even jeers. The speaker held out his hands in a calming gesture, and then tackled the issue head-on:

'Do I hear dissenting voices among you? Are these the very same voices who say that we are not ready for an extension of the franchise? Who say that having helped the middle-classes to gain the vote, that it is now right for them to shut the door in our faces? That we are not fit for this most austere of responsibilities?'

He scanned every section of the audience, ensuring that he had their undivided attention.

'I have only one thing to say to these people. One question to ask. *What* is the alternative? To remain oppressed forever? To surrender our dreams, and submit lamely to the yoke because we do not have the fire in our bellies to do otherwise? To allow the corrupt practices in London to persist, and endure yet more abominations like the New Poor Law? I say no! I say we should stand united, and demand liberation. Live and work like equal human beings. Raise our children into a world of possibility and opportunity. No longer bow our heads to the ground as serfs, but walk with heads held high, sure in the knowledge that our brothers-in-arms shall not forsake us. Because we are a band too big to ignore. We are Chartists, and we will fight. We will fight – and whatever it takes, WE WILL WIN!'

The cheers that rang out this time were so deafening as to obliterate any jeer that anybody could muster. Bessie surged forward, eager to sign her name with pride, but even more eager to talk to that amazing man who was now stepping off the platform. He could help her, she knew it. He had all the answers and the passion, but when she had forged her way to the front, he was not there.

'Where is he? Where is he?' she cried, and eventually somebody let her know that he was needed at another meeting near Ackerley.

Bessie shot off towards Somerden, but he was not even in sight. It was not until the outskirts of town that she finally caught a glimpse of him, hurrying along with a companion.

'Hey, stop!' she shouted, but the breeze snatched the words before they could get anywhere near their target.

Her chase became yet more frantic as she saw them veer into Market Square. No! She must not lose them now. But by the time she was in the square herself, both men had been swallowed up by the masses.

Where had they gone? There were so many routes. Did the stage take you up to Ackerley? No, it was not far enough to merit a stop. Or was it? She ran past Devett's, then the courthouse, and on into Rawlins Coaching Inn, but there was no sign of them. Running back into Market Square, she was beginning to despair when by some miracle she saw him. Not the speaker, but the other one, with the overcoat and hat, and that was good enough. He would know how to contact his colleague.

She kept her eyes glued to him as he weaved speedily through the hustle and bustle, and then disappeared into a nondescript house. Within seconds she was rapping on the door, and almost immediately a man answered, but he did not seem to be the right height or build for the person that she had been following.

'Have you just walked in here?' she checked, and he gave a blunt negative. 'Then can I speak to the gentleman who did?'

'Nobody's come in or out all day.'

'But I saw him, plain as I'm seeing you now.'

'You must be mistaken.'

The door began to close, so Bessie quickly put her hands out to stop it.

'I only want to ask about the speaker. Nothing else.'

'I've no idea what you're talking about.'

The man's face was now half-hidden, but she was able to identify fear in the part that was visible, and it made her finally realise the need for discretion. Heavy Petersham overcoat in this weather; brim of the hat pulled down low. This mystery individual wanted his membership of the movement kept secret. But she was not the enemy. Far from it.

'I understand what you're doing,' she whispered, 'but there's no need. I'm on your side.'

'You're in the way. And you've got the wrong house.' He kicked away the foot that she had lodged in the opening, and then forced the door closed.

Bessie looked up and down the street. What could she do? Go around the back? But what if the man left through the front? And what if he was leaving through the back right now? She simply had to get in there. Knocking again, she pasted herself against the brickwork on the other side of the drainpipe, and waited for the door to open once more.

'Look – I've already told you,' snapped the doorman, but then stopped because nobody was there. Stepping forward, he glanced around, and Bessie stole the chance to dart into the house, and up the stairs.

'I just want to talk. I'm not a threat,' she promised, bursting through the first door at the top, and finding a gentleman with his back to her. 'Please forgive me, but I need a name, that's all, and then I'll forget I've ever been here.'

'A name?' said a familiar voice as the other man rushed in apologetically.

'I'm sorry sir. I tried to stop her, but she tricked me.'

'Don't worry Medwin.' The individual turned around. 'You're very good at tricking people, aren't you Mrs Bateford?'

'Oh dear God!' exclaimed Bessie as Gil Tremaine smirked at her. 'What the hell are *you* doing here?'

'I could ask you the same question, but you'd probably tell me it was none of my business.'

'Yes I would, and I'd be damn well entitled. Nothing that happened in that field is any of your concern. Do you hear me?'

'I hear you, but I can't profess to understand you. Although that's not much of a surprise.'

'You understand perfectly well Tremaine. You were at that meeting, same as me, and you had no right. You had no right!'

'I don't suppose you could be a little more vociferous, could you? I'm not quite sure they caught my name at the far end of the street.'

'What's the problem? Afraid you might be exposed as a spy? All alone in a poor part of town with none of your chums to guard your back. Draw the short straw, did you?'

'What in the name of sanity are you jabbering on about?'

'You!' snapped Bessie. 'Donning this ridiculous disguise so you can inform on people. Reporting back, naming names, so they'll all be sacked for following a cause.'

'I'm not getting anybody the sack, you mad creature. Besides, if this were indeed part of some aristocratic conspiracy to see Chartist sympathisers struck off the payroll, we'd have sent a footman. My lot aren't known for getting their hands dirty.'

'What were you doing then?'

'Being a sympathiser myself.'

'You!'

'Yes, me!' Gil tipped his head back, and rolled his eyes.

'But that talk was aimed at workers. Ordinary men and women. "Trapped in a cycle of hereditary poverty". That's hardly you, is it?'

'I don't quite fit the bill, I grant you, but I still support the sentiment.'

'You support us winning the vote? The likes of me having a say?'

'The Charter advocates a vote for every man twenty-one years of age, of sound mind, and not undergoing punishment for crime,' explained Gil perfunctorily. 'And in my opinion it is outrageously ambitious, so I'm afraid the chances of *you* having a say in the near future are rather slim. But yes, I support an extension of the franchise.'

'Then why not be open about it? Why skulk around like this?'

'I often do my best work while skulking.'

'So it wouldn't have anything to do with the fact that you're scared?'

'No it wouldn't.' He peered around the side of Bessie, to where his friend was still standing in the doorway. 'You can leave us to it now, thank you Medwin.'

'Oh . . . right. I'll be downstairs sir.'

He reluctantly left, and Gil addressed himself once more to his uninvited guest.

'Pray tell me – what exactly am I scared of?'

'Being ostracised of course. It's all very well sitting at dinner and spouting a few choice remarks on our behalf. That's an endearing idiosyncrasy, isn't it? But to actually get out on the hustings? Well that would surely alienate far too many rich and important people.'

'I'm sorry to dismantle your finely-formed argument, but alienating people has never been something which has particularly preoccupied my attention.'

'Prove it then,' challenged Bessie. 'Step out into the sunshine, and declare your allegiance to the Chartist movement. Stand up and be counted!'

'Right now?'

'Yes, right now. Out there on the square.'

'Alright. How about I make you a deal – I'll shout it from the steps down there, if you shout it from the steps of Bateford Hall.'

He received no response.

'What? Don't you fancy it?'

There was nothing in this world that Bessie fancied less. She knew how Arnold viewed radicals of any kind.

'Now why are glass houses suddenly springing to mind?'

'I've no idea Mr Tremaine, because our situations are utterly incomparable.'

'Really? I'm not so sure that they are.'

'I can't risk doing something provocative, and you know it.'

'But presumably Arnold still doesn't know who you are, which means that your declaration of allegiance shouldn't imperil you in the slightest. You *were* Miss Arabrook after all – an artisan's daughter, who now believes in the advancement of fellow artisans and other working people. What could be more reasonable?'

Bessie looked down.

'But of course it's a different picture if you're . . . scared.'

'Oh very sharp Gilmour, very sharp.' She turned to leave.

'Why exactly are you here anyway?'

'That's none . . .' She stopped. 'It doesn't matter.'

'It mattered a few moments ago.'

'And now it doesn't.'

'Just like that?'

'Yes, just like that.'

'Didn't you say something about a name?'

'Alright! I wanted the name of the speaker.'

'Again I ask – why?'

'Because I thought he might be able to help bring down my husband.'

'Ah-ha! So you persist in harbouring that little objective then, do you?'

'Well I didn't marry him for his looks.'

'Oh come now, he isn't that bad.'

"You want to see him from my angle", thought Bessie, but bit her tongue.

'I can give you the name if you want?'

'There's no need any more.'

'Can I be of any personal assistance then?'

'No. If I do anything, I'm doing it by myself. I never know when you're going to get bored.'

'I provided you with financial assistance for a very long time Mrs Bateford.'

'Yes, and then you cut it off, and now all the families are starving. How does that sit on your conscience?'

'It may surprise you to know that they're not actually my responsibility.'

'No, they're mine, and the debt I owe to you is also my responsibility, which I can assure you is not something that I've forgotten.'

'So you still have faith in finding all those hundreds for me one day?'

'Yes I do!' Bessie turned away again.

'The money isn't really a concern, but I do expect something from you, if you can manage it.'

She paused, half-in and half-out of the door. 'What?'

'Your silence.'

A smile spread over her lips. 'So you *are* scared.'

'Not of alienation.' His voice was stern. 'But I think that a healthy aversion to the gallows is rather a good thing, don't you?'

'The gallows? So they're hanging people for standing in a field now?'

'Not your type of people, but . . .'

'*Your type* are another matter. Of course they are,' confirmed Bessie flippantly. 'Different rules apply.'

'Yes they do, and if you abandoned your class bias for a minute you might realise quite how unusual it is for somebody like me to associate with a cause like yours.'

'So we should be honoured that you lowered yourself to our degree, is that it?'

'No, but you should understand how things are viewed by the authorities. When working people mass together, they think rebellion. Must stamp it out. If a rich man's offering support, they think traitor to his rank – revolution. I'd be on a prison ship before tea-time, and as nice as Botany Bay sounds, I don't actually have any present wish to visit.'

She was about to argue that it was all melodramatic claptrap, but then remembered what had happened to the farm labourers in Tolpuddle. Seven years transportation just for swearing a private oath – and for wanting an adequate wage. The men had since been pardoned, but that was not the point.

'You don't believe me, do you?' attacked Gil, and Bessie was poised to refute him, but then those comments from her wedding-day jumped to the fore, and she refused to provide him with any agreement whatsoever.

'Alright,' he continued. 'You go ahead and tittle-tattle if you like, but don't let it come as a shock to you if you see me hung, drawn and quartered in Carrow Square. With, I might add, the drawing and quartering taking place while I'm still very much alive.'

'Don't worry Mr Tremaine, you can carry on masquerading as whatever you like. You've kept my secret this long, so I at least owe you the decency of doing the same.'

'You surprise me Mrs Bateford.'

'Please stop calling me that. I'm no more a Bateford than you are.'

'That isn't strictly true.'

'Well it will be "strictly true" at some point in the future.'

'Why? Are you planning on killing him?'

'The thought had certainly crossed my mind.'

'So I might yet be meeting you on the gallows?'

'Indeed you might.' And with that, she waltzed out of the house and down the street, with every step wondering how she could have been so blind for so long. All these weeks, and the months before, staggering around in a fog, and it had taken the likes of Gil Tremaine to show her the way.

There was no need to contact some distant factory inspector who might turn out to be overworked, inefficient or even corrupt. All she had to do was make Arnold *think* that he was under investigation. A masquerade. That was all it required. An elaborate masquerade.

Her feet began to skip along as the pieces of a plan merged into one. It was only as she walked up the drive of Bateford Hall that her brain finally came down from its cloud of discovery, and she thought about her surroundings. Her attire was not appropriate for the main entrance, but at least there was nothing untoward in her possession. All the food was with Seamus, and she might be lucky enough not to come across anybody until having changed.

Unfortunately that thought lasted for only a few seconds before being swept aside by the sound of hooves on the pebbles behind her. But it was not Arnold. She turned around to see a stranger.

'Excuse me Miss, I was wondering if you could help me.'

He alighted, and led a magnificent grey horse towards her.

'Do you work here?'

She was not sure how to answer that, so simply provided an affirmative.

'I'm looking for a woman by the name of Freya McNeill. I was led to believe that she might be working in Somerden, and so I'm trying the various employers.'

'Freya? There's nobody here by that name, but I'm not sure about the factory.'

'Factory?'

'The cotton mill.' Bessie pointed in the relevant direction.

'No, I think if she's anywhere, she'll be in the house.'

'Then I'm sorry, I can't help you.'

'What about Templeton? She may well be known as Freya Templeton.'

'Sorry. No Templetons, and no McNeills.'

'Oh.' He suddenly had the look of a man who had gone from believing that his journey was nearing its conclusion, to realising that he was probably still at the very start. 'Could you tell me how many female domestics are employed here?'

'Six.'

'And are any of them above average height, with auburn hair and piercing green eyes?'

That sounded a lot like Dolly. 'Why are you interested anyway?'

'Because she left her previous position in rather a hurry. There are some wages owing to her.'

Bessie did not believe him for a second. 'Sorry,' she said again. 'No Freyas, and no auburn hair.'

'Well if anybody hears anything, could you let me know? I'll be staying at the coaching inn for a couple more nights.'

'Certainly. And your name is . . ?'

'Emerson. Kent Emerson.' He offered it after a slight pause, and then stepped up into his saddle, and rode away.

Bessie stood thinking for a minute before heading in through the rear entrance. She really ought to concentrate on herself, but the curiosity was simply too powerful. Going in search of Dolly, she finally located her in Harris' bedroom – putting away laundry in the chest of drawers.

'I've just met a stranger who might be looking for you.'

'Me? I don't know why anybody would be looking for me.'

'He was interested in a woman matching your description.'

'I'm sure there are many around here who match my description,' said Dolly. 'What did he want?'

'To give you some money. Apparently you left your previous position without being properly paid.'

'Oh well it must be somebody else then. Nobody owes me anything I'm afraid. Did he give his name by the way?'

'What does it matter if he has nothing to do with you?' countered Bessie, hoping to draw Dolly's attention away from the handkerchief that she had already folded twice. But it was only the name itself which did that.

'Emerson. Are you sure?'

'Yes, and he was riding a grey steed.'

'Grey?' repeated Dolly, with a flash in her eyes that Bessie could interpret so vividly. But why would the mere colour of a horse provoke panic?

'What did Mr Emerson look like?'

'Tall, smart, dark hair.' Bessie walked forward and placed a hand upon the laundry-maid's arm. 'If you're in any sort of trouble, please tell me. I might be able to help.' Dolly was probably some ten years the senior, but Bessie talked like the mother figure.

'I'm not in any trouble Mrs Bateford.'

'I've told you – it's Elizabeth. And if I'm not mistaken, you're . . . Freya?'

'I don't know what you mean.' Dolly snapped the words, and before Bessie could argue to the contrary, Arnold's butler appeared in the doorway.

'The Master wants to see you.'

'I'll be there in a minute,' she replied.

'He wants to see you immediately,' came the clarification, and Bessie knew that everything else would have to be left until later. There was also no opportunity to change, but hopefully she could provide an adequate explanation for her current state.

The butler strode down the stairs, opened the drawing room door, and she entered quite calmly. All of the recent excitement meant that she felt perfectly capable of coping with a situation like this.

'Where have you been?' demanded her husband, turning away from the window, and making no attempt to mask his anger.

'Out for a walk. It was such a lovely afternoon, and I put this old dress on, for fear of snagging one of the others.'

'Where did you go?'

'Around the fields at first, but then I ended up wandering all the way into Somerden, before turning around and coming straight back.'

It was true, but she had the sense that her bright and breezy account was only heightening his rage.

'Did you see anybody?'

'No. Except in passing of course.'

'You're lying.'

'Lying? Whyever would you think that?' She could not possibly mention the Chartist demonstration. If he heard murmurings of another one, he would set the dogs on them.

'Because it's so bloody obvious, that's why!' He stamped his foot, and the reverberation carried right across the room. 'You've been with another man, haven't you?'

'No! Arnold, I wouldn't!'

'Who was it? Munroe? Thomas? Give birthday boy a little treat, did we?'

'Thomas? I don't know where he is.'

'Yes you do.'

'I don't, I swear, and even if I did, I would never betray you. I accepted your proposal quite willingly.'

'You accepted because you had no choice, and now you think you can make a laughing-stock out of me.'

'I'm not making a laughing-stock out of anyone. I only went for a walk.'

'A walk without your wedding-ring eh? A walk that caused a wild flush to settle in your cheeks.'

'It . . . it was warm.'

'Get upstairs,' he ordered, advancing upon her.

'No, please Arnold.'

'I said get upstairs.' And before she could dart away, he had grabbed her by the hair, and was using it to drag her all the way into their bedroom.

'Please,' she begged when he let go, and was undoing his belt. 'Not on the Sabbath.'

'The Sabbath sounds like the ideal day for teaching whoring sinners a lesson.'

'I'm not a whore,' she retorted, with defiance bordering on stupidity, but there was still too much Cullen in her not to fight. If the staff were listening – and no doubt they were – then they would not be hearing her take it submissively like the first Mrs Bateford.

'You are what I say you are,' he growled.

'But I haven't done anything wrong. I went for a walk, that's all, and if I'd known you wouldn't like it, I would never have left the premises.'

'You knew damn well that I wouldn't like it, which is why you put on this old tat, so you could sneak around and avoid detection.'

'No Arnold, I . . .'

'Get it off.'

She hesitated.

'I said take the thing off!'

The glare was sufficient to make her obey, before he snatched it from her grasp, ripped the others from the wardrobe, and stalked from the room. Whatever he was doing, it was the end for those dresses, and it filled her with an even more powerful hatred. Josiah had handed over precious savings to buy that material, and now Arnold was destroying it, like he destroyed everything else.

'There was no need for that,' she declared when he returned. 'You have this all wrong.'

'Oh have I? So you're telling the truth, are you? You saw nobody, except in passing?'

'That's right.'

'Then who was that man outside?'

'I don't know. He was looking for somebody, but found he was out of luck.'

'You're lying to me again!'

'I'm not!'

'I know a lying whore when I see one.'

'And it sounds like you've seen plenty in your time.' She stepped back the moment that she had said it, almost as stunned as he was.

'What did you say?'

'I . . . I . . . nothing.'

'Tell me what you said!'

Bessie had been here before – with Garrick – and when he had demanded a repeat, she had hurled it at him. But she was not about to make the same mistake twice. 'I'm sorry Arnold. I didn't mean it, believe me.' She hated the pitiful whine of her own voice, but she really did need him to stop this now.

'Sorry? You're not sorry. But you're going to be.' He lunged forward, seized her by the throat and threw her onto the bed – with such a force that she fell off the other side and hit her head. For a moment she had no vision, and no idea of where she was. But then Arnold hauled her up, and as his bulbous body sank down on top of her, she knew exactly where she was, and the hell into which she was being pitched.

CHAPTER FOUR

To describe herself as sore the next day was putting it mildly, but Bessie was still required to attend breakfast as if nothing had happened. As if her husband had not just accused her of the worst moral crime imaginable.

The meal itself was typically awkward, and she could tell that Charles had sensed the change in atmosphere. He was dying to know the cause, but she had no intention of satisfying his curiosity, and presumably Arnold was not about to admit that his wife of less than two months had already defiled the marriage-bed. She assumed that he would keep a very close eye on her as a result, but that was not in fact the case. For most of the morning she was left to her own devices – although wherever she went, the butler seemed to pop up. That planted a rather mischievous thought in her mind, inciting her to stride down the front steps and really send Arnold into a spin, but self-preservation prevailed. She actually had no desire to provoke a recurrence of last night – at least not for a considerably long time – so she frittered away the hours until summoned to his study at noon.

'I want you to learn how to ride,' he announced. 'You should find your predecessor's riding-habit in the attic, along with other bits and pieces, and a pair of boots are to be delivered this afternoon. Your instructor will be an overseer from the mill. He is coming to work here as an under-butler – and will live in.'

The last two words were emphasised, and Bessie simply stared in confusion. An extra member of staff was indeed a good idea; poor Duncan had been run ragged since the disappearance of Yates. But why exactly was she being rewarded in this way? The very next day? Thankfully – and rather unusually – Arnold provided her with the answer:

'I've been invited to join the local hunt, and although you will not be participating yourself, I expect you to play a fully active role in the social scene.'

In other words – he was not leaving her here for hours on end, dallying with goodness knows who. Bessie smiled as she realised that perhaps there were some advantages to being dubbed a Jezebel. If it meant that she could escape this house and experience the open fields on just one occasion, then last night was most definitely worth it.

'I suggest you set to work on altering the clothes. Your first lesson will be tomorrow.' He leaned back in his chair, and looked out of the window. 'Good. Your instructor is on his way now.'

She had no view of the drive from where she was standing, but soon a knock came on the door, and a man entered. Her eyes instantly flashed across to Arnold, and saw that a smirk of domination had taken up gleeful residence. This great hulk of an overseer was not here to be an under-butler; he was here to keep her in check, to intimidate her into towing the line. And it was already working. Because she knew him. She even knew the taste of his blood.

This was the man whose hand she had bitten on Ulmers Hill. The one who had taken his revenge by testifying to her having sticky fingers in the silverware. She thought that he must have moved on, left the district, when all this time he had been within spitting distance – gaining pleasure from inflicting pain on others, and now the pain was coming right up to her door.

She took a breath. It was important to breathe. Her appearance had changed dramatically – she had to remember that, and now she was Lady of the Manor. Nobody would ever equate Elizabeth Arabrook with some outspoken maid from the valley.

"Get a grip", ordered a voice from deep inside. "And stop looking so ridiculously guilty".

'Elizabeth, this is Rufus, one of my most trusted assistants.'

Yet more emphasis from Arnold as she nodded, and the overseer nodded back.

'Have you settled into your new quarters Henderson?'

'Yes sir, and I have transferred my responsibilities at the mill.'

'Excellent. Mrs Bateford will require some things from the attic, and then you should be on hand in case she needs anything else.'

'Certainly.' Henderson left the room, knowing which chin-twitch indicated dismissal, and Bessie managed to follow, even though her knees were buckling.

Why was she in such a state? She had entered the lion's den and confronted four Bateford males, so everybody else ought to be a breeze. Maybe it was the trauma of last night finally hitting home, or the sheer size of this man. He gave her a horrible reminder of being outnumbered and overpowered on that Hill, and the thought of him now watching her every move made her feel totally suffocated. It also made the implementation of her plan a hundred times more difficult, but what could she do? Arnold's word was Law.

Having been bored with nothing to think about, she now had far too much to think about, and Dolly had upped and vanished. The laundry-maid had never lived in, and nobody had given much thought to where she went once her shift came to an end, but she had presented herself on time every day for the last ten months. Until today.

Bessie was intrigued – and concerned. If only she had the luxury of being mistress of her own actions, she would go to that coaching inn, talk to that man, and get to the bottom of all this. But of course she was only mistress in one very primitive sense, and it was probably best left alone anyway. So she put it out of her mind, and instead took a needle and thread to the buff-coloured riding-jacket of Jane Bateford. It felt awful to pick through a dead woman's clothes like this – as if dancing on her grave. Except dance was obviously completely the wrong word, because there was no joy at all to be gleaned from sitting in Arnold's drawing room with the likes of Henderson prowling around outside.

He kept on prowling for most of the afternoon, while she kept on sewing, and then dinner came around again, with Harris drinking to excess, and Bessie choosing to join him in a glass of wine. She had been instructed to wear red, and that in itself meant the need for a shot of something strong. And twenty-four hours later, she would need something stronger still.

Her first "lesson" turned into a complete nightmare, and that had nothing to do with the horse. He was called Duke – a docile old thing, with a lovely chestnut coat, and a beautiful white star on his forehead. Swishing away a few flies occasionally, he otherwise stood in sleepy-eyed submission awaiting instruction, and she learnt how to give a few of those instructions – having grasped the fundamentals, like climbing into the saddle.

It was not dignified to spread one's legs apart and straddle such a beast, she could understand that, but really and truly whoever thought it feasible to control a horse with both feet on the left-hand side? By the time you were sufficiently settled, and no longer at risk of sliding off, it was quicker to walk to wherever you were going. But Arnold wanted her to ride, so ride she would, and it was another glorious day. She really did try to enjoy it, despite Rufus constantly staring at her. What on earth was causing him such a problem? She simply could not work it out, and that preoccupation continued until he put a stop to it in the most dreadful of ways.

It happened right at the end, when she was preparing to hand over the reins, and go inside. That action in itself was an uncomfortable one, even with a ruffian who deserved no better. Aristocrats handed over belongings – be it animals or luggage – for some lackey to deal with, while they partook of refreshments followed by a lie down. She hated turning into that kind of person, but it was the words accompanying her action which pitched her into disarray.

Staring even more piercingly than usual, Rufus Henderson sniffed up and said: 'Haven't I seen you somewhere before?'

Six little words, nine little syllables, but they ripped the ground from beneath Bessie's feet and sent her spiralling into a tunnel of despair.

Heaven knows how she managed to muster any sort of speech, but an uppish retort of: 'I shouldn't think so,' eventually issued forth, before she stomped back to the house as if it had been impertinent of him to even make the suggestion.

Then she hurried up to her old room, and sank down by the wall. Was it really as bad as it seemed? Had she done something to trigger off the beginnings of a recognition? Or was she simply reminding him of somebody else? Had she responded correctly? Or put him on even higher alert? What should she do? Was there anything *to* do? Could she act in a way that was even further removed from Bessie Cullen? Or would any alteration of her approach now be the worst thing imaginable?

So many questions, and over the coming hours she came to realise that there was only one answer. She had to get rid of him. But that provoked yet another question. How? He was not likely to leave voluntarily, which meant that she had to force him out. But he was one of the most loyal of Bateford lackeys – "trusted" – so would not be dismissed purely on her say-so. She had to convince Arnold of the need to do it himself, and perhaps recent events had already lit up the way.

She had been branded adulterous, so now it was time to show that all her protestations of innocence were indeed false, that she had given her love to another man. The penalty for such treachery would presumably be a repeat of Sunday night, and although painful, she would come through it. Whereas the man who had led her astray? Defiled her? His punishment would be banishment, or even worse.

The next couple of days were taken up with arranging all the details inside her head, and then she began to lay the foundations – asking Arnold about "Ruff's" whereabouts, expressing the view that he was a most welcome addition to the household. Showing a decidedly unsubtle, and unhealthy, interest in their burly bruiser from the factory. And when that was done, it was time for his day of judgement to dawn.

She had fixed upon Monday out of fear of leaving it any longer, but then the weather turned, and in the end it was Thursday the thirteenth. Her stomach rumbled with anxiety the entire morning, but there would be no more delaying. Her lesson was set for three o'clock, and time-tabled to last exactly an hour. Not a minute longer. Arnold was a stickler for punctuality, and especially so since the day of her supposed transgression. But today she was planning on being more than just a minute late – and Duncan would be on hand to provide an explanation.

Going in search of her footman friend shortly before the lesson, she told him that if enquiries were made, he was to say: "I don't know about Mrs Bateford at the moment, but I believe she was below-stairs earlier on".

'But,' began Duncan with a frown. She was not allowed to be below-stairs. The Master's rules on separation were well established, and strictly enforced. Family did not consort with staff, and she was no longer a member of staff. He wondered whether to remind her of that particular fact, but instead asked: 'You really want me to do this?'

'Absolutely,' she replied, and made it clear that he would not get into any kind of trouble.

Eventually his agreement was secured, and she embraced her lesson with enthusiasm, taking Duke further than he had ever been before. Rufus did not like it, but he was her instructor, not her controller, and he knew it. Besides, it was Duke doing all the leading, not the other way around. She was nowhere near proficient enough to be in full command of such a magnificent animal, and hence she was utterly at a loss to stop him when he chose to take her across the brook.

It was the perfect spot. On the other side was a clearing within a forest, and beyond that was Tremaine land. Rufus would not know which part of the forest had swallowed her up. Of course he could track her, but it would take a while – and that was all she needed. Previous trips had enabled her to gauge approximately how long it would take to get back to Bateford wood, and as she tethered Duke to Thomas' favourite tree, she was right on time. Now for stage two – into the house, and Henderson's room – unseen.

The first element was easy, she had done it on many an occasion before; and there was a significant chance that part two might not be too challenging either. As a nursemaid she had become familiar with which bedroom belonged to which person, so locating his actual lodgings ought to be quite straightforward. Tess and Constance would usually be an obstacle at this hour, but with Dolly having disappeared, and no replacement yet secured, they were sharing the laundry as well as attending to their other duties. Agatha was upstairs with Ella, and it did not matter if Duncan or Mrs Evans saw anything untoward. So that only left Mrs Muir and the butler.

The latter often handed over responsibility to Duncan at this hour – to have a rest before returning to his post early in the evening – and that would be ideal as long as he took a proper time-out, putting his feet up in his own room, rather than having a cup of tea at the kitchen table.

As for the housekeeper, hopefully she would have dreamt up some excuse to be above-stairs and out of the way. It inflated Mrs Muir's sense of self-importance to frequent the family areas as often as possible, so she would supervise the maids unnecessarily, or finalise a grocery order in one of the spare rooms, and there was no reason why today should be any different.

The chances of evading detection were therefore quite good, and as Bessie peered through the back door to find that only the cook was in attendance, she knew that this was to be her lucky hour.

'Good afternoon,' she declared brightly, pretending that it was perfectly normal to waltz through in her riding-habit and boots. She did not offer an explanation, nor ask Mrs Evans to keep an eye out, because this would all be done within half a minute.

There were only two rooms to check, and although the first proved to be empty, the second showed the right signs of occupation. Removing her "important item" from an inside pocket, she placed it under his bedstead, helped herself to a pair of his trousers, and then scurried back into the open air so fast that Mrs Evans was left debating whether she had seen anything at all.

Creeping around to the front of the house, Bessie then hovered near the ivy, waiting for Arnold to appear. It did not take long. Presumably the hour-hand had clicked onto four, and it was time to hunt her down. Striding out of his study, Arnold went straight over to Duncan, and although Bessie could not decipher the words, she could decipher his very next move. As soon as the footman responded, Arnold marched – without hesitation – in the direction of the back stairs. He had not seen those stairs in years, probably not since he was a boy, but with a little help from her friend she was encouraging him to chart new territory. Arnold Bateford had taken the bait, and now all that remained was for her to rejoin Henderson, and wait for the sparks to fly.

Scampering over to the wood, she pushed the trousers deep into the hollow of an old tree-stump, before using it to launch herself back into the saddle. Heading down towards the valley, she then cut away north-eastward, and managed to arrive at her chosen point just as Rufus was galloping over the brow of the hill.

'What happened to you?' she exclaimed, sounding both excited and affronted in equal measure. 'I ended up riding all by myself.'

'Which was surely your intention,' he grunted, but she pretended that it was lost on the breeze.

'Duke took it upon himself to show me the valley, and I found myself utterly powerless to refuse. In fact I became quite distressed at one point.' She laughed like a nervous little girl, and then continued to jabber away as they neared the house, the perfect picture of happiness – until Arnold came storming down the drive, and it was time to ram some nails squarely into this Henderson coffin.

Steering Duke next to Rufus' gelding, she declared: 'It was *such* a relief when I saw you again,' and promptly placed her hand upon his arm, before drawing it back as if caught out. 'Oh Arnold!' she cried, trotting up to her husband. 'I'm so sorry we're late. We ended up rather lost.' She slithered down from the saddle, and pushed a lock of hair out of her eye – to convey that she had enjoyed a very wild time indeed.

'Get in the house.'

Bessie leaned away in apparent shock. 'Are you angry Arnold?'

'I said get inside.'

He did not place a finger on her, but the force of his displeasure was enough to propel her up the steps as he stalked from behind, with Ruff bringing up the rear. The moment that they were over the threshold, she shot upstairs, and Arnold turned on his henchman.

There were no words at first, and Rufus knew what that meant. He braced himself for the eruption, although was utterly perplexed as to why he should be the subject of one.

'You've had your hands on her, haven't you?'

'What?'

'What? Don't "what" me, you rotten swine. You've had my wife.'

'No I haven't!'

'Then how do you explain these?' Arnold advanced, silk stockings in hand, and Rufus stared at them with the wide eyes of ignorance. 'They were found under your bed.'

'My what?'

'Bed! How did they get there?'

'I don't know. I've never seen them before in my life.'

'So they developed a mind of their own and walked down by themselves, did they?' Arnold raised a sardonic eyebrow.

'No. Of course not.'

'How then?'

'I . . .' Rufus was about to reiterate that he had absolutely no idea, but suddenly the events of the last hour began to slot into place. 'Because she put them there.'

Now it was Arnold's turn to exclaim: 'What?'

'Your wife. She crept back during the lesson, and put them there. On purpose.'

'You mean that she left them there after one of your little liaisons.'

'No! I lost her up by Tremaine's forest, and only found her just now, all-smiles, and acting weird. She planted those things deliberately for you to find.'

'And why the blazes would she do that?'

'Because there's something wrong. I don't know what it is, but I know her from somewhere. She isn't who she says.'

'She's my wife, that's who she is.'

'But she's playing games. Can't you see that?'

'All I can see is you trying to squirm off the hook.' Arnold began to twist the stockings into a ready-made noose, and Rufus backed towards the door.

'I've served here for years. You've only known her a few months. Why won't you believe me?'

'Because it's nonsense. Why would she provoke my wrath, when she knows exactly what I'll do to her?'

'Because all that matters is what you're doing to me! She's probably up there now laughing at us.'

'Laughing? Yes, that's right, isn't it? You've both been laughing, haven't you? It was *you* that Sunday! Christ, and then I brought you into this very house! How long has it been going on? Weeks? Months? Was it you she was seeing on those weekends away?'

'What weekends? I don't know what you're talking about.'

'Don't you?' A frozen look spread across Arnold's face. 'Well maybe you'll better understand the talk of my fists.' He pounced, and Rufus fell against the door-frame in a desperate attempt to flee.

Bessie heard the sound from upstairs, and grinned from ear to ear. Whatever was being done to Rufus

Henderson, he deserved it; and the same went for Arnold too. Rufus was by far the bigger man, could easily dominate any fight, but was unlikely to even try. He had the servile mentality of a hired brute, and turning on his master was not in his nature. So Arnold would soon be up to deal with her, and that meant she needed to prepare – both for the pain, and for the final part of her performance.

Removing her riding accessories, she put them away, and then sat on the end of their bed, manufacturing a look of apprehension as footsteps sounded on the landing. It was indeed Arnold, and he had bloodied hands.

'Oh dear Lord,' she exclaimed, rising to her feet. 'Are you hurt?'

Arnold's top lip literally rippled with contempt.

'Wh . . . what about Mr Henderson? What have you done to him?'

'You should be more concerned about what I'm going to do to you.'

'Why?'

'Don't act dewy-eyed Elizabeth, or I swear to God, I'll kill you.'

'But I don't understand.' It was an intentionally pathetic statement, and she offered little resistance as he pinned her down.

'How the hell did he get hold of these eh? Tell me! How?' Arnold spat the words down upon her, and held the stockings right over her face, so that Henderson's blood dripped onto her cheek.

'I . . .' She had an answer all set for this question, designed to make her appear impassioned and yet dreadfully duplicitous at the same time. But his chokehold was just that bit too tight, and she thought better of it. 'Please Arnold. Let me go.'

'Not until I have some answers. How did they get there?'

'Where?'

'His bedroom!'

'I don't know. He must have taken them.'

'You're lying.'

'I'm not.'

'Yes you are. You've been meeting him, haven't you? How many times? Ten? Twenty? Whenever my back's been turned?'

'No! Arnold, why would I ever do such a thing?'

'Because you're an ungrateful little slut, and you can't help yourself.'

Bessie had managed to wriggle so that Arnold's grip was not directly over her windpipe – and it was a good thing, because he pressed down in order to propel himself back onto his feet. Then he snarled at her for a full minute, before pushing the braces off his shoulders – and *that* was when her act faltered.

Whether it was a deep-seated satisfaction that this was actually proceeding exactly as anticipated, or the irony of those forget-me-nots embroidered on the straps of Arnold's braces, but a look of self-assurance flashed across Bessie's face, and he saw it. In that instant he realised that she was not afraid of him, not one bit; that what he had done to her last time had not even left a mark. Well this time he would not leave a mark, he would leave a bloody great welt.

Pulling the braces back up, he stalked out, and Bessie realised that something terrible had just happened. What had she done? What was he going to do to her? Should she try to escape? So many questions again, but no answers until one was suddenly presented to her – in the form of Duncan.

Ordering the bewildered footman into the room, Arnold ripped the coverlet and duvet from their bed, held out the offending stockings, and barked three words: 'Tie her up.'

'But . . .'

'Just do it.'

Duncan inched forward, and Bessie decided that it would probably be a good time to start pleading – for real.

'There's no need for this Arnold. Please.'

'There's every need,' he growled, before issuing Duncan with very specific instructions: 'One hand to that post, one to the other, and you've got sixty seconds starting now.' He was referring to the decorative pieces of wood on either side of the head-board, and promptly pulled out his timepiece.

With quivering fingers, Duncan forced himself to lift Bessie's right wrist, and she nodded to tell him that he should do as directed. This was her battle, *her* game that she had chosen to play, and nobody innocent was going to suffer for it. Besides, she could handle this. It could not be as bad as prison, or the night that Thomas had left, or when she had been told that her baby brother was dead. So many bleak memories, and she called upon every last one in order to construct a coat of armour strong enough to repel any onslaught.

'Twenty-nine, twenty-eight, twenty-seven . . .' Arnold was counting down, and also speeding up, as Duncan crossed to the other wrist.

Bessie knew that the first knot had been left loose, and her heart ached with thanks, but she was not about to land him in trouble by breaking free. This was one time in her life when she simply had to take the medicine. Rufus was either dead or gone, and she would presumably live to fight another day. Nothing else really mattered.

'Five, four, three, two . . .'

Duncan finished with a second to spare, and sprang up, back straight, awaiting his order to leave – but was in fact given an order to fetch.

'Get the cat.'

'The what?'

'Cat man, CAT! Do I have to keep on repeating myself?'

'No sir, of course not sir.' Duncan hurried from the room, and a minute later, he was back with the cat-o'-nine-tails. It was kept in the top drawer of the dining room sideboard. Nobody could fathom why, but they all knew about it. Except Mrs Bateford. Until now.

Handing it over, the traumatised young man then received his marching orders, and without daring to look at Elizabeth, he obeyed.

Arnold then spent an inordinate amount of time unravelling his leather whip, manipulating it, stroking it, practically caressing it, as if revisiting a most treasured possession. Bessie twisted her head around to see what he was doing, and then turned away when it became unbearable, but Arnold quickly seized back her attention. He lashed the end of the bed with such force that the reverberation ran right through into her bones, but she knew it would be nothing compared to the impact that was coming.

Now she felt scared, really scared. How many strikes was he going to make? Could she take it? Or was she at risk of actually dying here? She should have left with Thomas when she had the chance. Even after he ran, she should have gone. What in the name of sanity was she doing here?

Closing her eyes tight, she tensed, but nothing happened, and eventually she had to open them again. Arnold was next to her, the whip hanging down, dormant but ready.

'Have you ever come across one of these Elizabeth?'

She swallowed, and shook her head.

'Then let me introduce you. This little feature here – you see it? It runs all the way along. Nine times. Nine beautifully-constructed knotted lashes. To give the whole thing that extra bit of punch.'

He drew his arm back, and hit her with such force that it jarred his wrist, but for the first couple of seconds Bessie felt absolutely nothing. Her suit of armour was working its magic. She was immune. It even flashed into her mind that perhaps she should scream – convey agony, because otherwise he would find something worse. But within the blink of an eye, there was no question of pretence. The pain seared through her like a fire, and her lungs emitted a cry loud enough to wake the dead.

'Ah good,' concluded Arnold. 'You felt it.'

Placing the whip down, he put both hands at the nape of her neck, and tore the clothes from her back. Even her undergarments. Then he ran his fingers over her skin, almost gently, as if tending the wounds of a loved one.

'It's amazing how strong these habits can be. Barely a mark, but that'll soon change. Unless of course there's no need. Are you sufficiently sorry Elizabeth?'

She wanted to say that he could go to hell, but instead whispered: 'Yes Arnold. It's enough.'

'You'd like me to stop already?'

'Yes. Please.'

'Oh what a pity then that I can't. You see – each of these knots represents a day of our marriage, and how long have we been joined together now? Come on, you're a governess – you can count, can't you? Fifty? Fifty-five days? Yes, that's it. And we've only covered nine so far.'

He hit her again, but this time there was no scream. Bessie clenched her teeth so tight that not even a whimper was allowed to escape.

'What? Didn't that one hurt?' He rubbed his hand over her back again, and the sweat of his palms seeped into the cuts until they were literally stinging beyond belief.

'Such lovely smooth skin, and already such a mess. Apart from this bit down here.' He thrust his hands down the inside of her skirt, and then pulled outwards until all of the new stitching snapped. Then he flicked the whip a couple of times on the floor, before flexing for strike number three. But it did not come. Right at the last minute he stopped – because Bessie had moved. Trying to deflect the full force, she had shifted slightly to the side, but Arnold was not having any of that.

Leaning down until his face was right up against hers, he rasped: 'Move again, and I'll carry on until there isn't an inch of skin left. Understand?'

She lowered her head, but that was not enough.

'I didn't quite catch that. What did you say?'

'I . . . er . . . yes.'

'Yes what?'

'I won't move,' she promised. Her eyes had watered so much that they were swimming with tears, but she would not let them drop.

'Excellent,' declared Arnold, pursuing the sarcasm with relish as he stood upright once more. 'You're getting the hang of this now. Right, where were we? Eighteen. Yes, that was it.'

He proceeded to inflict three more blows, but fury quickly replaced the sarcasm, because she refused to utter a single sound. He could not understand it; he was hitting her with all his might. She could not understand it either. Why defy him in this one regard when she was submitting in every other? Was it simply in her nature to keep on fighting even when the cause was lost? To try and stand even when her feet were sinking fast? Or was it because another pitiful wail would be an affront to all the misery that the Cullens had ever suffered? An insult to the memory of little Pauly who had died before he had even taken his first breath.

No. Both statements were true, but she could not lay claim to either of them. She was biting her tongue, and practically through it, because all other submissions were mere whispers, for Arnold's ears only. Whereas a scream would involve the whole household. The first one must have echoed around the ears of Constance and Mrs Muir, and there was too much stubborn pride coursing through Bessie's veins to allow it to happen again. So she buried her pain deep inside, and Arnold stalked from the room with the frustration of a horseman battling a mare he was determined to break. When he returned, it was to explore a theme that he had already introduced – salt in the wound. Pounding a handful of the stuff in a pestle and mortar, he tipped the granules into some water on the wash-stand, and helped himself to a strip of her torn clothing.

Bessie watched as he dipped it into the briny solution, first one side, and then the other, so carefully, so deliberately, before carrying it across the room, and slapping it onto her skin. It was hard to put into words what it felt like as he covered every inch of her back. Like a thousand needles were being pushed without mercy into every bleeding lesion. But still she did not give him the satisfaction that he sought.

Taking the cat in hand, he was nearly tempted to throttle her with it, but instead took one final strike. He had held it back for this moment, so that each of the lashes would drive the salt so deep that she would never forget the feel of it. Yet *still* there was nothing. He stomped his way back to the door, unsure of what to do next, until suddenly struck by the arithmetic of it all. Six cracks of the whip, nine lashes – that made only fifty-four days. There was one day unaccounted for.

He swung around and hit her again. It was from the other side of the bed, and with his weaker left arm, but it took Bessie by surprise, and that caused a cry of defeat to ring out before she could fight to stop it. A heavy silence followed – as if cementing the significance of that moment – until Arnold let the whip drop from his hand, and the tears finally dropped down his wife's face.

'Betray me again, and you'll get the same. If we've been married ninety days, you'll have ten. If it's nine hundred, I'll flex my wrist a hundred times. Although I dare say you'll be dead before I get anywhere near the end.'

Arnold concluded his declaration with what sounded like a snigger of amusement, before crouching at the head of the bed and forcing her to look at him.

It was not followed by his usual demand for consent. He did not seek a nod, or words of compliance, nor any vow that she would mend her ways. And she did not offer him any such assurance. The look was enough. They both knew that from that moment on she would do absolutely everything in her power never to incur a repeat of this day again.

CHAPTER FIVE

For Bessie a period of solitude followed the stare. Arnold left, and an hour passed before Duncan was permitted to enter. There was anguish etched into the creases of his forehead, but he had kept away until given the instruction. Sixty minutes of standing to attention in the hall, wondering and wondering. Why had he agreed to give that message to Mr Bateford? He should never have done it. Why had Elizabeth *wanted* him to do it? Was she still alive? What about Mr Henderson? There were spatters of blood on the pebbles outside, but no other sign of him. Had he left? Was he coming back? Had Elizabeth done something inappropriate with her new teacher? And did it merit a whipping if she had? No, never, and he should have said something. He should have refused to fetch the cat, refused to tie up a female. But he needed this job. Ma needed the money, and that thought in the back of his mind rendered him devoid of any backbone that he might otherwise have been able to muster.

So he had stood there in spineless submission, until eventually issued with a long list of orders. Arnold wanted his wife removed from their room immediately, and put into her old bed, where she would be allowed to "recuperate". Fresh water and towelling were to be provided, but she would tend to herself. No other assistance was to be made available. The soiled sheet needed to be washed, along with her clothes, before the latter were returned to Elizabeth – complete with sewing kit – in order for her to mend them to a professional standard.

The water on the wash-stand was to be replaced, and Arnold requested that his Jacquard-woven silk waistcoat be put out ready for him before dinner, along with his best shirt. Elizabeth would remain in her old room for exactly five days, and was barred from leaving during that time. Her meals would be brought to her, but there would be no other contact until Tuesday afternoon. At that point she would be able to resume her usual duties, returning to the master bedroom, and preparing for the evening – where she could wear any dress of her choice, as long as it was red.

Duncan's body was swept with relief as he tried to absorb the mass of information. If Elizabeth was expected to be up and about in five days, then she could not have suffered too badly. It was only when he laid eyes on her back that his relief turned to horror once more. The criss-cross of cuts was invisible, but he could see blood. So much blood. Like somebody had filled a pail from the slaughter of an animal, and deluged her with it. He could smell it too, congealing in the warm June air. But thank God it *was* congealing. Nobody could afford to lose a drop more than that.

As he inched forward, he was still not convinced that she was actually alive. Her body was slumped to the side, head bowed, eyes closed. But as he drew near, he finally detected small signs of breathing, and instantly looked away. The torn clothes had dropped down, leaving her exposed, and making him feel decidedly uncomfortable.

Untying her wrists, he eased her off the bed, and draped the coverlet around her as quickly as possible.

She did not flinch, but neither did she seem to care whether he covered her or not. Steering them towards the door, he then helped her out onto the landing, where they proceeded under the watchful gaze of Mrs Muir – and Harris. The latter had not set out to appear at this moment, had not been listening at keyholes and peering through cracks in the door like certain others. He had endured the misfortune of hearing the earlier events, and had waited until he thought it was safe to venture out. Now that he realised otherwise, he promptly withdrew. There were enough images in his head from when his mother had been alive, and he had absolutely no desire to embrace any more of them.

Mrs Muir on the other hand, was not about to go anywhere. She was hovering near the top of the stairs, and when Duncan's direction became clear, she moved towards the nursery door to get a really good look. Constance and Tess had been given strict instructions to focus on their work, but Constance had heard the click of the door, and joined the scene too. They both stood unblinking, eyes peeled, absorbing every detail of this nursemaid who had risen to such prominence, only now to be rendered pitiful and worthless. The dishevelled hair, tear-stained face, the state of the sheet, that smell of bloody defeat – it was all exactly as Ida Muir had predicted, and satisfaction permeated her very soul. She even indulged in a conceited smirk as Duncan ushered Elizabeth into the room, and closed the door behind her.

'Tell me what happened,' snapped the housekeeper at once, but Duncan simply shook his head. He had done little else for Elizabeth, but the one thing he could do now was keep his mouth shut.

Aggravation instantly burnt in Ida's breast, and she reminded the footman of her senior position, but it made absolutely no difference. What was she going to do? Report him to the Master for keeping the Master's affairs a secret? Duncan knew that she did not have a leg to stand on, and reminded her in turn that he was following Mr Bateford's orders, and Mr Bateford would surely not like to hear of any interference. That – along with footsteps on the stairs – sent Mrs Muir scurrying back down to the kitchen, and Constance back to her chores.

As it turned out, it was Bateford junior – Charles making a surprise visit home from the mill, but Duncan still took precautions in case Mrs Muir should reappear. Particularly with the cat-o'-nine-tails. He cleaned it in situ, and hid it under a pillow as he rushed it back to its drawer. Then he changed the water in the wash-basin, and returned the pestle and mortar to the kitchen, trying not to imagine how on earth that could have featured in Elizabeth's ordeal.

Once the main bedroom was fully back to normal, he knocked respectfully on her door, and provided water and towelling – followed by her nightdress. It was the only item of clothing that she was allowed for the next five days, and she stared at it as he placed it on the end of the bed. Now was probably not the right time, but he relayed the list of rules as well, wanting them out of his head, but they seemed to pass right over hers. He made another attempt the next day, but received exactly the same impression. When her eyes were not shut, they were vacant, and she was also refusing to eat.

He had taken it upon himself to bring the food to her, making out that it was Mr Bateford's express instruction, and it was always Mrs Evans' finest fare – hot and inviting, but Elizabeth was not even the remotest bit interested. He had resorted to eating it himself, afraid that the cook might be offended – or end up worrying more than she was already.

When it came to Sunday morning, he decided that something really had to be done. Elizabeth had not eaten a morsel in three days, and she was not of a size where she could be living off her back for a week. As he stopped outside her room, he put the finishing touches to a small speech. Encouraging yet firm was the general theme, and he must not take no for an answer. Knocking gently, he expected to wait for a few seconds as usual, then knock again, before pushing the door open. But today was different. She actually answered, and his stomach gave a gurgle of hope. Surely that had to be a good sign?

Yes it was. He entered to find her sitting up – in a chair – wearing her nightdress, and she was sewing. Until now he had always found her curled up in the same position on the bed, still wrapped in the sheet, and showing no apparent signs of ever wanting to move.

'Good morning,' he said cheerfully, as if she had recovered from nothing more than a minor sniffle.

'Good morning.'

'Shall I place the tray down here?' He indicated the nearest flat surface, but she set aside her ripped riding-skirt, and patted her lap. 'No, I think I'll have it here.'

'Oh . . . excellent.' He beamed, and as she smiled back, he felt himself suddenly becoming so much lighter. But then he glanced in the direction of the water, and the change in its colour drained all colour from his own cheeks. Elizabeth had clearly made some attempt to clean the mess that was now her back, and it provided a horrible reminder of what had happened – and the part that he had played.

Placing the tray down as directed, he stepped back, clasped his hands in front of him, and said simply: 'I'm sorry.'

'Sorry for what?'

'For giving Mr Bateford that message.'

Bessie almost said: "What message?" Thursday felt like such a long time ago. 'But I asked you to do it.'

'I know, it's just . . . *why* did you ask me?'

'I can't really explain in a way that will make any sense Duncan. All I can say is that you did as I requested, and I'm indebted to you for it.'

'Indebted?' he exclaimed. 'How can you say that after what he did to you? I never should have fetched that thing. I never should have tied you up, I . . .'

'It's fine,' said Bessie, her voice soothing but also slightly stern. 'When my husband issues you with an order, you should follow it without question. My fault has been to do otherwise, but I now know better, and hopefully you will not be finding yourself in that position again.'

Duncan had no idea what to say. He could hardly reply: "Good", or "Thank you", because that would suggest some sort of benefit to recent events – in quelling her rebellious nature.

It had been there ever since her first day at the Hall. They had all been able to see it, and certain people had even suggested that it was the reason why Arnold married her. Reminded him of those passionate ladies down Holliston Road – only she was even better, because she was free.

Thankfully Elizabeth distracted him from that rather disagreeable thought by asking after Isabel, but that pitched him onto another subject where he was completely at a loss. He had seen the youngest Bateford only three times in her life, and had certainly not come across her in recent days. But Agatha had not reported anything untoward, so he said simply: 'She's well,' and hoped that it was true.

'Good. I'm very glad.'

'Did I mention that Mr Bateford wants you to remain in here until Tuesday afternoon, and then prepare for dinner, wearing one of the . . .'

'Red dresses,' completed Bessie, which made him even more curious as to its significance. 'Yes you did. Can you do something for me Duncan?'

'Of course.'

'Can you give my husband another message? Tell him that I am thankful for the time that he has given me to recuperate. That I look forward to wearing his favourite colour again. And I respectfully request his permission to resume my place at his side tomorrow evening, a day early.'

'Oh . . . right . . . yes.' Duncan repeated it to himself, and then shot off, returning shortly with an assent.

When Arnold heard the transmission, he was both surprised, pleased – and deeply suspicious. He had broken her on Thursday, there was no doubt about it, and her words seemed to confirm it. But they could also be a declaration of defiance. "I don't need all these days to recover, because you didn't really hurt me". And if that were indeed the case, then it was best dealt with immediately – which was the main reason why he said yes, and why he was in the dining room at ten to seven, ready to watch her every move. Would she present herself with only seconds to spare, making her usual point? Would she stare down the table at him with that false look of respect which she manufactured so well?

The answer to both was no. She arrived less than a minute after he did, and her first action was to smile – in a way that seemed sincere, and indicative of relief.

'Thank you for letting me attend Arnold. I am most grateful.'

It took him a full minute to respond, with a nod, his suspicions stoked to their highest degree, and convinced that he would soon detect the tell-tale signs. Typically it was during their main course. Her attention would stray, and it would look like she wished to be a thousand miles away from him. And at least once every mealtime, he would catch a glance in his direction that was far from cordial.

But today he saw neither. There was nothing poisonous in her eyes, in fact there was nothing at all. They seemed somehow . . . dead, and he was not sure that he was happy about it. He had wanted to beat obedience into her, not beat the life out of her. Wilful was bad, but a certain wildness was rather stimulating. One thing was for certain – he would receive enlightenment when he got her upstairs. She was repulsed by the feel of him, he knew it so well, and there was no way that she could keep it under wraps.

With such a truth in mind, he was therefore both amazed, and frankly insulted, when their bedroom door closed, and his wife made the first move towards intimacy.

'You can drop the act now Elizabeth.'

He expected her to deny that there was any act, but she merely blinked, as if in acquiescence.

'I know you want to get back in my good books, and so you should, but this is going just a bit too far.'

Bessie swallowed. 'I *am* trying to earn your approval yes, but you're right – it is also time for honesty. Do I have your permission to speak freely?'

He debated it for a moment, before coming to the conclusion that he was sufficiently intrigued to hear her out.

'I never wanted to marry you Arnold. I did it because I felt that I had no choice, and the thought of our first night together was really quite terrifying. That is not the case any more, but I am sure you can appreciate that at times it still remains a far from comfortable experience. I know you probably won't believe this, but I have never been unfaithful. On the Sunday when I went out for a walk – I returned in a somewhat . . . excitable state because I had come across a gathering in the fields to the west of here. The speaker was calling for workers' rights, and I have to admit that in that moment I supported their ideals, and was afraid to tell you in case you had them run out of town. While as for Mr Henderson, I pretended to like him, but actually found him a thoroughly odious individual, and am now glad that he's gone.'

She drew breath. 'So I can assure you that I have honoured this most important vow to the letter, but I also know that I have not performed my other vows as I should. I have not always acted appropriately, and Thursday has made me realise that I am entirely at fault for that. Ultimately I walked down the aisle of my own free will. I was not press-ganged into it, and although this is not the life that I had envisaged for myself, it is an extremely comfortable one, and one which I now wish to embrace. In all regards.'

Pausing again, she then made a final declaration: 'I want to forget the past, and everybody in it. I want to move on from what happened between us, and simply concentrate on being a proper wife to you. So my conduct tonight is – as you suggested – entirely out of character, but nevertheless genuine, and I hope you will believe me when I say that it is an indicator of the behaviour which you can expect from me in the future.'

Her eyes had been locked on him throughout, and they remained so now as he walked towards her. Every word was the truth, and he could see it – even though his gut was grumbling at him to the contrary.

'Are you scared of me?' he asked, stopping less than a foot away.

'Yes,' she replied, equally direct, and with more than a little apprehension.

'Good. Every wife should be in awe of their husband, and you more than most. I've brought you out of nothing, and don't you ever forget it.'

'I won't, I promise.'

'I mean it. The day you stop fearing me is the day you die.'

'I understand, really I do.' She had a feeling that he was going to hit her to make sure that his point was reinforced, but instead he tipped his head to one side, and his lips spread into a type of smile that she had never seen before.

'As long as you keep to these ground rules Elizabeth, then I don't mind if you wish to . . . well . . . frankly express your gratitude in a more overt manner in future. In fact I consider it a fundamental facet of your apology that you seek to indulge me on a much more enthusiastic basis from now on.'

He stepped back, leaving her to resume her approach, and after only a brief hesitation, she did.

She did it the next night as well, and the next, and kept on doing so over the days that followed – especially leading up to the night of Mrs Forrester's party. Arnold had been wavering about whether to attend, but Bessie put in a most persuasive appeal, and he decided that flaunting his newly-demonstrative wife would be relatively diverting for a few hours. Bessie had much the same thing in mind – namely turning her thoughts away from the last weeks, and turning them instead to a certain Sylvia Chaloner. The widow who had not considered a governess fit to sit in fine company, would have to face the sight of her at one of Mrs Forrester's famous gaming-tables.

It is *the* event of the season.

Bessie could recall the disparaging sneer as if it was only yesterday. Well there were four such events each year, and there was no way that she was going to miss this summer instalment. Fixing her hair in the most attractive style possible, she selected the dress which accentuated her positive features to best effect, and Arnold even supplied a sapphire necklace that had belonged to his grandmother.

The dress was not red, or indeed any variation on red, but the need for a distinguishing dye had diminished with her recent agreeability. Her gown was a brocaded silk of deep blue – always a good match for dark hair – and as the Bateford carriage pulled up outside a grand mansion on the edge of town, she felt like Cinderella arriving at the ball.

Charles and Harris were also in attendance. The invitation had requested the presence of Mr Bateford and family, but they all knew who was the star attraction. Would Arnold really bring his trumped-up commoner wife along? Yes he would, and that trumped-up wife was determined to enjoy herself to the full.

Unfortunately like most things in life, the more you looked forward in expectation, the more things turned into a disappointment, and that proved to be the case here. Initially at least. They were last in, and although it was not by design, Bessie thought that perhaps it might be a good thing. Ensure a dramatic entrance, and indeed all eyes turned to stare, with the many up-and-down looks giving her some manner of satisfaction. Of course the looks coincided with murmurs of derision, but that was all part of the fun, and as a parlour-maid nobody even noticed that you were in existence, so disapproving attention was better than no attention at all. The problem was that the looks came from firmly established corners of the dining room. Everybody had settled into their traditional cliques, so the Batefords were forced to make do with a little clique of their own, and that was rather limiting.

Mrs Forrester was not in favour of big sit-downs – took up far too much time. It was a case of munch and mingle for a while, and then to the card-tables! The amount of money which changed hands at some of her parties was of quite notorious proportions. It was even said that a wife or two had been lost on nights like these, and Bessie did find herself hoping that Arnold would not hand her over as part of some I.O.U. She was fairly certain that her place was secure, but when he walked off to converse with Stewart Munroe of all people, she did feel rather neglected. And when Charles then wandered off too, she felt positively isolated.

'You aren't going to leave me as well, are you Harris?' She accompanied her question with laughter, trying to make light of the situation, and was filled with a swell of affection when he replied:

'I was about to ask you the same thing.'

'You know something Harris – we don't talk anywhere near enough.'

'You mean . . . to one another?'

'Yes. We've lived under the same roof for nearly a year now, and yet only had a single proper conversation. Or perhaps two at the most.'

'True,' he agreed, as if rather wistful, and then his cheeks flushed. 'You haven't told Father anything, have you?'

'About what?'

'About our proper conversation.'

'Oh you mean . . .' She almost uttered the critical word Isabel. 'No. Of course not.'

'You must never tell him that you know, never tell anybody. And she can't find out who she is. It would spell disaster.'

'Nobody will hear a thing from me. I gave you my word, didn't I?'

'Yes, but that was before you married one of us. I never expected you to do that.'

"Neither did I", thought Bessie, before offering further reassurance: 'My word still stands. In fact even more so. I could never betray the confidence of my favourite stepson, now could I?'

'Are you sure about that?'

'Yes. My lips are sealed.'

'No, I mean about being your favourite. I thought you'd taken rather a liking to Thomas.'

'Whatever gave you that idea?' She turned away as her own face flushed, and cast her gaze in the direction of Gil Tremaine, who yet again demonstrated that he had no interest whatsoever in looking at her.

'I sensed something. On quite a few occasions actually.' Harris set her with the keen focus of a man whose sudden thirst for gossip needed to be quenched.

'I'm afraid you're mistaken,' she replied, trying to do casual, but failing miserably.

'You're blushing. I'm right, aren't I? Is that why Thomas left? Because you chose my father over him?'

'I have no idea why Thomas left.'

'But you must have. It's too much of a coincidence, him going the very same night that you gave Father your answer.'

'Really Harris, you're seeing things that aren't there.'

'Am I? I don't usually. I told you that Ruth Padstow had her eye on a Mr Sherman, and I was right. She's here with him tonight.'

'I'd noticed,' said Bessie. The sight of dear "Ruthie" had brought back a host of painful memories, and she had successfully been blocking every last one until Harris had picked up this topic like a dog with a bone.

'Did Thomas speak to you before he left?'

'No,' she snapped before realising that irritability conveyed guilt, and she ought to remain pleasant. 'I was really rather ill, if you remember?'

'Oh yes.'

'It was quite a miracle that I was able to walk down the aisle at all on your father's special day.'

'You didn't think of delaying, hoping Thomas might come back?'

"Good grief", thought Bessie – and not for the first time when it came to Harris Bateford. This lad was sharper than he looked. 'Naturally I was hoping that he would attend, for Arnold's sake. But actually I was more interested in whether your sister Cynthia might appear.'

That ought to throw him off-course for a bit.

'Cynthia! You *are* joking?'

'No. Not at all.'

'But I told you what happened over . . . you know who.'

'Yes, but weddings usually bring people together, don't they? Create something of a thaw.'

'Thaw?' hissed Harris. 'Not even the heat of a thousand furnaces could thaw Drew Roscoe.'

'Intractable sort?'

'Not especially. He simply hates the name Bateford.'

'But if he talked to Arnold, I'm sure they could work things out. He lives quite close, doesn't he?'

'About . . . six or seven miles.'

'Ackerley, isn't it?'

'That's right.'

'I forget – is that to the east of Somerden, or the west?'

'South,' informed Harris, giving her a sideways glance. 'If you're hatching a plan for some sort of reconciliation, I'd better stop you right there. It's *never* going to happen.'

'Pity,' mused Bessie. 'And I don't just mean for Arnold's sake. Presumably you miss seeing your only sister.'

"Not especially", was the response which sprang to mind, and when he appeared to struggle for words, Bessie quickly added:

'That was a slip of the tongue by the way. I'm aware that Isabel is also your sister. Publicly at least.'

'Oh . . . right . . . no, I was just thinking that perhaps Cynthia is best off where she is.'

'Why?'

'Well she was like I told you . . . headstrong. In fact when it came to . . .' He mouthed the next two words. '. . . Luke Cullen, she was downright mutinous. Sent Father crazy, and you know how he doesn't like being flouted.'

Indeed she did.

'I'm glad that you don't seem to be having any such problems yourself at the moment.'

'Me too,' agreed Bessie with palpable force.

'I was a bit worried when you became acquainted with the . . . you know?'

'No,' she frowned, being reminded of Harris' rather frustrating love of playing "Fill in the blanks".

'Of course you do.'

No, she still did not. 'Please Harris, I'm starting to feel really quite tired.'

'The cat.'

'Oh!'

'It *was* the cat, wasn't it?'

Bessie coughed and looked down. She tried very hard not to think about that thing, or the fact that her back would forever be scarred, like a brand.

'You want to use some of Meredith Critchley's liniment. Mrs Evans can probably get hold of it for you, and I know it works wonders. My mother used to swear by it. God rest her soul.'

Bessie lifted her head back up, and tried to appear grateful. Harris was well intentioned – that much was obvious – but the thought of receiving advice about the sores of inter-marital conflict from the son of your predecessor was frankly depressing. And moments later, the evening became even more depressing when the sound of a piano reached her ears. Several of the guests had called upon Sylvia Chaloner to abandon her own need for sustenance, and entertain them with her fine singing voice. It required much cajoling, but eventually – with a sigh – she accepted that she could not refuse their earnest petitions.

As far as Bessie was concerned, "singing" was a bit of a stretch. Cat and strangle would be a far better description, although she had to admit that her own ears were listening against the backdrop of a very cattish state of mind. And after the second ditty, she was able to appreciate that at least the noise had put an end to the discussion with Harris. A discussion which she had herself instituted, and which she would think twice about ever instituting again.

Watching Gil's discomfort as he turned Sylvia's music also managed to lift Bessie's mood. He kept nibbling at something off his plate between turns, trying to make his partner aware that she was keeping him from his food. But she persisted in entertaining, and when it looked like she was set to suck the life out of a fourth aria, he was compelled to clap his hands and declare: 'Isn't it time for cards?'

Thankfully Mrs Forrester had formed exactly the same opinion, and ushered everybody through to the gaming-area. It encompassed the drawing room *and* the library, and even into an annex-cum-billiard room, with all the furniture pushed back to leave space for eight big baize-covered tables. Each one had a pack of cards, score-card, plus pencil, meaning that everything was set for a grand competition. "Take to your places and begin!" was the cry which Bessie expected, and she was so relieved not to have to be one of those responding. Her knowledge of cards was decidedly patchy, and Harris was much more interested in watching the interaction between various couples in attendance, so they would both sit it out, with Arnold and Charles representing the Bateford family.

Having not been particularly bothered about whether or not he attended, Arnold's eyes became suddenly fixed with a rather scary focus once he could see the baize. Did they really need to win money that badly, or was it simply about getting one over on the others? Bessie chose not to analyse that question too deeply, and when she was struck by an image of the Whitsons in their tiny cottage with meagre rations, she blocked it out completely.

Taking a standing-place by her husband's side, hand resting upon his shoulder, she prepared to spend the next however-many-hours in a position of support, becoming increasingly bored, and ever more regretful that they had not stayed at home. An important lesson had been dealt to her this evening. If you went out purely with the aim of showing off, then you would find the sense of achievement probably very fleeting, and seldom worth the overall effort. When the maids passed through to begin clearing the dining room, Bessie even found herself envious that they had something to do. Little did she realise that Mrs Forrester was soon to ensure that *everybody* had something to do.

A significant amount of effort went into organising these revelries, and Mrs Forrester prided herself on always getting the numbers just right. For instance, when she sent out twenty invitations, she already knew which four would turn her down. Usually it was because they had lost too much money the last time around, and so could not afford to repeat the experience. Or occasionally it was due to some other problem – marital, emotional, or even sexual. She was the first to be in the know. In fact sometimes she even had the facts in place before the participants themselves were fully aware of what was going on. But then occasionally, like tonight, she was thwarted.

When she had dispatched an invitation to Bateford Hall, she had not actually anticipated that the sons would be joining their father. You did not bring children to gatherings like these, even those that were fully-grown. At first, however, it was no problem since Elizabeth and Harris showed no interest in becoming involved. But then Mrs Kirkpatrick went and had one of her funny episodes, forcing Mr Kirkpatrick to take her home, and that threw the whole thing completely out of kilter.

At intervals of every twenty to thirty minutes, a designated couple from each table would stand up and move to the right, taking on fresh opponents, and ensuring that every pairing played eight different matches. But now there were going to be two people sitting out at every turn, like a couple of wallflowers. As well as disrupting the flow of play, it would look dreadfully untidy, and in Mrs Forrester's ordered mind, untidy could not be tolerated. So there was only one thing for it. Harris and Elizabeth would have to be pressed into service. Like it or lump it.

Bessie most certainly did *not* like it. Yes she was bored, but not at a level where she wished to appease it with playing whist. She had no idea of how to play whist, and although watching Arnold for the best part of an hour had left her with the impression that it was not the most difficult of pursuits, it did seem to require an understanding of what your partner was thinking. Bessie had no idea what Harris was going to say next, never mind what he was thinking. As a result they were liable to play atrociously as a pair, represent Arnold very badly, make him angry, and undo all the good work of the last two weeks – which absolutely could not be allowed to happen. Bessie was adamant about it. She was just going to have to refuse.

Of course that was much easier said than done, and as far as Mrs Forrester was concerned, it was a practical impossibility. She was one of those women who could have you signed up to a hundred things before you even realised that there had been any agreement on the first one. And when Arnold then waded in with: "You mustn't obstruct the hostess", Bessie's final attempt at refusal was demolished.

Before leaving the field of battle, the Kirkpatricks had lost their first two matches, which meant that Bessie and Harris started off with two defeats against their names. That mattered because when everybody had played eight times, the two couples with the most victories battled it out for the ultimate crown. Obviously being hailed as "Forrester's Winning Whistlers" was of the utmost importance – although the currency changing hands also gave things an extra edge. Within each game, you could gamble as much as you wished – or as much as your opponent was willing to match. Or alternatively you could simply play for sport. Money was not essential, but nobody would know it from the atmosphere. Hundreds of ordinary men and women starving elsewhere in the town tonight, just streets away, and yet here at Mrs Forrester's the gentry were throwing around cash like it was going out of fashion.

Bessie knew that she ought to be enraged, but was too preoccupied with the horror of throwing *Arnold's* cash around. He was in a good enough mood to give Harris a five-pound stake, although accompanied his generosity with an order to bring it back with interest. She tried to suggest that such a return was most unlikely, pitting themselves against experienced veterans of the game, but that did not seem to register, and all she could do was hope that her husband continued to play at a sufficiently high level to make their own loss irrelevant.

There was no doubt that it was going to be a loss. Things started badly, went quickly downhill, and by the time they were forced to entertain Gil Tremaine and Sylvia Chaloner, Bessie and Harris only had thirty shillings left.

'You don't believe in playing for high stakes then,' commented Gil as he sat down. 'That surprises me.'

"Oh dear God", thought Bessie before chiding herself for being so silly. You could not be offended at a person's lack of interest, and then have issues when they finally realised that you existed. 'No, I enjoy high stakes as much as the next woman,' she replied pointedly. 'It's simply that we're not having the best of evenings, are we Harris?'

Harris shrugged, and looked anxious. He was always cowed into timidity by the presence of other males, particularly one as commanding as Gil, and Bessie was heartily glad for that.

'We were surprised to see you here,' observed Sylvia. 'Thought you might be rather overawed by such an eminent occasion, having only recently been admitted to our social circle.'

There were definite hints of malice in those sweetly-spoken words, but Bessie chose to let it pass, and said: 'Thank you for your concern.'

'Oh rest assured, we are all deeply concerned. With your background being what it is.'

'My background?' repeated Bessie.

'Yes. Well you have to admit that an upbringing of . . . what was it your father did again?'

'He was a tailor.'

'Ah yes, now I recall. Well of course it means that you're in no way equipped for a stage like this.'

'And why is that Mrs Chaloner?'

'I hardly need spell it out, do I? You were clearly not destined for this life, so were not appropriately . . . tutored. In singing, general etiquette, and the like.'

'Talking of singing, I must admit that I found your own attempt quite engrossing. In fact it was impossible to tear one's ears away,' remarked Bessie, but Sylvia deflected the sarcasm with a deft touch:

'Thank you. Gil is always encouraging me to strike up a tune on his pianoforte. Says my voice soars like an angel.'

'Does he now? I can just picture it.' Bessie raised her eyebrows in Gil's direction, and he smiled lackadaisically in response.

'Presumably you've never sung yourself?' pursued Sylvia, and promptly answered her own question before Bessie had a chance. 'Thought not. And you see, that is why you have our deepest sympathy.'

'*Our?*' queried Bessie, beginning to feel just the slightest bit inflamed.

'Yes. Gil and I. Thrown into this world, with alarming speed, it must be rather frightening. I mean it was only by accident that you were compelled into being a governess in the first place. Otherwise you probably would never have even walked through the doors of Bateford Hall.'

'And by accident you mean my father setting fire to himself and everything else in a drunken stupor,' clarified Bessie, which left Sylvia temporarily startled. 'Isn't that the view which you've formed of him?'

'I don't recollect forming a view at all,' replied the widow dismissively.

'So glad. Wouldn't want to be thinking that you were the judgemental type.' Bessie pursed her lips. 'Actually, far from being overawed, when you've had experience of dealing with the demands of little ones on a daily basis, a roomful of adults seems rather tame in comparison.'

Sylvia had previously bristled at the mention of children – since she did not have any – but this time it had no such effect. She simply made the stinging observation: 'So your hands always shake like that, do they?' And then asked Gil to fetch another glass of wine.

It was first blood to Chaloner, but Bessie was not about to leave it at that. She spent the next five minutes searching for a way to even the score, but achieved nothing more than making her game-play even worse.

'Are you aware of the general aim of whist?' enquired Gil.

'I believe so,' replied Bessie, countering his amusement with a strained smile. She had the main elements in place anyway. Collecting tricks seemed to be the thing. One trick equalled one point, the first six tricks did not count, and the first to five points won a game. All quite simple. What was perplexing was this concept of trumping, and somebody had said something about winning points for honours, whatever they were. Of course selecting which card to play, and when, was also rather a troublesome issue. 'I must confess, however,' she added obstinately, 'that my life to date has been occupied with serious matters, not trifling with mere sport.'

'But even serious matters can turn into a sport, can't they? Especially if you lose track of where you're going.'

'Indeed, and even more so if you never had a track to begin with.' Bessie was fully aware that Elizabeth Mary Cullen was becoming more and more of a distant memory, but she was not about to let him lambast her for it.

'How is everything up at the Hall?' asked Sylvia, directing her question towards Harris in an attempt to break up this brief, but worryingly potent exchange between Gil and the governess.

'Fine, thank you.'

'It must have been rather an upheaval, having a stranger enter your family. Bound to lead to friction?'

Harris glanced at Bessie, and she hoped to goodness that he was not about to start discussing liniment remedies. Mercifully all he said was: 'Not really,' and recognising that he was not about to be amenable, Sylvia turned her attention back to Elizabeth:

'I suppose there'll be more of an upheaval soon, when you begin to add to the family yourself. I'm sure you can't wait.'

Childbirth was very much something that Bessie could happily wait a long time for.

'Lots of little Batefords running around,' added Gil with a tilt of his head. 'What a charming thought.'

Bessie chose to swallow rather than reply.

'When I first met you on the stage from . . . now where was it?' Gil knew that she would still be terrified by the mention of Henningborough. Always made people think of those prisons – and prison*ers*.

'Thurleigh,' she growled.

'Of course, that's it. I can't imagine back then that producing Bateford heirs could possibly have been something you foresaw in your future.'

'Obviously not . . . *Gil.*' She was not in the mood to be familiar, but it would irritate Sylvia, so was definitely worth the effort. 'How could I possibly envisage that I would be lucky enough to capture the heart of a man such as Arnold?'

'Capture? Yes . . . that's a good word. Certainly someone has ended up rather . . . entangled.'

'What a cynical tone,' laughed Bessie, as if sorry for him. 'But you're right – love is indeed a snare from which few escape. And very few ever want to escape.' She looked towards Arnold with fondness. 'I'm surprised that you have not yet formalised your own feelings. Surely you've been expecting a proposal for quite some time Sylvia.'

The widow's face became crimson in an instant, and Bessie was fairly certain that there was shaking from those slender fingers which had never seen a day's work in their life.

'Why don't you do it here tonight?' suggested Bessie, capitalising on her upper hand. 'It's the most perfect occasion for making such a grand announcement.'

Sylvia did not say anything, so attention turned to Gil.

'I think a man should propose at a time of his choosing. Not when some mischief-maker thinks that he ought to.' The eyes had gone cold, and that jawbone was pulsing again.

'Mischief-maker? Really Gil, you read me all wrong. I am merely concerned that poor Sylvia here has been waiting long enough.'

'I am not waiting for anything,' she snapped. 'Gil and I are a wonderful team, as is shown by our performance tonight. We already have four victories to our name, and look set to repeat our famous triumph of last autumn.'

Bessie was all set to say something caustic, but then detected real hurt in Sylvia's eyes, and felt strangely sorry for her. 'Congratulations,' she offered instead. 'I doubt I shall ever match your achievement. In fact we might as well keep our last pound Harris, since we seem certain to lose it at this table.'

'What a pity,' remarked Gil. 'I'm looking to win all the shillings I can. My finances took rather a hit a couple of months ago.'

While Bessie focused intensely on her cards, Sylvia said: 'What hit? You didn't tell me anything about a hit.'

'I didn't wish to worry you. And anyway I have it on good authority that my loss is only to be a temporary one.' Gil paused. 'What do you think Elizabeth? When something is lost, is it lost forever?'

'No,' she replied instinctively, but then qualified her response. 'But unfortunately circumstances sometimes do change, and often against our better wishes, things can become irretrievable.'

'Really?'

'I'm afraid so.' She was telling him that he might never see his money back. The hundreds that she had stolen and lost to that masked man, as well as the months of support that he had provided to the workers.

It pained her, deeply, but it was true, and they both now needed to accept it.

Thankfully he seemed to accept it better than she did, and soon it was time for him to move on, and for Bessie and Harris to face a new challenge. Every match was decided on a best of three basis, and until now they had always lost after the second game, but suddenly out of the blue they won one. They also recouped two pounds of their money – from none other than Stewart Munroe.

He had attended the party with a young lady on his arm who knew even less about whist than Bessie, and having *two* twenty-something females at his table was enough to send Stewart's concentration right out of the window. Bessie ended up wishing that she had wagered even more. Certainly at her next card-party, if she came across a widower or husband with a roving eye, she was going to play her hand to full effect.

It was impossible to implement such a strategy immediately, however, because the next couple were Ruth Padstow and Mr Sherman. Unlike Stewart's companion, Ruth did indeed know how to play, and Mr Sherman most definitely did not have a roving eye. In fact he was what could be described as "a very pleasant young man". And when Bessie was able to get past those painful memories of Thomas mooning over Ruthie, she had to concede that Ruth was rather nice too. Albeit sad – especially when asking after Thomas. It was a deliberately casual enquiry, but the wound was plain to see.

Ruth had been made to feel extraordinarily special over a series of dinners earlier in the year, only to hear absolutely nothing from Thomas since the beginning of March. Why? What had she done wrong? Bessie could see the self-doubt, and was instantly consumed by guilt.

Ruth had been used; there was no other word for it. While Thomas Bateford had been fighting his emotions, and Elizabeth Arabrook had been ignoring her own, this young woman had become a pawn, and it was cruel. In fact it was unforgivable, and all Bessie could do now was to take great pains in convincing Ruth that she had not been individually snubbed, but that Thomas had turned his back on them all:

'Left in the middle of April, just like that, and hasn't been back since. We don't even know where he is. Haven't heard a word.'

Ruth's bottom lip dropped with surprised relief, before quivering with concern. 'Why? Why would he do that?'

Harris proceeded to offer up an explanation which made an extremely explicit link to the nuptials, but Bessie twisted it by suggesting that Thomas was unhappy about somebody taking his mother's place so soon after her death.

As she said the words, Bessie appreciated the significance of them for the first time. She had indeed filled Jane's shoes less than a year after the funeral, and presumably that was another thing causing Thomas to hate her from afar. She wondered where he was. It was probably best that he was gone; it might never have worked out, and things were currently fine with his father. But it did not stop her thinking about him from time to time, and hoping that he was well.

To take everybody's mind off the subject, Bessie turned her focus to Mr Sherman, asking a series of absorbed questions, and trying to convey to Ruth that she should concentrate on the man who was here, not pine after the absentee. Regrettably it had little effect.

There was no warmth at all emanating from Ruth towards Mr Sherman, which was rather cruel in itself, because he was clearly becoming utterly devoted. By the time they left the table, Bessie felt really quite depressed. Having been exploited by Thomas, Ruth was now doing the same with somebody else, and so the world went around. It seemed that everything came back to where it started, including the Batefords who found themselves reunited for their final game.

Obviously Bessie and Harris now lost on purpose, and Arnold received his money back. He did not seem remotely concerned that it had been cut in half, and that was because he had seven wins to his name, which would surely put him onto the top table. Bessie was pleased at first, but that quickly faded. If Sylvia's claims were accurate, then there was a good chance that she and Gil would end up as the opponents, and Gil was a mean player. Sitting there with eyes almost drooping, it was like he was hardly paying attention, but his mind was sharp. As sharp as that dagger which he had once held to her throat.

She occasionally pondered why somebody would share a bed with such a thing. Was he actually in fear of his life? And if so, from whom? Did it have any connection to his support for the Chartists? No, she was still not convinced that his support in that regard was genuine, but the one thing she *did* know was that he was a genuinely good card-player, and it left her afraid for Arnold's fate. Surely it was better never to reach the final showdown, than to reach it and be defeated?

Well she was soon to find out – because within a matter of minutes Mrs Forrester announced that the winning couples were indeed as suspected, and would proceed to do battle for the ultimate crown. Bessie thought that everybody else would take that as their cue to leave, but apparently it was traditional to gather around and watch. Show the appropriate sportsmanship – and also partake in a last glass or two from the fine collection of beverages on offer.

An excessive amount of drinking had already taken place, and with only side-nibbles for accompaniment, it was amazing how some of the guests could still stand up straight. Harris was one of those wetting his whistle on a regular basis, but he was so accustomed to topping himself up, that he was holding together really quite well. Whereas Bessie had been avoiding it completely. There was enough danger of her tongue running away with itself when she was sober, but intoxicated? In front of Arnold? It did not bear thinking about.

The leading competitors had also largely spurned the spirits, and now took their seats at the main table in the library. It was all or nothing from here, and the rules had changed. Instead of best of three, it was now the first to thirty points, and that made Bessie almost groan with frustration. If things were close, they could be here for another hour yet. And of course as luck would have it, the match was very close indeed. With the clock chiming one in the morning, the score was twenty-eight versus twenty-six – in Bateford's favour. One more game, and the result would be in.

Middle-class manufacturer against upper-class landowner. New money taking on old. Capitalism confronting feudalism. The symbolism could not be greater, and the stakes could not be higher. There had been no smaller wagers along the way, it was all on this one hand, and Arnold was betting his entire winnings for the evening – plus a sight more besides. If victorious, he would double his money. If not . . . Bessie did not wish to contemplate "if not". He had to win, that was all there was to it.

Like most people, she was not sticking to a single position, but circling the players in order to get a good look at their cards, and as they each picked up the final thirteen, her fingers were crossed.

"Let them be good. Please". She focused upon Arnold. Two Aces. Brilliant. Then she looked to Charles. No Aces, and only one King. That was bad. Overall it was probably even, which meant that it was down to whoever played their cards to best advantage. Who would it favour? Sylvia certainly looked intensely driven, and seemed to be blinking in a most irregular manner, probably giving Gil some signals. Was that allowed? Were Arnold and Charles doing the same? What would be the result in a few minutes time? Bessie almost could not bear to watch.

The first six tricks were played, and then it was onto points. "Please give us the first one", she begged, but her prayers went unanswered. It was won by Gil and Sylvia, as was the next, but then things swung back towards the Batefords. Twenty-nine versus twenty-eight.

"Please don't let it get to twenty-nine all". Her head dropped as the palpitations became overwhelming – and she prepared to wait for the sounds of victory – be it Sylvia's shrill squeal of delight, or Arnold's . . .

There was no need to imagine what that might be, because suddenly there it was. A great bellowing explosion of joy culminating in two little words: 'Got you!'

Her husband had done it. He had actually done it.

'You're going to have to dig into those over-sized pockets of yours Tremaine.' Arnold flicked his fingers in a "Give it to me" sort of action, and once he had the wad of notes in hand, he began to count them out, one by one, placing them down onto the table.

Having offered up several prayers of thanks, Bessie now wanted to say: "I'm sure you haven't been diddled", but could not quite summon the courage, even by way of a joke. Mercifully Gil seemed to take it all in good heart – which was more than could be said for Sylvia. She scraped her chair back, and stalked from the room – apparently in pursuit of her pelisse.

'I fear I didn't play that last hand too well,' remarked Gil, scratching under his chin, and sighing.

'Don't worry, she'll forgive you – eventually,' said a voice from the throng, which prompted a reply of:

'I wouldn't be too sure.'

'She simply has to accept that she lost to the better men,' crowed Charles, who was experiencing one of the most rapturous moments of his life. Brother Thomas gone, the position of number-one-son now his own, and he was not only filling it with ease, but also steering their father to a famous triumph. Nothing could feel better than this. Nothing on earth. And whenever Charles was happy, Harris was too, which meant that the Bateford family practically floated out of the room, riding the crest of a magnificent wave.

'You see Munroe, told you we were on the up and up!' Arnold shouted it across the hall, and Stewart was forced to nod in agreement, while Bessie watched with confused concern. Could these two men possibly have buried their differences? After everything that had happened? After Munroe's anger at almost being duped, and Arnold's fury over his name being dragged through the mud. It made no sense. Unless it was simply a case of Arnold feeling able to embrace anybody, even his mortal enemy, when basking in the glow of victory.

It was impossible to debate it because Arnold realised that he had left his cigar case behind, and she quickly offered to retrieve it. Gil had remained in the library, which meant that it would hopefully be possible to have a quick word. Of course it was dangerous to be caught alone with any man, but she had Arnold's express consent, and it was not going to take long. In fact there was only one question on her lips:

'Did you let him win?'

Bessie put it to Gil as soon as she was through the doors, and when he had stretched sufficiently, he sat up and replied with a question of his own:

'Now why would I do a thing like that?'

'I don't know, but you seem to be taking it awfully well.'

'I guess that's just the sort of fellow I am.' He rolled his cuffs back down, and straightened the front of his shirt. 'Besides, it's probably for the best. I'm not sure defeat was something that you could handle.' Indeed if he had to use one word to describe the look on her face during that last hand, it would have been frenzied.

Bessie blushed, irritated to think that she had been so obvious. 'Naturally I was supporting my husband tooth and nail. As any wife would.'

'Particularly one as demonstrative as you.'

'Demonstrative?'

'Yes. Anybody would think you'd fallen in love with the old goat.'

'He's my husband.'

'So you've said.'

'I owe him my affection.'

'Do you now?' Gil raised his left eyebrow. 'That didn't appear to be the state of things earlier in the month. Planning to bring him down, weren't you?'

'Shush! That meeting never took place. For your sake, *and* mine. Anyway things have changed since then. I have a lot to be thankful for.'

'Really? Pity the same can't be said for your father.'

'You . . .'

'What? Truth hurts, does it Mrs Bateford?'

Especially when it was as close to the bone as that. But Bessie was not about to get into a spat. 'You forget Gil, I am an orphan.'

'What are you really playing at?'

'I'm not playing at anything. I am merely enjoying my evening. Or at least I *was*, and now I'm looking for my husband's cigar case.' Scanning around, she could not find it, until spying it upon one of the chairs. She leaned down, but on her way back up, a hand gripped her above the elbow.

'I'd be careful if I were you.'

'And why is that?'

'Lest you get just a little too carried away.'

'Practise what you preach Gil Tremaine.' She wrestled her arm back, and headed over to the door, which was a good thing because it meant that she was well away from Gil when Arnold reappeared.

'Sorry darling,' she smiled. 'I was held up by Gil lamenting the extent of his losses. I fear you've pitched him into a state of considerable melancholy.'

Arnold was so pleased to hear it that suspicion did not enter his mind. 'Don't panic Tremaine. You'll have the chance to take me on again – in three months time.'

Gil tipped his head in a wry act of gratitude, before Sylvia walked in – or rather "stormed" in. Barely acknowledging her opponents' existence, she marched over to Gil, and thrust his coat at him.

Aware that she was probably entitled to be somewhat vexed, he did not labour in getting to his feet and putting it on. Then they approached the door, where Arnold had generously stood waiting. The other guests were concluding their goodbyes to Mrs Forrester, which left Arnold desperate to make the most of this last few minutes of gloating. Plus he wished to discuss the Somerden Hunt.

When he discovered that Tremaine was not in fact a member, his evening was rounded off to utter perfection. A good deal of business was done between the members of "The Pack", and Arnold had wanted to be a member for years. Ultimately last year's reputational damage had forced him into paying for the privilege, but there was an increasing trend towards some form of subscription, so he was not alone, and it was worth every penny.

'Presumably you won't be joining Arnold,' commented Sylvia, looking to resurrect her evening by returning to her favourite subject of "Elizabeth Bateford isn't fit for the upper echelons of society".

'On the contrary, Elizabeth can handle a horse very well,' replied Arnold, leaping to her defence, and causing Gil to mutter:

'Now why doesn't that surprise me?'

Bessie's instinct was to find a tart retort, but she chose instead to deflect attention. Arnold was in such a good mood, and she wanted it to stay that way – which indeed it did over the coming days. In fact it was reinforced when his field-hunt coat arrived, complete with gilt brass buttons emblazoned with S.H. His glee was almost childlike, and he even allowed her to go out riding again.

The main motivation was that she not show him up with her inexperience, but Bessie liked to think that it reflected the establishment of some sort of trust as well. Restricted trust that is. There was no instructor any more, and she had to ride at the front of the house so that he could keep an eye on her. But it was freedom nevertheless, and she enjoyed every jaunt, including the one on the first of July – when the Bateford carriage appeared halfway down the drive shortly after she had set out.

Was there something wrong? She galloped over, but discovered that it was simply business. Arnold needed to go into town, which meant that her practice would have to be curtailed. Not immediately, but she must return inside soon and prepare, because he may well be bringing guests back for dinner.

Bessie gave a warm smile of compliance, and then resumed her efforts to scale the little jumps that she had erected. They were not high by any standards. Indeed Ella could probably hurdle them, but Bessie did not want Duke having to lift his feet too far off the ground.

Ten minutes later – when sure that Arnold had no intentions of doubling back – she left Duke grazing in the meadow, helped herself to a different saddle, and hurried off into the wood. Making her way to the tree-stump where she had stored Rufus' trousers, she pulled them out, put them on, and rushed back. The trousers were far too large, but she had pins to take care of that, and soon felt relatively comfortable. Then it was time to get her feet into those stirrups, ride like a man, and fly like the wind.

Heading towards Somerden, she had to slow up as they skirted the actual town, and then went south, asking for directions once the surroundings became unfamiliar. Bessie knew that she could not be far away from her destination. Harris had said six to seven miles, and there was a fair distance behind her already. A small-holder answered her queries, and soon Ackerley was rising up on the horizon. It was a collection of stately homes, nothing more, and as Northcliff came into view, she stopped, breathless.

Duke had done brilliantly to get her here, but now it was time to play her own part, and was she really sure about what she was doing? Her brain had given it a lot of thought, been over and over it time and again, but still there were doubts. Too many doubts, but too late to do anything about them now. Encouraging Duke to stir himself once more, she cantered forward, before tying the reins loosely to a laburnum tree at the top of the drive. He would happily stand there all day, but she had to take the precaution, just in case a passing filly caught his attention, and he wandered off. Then she ascended the front steps, but a liveried individual appeared in the doorway, barring her admittance.

It was no wonder. The horse was sweating, Bessie was sweating, the trousers were those of a man, and her hair was a mess. Not exactly the class of person normally received at Northcliff.

Unsure of what to say, Bessie decided to be brutally direct, and tackle all his misgivings head-on: 'Good afternoon. I know you're thinking that I seem rather misplaced, but I assure you that this is the house I am looking for. I need to speak to Mr Roscoe, on a matter of considerable importance, and he will most definitely be interested in what I have to say. Even if that seems unlikely at this point. If it helps, I can wait out here while you consult him.'

The butler did not move at first, but then eventually closed the door and retreated across the hall. It was not within his remit to decide who ought to be turned away, even though he wished that it was. His duty was simply to report or convey – messages or people – and a minute later, he was back with Mr Roscoe. And it was clearly Drew, not Mark.

Bessie had so much flitting through her head that she did not form any immediate opinion of Cynthia's husband. Drew on the other hand, formed a very definite opinion of her, and it was not favourable.

'You wish to speak to me?'

'That's right. And your father should probably hear this too.'

'I'm afraid that will be rather difficult. He died a few weeks ago.'

'Oh. I'm sorry. I didn't know.'

'What exactly is this about?'

'It's a somewhat complicated matter, and quite private in nature. Could we possibly speak alone?'

After a slight purse of the lips, Drew instructed his butler to withdraw, and directed her to get on with it.

'I suppose it's best if I first tell you who I am. It might come as a bit of a surprise, but my name is Elizabeth. Elizabeth Bateford.'

Drew's nose wrinkled as if her musty smell had suddenly wafted in his direction. 'I do not deal with people bearing that surname,' he declared, and turned away.

'No, please don't. This thing between you and my husband needs to be resolved. Surely you can see that?'

'Husband?' Drew turned back with a frown. 'You mean . . . Arnold?'

'Yes.'

'Arnold? And you? My God, I knew he'd married a . . . But I never thought . . .' He did not finish either sentence, and Bessie was extremely grateful for that.

'Please just hear me out. That's all I ask. Five minutes, and I'll be on my way.'

Drew took his time having yet another look at her, and then through either pity or intrigue, he pushed the front doors open. 'I do not conduct my business in the open air,' he declared, and she scurried up the steps before he could change his mind.

Once inside, she was led into the nearest room, and then Drew stood near the empty fireplace, legs apart, and arms folded. 'I'm listening.'

'Thank you. I would be appreciate it if you could keep on listening until I reach the end. Even if you find my statements shocking, or they cause offence, it is only at their conclusion that they will make any sense.'

He blinked a few times, but ultimately gave his consent, and honoured his word until she paused long enough to indicate that there was no more to be said. His face had remained impassive throughout, but now it took on a look that was not exactly encouraging. 'You really expect me to believe a word of that?'

'Yes, because it's true.' Bessie said it with passion, but knew that it was nevertheless lame, so she added: 'Everything fits with what you already know, and in any areas where you are unsure, you only have to consult your wife.'

His wife had gone to Pelton for the day, and he would not be consulting her on this anyway. At least not yet.

But Bessie's tough declaration settled in his mind one or two issues about veracity.

'So let me get this straight.' He unfolded his arms, freeing up his fingers for some counting. 'You want me to provide you with a man who will happily participate in a brawl, another two men who can provide a supporting role, a young lad, a bowl of water, a substantial sum of money, a kidney from my kitchen, and my patience.'

'That's right.'

'And what makes you think that I might be willing to do any of these things?'

'Because you're a man who's guided by instincts, and your instincts are telling you that it's a good idea.'

'That's where you're wrong. I am a man guided by caution, and that caution is suggesting that I send you promptly on your way.'

'But you don't always have to pay heed to suggestions,' replied Bessie. 'And if you love your wife, then you'll do as I ask.'

It was totally impertinent, but Drew did not issue any rebuke. He did indeed love Cynthia, but he was not always sure that she felt remotely the same. Perhaps this was his chance to secure her affection. Or perhaps it was the worst idea that he had ever encountered.

Bessie could see him locked in debate, but did not speak. She had put her case, and now it was for him to decide – although when his answer came, it was more of a qualification than a decision:

'I can certainly give you the water for your horse, along with a pig's kidney, although goodness knows why you need one. But as for the rest? I will have to take time to consider it.'

'That's fine. Your actions in the future will show me your intentions.'

There were two main reasons why she was not willing to plead. One: because some of those doubts had resurfaced, and half of her suddenly wanted to hear a negative. And two: because she had to get back.

'Thank you again.' She moved towards the door, and when Duke was sufficiently revived, she prepared to leave.

Drew Roscoe was still standing in the same room, although had now taken up position by the window, and nodded as she stared. That was to bid her goodbye. But then five seconds later, he did it again – and that was his answer. Her mission had been successful, things would soon be set in motion, and from this point on, there would be no turning back.

CHAPTER SIX

There would also be no way of creeping back into
Bateford Hall. Presumably Arnold had told the butler
that his wife would be returning from practice within the
hour, and she had been far longer than that. Of course
she could attempt to spin some sort of yarn, but it would
undoubtedly be relayed to Arnold, and he would not
accept her verbal reasoning. Not in a month of Sundays.
He would jump to the conclusion that she was up to her
old tricks again, and that damn cat would reappear.
They had now been married for seventy-three days, so it
would entail two extra lashes this time – including one
for the day unaccounted for. Her body simply could not
take another nine strikes. In fact she sometimes
wondered whether the deepest welts would ever stop
smarting. So in order to avoid that particularly
unpleasant fate, a very persuasive action was required,
and first she needed to get changed.

Leaving Duke in the field below the meadow, well out
of sight of the house, she swapped the saddles back, and
returned Rufus' trousers to their tree-stump hollow. It
had kept them concealed until now, so was obviously a
good spot. Then she put her riding-skirt back on, and
unwrapped the kidney. No blood had seeped out, and as
she moved to pick it up, she suddenly realised that blood-
stained hands would look completely wrong! Some
thoughts really were life-savers. Uttering a little prayer of
thanks, she wound Rufus' trouser-leg around her hand

until it could act as a thick glove, and *then* began dabbing blood onto her temple. It felt awful to touch her face with material which had once been so close to Henderson's posterior, but there was no alternative, and having squeezed more blood from the kidney, she kept on dabbing until her hair was fully matted. If Doctor Stanbury were to examine her, he would find no cut, but that could be explained by concealment in the hairline. Or at least she certainly hoped so.

On her way out of the wood, she threw the kidney into the peat-bog, watched it sink, and rejoined Duke. It was hard to say whether anybody had been out looking for her yet, but just in case, she was going to pick an area where she was allowed to roam, but which was not immediately obvious. A place easily overlooked, and there was only one option which sprang to mind.

It was on the south edge of the meadow, where the gradient dropped away sharply, and could give you a bit of a shock if you were taken unawares. There were also a few rocks in the dip, and Bessie rubbed herself against one of them, transferring some of the blood that was trickling down her neck. Then she pressed the side of her body against the soil, and prepared to take up position. The story would be that naughty old Duke had thrown her off, where she had impacted a rock, and lain unconscious ever since. Before adopting her final resting pose, she kicked off a shoe, to suggest that it had been caught in the side-saddle during her fall, and then she waited – and waited – and waited.

Time was bound to pass much more slowly than usual, she understood that, but it seemed to be hours rather than minutes that were ticking by as she was plagued by what must have been a thousand small flies.

She should have anticipated it, being daubed in blood, and even Duke got in on the act, trying to lick her face. It was most considerate of him, but she really did need some blood left for Arnold's arrival – whenever that might be.

Obviously he was still in town, and that was a good thing – it had enabled her to settle in, but as time progressed, she began to wonder what could possibly be keeping him so late. Was there a chance that he might not make it back this evening, that she might be out in this meadow all night? She did not fancy a hard clod of earth for a pillow. Nor did she fancy spending the next twelve hours picturing what he might be doing – and with whom. There was no question that he was familiar with Somerden's notorious quarter. How else could he take Cynthia there? Take his sixteen-year-old daughter to a brothel, for tips on masking the loss of her virginity. It was almost impossible to believe that he had done that.

Other issues, doubts and miscellaneous cogitations visited her in rotation until at last she heard voices – and thankfully one of them was Arnold. He was back, and not exactly happy, but hopefully he would soon encounter Duke wandering around, and begin to appreciate that his wife had been the victim of a misadventure, *not* the perpetrator of some heinous misdemeanour. The search for her began in the north-east corner – she could tell from the way that the commotion carried on the breeze – and they seemed to be making heavy weather of it. She was almost tempted to shout: "I'm over here", but eventually they located her of their own accord.

Appearing lifeless was of primary importance, but when they had moved her head a couple of times, she decided that a small response was necessary. Otherwise there was a risk that her lids might open involuntarily, and everything could look dreadfully false. So she mumbled deliriously, and allowed her eyes to roll as she was carried back into the house. One of the two remaining overseers had been summoned since he could do the job single-handedly, although it was a particularly undignified experience. Being hoisted over somebody's shoulder was most unladylike, not to mention uncomfortable when that shoulder began to dig into your ribs. And then she suffered the ultimate ignominy of being tossed onto Arnold's bed.

Even if they were married for the next forty years, she would still view the master bedroom as Arnold's domain, not her own, but the fact that she was carried into that room, rather than any other, was a very good sign. It meant that he was not angry, and over the coming days there were no signs of suppressed anger either. Indeed he seemed most impressed with the effort that she was making to be mobile again as quickly as possible. She did not make it *too* quick of course, for fear that it would look suspicious, and also because she needed the other parts of her body to recover. Having never travelled those many miles before, her thighs were more than a trifle stiff, and lying in the sun for a long time had not done her face much good either. But by the time they had reached the weekend she was up and about again, and ready in the event of any visitors coming to call.

When a man did finally present himself at Bateford Hall, the phrase "come to call" was probably not particularly appropriate for the situation. She was in the drawing room, engaged in her favourite pursuit of knitting, when the sound of crunching pebbles reached her ears, and as she pulled the curtain back, she saw a tall thin individual marching resolutely towards the front door. He was flanked by Charles and that overseer with whom she had become fleetingly acquainted – and they both looked intensely morose. Bundling the wool off her lap, she dashed into the hall just in time to hear a request to speak to Arnold, and while the butler disappeared upstairs, she was able to assess this stranger. Well-dressed, but not in an expensive way, he had a pale and rather strained face, and a light in his eyes of feverish zeal.

Arnold was not normally on the second floor at this hour in the afternoon, but he had been struggling with back-ache since yesterday, and wanted to knock it on the head before dinner. Unfortunately he had enjoyed only limited success so far, and therefore was not in the mood to be dealing with problems. As he approached the bottom stair, the glance which flashed in Charles's direction could accurately be translated as: "What the hell's the point of keeping a dog if I still have to bark myself?"

All that Charles could do in response was offer a grim shrug. There were many problems at the mill, and he relished dealing with them each in turn, but this was not of your average come-day go-day variety, as Arnold was soon to find out.

'What is it?' he snapped.

'My name is Frank Verrell. I am the factory sub-inspector for this region of the North Midlands, and I am here to inform you that your mill is breaking the law.'

Arnold's expression was blank at first – both with surprise, and also a drowsy stupor, but then tedium quickly moved in. These little irritants came along from time to time, and could usually be dispatched with a minimum of fuss. 'I'm afraid you must be mistaken.'

'Are you aware of the requirements of the 1833 Factory Act Mr Bateford?'

'Yes, fully aware.'

'Then you will know that no child under the age of nine is permitted to be employed in an establishment such as your own, and that there are strict limits to the weekly working hours for those above that age. Namely no more than forty-eight for those under thirteen, and a sixty-nine-hour limit for those . . .'

'Yes yes, I know all this.'

'Well that renders me rather confused, because your mill is in breach of not just one of those provisions, but all of them, and under the law that requires me to issue you with a notice of impending penalty.'

Arnold pursed his lips. He was loath to even entertain the notion of paying this weedy officiary, but if it meant getting back to bed without further ado, then perhaps it was worth it. 'So how much do you want? Ten pounds? Twenty?'

'Try a thousand.'

'Thousand!'

'Yes. And guineas, not pounds.'

'You haven't even got the authority to name such a figure, never mind expect me to pay it!'

'In times past, you may well have been correct, but these new discretionary powers mean that I have all the authority I need. And frankly I must say that your disregard for the regulations is on a scale more flagrant than I have ever before encountered.'

'I don't care,' slammed Arnold. 'You can take your regulations and your stupid little laws, and bugger off. Because you've got no proof.'

'That's where you're wrong again I'm afraid,' countered Verrell, in the sort of calm tone suggesting that he had danced to this tune before. Everybody who was brought to book reacted in exactly the same way, and he was happy to go through the motions, because he knew where they would end up.

'What? Have you been talking to some of my workers? Is that it?' Arnold raised his eyebrows contemptuously. 'Have they been giving you their usual tales of woe? Because that's all they are. Tales. When it comes to it, they'll never go against me. Never.'

'I don't need them to. I've had a boy employed as a piecer in your mill for the whole of these last two weeks, and he's been certified by our surgeon as being most definitely under-age.'

After his previous bullish statement, Arnold suddenly went rather quiet. 'One boy. What's that? Fifty pounds at most.'

'I believe I've already made it quite clear that this concerns significantly more than one boy. Indeed your entire force of child workers is being compelled to perform more hours than the law allows.'

'And how exactly is your surgeon going to prove that?'

'He doesn't need to. Under the 1836 Act, it is now compulsory for all births, marriages and deaths to be registered . . .'

'Exactly! 1836! You think my workers are all three years old, do you? You're a fool. They're too old to be registered, which means that you don't know the age of a single last one of them.'

'No,' said Verrell. 'But you do, and you've listed them most diligently in your wages book.'

'What?'

'Your wages book. Certain sheets of which have rather fortuitously found their way into my possession.'

Now it did not just dawn that this was slightly more serious than first imagined, it struck Arnold right between the eyes, and he retaliated in the only way he knew how. 'You're lying!'

'You don't believe that I have the sheets in question?' clarified Verrell.

'No I don't!'

'Then let me describe their arrangement for you. Names on the right-hand side, rather than the traditional left, which is reserved for the important details of age and hours worked. Presumably you wish to make sure that nobody claims an age older than they are, and receives higher remuneration as a result. There is also a rather substantial column outlining the fines your workers pay for breaching *your* regulations, and of course your name is repeatedly embossed along the top. Sound familiar?'

'Familiar?' Arnold shot forward. 'I ought to ring your bloody neck.'

'I wouldn't if I were you. The inspector knows that I'm here, and should anything happen, he will personally take control of this investigation himself. With the power to shut you down for a considerably long time.' Verrell had managed a quick side-step so that Bateford junior was between him and the senior version, but Arnold still had hold of a lapel, and kept a very firm hold as he growled:

'I'll have you arrested. Trespass. Theft. You'll be rotting with the rest of the vermin . . . *for a considerably long time.*'

'But I never said that I stole anything, merely that your documents came into my possession, and regrettably I am unable to provide a meaningful description of the individual who supplied them to me.'

If looks could kill, Frank Verrell would have found himself six feet under, but for the first time in his life Arnold managed to look and not kill – at least not yet. 'You get out of my sight, do you hear me? You get off my property right this minute, or I swear to God, I won't be responsible for my actions!'

'Good idea,' agreed Verrell, still the epitome of self-composure, but taking the precaution of backing away once his lapel was free. 'Give you time to think over what I've said – and to get the money together.' He finished with a smile, before deciding that it was probably too much, and hurrying off at quite a pace down the drive.

Arnold stared after him for a full minute – the calm before the storm – and then let rip, kicking the thing closest to him, which happened to be his own study door. In fact he made contact with such force that his foot went right through the panelling. Then, since it was ruined anyway, he went for strike numbers two, three and four until the door was shredded beyond recognition – meaning that the time had now come to make a human pay. Starting with that boy:

'Where is he?'

'Who?' replied Charles, which was the wrong thing to say, and completely unnecessary, but he wanted to delay the beating until his father had come down from this peak.

'Who? You ask me who! That boy of course. The little runt who's been in my mill for the past two weeks.'

'A . . . A . . . Angus Lynch. I think it must be him.'

'You *think*?'

'Yes.' Charles was trying very hard not to shake.

'And how exactly did this Angus Lynch come to find himself in my building?'

'He was looking for work.'

'Looking for work?' repeated Arnold.

'Yes, because his Pa had been let go, and his brother was sick, and . . .'

'Don't tell me – you felt sorry for him.'

'Of course not!' In fact if anything, Charles had felt all-powerful when dealing with such a pathetic figure who smelt like a midden, and kept saying sir in a desperately servile manner. To have control over the fate of the entire Lynch family had been rather gratifying, but it had also made good business sense. 'He was willing to work for only a shilling, so I took him on, and sacked the oldest Drayson lad. It meant a saving of thirty pence a week.'

'A saving?' Arnold looked like he was about to rupture something. 'Thirty pence a week against a thousand-guinea fine. You consider that to be a saving!'

'I never thought about it like that,' mumbled Charles with a legitimately injured tone. 'You've never paid the legislation any mind. In fact you've always been proud to flout it.' He paused, recognised that he was getting too bold, and added: 'Haven't you?'

'Yes, proud indeed. But I also have the sense to appreciate trouble when it's stark staringly obvious!'

'But how could I have known that trouble was coming?'

'By engaging that pathetic excuse of a brain of yours. Every woman in that place is carping about four and a half shillings a week. "It's starvation rations. However will we cope?" Their children get a shilling less, and the youngest even less than that. Then some whipper-snapper pops up, happy to accept nothing at all, and you don't smell a rat!'

Arnold's voice was booming so loud that the house was almost shuddering, and Charles wanted more than anything to cower back a few steps, but he could not do it, not with so many eyes watching – including those of Harris who had now crept onto the scene. 'I . . . I . . .' he stammered, but ultimately could not find a sentence, so Arnold moved on sarcastically:

'That accounts for the boy then. But would somebody care to explain how my documents have ended up in the hands of Frank Verrell?'

Both Charles and the overseer looked down at this point, and Bessie could not help thinking that Arnold would have been better employed putting his youngest son in charge at the mill. If something appeared too good to be true, it would definitely alert Harris' attention. Mostly because he would be intrigued as to why.

'I'm waiting,' growled Arnold, and it forced Charles to confront the issue.

'I think the office may have been . . . breached.'

'You *think*?'

This time Charles did not even have the courage to say yes, but simply swallowed in response.

'And did anybody think it might be a good idea to tell me?'

'There was no need. I didn't . . .' Charles stopped himself in time. 'There didn't appear to be anything missing.'

'Well appearances can be deceptive, can't they? And they sure as hell were in this instance!' Arnold clasped his son's head between his hands, and then slowly closed those hands until he had a clump of hair in each fist. 'One thousand guineas. One *thousand* guineas!'

The first iteration of that amount was angry and resentful, the second was almost despairing – because he knew he did not have it. Even with the winnings from Forrester's party, he would have to sell an asset before he could reach it, and that was shameful. A man in his position ought to be able to lay claim to ten times that figure with nothing more than a click of his fingers.

'Please Father, I'm sorry,' whispered Charles, afraid that those clumps of hair were about to be ripped from either side of his head. But to everybody's surprise, Arnold let go – although with a shove that sent his son crashing to the floor.

'I still haven't heard an answer to my original question. Where is he?'

Since Arnold was staring straight at him, the overseer felt obliged to reply: 'We . . . er . . . don't know. He hasn't been in today.'

'And does he often take it upon himself to have a day off whenever he feels like it?'

'No sir.'

'So you last saw him yesterday evening?'

'Yes sir.'

'And what happened yesterday evening? In fact what happens regularly on a Tuesday evening?'

The overseer knew that he had already said far too much, Charles was still on the floor with no apparent desire to get up, so the question was directed towards Bessie.

'The workers receive their pay,' she replied in a voice full of sympathy, showing that she understood how her husband felt, and that he had every right to be furious.

'Exactly. Pay-day! Which means that this little bastard wormed his way into my mill, stole my records, hightailed it without so much as a by-your-leave, and I've gone and bloody well paid him for it!'

Nobody considered it wise to endorse the truth of that statement, but the silence only made Arnold even more irate. In fact he swung around with such venom that he almost sent the butler flying.

'Get out of here Bellamy. You don't need to be a part of this.'

'Certainly sir.' The butler headed off down the back stairs – without question, and with speed, as always – and Arnold was left to breathe heavily.

The first Bateford on this site had taught his son that treachery must be stamped out with ruthless force, and Arnold had lived by that law from an early age. But Bellamy Jones had never shown even a flicker of disloyalty in all the years of service, and Arnold suffered a tinge of regret that he had almost struck him in anger. It was only a tinge, however, and soon normality was restored.

'Does that seem fair to you? That I pay for the privilege of being fooled?' He hauled Charles out of the corner where he had taken up residence, and shook him quite violently.

Once the shaking stopped, Charles winced, and debated what could possibly be the right move. To speak or not to speak. That was the question, and he did not care which was nobler, only what might turn out to be safer. But before he could decide, Arnold altered the grip that he had on his clothes, and literally threw him out of the house.

It was a fifty-year-old man against a twenty-year-old youth, but real spite could generate amazing strength, and Charles was lifted off his feet, sent hurtling through the air, and landed in an unsightly heap on the drive. Realising that it had made him feel just the slightest bit better, Arnold prepared to do the same again, although not with quite such a spectacular effect. The overseer was a heavy man, and nobody was about to lift *him* off his feet, but the push towards the door was enough to send him tripping down the steps, where he ended up in the same spot as Charles. In fact Charles involuntarily acted as the perfect-sized cushion to soften his fall.

'Get down to that mill and squeeze more out of those people than you've ever squeezed before,' ordered Arnold. 'I want full capacity to *mean* full capacity, and I want blood, sweat and tears. Starting with yours!'

'Yes sir.' The overseer scrambled up and ran down the drive, fully aware that he had been let off lightly.

'What are you waiting for?' Arnold snarled at his son, who could not have answered if he had wanted to. Seventeen stone of overseer had punched the wind right out of him, but because of fear that something worse might happen, he eventually managed to stagger to his feet, and blundered away from the house, tripping over his legs like a disorientated Great Dane.

When Arnold finally turned round, Bessie had a horrid suspicion that he might go for the treble, but in fact he did not launch her or Harris into space, and instead went back upstairs to resume the resting of his back.

The moment that the coast was clear, Harris dashed over to secure answers about what had happened at the start, and Bessie happily obliged. Her stepson had provided vital information on occasion, so it was only fair that she return the favour. She did not, however, expect it to take the best part of an hour. By the time that

Harris had everything straight in his head, it was time to change for dinner, and her knitting would just have to wait until another day.

Upon reaching the top of the stairs, Bessie paused, nervous about disturbing Arnold, but he was not in fact asleep, only subdued, and persisted in that state throughout dinner and beyond. It began to worry her because it was the wrong type of silence. She was expecting morose, ready-to-lash-out-at-any-minute silence, but this was a thinking man's silence, and totally out of character. There was no doubt that Verrell was set to return, and also no doubt that Arnold would again refuse to pay, so there was plenty to ponder, but nevertheless it felt wrong.

When she came to think about it, his reaction after Verrell's departure was not right either. Yes he had beaten the door to a pulp, but the witnesses had largely escaped unscathed, and that was not the norm for Arnold Bateford. It continued to harass her the following morning, and then full alert was raised with the announcement that Stewart Munroe was coming to dinner – and she was to have a headache.

'It's a business dinner,' explained Arnold. 'Gentlemen only.'

What was that supposed to mean? What sort of business? And why Stewart? Somehow she managed to remain casual, promising to wait up – which caused Arnold to smile – but inside her stomach was churning. She simply had to know what was going on, and once the notion of listening through the wall had been banished, she knew that there was only one thing for it. Harris.

The three Bateford males went downstairs at ten to eight, an hour later than usual, but everything went out of the window for guests, particularly one that appeared to be a guest of honour. Stewart's carriage pulled up right on cue, and Bessie knew that the eating and drinking would take at least a couple of hours, so she went into the nursery. Ella was asleep, but it was wonderful to watch her, to feel close, and it also offered the perfect look-out for when the evening became interesting.

She imagined that at some point Arnold would wish to converse with Stewart alone, meaning that his sons would have to be dismissed. And true to form, that was the case. All she needed now was for them to go their separate ways – which they did – so she left it thirty seconds, and then raced along the landing to Harris' room. It was impossible to knock, but he would not be undressing yet, and as she dived in, she could not help thinking about the time when it had been Thomas' room all those many moons ago.

Harris jumped, startled, but then a sparkle quickly lit up his eyes. 'Do you want to hear all the gossip?'

'Oooh, yes please,' she replied, shoulders hunched in an act of eager anticipation, and was soon being informed that Stewart's investment – which had seemed completely dead in the water – was once again on the table.

'But why?' she demanded, trying to sound intrigued rather than irritated.

'Because of these railways. They're coming to Somerden faster than first thought. The line to Henningborough is already complete, and when it reaches us, they say it'll branch off here, there and everywhere. Apparently some Marquis is pushing it through, reckons Somerden is strategically important, and Munroe thinks that if he joins with Father, it could be . . . you know?'

'Mutually advantageous.'

'That's right. And now they're haggling over the exact extent of that advantage. Munroe is willing to pay for replacing the machinery, extending the size of the mill, and dealing with this Verrell business, but wants forty percent of all future profits as a result. While Father only wants to give him twenty-five.'

'I see.'

'If truth be told, I don't think Father wants to deal with him at all, but if he doesn't make the most of this railway, then somebody else will, and it seems the lesser of two evils, especially at the moment.' Harris paused before exclaiming: 'You do know who's behind all this, don't you?'

Bessie had missed most of that, too busy debating what to do next, but caught his last statement. 'Who's behind all what?'

'The inspectorate of course. Being investigated.'

'Who?'

'Thomas!'

'Thomas?'

'Yes. Father's convinced of it, and Charles is seething mad. Says Thomas always knew how much he wanted to run the mill, and is now out to subvert it. He also says that if he ever claps eyes on Thomas again, he'll kill him.'

'And he'd be well within his rights,' endorsed Bessie, aware that if she said anything remotely defensive of Thomas, or even neutral, then Harris would pursue his favourite theme of: "You liked my brother, didn't you?"

Her stepson was clearly eager to talk some more, but time was now of the essence, and so she had to fob him off with a promise to continue their conversation the following day. Then as soon as she was back in Arnold's bedroom, she removed her clothing, and put on a nightdress. It was imperative to stop this deal in its tracks, which meant speaking to Stewart, but she could not attempt her usual manoeuvre of sneaking off in the coming days. That ploy had already been pushed to the limit, so she had to do it here, tonight. But if she went downstairs with a complaint of ill health, somehow diverted Arnold, and talked to Stewart, then Arnold would know exactly what was going on if the deal later fell through. So once again that left only one avenue open – to get Stewart on his own, without Arnold ever knowing about it.

She felt like a cat with nine lives. Not only were they running out, she was not even sure that she had any left. But an idea was forming in her mind, and it might just work. Creeping back along the landing in her bare feet, she hurried down the stairs, managed to avoid being seen by the butler, took a sharp left turn, and made her way into the family's water-closet. Stewart would undoubtedly have consumed a healthy volume of port over the latter stages of the evening, and being of a certain age, surely he would need to pay a visit before embarking on his journey home. All she had to do now was pray that he had not already paid that visit, or indeed that Arnold did not decide to pay one first.

As she stood there with fingers crossed, the convenience of her surroundings hit home for the first time in many a month. She was able to come down here, do her business, and never encounter it again. All because of a cesspool in the basement. Such was the luxury of privilege. While working people had to face the overflowing privy every day, and the putrid smells of human waste. Night-soil they called it, because every few months – under cover of darkness – a dealer was supposed to come and cart it away, but if he could not gain access, then it was left to pile up – and up – and up.

How could those who lived so well be utterly oblivious to those who did not? Was it because they had learnt to think of nothing except themselves? Probably, although her conclusion held very little condemnation. She had come to understand now how easy it would be to fall into the same trap herself – assuming that she had not already done so. But such thoughts were for another day. She needed to prepare the arguments to put to Stewart, and having been through them only the once, footsteps approached, and the door was suddenly opened.

Quickly putting a finger up to Stewart's mouth, she drew him inside, and managed to keep his initial exclamation to a whisper.

'What a lovely surprise Elizabeth. I thought I were to be denied the delights of your company this evening.'

'Thank you Stewart, but I don't have any time for niceties. There is an absolutely enormous favour that I must ask of you.'

'Ask away. You should know that I can never refuse a lady in her nightwear.'

Good. He was in the right sort of mood. 'Am I correct in thinking that you are again considering a financial stake in the mill?'

'Indeed I am.'

'Well I really must petition you against it.'

'Don't worry Elizabeth, it isn't like last time. I'm fully apprised of the state of your husband's business. Nobody pulls the wool over my eyes twice.'

'Actually,' confessed Bessie, 'it is for *myself* that I am concerned. If you provide Arnold with this assistance, then the mill will prosper, and I cannot afford for that to happen.'

'You do not wish for your husband to be a success?'

'No I do not.'

Stewart frowned. 'What a curious thing for a wife to say.'

'But it is precisely because I am a wife that I must say it.' She lowered her head for a moment, as if driven to confront something dreadfully uncomfortable. 'Arnold is, as you are probably aware, a regular visitor to a certain . . . part of town.' She left Stewart to fill in the actual place-name, but when he remained silent, she was forced into it: 'Holliston Road.'

'Ah, I see.' He had never actually been tempted in that direction himself, preferring his amours to be a little closer to home – usually from among his own pool of staff.

'Even if I am attentiveness itself, he still persists in seeing those . . .'

'Whores?'

'I was going to say: Ladies of ill repute. And the only thing that stops him from seeing even more of them is that he is preoccupied by worries at the mill. But if you remove those worries, then he will take himself there morning, noon and night, and the risk of him being exposed as a . . . as a client, will soar to a truly terrifying level.'

Stewart placed a calming hand upon her shoulder. 'I am sure that it will not come to that.'

'But *how* can you be sure? The magistrates are taking a harder line. I have heard of raids in Henningborough, of men scurrying through the back alleys in desperate bids to avoid escape. And with this new railway, surely the magistrates in Somerden will be keen to clean up the town?

A raid will be organised, I know it, and Arnold will be held up for public ridicule, with our reputations ruined.'

She stopped, breathless, the perfect picture of pain, and Stewart began to look the picture of sly manipulation.

'I appreciate your plight Elizabeth, and certainly there are many other businesses with which I could invest, but Arnold is offering a thirty-five percent share of the profits for only a relatively minor outlay. That is not an opening which comes along every day.'

'But aren't there more important things in life than money?'

'Perhaps,' he conceded. 'One or two, and the fragile fears of a female are not to be dismissed lightly, but as I say, this is a golden opportunity.'

'What if you were to receive . . . say . . . an opportunity in another sphere?'

'If that were indeed to be the case, then I would need to consider my position very carefully Elizabeth. I am not a blinkered man, but it would depend on what this other sphere might be.'

Bessie swallowed. 'You need to understand that my problem with these women is not simply because Arnold spends so much time with them, but because of their status.' She raised her eyebrows, but it was clear that Stewart either needed, or wanted, her to be more explicit. 'In other words – I am not affronted by the concept of . . . shall we say . . . extra-marital dalliances? But they should be done within one's own class.'

Stewart grinned. 'Variety is the spice of life, but only as long as it's safe?'

'Exactly, and I hope that I am not impertinent in suggesting that there has been a little . . . spice . . . between us, since our first meeting.'

Stewart licked his lips. 'And I hope that *I* am equally devoid of impertinence when I suggest that I would very much like things to become a whole lot spicier.'

'That is music to my ears Stewart. Music to my ears.' She leaned up, inviting his kisses, and when that was over and done with, she set to organising some details.

Obviously withholding investment for a second time would mean that Stewart was not high on the list of those welcomed at Bateford Hall, so Bessie had to find a way to get herself to his house – and Mrs Forrester was it:

'You should refuse your next invitation, while I will ensure that Arnold accepts ours. Then once we arrive, I shall be struck by some malady requiring me to rest in one of the rooms upstairs. Arnold will be locked into defending his whist title for at least two to three hours, giving me plenty of time to slip away.'

'And my house is only a short carriage-ride from there. I shall send my driver to collect you, and we shall have a full two hours together.'

'Splendid.'

'You're sure that your husband will not think of checking on you?'

Consumed by the desire to beat Gil again, Arnold would not even notice her absence. 'Absolutely positive,' she replied, believing that it was all sorted, but then Stewart went and added – in a voice filled with frustration:

'But it is many weeks until Mrs Forrester's next get-together, and that is an awfully long time to wait.'

'I know,' she agreed with sympathy. 'But some things are worth the wait, and you will be worth it, won't you Stewart?'

'I have had no complaints in the past.'

'Good, because I shall ensure that you have no cause for complaint with me. But you must go now, before we get caught.'

'Men often take a considerable length of time in these places after a meal. There is no rush.' His hands slipped south, and a couple of minutes later, when she had tolerated about as much groping as she could stomach, she reiterated a sense of urgency. Before he would go, however, Stewart wanted something else firmly established: 'I hope I can count on the fact that this will be the first of many such assignations?'

'Of course,' she assured him, but knew that her words had not come across as sufficiently convincing, so added: 'Having had to wait all these weeks for you, I shall be quite . . . insatiable.'

That did the trick. 'Until the tenth of October then,' he concluded.

'You already have the date?'

'Yes. Our dear Mrs Forrester always holds her autumn party on what would have been her late husband's birthday. He was staunchly opposed to any sort of gaming, so I fear that it's an act of defiance rather than tribute. Anyway it also happens to be the day before my youngest son comes of age.'

'Will that be a problem?'

'Not in the slightest. I shall send him out with his brothers for a pre-birthday drink at a friend's house. It will be ideal.'

'Oh good.'

'You know something Elizabeth? I've never really liked Mrs Forrester very much, but now I'm suddenly developing quite an affection for her.' He turned to leave with a satisfied smirk, before turning back. 'And there's

Mr and Mrs Coombes too. We can play the same trick at their party.'

'I can't always be arriving in good health Stewart, and then falling ill within ten minutes. Arnold is not a fool.'

'True. I may have to attend as well, and we can snatch a few moments wherever possible. We might come to find ourselves intimately acquainted with a whole host of water-closets all over town.'

'How disgracefully . . . daring,' she replied, face flushed with excitement, when the word which had first sprung to mind was: Grotty. 'Until the tenth then?'

'I shall be counting the days.'

Stewart finally left, and she was able to straighten her nightdress, and think about how best to get back to bed. The main staircase was really the only option from this point in the house, and to go unnoticed required the butler to be standing in exactly the right spot in the hall, and for nobody else to be in attendance. Having hovered in the shadow of the staircase for more than five minutes, that first element was in place, but then Arnold went and appeared from the study.

His mood was jovial, which suggested that Stewart had sensibly held off from announcing the bad news tonight, but things were about to turn very bad for *her* if she could not get upstairs first. Yet another person appeared on the scene – Duncan – summoned to bring Munroe's carriage around to the front. The Bateford stable-boy had already been sent home, so the poor footman was acting as general drudge again – but thankfully he would receive assistance from Munroe's driver who had just finished his fourth cup of tea in the kitchen. Arnold's butler went with them to supervise, so that only left Arnold himself, who had been joined by

Stewart. If only they would walk outside to say their farewells, but they seemed to have no intention of doing any such thing – until Stewart glanced in her direction, saw half a face peering through the banisters, and recognised her predicament.

'It's a brilliant moon tonight. I wonder Arnold – could I trouble you for a walk down to the mill? Get a good look at the structure close up.'

'Why of course Stewart. We can enjoy a cigar on the way.'

There was no need to fetch coats as it was a muggy evening, so they simply exited the building, and Bessie shot out as if somebody had lit a fire beneath her. Reaching their bed within a matter of seconds, she sank onto it, and was swamped with a sense of safety. Never in her wildest dreams could she have imagined that the smell of Arnold's sheets would engender such an emotion, but when he appeared, it was rapidly replaced with a very different one.

Fear was not the word for it, because he suspected nothing, and was almost as happy as when he had won that final hand against Tremaine and Chaloner. Satisfaction was not the word either, even though she had pulled off something of a master-stroke at short notice. The emotion that she was battling was in fact one of shame – tinged with a little guilt. Was it right to be doing what she was doing behind Arnold's back? And did the end ever justify the means? She was offering up carnal relations to one man, and engaging in carnal relations with another, merely to pursue her own agenda. Talk about ladies of ill repute, she was swelling the ranks – and also taking Louise's advice to the limit. Bessie Cullen was a prostitute in all but name, and the thing which worried her most was that she seemed to be rather good at it.

CHAPTER SEVEN

Usually things felt much worse in the cold light of day, but when Bessie woke, she was actually able to push negativity aside, and share in Arnold's optimism. For as long as it lasted that is. By mid-morning Munroe's message had arrived, expressing thanks for the opportunity to invest, but regretting that he would have to give it a miss on this occasion. He hoped, however, that relations could remain on a friendly basis, and he looked forward to doing battle once again at Mrs Forrester's autumn party.

Bessie knew that the final element was for her benefit, but thought that perhaps it might help as far as Arnold was concerned. A reminder of his greatest triumph would surely put him in a better mood? No. In fact it had exactly the opposite effect. Munroe was adding insult to injury by bragging about money on cards when it should have been going into the mill. It was a blatant act of provocation, and indeed within a couple of minutes, Arnold was convinced that there had never been any real intention of investing in the first place. Then when neurosis completely took over, he claimed that it was all Thomas' doing, pulling strings from afar. Having condemned his son for being something of a "disappointment", Bessie was amazed to hear Arnold crediting Thomas with quite so much influence. But of course she kept her opinions to herself.

Charles was lucky enough to be at the factory, but she and Harris were in the dining room when Arnold received the bad news, and as he stalked in, it was immediately obvious that the Arnold of old was back. Harris sank low into his chair, and watched it all with a look of considerable panic, hoping to go unnoticed. He had witnessed such eruptions before, but a sibling had always been on-hand. Now apart from Elizabeth, he was all alone, and that left him feeling not just vulnerable, but utterly defenceless.

Keeping his mouth shut was the best policy, and no movement whatsoever. Statuesque was the word, but today Arnold was not in the mood for silence. When he railed about being the victim of a conspiracy, he wanted whole-hearted endorsement – which Elizabeth provided, and poor Harris tried his best, but everything came out sounding wrong, and he was heading for a cuff around the ears when visitors arrived just in time. Frank Verrell was back – with two assistants – and a strong thirst for cash.

The butler attempted to bar their entry, but to no effect, and within seconds the trio of impostors were standing combatively in the face of the Bateford trio. There was no doubt that Frank was of a slender build – or "weedy" to use Arnold's scathing description – but the same could certainly not be said for his assistants, and that gave Frank the courage to continue with the calm confidence of last time.

'Well here we are again,' he commented cheerfully, doffing his cap in Elizabeth's direction. 'Please forgive the intrusion Miss, but there is the small matter of criminality to be cleared up.'

'It's Mrs, not Miss,' growled Arnold, and Frank glanced at Harris. Presumably he must be the husband, although he did seem a little on the immature side.

'She's my wife, you ignorant pig.' Arnold stomped towards his enemy, which was either very brave or very reckless, considering that he was outnumbered three to one.

'I stand corrected,' replied Frank, tipping his head to suggest that he was really quite impressed – before adding: 'I suppose money can buy you almost anything these days. No offence ma'am.'

Bessie stood up. 'If you're insinuating that I married my husband for his money, as certain others have done before you, then I am very much offended, and *you* are very much mistaken.' She finished right next to Arnold, and Frank managed to cough his way through an apology, before concentrating on matters that were more within his remit.

'So do you have the money then?'

'No.'

'No? I thought I made it perfectly clear that not paying is not an option.'

There were no words from Arnold, and Bessie knew better than to speak on his behalf. Harris was now safe on the far side of the table, and more than happy to stay there.

'I really can't understand why you're adopting this obstructive attitude,' grumbled Frank with a disappointed puckering of the lips. 'It isn't as if we're talking about a particularly large sum.'

'Not large?' retorted Arnold. 'For minor breaches of a law that should never have been passed, it's a bloody outrage.'

'Well of course you're entitled to your opinion, although I must take exception to the use of that word minor. And in the grand scheme of things, a thousand really isn't very much at all. Indeed it is only the same as my inspector receives annually in income – pounds that is – and frankly I am far more deserving.'

Frank chuckled to himself. Frank is frankly deserving. That had a certain ring to it, but Arnold certainly did not see the funny side:

'This has nothing to do with any law. You come up here on your high horse, spouting provisions when all you want is money for yourself. You're nothing but a greedy little blackmailer.'

'I am not greedy!' corrected Frank. 'If I was greedy, I'd have demanded ten thousand. And before you start talking about extortion, I'd take a long hard look at yourself. Treating those workers like dirt, then threatening eviction if they complain, but when somebody does the same to *you*, you're shouting indignation from the rooftops. Rather hypocritical, don't you think?'

'Hypocritical or not, I *am* shouting indignation from the rooftops, and I'm not paying you a penny.' Arnold made the declaration with a perverse smirk on his face.

'Then you leave me with no choice but to shut you down. You'll be bankrupt by the end of the year.'

'I'm sure you'll try your worst, but you won't succeed in doing any such thing.'

'I succeeded in gathering the evidence I needed,' retaliated Frank, 'and when I put it before my superiors, they'll come down on you like a ton of bricks.'

'I don't believe you. I don't believe that any of you have the power to do anything to me at all.'

'You'll just have to watch and learn then, won't you? Watch as the bills roll in, and there's no hope of paying them because your business is closed and there's no way of opening it again. Watch as your suppliers demand payment, and become so infuriated by your refusal that they take action to see you in a debtor's gaol.'

'Get out,' snapped Arnold as the truth of those words suddenly began to sting.

'No. This time I'm not leaving without my money.'

'You'll never get it!'

'I'd start preparing for a nice long spell behind bars then. And don't go thinking that your friends will help you out. In my experience, well-to-do folk don't like to be associated with the demise of those around them. While as for your lovely wife here, can you really see her hanging about when there are so many better offers out there for a girl of her particular attributes.'

Bessie slapped Verrell soundly across the face, but her husband did much more than that. Ramming the sub-inspector so hard that he crashed onto the floor, Arnold then began pummelling him about the face. Verrell's assistants jumped in to provide some sort of defence, but one was thrown backwards, the other elbowed in the eye – and by the time they had recovered, Frank's face was the most terrible mess.

Finally hauling Arnold off, the two assistants held him at bay by clamping both arms by his side, which enabled Frank to scrape himself off the carpet and swear vengeance. It was hard to tell precisely what he was saying because his mouth kept filling with blood, which he spat out at regular intervals, but the general gist was that Arnold would rue this day for a very long time.

With one last glare at the obstructive Batefords, he retrieved his cap, and staggered from the room – followed by the assistants when enough time had lapsed to give him a decent head-start. Bessie was sure that another door would now bite the dust, or an item of china-ware be smashed to pieces, but actually nothing happened. Having done what he wanted to Verrell, and with Munroe presently pushed from his mind, Arnold's anger abated – and surprisingly did not return. He was confident that he could thwart this sub-inspector with mere inactivity, that if he ignored it for long enough, the issue would simply go away. Was that insanity or mere arrogance? Bessie could not decide, but the appearance of Drew Roscoe on Wednesday morning brought the whole affair back into sharp focus.

She was in the bath at the time, which was dreadfully inconvenient, but totally unavoidable. Having put it off, and put it off, Arnold had ultimately insisted that she have a wash. But when she heard Drew's barouche draw up, she was out and dressed quicker than you could say: "There's still soap in your ears".

Reaching the bottom of the stairs, she was soon pleased to find that she had not missed anything. Harris was hovering in the hall, and rushed over to her immediately.

'You'll never guess who's here.'

'Who?' shrugged Bessie.

'Drew Roscoe.'

'No! But I thought you said he'd never . . .'

'I know, I can't believe it either, but he's here, in the drawing room, and Father's keeping him waiting.'

'Good Lord,' she exclaimed, while trying to think what to do next – namely how to hear what was being said once this meeting took place.

'How are we going to listen in?' asked Harris suddenly, and Bessie smiled at a man after her own heart.

'I've left some knitting in there, so I think it's best if you go in and look for it, get talking, and then I enter after a short delay. That way we'll both be in the right place.'

'But what if Father decides to take Drew over to his study?'

'Well then we'll . . . have to improvise.'

'And what am I supposed to talk about?'

'You could perhaps ask after your sister?'

'Oh yes,' replied Harris as if such a thing were a revolutionary concept.

After a few more words of encouragement, he moved off, and it was not long before Bessie glided in, majestic as the Lady of the Manor ought to be.

'Have you found it yet Harris?' she asked, before stopping as if surprised. 'I didn't realise we had guests.'

Drew rose to his feet. 'It's Mrs Bateford I presume?'

'That's right.'

'I'm Drew Roscoe. Pleased to meet you.'

Bessie accepted his hand, but took great care to avoid any sort of eye-lock, even a momentary one, because Harris noticed such things.

'Is that Roscoe as in Cynthia's Roscoe?'

'Indeed. I am her husband.'

'Oh dear.' Bessie clasped her face as if dreadfully ashamed. 'It must seem awful to you that I have never met her. My own stepdaughter. I do hope that she is well?'

'Yes, very well.' Drew turned to Harris. 'Is your father genuinely engaged in matters of pressing importance, or is he deliberately keeping me on hold?'

Harris did not have a clue what to say to that, so Bessie stepped in. 'My husband is never anything other than completely genuine, I can assure you. And he would never keep a guest waiting unnecessarily.'

'But I am no ordinary guest,' argued Drew. 'Surely you are aware of the bad blood?'

Harris flashed a warning frown at Bessie, who replied demurely: 'I am aware of a breakdown in relations, but am not exactly au fait with the details.'

'No? I am surprised that your husband hasn't shared them with you.'

'My husband shares many things, but I do not pry into a subject which is clearly a painful one. Perhaps you would care to enlighten me instead?'

'Perhaps another time,' he replied, and turned his attention to the door, which eventually opened.

Arnold did not appear irritated that his family were present, in fact he seemed rather pleased as he declared: 'Ah Roscoe, I see you've met my wife.'

Bessie again ended up feeling like the prize cow on parade, but if it meant that she was able to stay in the room, then it was a small price to pay.

'Yes, indeed I have had the pleasure,' remarked Drew in a distinctly frosty tone.

'And what has earned us the pleasure of *your* company?' enquired Arnold.

'I've been hearing that you've had a bit of trouble of late.'

'Trouble?' came the wary repeat.

'With the inspectorate. Apparently there's some chap in town talking to the magistrates with a view to having you arrested.'

'Arrested?' That repeat was not so much wary – as worried.

'Yes, by all accounts he took exception to your attempts to rearrange his face.'

'And I suppose you've come to gloat, have you?'

'It did cross my mind,' conceded Drew. 'But actually I've come with a proposition that could see this man out of your hair for good.'

'What makes you think I can't clear him out of my own hair?'

'Perhaps you can, but he's now looking for three thousand guineas before he'll go away, and it seems you viewed it as extortion when he only wanted one.'

Arnold gulped. He could not find three thousand, not this side of a blue moon, and although he would love to send Roscoe packing this very instant, he ultimately decided that listening did not mean accepting. 'I'll hear you out,' he replied. 'Through here.'

Harris' heart sank as Drew followed Arnold out of the room and over to the study.

'What are we going to *do*?' he hissed, but try as she might, Bessie could not find any reasonable excuse for knocking on that door. They would simply have to deduce what they could from their current positions, and actually it was a fairly easy task. Drew exited the house less than four minutes later, stony-faced, and when Arnold surfaced, he was much the same.

'Can't have been a very good proposition,' observed Harris, and Bessie simply nodded.

She knew exactly what that proposition would be, although had left Drew to work out the actual figure. It was designed to be initially dismissed, but then grow on you after a couple of days. Grudgingly enticing was the aim. She also knew that Arnold would never tell her if she came out and simply asked about it. He had to make the decision to talk himself, and true to her prediction, he gave voice to what was on his mind the very next night in bed:

'He's offering nine and a half thousand for the mill, the Hall, the land, everything. Wants to buy me out, when he knows damn well that they're worth at least double that.'

'What did you say?'

'I said over my dead body.'

'Good. I don't know how he had the cheek.' She draped her arm over his belly, and snuggled up against his shoulder. 'Why exactly is there such animosity from his end? I can't understand it.'

'He's a malignant individual, that's all. Can't step out from the shadow of his father,' criticised Arnold, and it was clear that Bessie was not about to hear any more.

It did not bother her. She had not expected an answer anyway, but had posed the question simply in order to reiterate that she knew nothing of the ins and outs. And since Arnold obviously wanted it to stay that way, they both soon slipped into slumber.

One thing which *did* bother Bessie was that she might say something in her sleep, reveal her true intentions, so it was always a relief when Arnold woke in the same mood as when he went to bed – which was indeed the case the following morning. He was determined to brazen this out. The magistrates could not arrest him. Many were manufacturers themselves. He was one of them! It was inconceivable. That conviction did wane a little when he went into Somerden on the Friday, and found that Drew was not exaggerating about all this talk of the town. But talk was one thing, actions very much another. Nothing would come of Verrell's complaint, he was totally and utterly convinced of it.

Bessie had expected Arnold to be stubborn, as stubborn as a mule in fact, but the threat of imprisonment ought to have been enough to tilt him into submission. Now she realised that the threat was not even credible as far as he was concerned, and frankly Drew had gone far too low with his offer, so that left her in need of drastic action. She had to make incarceration happen, simple as that, and there was only one man who could help bring it about. Firstly, in order to see him, she would have to employ the "Stewart ruse" – sneaking off when a dinner party was underway – and thankfully the Llewellyns were hosting one this very weekend.

Arnold would usually have needed a lot of cajoling before being willing to attend, but actually he considered this particular night to be of the utmost importance. Part of his "front it out" approach. Show no fear. Bessie praised him for his warrior-like attitude, and pledged to do her best in support, which indeed she did. Her performance during the meal was exceptional, despite having to endure the company of Vernon "all workers are slackers" Llewellyn. For a man who did nothing but eat and drink, it was amazing that he felt qualified to say such a thing on such a regular basis. But eventually the torture was over, and the ladies separated from the gentlemen.

This was her chance. Muttering an almost inaudible excuse, she made tracks for the back entrance, and was soon out onto the street. Most of these houses were built to exactly the same model, and having lived on both sides of the dividing line, it was easy enough to find her way out. Hurrying along the pavement, she turned the corner, and there he was.

'Thank you so much,' she beamed as Fraser Matthews greeted her with a warm embrace. It was quite an intimate welcome for two people who did not really know each other that well, but it felt as if they had shared a bond forever.

'It is absolutely wonderful to see you again,' said Fraser, eyes misting over. In only a few days it would be the anniversary of his daughter's death, so that made it a difficult time anyway, and this young woman was such a powerful reminder of the spirit which had been so cruelly snatched from him. Poppy Matthews and Bessie Cullen would have been firm friends if they had ever met, he just knew it.

'You look well,' he declared with relief.

'Thank you, and I hope the same can be said of you?'

'Yes, not too bad,' he replied with a tired smile.

'I'm sorry that I cannot stay for long, but I need to ask you to do something for me.'

'Anything. You know that if it is within my control, I will make it happen.'

'Good, because I need you to arrest Arnold Bateford.'

'Bateford? What has he done? Has he hurt you again?'

'No, he's . . . well . . . there's no easy way of saying this. He's my husband.'

'Your husband!'

'Yes.'

'But wh . . . what? I mean . . . when? How?'

She stopped him before he could get to why. 'It's complicated, and I promise you that I'll explain everything once this is over, but for now I need you to trust me.'

He had condemned her to twelve months in Henningborough gaol, full well knowing that she was innocent. Yes, he owed her a leap of faith. 'What is the charge then?'

'Assaulting a government sub-inspector.'

'And the name of this sub-inspector . . ?'

'Frank Verrell. Only he isn't real, Arnold simply thinks that he is.'

The lines along Fraser's forehead become pronounced with confusion, but Bessie did not have time to go into it.

'I know this sounds crazy, but it won't get anywhere near a trial, so Arnold will never find out, and I just need him locked up for a couple of days, that's all.'

Fraser chewed on his lip.

'Please? I really have to get back.'

'And you can assure me that there will be no trial?'

'We won't even get close to one.'

'Then how can I possibly refuse?' Fraser accompanied the question with an anxious shrug of surrender, and Bessie planted a kiss upon his cheek.

'So how long exactly do you want him to be held in one of my cells?'

'I'll be able to tell you that once he's in there, but it really shouldn't take many days. And remember – it's Frank Verrell bringing the claim for the damage to his face.' She gave Mr Matthews a kiss on the other cheek, before adding a final thought as she turned to leave: 'I don't suppose you could see to it that Arnold is put in my original cell?'

Fraser hesitated for a moment, but then his lips spread into a guilty grin. 'I think that such a detail can probably be arranged.'

'Perfect!' She dashed off with a sense of achievement so overwhelming that it practically *swept* her back into the company of Henrietta Llewellyn, who did not even pass comment on the absence. Nobody else questioned it either, Arnold suspected nothing, and as they rode home, she was able to bask in the knowledge that everything would soon be moving again, thanks to the help of Mr Matthews – and Duncan.

She was not able to speak to the footman until the next day, but then expressed her heartfelt gratitude for a job well done. Not only had she asked him to convey a message to a man he did not even know, it had also been necessary to discover the magistrate's home address first – and all against the backdrop of what had happened last time. Duncan had understandably been reluctant to comply, but little did she realise quite how close he had been to actually saying no.

The word had been on the very tip of his tongue. He had opened his mouth with the absolute intention of expressing it, convinced that he was doing the right thing, until the look on her face had told him otherwise. There was just something about the way that she made these extraordinary pleas, as if everything was balanced on a precipice, as if her life literally depended on the outcome, and standing in her way was infinitely worse than any of the consequences might be. But surely there *would be* consequences. How could there not be? And his heart had been pounding to the possibility of them as she returned from dinner. In fact it had kept on pounding at exactly the same rate the next day, even after Elizabeth had thanked him, and it was only on Tuesday that he finally began to relax – which was precisely when everything blew up.

He was not a witness to the main event, did not see the arrival of the constables, or all of the disruption at breakfast in order to remove Arnold on the order of the magistrates. It was only the aftermath that he came upon as the prison-van made its way back down the drive.

It was an ugly conveyance, little more than a wooden box with an arched roof, and Arnold raging through the bars. When the raging became indistinct, Charles began to rant in every direction instead – although not actually saying anything that constituted an instruction. Harris was speechless as usual; in fact it looked like he had been hit by a rebounding door. And Elizabeth was ringing her hands, pleading for somebody to do something, to find some way to save her husband from the dire fate which awaited him.

Duncan studied her reaction intensely as a particularly disturbing notion took over his brain. Thirty-six hours ago she had met with a magistrate behind the Master's back, and now the Master had been arrested. What did it mean? Surely . . . no . . . it could not be . . . no . . . that did not make any sense. Mr Matthews was a friend of her uncle's in Thurleigh, and there was no doubt that Mr Bateford had assaulted the inspector man, so it was natural that she would turn to a family friend in time of need. Yes, that was it, and Mr Bateford had been kept in the dark in case the meeting was unsuccessful, which had obviously proved to be the case.

Once Duncan had fixed it all properly into place, he was able to calm down, and Elizabeth's torment was enough to allay any residual concern. She was clearly worried sick, and her mood did not even begin to lift until Thursday evening – with the news that she would be able to see Arnold the next morning. Unfortunately that same news pitched Charles into a very black temper indeed.

If his father were to be allowed only the one visitor, it should be his son, not the wife who had only become a wife a matter of weeks ago. The fact that it was her birthday on that Friday the second of August was utterly irrelevant. *He* should be the visitor, but there was nothing he could do – besides accompany her of course. He did not like her, and he did not trust her, and there was no way that she was going it alone.

When they reached the courthouse, Bessie deliberately went up the main steps, and left it to an attendant to take her back out and around to the side. It was vital that she did not show any knowledge whatsoever of this building, and when Charles stepped from the carriage as she reappeared, there was a certain level of apprehension in her blood. If this pigheaded stepson had it in mind to escort her all the way up to the door, and that door were to be answered by the same man as last time, then she could be in serious trouble.

The apprehension grew as Charles showed no signs of returning to the carriage, and did indeed proceed to walk her right up to the basement entrance – which was again manned by one Callum Proctor. By way of precaution, she had opted to wear a low-brimmed hat, and it was either that, or the fact that the gaoler saw so many people in a four-month spell, but he did not recognise her. Not only was it a huge relief, but she was then able to enjoy the sight of Charles having the door shut in his face, before being led along the row of cells to Arnold.

It could have been a potentially painful experience, revisiting so many difficult memories, and thinking of the family life that she had enjoyed before all this misery began. Not a perfect life, but comforting nevertheless, and something that she might never know again. But today was her birthday for real, not merely in the fantasy world which she had created. She was nineteen – or twenty-two as far as Arnold was concerned – and she was going to savour every minute of her special day.

Callum stopped exactly as anticipated, unlocked the door, swung it open, and then returned to his post. There was no danger of Arnold escaping because one leg was chained – as hers had been. He was also hot – as she had been, but the one dirty window was now clean, so he had the luxury of a little more sunlight.

'Oh Arnold, what have they done to you?' she cried, stepping into the cell as her voice cracked with the distress of it all.

Crouching down beside him, she expected her sympathy to be swept aside by a loud explosion of anger, but he actually did the one thing she would never have imagined – he leaned his forehead against hers, and kept it there. Three days of the hell which others often endured for years, and he had been brought to his knees.

'We've been trying to persuade the magistrates to release you,' she explained desperately. 'But they won't do anything as long as Verrell persists in his claims, and he won't alter course no matter what we say.' She did not mention Drew Roscoe, but left a nice big gap for Arnold to fill.

'Is Roscoe's offer still on the table?'

'Yes. Why?'

Arnold turned away, and she waited for the reluctant declaration of acceptance, but he could not bring himself to do it:

'My father founded that mill, built it up himself, brick by brick, and I won't just give it to that lowlying scum. I tell you I won't do it!'

'But if it gets you home,' she urged gently, drawing his head back towards her, and cupping his face between her hands. 'I want you with me. Especially today.' She eased forward, to whisper in his ear: 'I need you by my side.'

That ought to work some magic. Yet again she was offering herself up on a plate, but yet again she was wrong. Arnold would not budge.

'You'll have to break Verrell's testimony,' he declared.

'How?'

'By killing him if you have to.'

'Killing him? Well . . . I'm sure . . . perhaps Charles would be willing to try,' she replied, putting it onto her least favourite person, and putting Arnold right off the idea at the same time. He was convinced that his son would only make things even worse.

'I'll have my day in court then,' he concluded. 'They may have to try the case, but there's no way that any magistrate will imprison me, no damn way.'

The next five minutes were taken up with Arnold's defiant reiteration of that belief, and his plans for the stand, until Callum returned to say that time was up. Bessie reluctantly bid her husband goodbye, broken-hearted, and maintained the tearful act until reaching those steps leading up into court – where she found Mr Matthews waiting.

'Is it having the desired effect?' he asked, and she confirmed that they were indeed on the right track, although he could help push matters along by having a little word.

'Arnold is under the impression that somebody of his status will never be convicted,' she explained. 'If you could point out that assault is assault regardless of the accused, it would be very useful.'

'I think I can manage that.'

'And could you also suggest that it might be a fair few days before his case comes to trial?'

'What do you mean by a fair few days?'

'Oh there's no need to be specific, and if he becomes aggressive simply walk away, saying that you don't deal with refractory prisoners. The concepts will still be planted in his head, ready for him to dwell on in the darkest hours, and that's more than enough.'

'How long do you think this dwelling is likely to take?' he asked.

'The weekend ought to do it. I'll be back here on Monday.'

Until then she had two glorious days of looking woeful in front of Charles and Harris, but otherwise enjoying the company of Ella. Outside in the summer sunshine, meeting Duke, playing bo-peep, and generally getting reacquainted, because it had been quite a long time since they were properly together. If somebody were to report it to Arnold after his release, then she would simply claim the need for solace during her hours of distraction. And then, *very* early on Monday, it was back to business – and back once more to her husband's cell.

'No! I won't sell at that price. If I have to rot in here for a month, I will!'

When she saw the focus in his eyes, she knew that there was no option but to resort to Plan B.

'What if he revised his offer?'

'Revised?'

'Yes. I think he might be willing to not only pay off this Verrell nuisance, but also put money into expansion, and all in return for only a half-share of the mill.'

'You mean a partnership?' frowned Arnold.

'Yes.'

'Why?'

'Something about . . . railways heralding a golden era.' It was imperative that she did not outline exactly what Harris had told her about Munroe, and there ought to be no need. A word or two could conjure up a whole host of golden opportunities.

'But why is Roscoe suddenly willing to settle for half?'

'Because he realises he can't have any more. I think he was hoping to take advantage of our problems, but you've proved to be rather too troublesome.'

'And how come you know what he's thinking all of a sudden?' Arnold pounced, voice thick with suspicion, but Bessie was prepared to make her next answer very good indeed.

'The truth is – I've just come from his house, and I know you'll hate me for this, but I couldn't simply sit back and do nothing. It's been churning in my breast all weekend. How long you might be in here, what I'm going to do without you, and so I went to speak to him. But I told him point-blank what you thought of his offer, and it was then that he began to concede a bit of ground. I don't know whether he's conceded enough, it's up to you Arnold, but I had to do something. I need you back.' She leaned close to him, so that he could feel the rapid yearning of her heart. 'I need you back *so* badly.'

There was no doubt about the inference; the only doubt was regarding his response. He would either kiss her, or kick her into next week – but mercifully it was the former. In fact he kissed her more passionately that he had ever done before.

'Tell him I'll sign,' he announced when their lips finally parted.

'You will?' she exclaimed breathlessly.

'On the dotted line.'

'Oh Arnold, you've done it. You've held out, and you've won!'

A smirk of satisfaction spread across his face. 'I have, haven't I?' He would keep control of the Hall and the lands, and only had to share the profit that Roscoe money would help create. A half-share of future riches was better than a full-share of next to nothing – which was the present situation. 'I've got the better of them all!'

She took it upon herself to kiss him again, as if the wave of excitement had rendered her incapable of self-control. 'Shall I go to Mr Roscoe right now? Tell him what you've decided?'

'Yes, and then get me the hell out of here.'

She hurried off, supposedly for her second visit to Northcliff, but actually it would be the first that Drew heard about this abandonment of Plan A, and she was praying that he would find the change acceptable.

It was still so early that the Roscoes had not yet finished breakfast, but creeping out before Charles could join her had been absolutely essential. There would be enough danger in the driver knowing that she had paid only the one visit to Ackerley, but hopefully he was unlikely to strike up a conversation with Arnold. She herself did not even know the driver's name, but knew that he lived on the right side of the village, and earned extra by being called up whenever was necessary. Cheaper than having somebody hanging about drinking cups of tea all day, and it also meant that he was not viewed as "trusted" like Rufus. In fact Arnold usually acted as if the driver was merely an extension of his carriage, which was not very pleasant, but undoubtedly useful in this particular case.

Having been shown into the library, it took forever for Drew to appear – alone – and his first words were: 'What's happened? What's gone wrong?'

'Nothing, but I'm afraid I've had to modify your offer slightly.'

'Modify?'

'Yes.' She proceeded to explain, but before she could add that it would work out better in the end, he jumped in with:

'That isn't what we agreed.'

'I know, but doing it in stages will actually save you money. Arnold thinks that you have to find three thousand guineas, plus the cost of expansion, whereas we know different. You're about to own half of Bateford Mill, without having to pay out even so much as a penny.'

'But I don't want half, I want it all, and that's what you promised me.'

'And it remains my promise. I know how Arnold's mind works . . .'

'Forgive me for being rude, but it doesn't look it so far.'

'I admit that there may have been a few unexpected deviations, but the overall result will still be the same. I just need you to trust me.'

It was the second time recently that she had asked for a man's blind faith, and although the answer was again positive, there was significant reservation.

'I'm starting to think that we should never have embarked on this.'

Bessie swallowed. It was a bit too late for second thoughts now. 'We've done the hard part. It's only a case of holding our nerve.'

'It isn't that, it's about *why* we're doing this. If truth be told, I don't really bear your husband any ill will at all. My father had his money back, and I'm glad I married

Cynthia, even if it was part of some attempt to hoodwink me. I have no need, nor desire, to pursue revenge.'

'Good, because this isn't about revenge. It's about Isabel and the workers. Your wife will only be happy when she has her daughter back, and I'll only be happy when I've paid my debts to the women and children in that mill.' As well as the men who had lost their jobs as a result of her actions. She must not forget them. 'This is the best way to achieve all those ends in one fell swoop.'

'It seems an excessively convoluted way to me.'

Bessie chose not to take offence. 'I need you to be patient. Do you remember? I asked for that right at the beginning.'

'Yes, yes.' He sighed.

'Am I correct in assuming that Cynthia doesn't yet know anything about all this?'

'No, I'm not going to build her hopes up, only to see them dashed.'

'But I thought you just said you trusted me to deliver.'

'I do, but sometimes there are eventualities beyond our control.'

'True,' admitted Bessie, hoping that she had in fact covered all possible eventualities. 'At least we're now moving onto a phase where you'll be able to do a lot more. Or at least your men will.' She outlined exactly what was required, and then asked after Mr Verrell.

'Who?'

'Verrell. Frank?'

'Oh yes,' said Drew, brain brought back from the distraction of everything that needed to be organised. 'He's fine.'

'His face was an awful mess, and I had to slap him as well – for the purposes of authenticity. I do hope there won't be any lasting damage.'

'No. Most of the blood was because he bit the inside of his mouth during one of your husband's more accurate blows. But my physician has fixed him up, and after a very brief period of suffering, he's just been enjoying all the attention.'

'Attention which he thoroughly deserves,' said Bessie. 'He did an exceptional job.'

The tension in Drew's brow receded a little as he offered half a smile for the first time. 'I'm not sure I like the fact that my cousin is such a good liar.'

'Cousin?' The exclamation shot out before she could stop it, and then she chided herself for being such a snob. Why should it be acceptable to send in a member of staff, and not a member of your own family?

'Yes, Frank Roscoe. He was visiting from out of town, so I asked if he fancied helping, and he's never been one to turn down the chance of a bit of adventure. Plus he's had his eye on my barouche for quite some time, and now I have to buy him one. So you see – there *are* costs involved, and of course I've already agreed to give you an extra one thousand two hundred and fifty pounds, on top of anything I pay Arnold.'

'You can't expect to take over a man's life for nothing,' she countered, but there was nothing forceful in her voice, because there was no aggression in his. 'I'd better be going,' she then concluded, and stood up.

'So just to clarify – my next move is to have the legal documents drawn up, and to take them to the courthouse this afternoon.'

'That's right, and I've visited you twice today. Once when you discussed the revised offer, and once to give you Arnold's decision. And I was in a state of considerable distress the first time.'

'Unfortunately you seem to have plenty of distress to draw on Miss Cullen. Or can I call you Bessie?'

'No. It must be Elizabeth, and please push Cullen from your mind until this is all over.'

'Understood. But feel free to call me Drew if you wish.'

'Perhaps in the future, but for now it's Mr Roscoe.'

'Well then Mrs Bateford, I will bid you good day.'

'Good day.'

He escorted her out, and as she climbed into the Bateford carriage, a curtain twitched in the drawing room. Presumably Cynthia was intrigued about this unidentified female whom Drew wished to see alone. What would he say? Would Cynthia recognise the carriage? Or the driver? Bessie pondered the questions for a moment, before focusing on the more important matter of getting back to the courthouse, and letting the magistrate know that Arnold could now be released as soon as Drew Roscoe had paid his visit.

Mr Matthews was pleased to hear that he would no longer have to accommodate a Bateford male, and when Bessie again promised to explain everything soon, he did not press her. There was a part of him which preferred not to know how she had ended up married to the man who had decimated her family. Thanking him profusely, Bessie then took her leave, and made her way back home – to share the good news with Arnold's two sons.

To describe Charles as having his nose put out of joint would not have done justice to the impact of her announcement. His face literally drained of all colour, as if a sheet had just been draped right across it. For this intruder, this paramour, to think herself entitled to search for a solution was one thing. But to take it upon herself to visit Roscoe, and then to have her proposal accepted – it was simply too much to bear! Stalking down to the mill, Charles relieved both of his overseers of their straps, and began lashing about in every direction, but it did not help. No matter how much abuse he meted out, he could not get past that nagging question:

Was he always to play second fiddle like this?

It had been bad enough with Thomas, but now with a woman, a mere nursemaid. And a nursemaid who was increasingly inhabiting such a position of dominance. Indeed Arnold's infatuation was clear to see a few hours later, when they all shared in his "victorious" journey from cell back to civilian life. He could not stop touching her, on the arm, on the knee. It was repulsive, but Charles knew that he had to bury all of the anger, bury it way down deep, or risk incurring his father's wrath.

There was not even any respite during dinner. Changing the habit of a lifetime, Arnold suddenly decided that speech was now acceptable. Being deprived of company had made him eager to embrace it. Embrace *somebody* anyway, and Charles was forced to watch as the two of them built up to what was obviously set to be an ardent reunion upstairs. His suspicions of what would take place behind that bedroom door were both bitter – and fairly accurate. Bessie was at her most responsive yet, but not just because of the need to maintain her own act. It was also a result of the guilt that was slowly creeping back in.

If you did as you were told, Arnold was not actually the worst possible husband. Indeed he could be quite affable at times, and it was hard to keep remembering that he was willing to send innocent people to prison, to starve his workers, and play dirty tricks whenever necessary. In this cosseted existence, it was easy to forget almost everything, and that was one of the reasons why she had chosen to act now. Because if she had delayed any longer, even by as little as a month or two, she knew she might never have done it at all.

Guilt persisted the next morning – until it came time to change, and she shivered at the sight of all those welts on her back. Yet even then, her brain tried to argue his case. Was he not entitled to beat her if he believed that she was being unfaithful? She had deliberately provoked him with her antics over Henderson, had anticipated punishment, so was surely not entitled to be aggrieved when that punishment took a form which she did not expect. Was it bad to make excuses like this? Or was she finally exploring her own faults on a much deeper level? And what was the point anyway? It was all too late. Today was the day that life was going to change forever – and three o'clock was to be the hour.

Chapter Eight

Drew's barouche pulled up with a couple of minutes to spare – for a prearranged meeting where expansion was set to be discussed – but before he could even step out, Charles came careering past. Screaming obscenities, he ran right into his father's study, sank against the back of the sofa, and Arnold immediately demanded to know what the blazes was going on.

'He's double-crossed us,' panted Charles. 'That's what's going on. That bloody Roscoe's double-crossed us!'

Arnold's eyes became fixed – with belief, not doubt. His sons were many things – Thomas rebellious, Charles periodically inept, and Harris . . . well what could you say about Harris? But none of them were prone to wild exaggeration. 'How?'

'By suspending production in my half of the mill,' explained Drew, appearing casually in the doorway. 'And since it isn't feasible for you to run only half of the machines, I've shut down your half as well.'

'What? Are you insane?'

'No, I'm merely determined to secure what I originally asked for – the Hall, the land, everything.'

'And you think that . . .' began Arnold.

'I think that if I starve you of funds for long enough, you'll be forced to give in.'

'Over my dead body!'

'Yes, you've suggested that before, and I must admit that the more I hear it, the more tempting it becomes.'

'You'll never get away with it. I'll have my mill back up and running within half an hour.' He pushed Charles away from the sofa. 'Do it!'

'But he's put men on the doors.'

'Then get *more* men.'

"From where?" was the question which sprang to mind, but Charles could not say that, certainly not in front of Roscoe, so he hurried from the room, snarling at the enemy like his father.

'I appreciate that this must be difficult to take,' observed Drew, sensibly stepping out of the son's way, and stepping back even further as Arnold advanced. 'But you've never been one to exactly play by the rules yourself, so can have little cause for complaint.'

'You've picked the wrong man to mess with Roscoe!'

'On the contrary, you've the absolutely perfect man,' replied Drew, now calmly retreating far enough into the hall to reveal that he was not alone. Four aides were there – hopefully enough to deter any acts of violence, since he did not particularly fancy following Frank, and becoming acquainted with the taste of his own blood.

'Get out,' hissed Arnold. 'Get out of my house!'

'Of course. I respect the fact that a man's house is his castle, and I trust that you will do the same once it belongs to me.' Drew promptly made his way towards the exit, and Arnold watched, hands shaking, whole body shaking, but not actually knowing what to do – until that barouche began to move off, and clarity returned. The mill. That was it. He had to see it for himself, and within minutes he was there.

Bateford Mill had just the two entrances, north and south, and three men were posted on both of them, while his own overseers were standing a little way off as lame spectators. A steady flow of women and children was also meandering east, but not for long. That bell was going to be ringing out again before they could even reach the valley.

Striding back up to the Hall, he was informed by Bellamy that Charles had gone in the direction of Winscott, and for once in his life, Arnold approved of his son's actions. Everybody feared the name Bateford, and would answer the call for that reason alone. Removing his jacket with vengeful confidence, he gathered logs from the wood pile outside, carried them across the fields in a sling, and prepared to intercept a great throng – but a great throng was not exactly what greeted him. There were in fact only eleven men, as many labourers as could be found on the neighbouring farmland, and Seamus was among them.

Charles knew that many of the locals had wives in the mill, so had made it crystal clear that livelihoods were under attack. Seamus was therefore following Arnold Bateford, believing that it was best for his family, when indeed the exact opposite was the truth. If Bessie could have foreseen that one of her dearest friends would soon be poised to club one of Drew's men, she would have found a way to warn him off, but as it turned out, there was no cause for alarm because nothing untoward transpired.

Arnold stormed his way up to the north entrance, and the three guards automatically stepped aside, leading him to imagine that they were withdrawing in the face of greater opposition, but in fact they were stepping aside in order to let out a multitude. Roscoe had not just left six men, he had left sixty, and they promptly began to circle the mill like a ring of fire. Arnold encouraged his eleven labourers to start fighting regardless, but although they were not cowards, they were not stupid either, and chose instead to make their way back to the safety of Riordan's fields.

There was nothing else for Arnold to do except return to the house – with Charles pouring venom into his ear all the way along. This was a bleak day for the Batefords, very bleak indeed, but ultimately could be a good one for the second son. Elizabeth had brokered this deal, it was all her fault, and now she had to pay.

Unfortunately for Charles, Bessie was consistently one step ahead of him, standing right at the front door, and ready to neutralise Arnold's anger by volunteering for her own annihilation:

'Oh Arnold, I'm so sorry, I never thought, I . . .' Tears were streaming down her face, and without further ado, she rushed away from him, into the dining room.

Charles stared after her, and then stared at his father as if to say: "What are you waiting for? Throttle the little bitch". But before Arnold could decide whether to do so or not, Bessie was back – with cat in hand.

'Here, take it.' She offered it up to him, head bowed in meek submission. 'I deserve the worst you can give me. I deserve to die. I deserve to die.'

He took it, but then hesitated.

'Please?' Bessie peered searchingly into his eyes, and two tears dropped rather conveniently onto the floor. 'Please Arnold, put me out of my misery.'

There was another long pause during which Charles began to realise quite what a manipulator he was up against. But Father would see through this act of martyrdom. Surely!

No. Arnold spent a few more moments thinking, and then marched from the house – without even so much as a word of rebuke.

'What are you doing?' demanded Charles, setting off in hot pursuit, and oblivious to the impertinence of his question.

'Raising an army, that's what I'm doing. There are ninety husbands in those cottages of mine, and ninety wives are going to be sending them up here the minute they return from work. I'll overcome sixty, and I'll do it before the night's out.'

'What about Elizabeth?' He had to say the name, even though it was utterly loathsome. 'She's the cause of all this.'

'I signed the deed. It was my decision.'

'No it wasn't, it . . .'

'Not another word,' snapped Arnold, but this time Charles could not simply bite his tongue and submit.

'You beat the hell out of Mother on enough occasions, and she never did anything like this. What in God's name is stopping you?'

Arnold came to an abrupt halt. "Jane never satisfied me like Elizabeth". That was the truth of it, but instead of stating what they both knew, Arnold went on the attack: 'This is *your* fault more than hers. Employing that kid. Ignoring the obvious. If anybody deserves this thing, it's you.' He began to unravel the whip, and Charles stared in horror, before turning and running back to the house like a frightened child.

'You leave Elizabeth alone, do you hear me? Lay one finger on her, and I'll kill you. I'll kill you with my bare hands!'

Charles knew that his father's bellow held no empty threat, but he had to lay a finger on somebody. He needed to transfer this pain, and he needed it right now. Bounding up the stairs, he screamed out for Harris, but his brother was sensibly suffering from selective hearing loss.

'I think he might be downstairs,' suggested Tess, appearing from the master bedroom where she had been arranging some fresh sheets.

Charles was about to follow her direction, but then quickly changed his mind, and instead approached the maid who had been catching his eye of late. Successfully backing her into the room, he looked around. His father's bed – no better place, and no better way to quell this cauldron of anger. Why the hell should Arnold Bateford have all the fun? At his age.

Grabbing her by the hair, he yanked her towards him and prepared to tear the top of her uniform, but before he could even get any sort of fumbling hold, she did the one thing which he did not want. She began to remove the clothing all by herself. Perhaps if she showed compliance, she might move from maid to mistress of the manor just as easily as Elizabeth had done. But Tess had read the situation all wrong. Charles did not want her to be willing. He wanted her to claw and to scratch, and to whimper. He wanted to hurt her inside, and leave her begging him never to do it again.

'Get out of my sight,' he growled, and when she did not move, he shunted her out of the way, and stormed from the room. Somebody was going to suffer for this. Some day, somehow, he would leave his mark on this world if it was the last thing he did.

While he continued to boil, Arnold marched on towards the valley, collecting his two useless overseers on the way. They still had straps in hand, so with those whips and a whole lot of threats, Arnold set about the business of assembling an army. Any woman neglecting to send her husband to the Hall at nine o'clock this evening would see her family evicted with immediate effect. There was going to be a battle, and Arnold was going to make damn sure that he led the winning side.

When Bessie heard all this, she displayed overt indebtedness that he was solving the problem of her creation. And there was no doubt that it would indeed be a final, irreversible solution. 'Crush these men Arnold, and Roscoe won't have an ounce of authority left. *He'll* then have to comply with *you*,' she declared smugly, and he liked the sound of her words.

Privately she was as pleased as Punch that this was one of the many eventualities which she *had* predicted. A few hours later, just as the men were returning from the fields, Drew paid a visit to the valley himself, letting everybody know who was now in charge. There was an ongoing dispute with their previous employer, but it need not concern them. While matters were resolved, the cottages would become rent-free, and a truck-system had been instituted regarding wages. Vouchers would now entitle every woman and child to five shillingsworth of provisions per week from the village stores – the accounts having already been agreed with the various shopkeepers. Against that sort of generosity, there was no way that any of the men would be going anywhere near Bateford Hall. And that was how it proved to be. Nine o'clock came and went, without a soul putting in an appearance.

The overseers were instantly dispatched, and when they had made it back – after what was a steep uphill trudge on the return leg – they were almost too afraid to relate their findings. Fury, indignation, blind rage – Arnold's response was exactly as one would expect, but

Bessie saw something else there too. Almost bordering on regret. Perhaps he was beginning to realise that chickens always came home to roost, that the way you lived your life had a way of coming back to haunt you in the end. That you did not earn loyalty with the lash of a whip.

Whether he simply could not accept that particular truth, or could not face the look of disapproval staring down at him any more, but one of the first things Arnold did was to rip his father's picture from off the wall, and throw it onto the fire. As Bessie watched the flames ripple around the eyes of Arnold senior, she wondered what he had done to produce such a son. Instilled him with a ruthless ambition which turned people into irrelevant irritations? Or merely encouraged a healthy desire to succeed? Been a brute or merely strict? And what had his grandfather done in turn? Where did it end? Which generation was required to take some sort of responsibility? Louise was nice, and she was Arnold's sister. Presumably they had been raised in the same way, witnessed the same things. Certainly Thomas, Charles and Harris had lived under the same roof with the same parents, and shared no similarities whatsoever. Perhaps parentage had nothing to do with it. Perhaps siblings simply chose to be as different to one another as humanly possible.

Whatever had influenced Arnold during his formative years, there was no question that he would now be true to form. Confronted with obstruction, he knew only one conceivable response – to fight until he became dominant once more, and being as he could do nothing about the mill workers, he sacked nearly all of those at the Hall instead. Mrs Evans and Bellamy remained, but everybody else went, and the carriage and horses with them. Poor old Duke ended up in the hands of some hawker, and the stable-boy was also sent on his way.

The Batefords' stable-block had been struck by lightning two and a half years ago, causing a terrible fire which destroyed it. Thankfully none of the horses had been hurt, rescued from the creep of the flames by Thomas and the previous stable-boy, but it had happened at a time when the family finances were beginning to feel the squeeze, and so the proper replacement had never been built. A temporary shelter had stood in its place instead, and now Arnold even had that demolished, in order to use the beams for firewood. Bessie was flabbergasted at first, but then rather impressed by her husband's ability to adapt. He ordered a reduction in food consumption as well, and all non-essential items were ruled out completely. One way or another he was determined to make his outlays as small as possible, while Roscoe was paying a fortune to keep three hundred and fifty workers in self-indulgent inertia.

'We'll see who's starved of funds first,' smirked Arnold on more than one occasion, and prepared to sit it out. Bateford Hall was indeed his castle, the drawbridge had gone up, and this was a siege in all but name.

Bessie did not mind. In fact the departure of Mrs Muir, Constance and Tess was a decidedly welcome event. And the dismissal of Agatha meant that Bessie was at last granted her wish of caring for Ella. But the loss of Duncan was a severe blow. She managed to whisper a few words in his ear before he left, telling him to return the moment that he heard of a change in their circumstances. In the meantime, if he found himself struggling, he should go and see Mr Matthews. Hopefully the magistrate would not mind her taking such liberties, but would Duncan actually ask for the help of a stranger? That was the issue which troubled her on a persistent basis, but all she could do now was to try and block it out the best way she could – and to get on with her work.

There was an awful lot that needed to be done. Washing of clothes, cleaning of rooms, even taking food from the kitchen to the dining room, and the irony often brought a smile to her lips. She had started as a parlour-maid, then become a middle-class wife, and was now suddenly both at once. In many ways she was the happiest that she had ever been. There were plenty of chores to fill her day, but when they were done, she was permitted to sit at a good table, and rest in a good bed. It was the best of both worlds, and if it were to last forever, she would be quite content. Even dealing with Arnold was not much of a problem. Yes he was angry, but in an: "I'll win out in the end" kind of way, which kept him in positive mood. There were also a few hints that he was glad of her presence by his side, that he needed her, and apart from Ella, she had never experienced such a feeling before.

But of course it would not be lasting forever. Eventually somebody was going to crack, and Bessie began to think that maybe it would be best if it were Drew. A working partnership would mean closer ties to Cynthia, who would then be able to see her daughter, and it would also mean Arnold's powers reduced, with a better environment for the staff. In fact she began to wonder why she had not sought to persuade Drew of it in the first place. Why offer him the promise of everything when she was not even aware of what sort of man he was? He might not improve pay and conditions at the mill as pledged. He might be worse than Arnold. It was unlikely, but still possible – until Mrs Evans returned from the village with news that as they neared the fifth week of deadlock, Mr Roscoe was still covering the costs in the valley. He was a man of his word, and any attempts to convince herself otherwise were rendered unjust and in vain.

He was also a man of more resources than she had given him credit for, and he now chose to put them on grand display. Sending eight men up to the Hall, they placed a huge strongbox in the middle of the drive, and opened it. Coins were in there. Hundreds of gold and silver coins. They glinted in the sunshine, and were visible from every room overlooking the front. No words accompanied the action, but there was no need. It was designed to be psychologically damaging, and it worked wonders. Having reached the point where Arnold was convinced that Roscoe would soon be forced to break, he suddenly knew otherwise, and it left him broken instead. It also made him search for other ways to end this affair, and pushed him towards the most drastic of measures yet.

Bessie was checking on Ella after dinner, so was not around when it came to a climax in Arnold's mind. All she saw was a series of lights at the bottom of the drive as she returned from upstairs. It was nearly dark, and so it took some time to decipher that it was Arnold marching away from the Hall, and with a flaming torch in hand. Harris was there too, pressed into participation, along with the overseers – who had been kept on for security reasons, and now lived in the rooms vacated by

Tess and Constance. Charles also had a torch, and was bringing up the rear. He did not want to do this, did not want to destroy what was most dear to him, but defeating Drew Roscoe was the only directive right now, and there were few alternatives left.

Even as she realised who they were, and what they were carrying, it took several more seconds before it dawned upon her that they were planning to set fire to the mill. She screamed after them, hollered at the limit of her lungs, but it was too late. They were almost there, and she covered her face with both hands as panic engulfed her. What had she done? What if somebody died? It had been hot and dry for weeks. The place would go up like tinder.

'Oh dear God, please help me, please.' She kept repeating that prayer over and over again until a sound made her stop. It was the sound of Arnold returning, and finally drawing the fingers away from her eyes, she expected to see him silhouetted by a great big inferno in the background. But there was no inferno. The mill was not ablaze. At least not the part which was visible against the greying sky. It was in fact exactly the same as before – and that was more than could be said for Arnold.

He was wet. Drenched from head to foot. Harris was much the same, along with one of the overseers, while Charles and the other man appeared to have escaped with only a partial soaking.

What had happened? Had the heavens opened? Had God answered her prayers? Yes, but not quite in the way that she imagined. Instead of the heavens, some of Drew's men had opened a fair few barrels of water, and emptied them right over the advancing party. An attack on the mill had been foreseen from the very start, and

Bessie was not sure whether to laugh or cry as Arnold squelched his way past. In the end she shed a tear, both of relief, and also a little regret – sad that it had actually been necessary to bring him to this point.

With the chest of coins as well, it was suddenly blatantly obvious that Drew was now going to win, and the Batefords were merely putting off the inevitable. He had too much at his disposal, was far too sharp, and Bessie knew that she had advised him too well. It was therefore time to alter her approach and start to bring things to a close.

She began with the odd remark here, and the odd remark there, but gradually built up a picture portraying town as a glorious Utopia. Arnold could buy them a house, and they could live comfortably enough – far more comfortably than with this current millstone around their necks. Cotton may have been King for the last few years, but who was to say that such dominance would continue as they moved into the forties? It might become yesterday's news, but by selling to Roscoe, they were free to invest in whatever new commodity came to the fore as the economy improved. Be pioneers of something visionary.

Of course Charles did not like it. The loss of the mill would mean the loss of his role, and Elizabeth was exercising undue influence yet again, but she always had that one card up her sleeve which he simply could not trump. And by the time she had finished with her words and insinuations, Arnold was persuaded that he could sell with dignity intact, leave behind a hopeless cause, and at the same time unshackle himself from the long-held legacy of his father. Even Harris chipped in with an endorsement of Somerden life. He was simply desperate to leave this backwater. There was so much life and energy in town, and if he festered at this Hall for one more day, he feared that he might explode.

Fester was actually a fairly accurate description of their present state. The cesspool in the basement had not been emptied in a while, and odours were wafting up during the heat of the day. Charles did not mind, and put in one final plea to keep on fighting, but was utterly ignored. So instead he chose to focus on the one other project which occupied his mind – making somebody suffer, and that somebody was going to be Elizabeth Arabrook. Harris had told him about the welts, and the disappearance of Henderson on exactly the same day, so Charles set out to find the former henchman. No luck so far, but he had put out the word, and as Bellamy went to convey a message of parley to Roscoe, Charles walked into town to see if there had been any recent developments.

Shortly before Drew arrived, Charles was back, looking much happier because Rufus was reportedly close at hand – in Pelton of all places. Only a quick stage-coach ride away, and that ride would be taken at the earliest opportunity, but for now it was discussion-time, and Arnold kicked things off by putting his cards very firmly on the table.

'I'll sell you the other half of the mill for half of the original offer,' he declared, as if doing Drew a favour.

'My original offer was nine and a half, so four thousand seven hundred and fifty?'

'Yes.'

'What about the house and the land? They were part of that offer too.'

'They'll cost you extra.'

'How much extra?'

'Another five thousand.'

'And you really think that you're in a position to make such a demand?'

'I'm still the owner, I can make whatever demands I like.'

'So you want me to give you more than I offered some weeks ago, even though I already control half of the mill?' clarified Drew. 'I've also had to pay three thousand guineas to Verrell, pay your workers to wait around pending a resolution, and my own workers are also standing about doing not very much. Does that seem rational to you?'

'Nobody made you shut the damn place.'

'True, but from the look of your books it wasn't exactly making much of a profit anyway, and I *have* saved you a whole month's wages. You must admit that.' Drew was being facetious, and Bessie flashed a glare, warning him not to push it. 'I am, however, a reasonable man, so I shall give you what you ask for the mill. But in return I want the rest of your estate for fifteen hundred pounds.'

'Fifteen hundred! The cottages are worth more than that in themselves.'

'Hardly. They're dilapidated.'

'I don't care. I won't sell them for a pittance.'

This time Bessie's warning glare was extremely stern. It was absolutely imperative that Drew did not humiliate Arnold any further. Otherwise there was no telling what he might do. Luckily Drew had seen the signs for himself, and pulled back from the brink. At the beginning of all this, he had decided that fifteen thousand would be a very good deal indeed, so if he offered another three to four, on top of all his other costs, he ought to end up with around three thousand in change.

'Right. We've already agreed on four thousand seven hundred and fifty, which I'll round up to five, and then add another . . . say . . . three? Because I'm feeling strangely generous today. But that's as high as I'll go.'

Bessie looked to Arnold. It was the best that they could hope for, and their bargaining position was worse than poor. Nobody in the market for an investment would be interested in buying half of a non-operational mill from a man with whom the phrase "poisoned chalice" had become synonymous. Arnold realised that completely, but still he was not willing to sell – not yet.

'I'll accept nine thousand total. Guineas. And that's as low as I'll go.' He folded his arms, and Drew pursed his lips, licked them, and then pursed them again, but eventually said:

'You'll vacate within the week?'

'I'll be gone by Friday.'

'And you'll leave Isabel behind?'

'Isabel?' Arnold's eyes widened. 'I wasn't aware that she was part of this.'

'Cynthia would like to spend some time with her sister,' explained Drew, and the men in the room exchanged knowing looks, as if they had to keep the secret from the one person who was still in the dark.

'If you want her, you can have her,' dismissed Arnold, and Bessie had trouble in masking her anger.

Isabel was a precious, beautiful little girl, and handing her over to Cynthia was going to be unbearably difficult, but it was the right thing, so she was doing it. But hearing Arnold discard his own flesh and blood like some worthless rag was akin to stamping on all that pain, and made Bessie's blood run very cold indeed.

It was unclear whether he saw it and was prompted to speak out of a sense of consideration, or did it simply to irritate Drew, but Arnold then announced: 'She isn't Cynthia's sister, she's her daughter.'

Harris instantly winced in Elizabeth's direction, afraid that she would not act sufficiently shocked, but there was no fear of that. Bessie had thought that hell would have to freeze over before Arnold ever mentioned it, and her mouth dropped open accordingly.

'My daughter rebelled against her upbringing, and Isabel is the product of that,' he added in a severe tone, before turning back to Drew, who looked equally surprised. 'My wife has a right to know,' was the simple explanation, and Bessie found herself feeling uncomfortable. Arnold was including her as if she was really a part of this family, and yet two of the men present were aware that she had been in the know for quite some time.

'Thank you,' she muttered softly, and Arnold tipped his head as if to suggest that he awaited her private demonstration of gratitude later.

'But as far as the wider world are concerned, Isabel is Cynthia's sister, staying with us for a while,' stipulated Drew, which prompted Arnold to turn the corners of his mouth down in a vacillating action.

'Of course I'll try to convey that impression, but it is hard to know when one might suffer an inopportune slip of the tongue.'

Drew swallowed most deliberately. 'If you ensure that any such slip is avoided, I shall make it common knowledge that you came out of this dispute with . . . how can I put it? The upper hand? Which ought to assist you in future business dealings, should you wish to undertake any.'

Arnold pretended to give it some thought, but his mind was instantly in agreement. The Bateford reputation had been battered over the last year or two, and it would now be rather satisfying to prove a few people wrong – on the surface at least.

'Looks like we have a deal then,' concluded Drew when Arnold had finally acquiesced. 'That was all very civilised, now wasn't it?'

'For a man of your character, it was downright remarkable,' retorted Arnold, while making it clear that he would not be shaking hands.

'As you wish,' said Drew, and vacated the room, before returning moments later with some documentation. 'All that's left is to fill in the amount, and sign.'

'Forgive me if I don't take your word for it,' replied Arnold, and proceeded to examine every detail for hidden clauses. But it actually seemed above-board, and when he had entered the figure, he passed it back to Drew to sign first. 'When do I see my money?'

'As soon as you like.'

'First thing tomorrow then.' Arnold tried to push aside the rancour of knowing that Roscoe could lay his hands on thousands with such ease. Instead he focused on the future. One day people would be able to say the same about *him*. A townhouse would not cost a fortune, and there would be plenty left. He could make it grow and grow, until he was the most powerful man in town. Elizabeth was right, he was being liberated from his past, and casting off the shackles of all this bother. He was heading for a bright new future, and as he stamped his Bateford mark, he did so with considerable gusto.

'Friday it is then.'

'Cynthia and I will arrive around three,' said Drew.

'And I'll give you the keys,' agreed Arnold, before pointing out that the first task for any new owner would be to empty the cesspool.

'Thank you for the tip,' replied Drew dryly, and took his leave.

Friday the thirteenth of September. That was the day. Everything had materialised as planned, despite the unexpected deviations, and now all that remained was to prepare for the final act. Bessie had set her sights on transferring the mill to Drew, giving Isabel back to Cynthia, and then walking out of Arnold's life. She had mapped it out to the very last detail, including her bold declaration of what had really been going on for this past year. 'I'm Bessie Cullen, and I've taken the things that you hold most dear, just like you did to me. I'm the reason you couldn't secure investment, I'm the reason you're having to sell. I hate you, everything about you, and I hope you rot in hell.'

But now when she said it in her head, it did not hold the force that it once had. Did she still hate him? She *should*, but was it right to do any more to him as a result? He had inflicted something bad on each of the four Cullens – four unconscionable acts – but did driving Luke from the district really count as one? Surely any father would be furious if their daughter behaved as Cynthia had done. And as for imprisoning Wilf, that was for a crime that Wilf had actually committed, even if the sentence had been horrendously excessive.

In return she had blocked investment not once, but twice, and was now forcing him to relinquish his home – although he was receiving compensation for that. Did it make them all-square? Did he deserve to know that he had married an Arabrook who did not even exist, that their marriage was a sham, and that she was the person who had incited Drew's actions? Perhaps. But then again, perhaps not.

Was it better to simply keep quiet? She had got away with it, nobody suspected, so she could move into town, and continue living with Arnold. Goodness knows what she would do about Munroe, but she could handle him in some shape or form, and otherwise life would progress as normal. But *why* would she be staying? That was the question. Ella could no longer be the motive, so what would it be?

Friday the thirteenth of September. The days raced by, and many of their belongings were taken in a series of baggage-waggons to a new place on Erskine Avenue. The time for her decision was fast approaching. What was happening to her? Why this doubt? What was she thinking? What did she want? And what the hell was she going to do?

CHAPTER NINE

Thomas left the ironworks at the end of another day, with his mind made up. He had been thinking about it for several days – and thinking in that place was a distinctly bad idea. Avenues for death lay all around, but he had kept one eye upon the dangers, and settled himself upon what to do next.

He had been living this life for five months now. Nearly five months anyway. For the first few days he had simply wandered around Somerden in a daze. No money, no food, no clothes except the ones on his back, but he had not felt the lack of anything. A numbed fury had blocked out the need for all normal human comforts, and sent him around in circles until the date of that wedding had reached his ears. Then he had made a bee-line for the church, and stood watching from the trees. Watching her arrive and pause outside the gate, ribbons fluttering in her hair. Watching her look in his direction, and almost stare straight through him. Surely she would not do it. Surely she could not trample on his heart like this. Any moment now and she would begin to move. Move and come running, and he would be there to scoop her into his arms. But she had not moved, at least not towards him. Turning so calmly, walking so austerely, she had advanced into the house of God and pledged herself forever to the devil.

In that second he could have killed her. He had lunged forward with his hands twisting, twisting around her neck, and fingers clawing as if at her eyes. Could she not see what she was doing? Could she not see!

She had made him fall in love with her, only to stick a knife into his back, and give herself to another man. How could she even contemplate it? The girl who had always seemed so shy and nervous of such things, and now she was set to consummate vows with a man old enough to be her father. The man who had imprisoned her *own* father. Had she forgotten? Had she thought of nothing as she said those fawning words of acceptance? Had she been looking for a proposal from the Master of Bateford Hall all along? Was the eldest son simply not good enough for her?

She deserved to die. Totally, absolutely and completely deserved it. But no matter how much he hated her, and how powerful the venom that was currently coursing through his veins, he could not bring himself to do it. So there had to be another way, and as he had walked back to town with those church bells ringing in his ears, he had churned over the options one by one.

The obvious route was to expose her. Mrs Arnold Bateford, born Arabrook. Only she had not been born an Arabrook, and he could make sure that her little house of cards came tumbling down. The look on her face as he told Arnold that she was a Cullen. The look on *Arnold's* face. Not only had he hired his enemy, then promoted her, he had wedded and bedded her too. The explosion would be so immense that Bessie would be dead before the ashes had even fallen from the sky. But when was best to do it? In a day or two? Or leave it weeks? Leave her to endure the agony of being Arnold's wife. Because it would indeed be agony. Every minute of every day – and every night.

Or perhaps that was just a bit too severe. She had already suffered for being a Cullen, suffered because of the folly of Luke and Cynthia. And he had vowed never to tell a soul. His word really ought to be his bond, even in these circumstances. Yes, he would find an alternative. An alternative which involved somebody else. That would hurt more – and Ruth Padstow would hurt most of all.

He had sensed the flow of jealousy whenever the Llewellyns visited with Ruthie in tow. Bessie Cullen was not as cold-hearted as her actions seemed to suggest. She did feel something for him, he knew it, and he could make her feel the pain of it. He could return, pretend that everything was fine, and Arnold would gladly welcome him back if he promised to woo one of the Cheshire Padstows. And then the day would come when Bessie would have to watch *him* go to church. Think of *him* on his wedding-night with his new bride. Treat like with like. That was the way, and it was perfect. Except for the fact that he would then be tied to Ruthie forever. And more importantly, she would be tied to him. He would make her his wife, and make her a victim at the same time. A victim of something which had nothing to do with her, and over which she had no control.

Was he really vengeful enough to be quite so cruel? Or could he achieve the same ends by different means? Go back, but woo *Bessie*, make her admit to the love that she had for him, make her act on it. Then once she had done so, he could throw it back in her face. Tell her that she had been seduced out of hatred, not love, that he would not have her now if she was the last woman alive, before promptly walking away – and taking Ella with him. That would absolutely be the icing on the cake.

Although of course he could do it even now. Sneak back in while the house was sleeping, and snatch Ella, make Bessie wake up to the realisation that she had married for nothing. The child was lost, and all that remained was Arnold – and a growing self-disgusted emptiness which would one day suck the life out of her.

In the meantime, he would have his beautiful niece to love in her stead. He could write to Cynthia, tell her that Ella was safe and being cared for. But how exactly could he care for her when he had to work? For the very first time in his life, he had to find employment in order to eat – and that was the one thing which Bessie Cullen had considered beyond his capabilities. It was the issue above all others which had dictated her decision. She had accepted Arnold because she could not envisage an existence with Ella away from the Hall. She could not imagine how a Bateford, any Bateford, could slave all day long to provide for them both. But he could! He could work the shifts of ten men if necessary, and he had set out to prove it.

He had taken the worst job in Henningborough, the job shunned by all others, and for five long months he had faced the torturous heat from those furnaces until his brain had yearned for the iciest storm of winter. He had stirred the molten iron hour after hour, turning and twisting it with that spoon-shaped rod until it felt like his skin was on fire. He had lived in hell, and followed it up every night by sleeping where not even the lunatics would sleep. He had washed in the river, and stepped out wondering whether he was dirtier than when he had gone in. He had been passed by fine ladies and gentlemen in the street who had turned up their noses as if he was scum of the earth. He had bled poverty until he could bleed it no more, and every evening he had stood in front of that women's prison, trying to figure out how on earth he had come to this point.

Had he been mad when he wanted Bessie Cullen as his wife? Or mad when he wanted to kill her? Would he ever know sanity again? And would going back solve anything at all? Could it make things even worse? What if he discovered that she was carrying a baby? His own half-brother or sister. Or worse still – what if he discovered that she was happy? Could he control himself? Did he even know his own strength?

So many questions, and so few answers, but the one thing about which he was certain was that the time for debate had gone. It was time to buy that new set of clothes, pay that lady on Padgett Street for a bath and a hair-cut, and buy his ticket back to Somerden. Whatever else he did, he was going to show Bessie Cullen that he had survived, and exactly how he had survived. And *then* he would decide on his revenge.

Little did he realise that he was not the only one with such a thought in mind. Bessie woke on Friday morning, trying to remind herself of exactly how she had felt when Josiah first told her of the vacancy at Bateford Hall. The clarity of her convictions, the absolute hatred in her heart, rather than the muddied mess in which she was now submerged. While Charles woke in a fever of excitement, seized by the glorious range of possibilities presented to him as a result of Rufus Henderson's suspicions.

Could Elizabeth Arabrook possibly be Bessie Cullen in disguise? It seemed so utterly preposterous. He had seen her himself, in court, with his own eyes. That was not the same person, simple as that. But Rufus was convinced of it, and there were certainly a few things which did not add up. Like her failure to produce any family at the wedding for one. None of them had ever met even a single member of her family. Not once. Did that point against her being this "Arabrook" woman? Possibly, but why exactly would she want to be here? Out of a desire to kill her enemy from within? Or because she drew a perverse satisfaction from enjoying the high life, with all of them totally unaware of the truth.

Becoming Mrs Bateford must have truly blown her mind. A girl from the valley allowed to sit at their table. No wonder she was savouring every minute of it. But would Father believe such a revelation? He was not even willing to punish her over what they were suffering at the hands of Roscoe. And belief would entail an acceptance that he had been duped, which was not something that Arnold Bateford would come to very easily. Perhaps it was best to keep him in the dark. Yes. Perhaps there were better ways of manipulating the full and wonderful potential of this situation.

Charles debated it over breakfast, while Bessie debated her next move. Whatever she did, she needed Ella out of the way. The question was how best to achieve that, but thankfully Arnold provided the simplest of solutions by retreating to his study after breakfast – and staying there. He wanted to be alone, which was perfect. It meant that she could gather together Ella's belongings, carry her stealthily down the back stairs, and set off.

Mrs Evans was of course in the kitchen, and Bessie had a quick word first, asking her to take herself out for the day. The cook was not in fact moving to Erskine

Avenue; she was staying behind because Drew and Cynthia were taking up residence on a temporary basis, to ease Ella's transition. The toddler would soon have to face a lot of new people, and a new place would probably be too much.

'Why?' asked Mrs Evans, looking down at the main kitchen table by way of pointing out that she had lunch to prepare, not to mention dinner for the new owners later.

'Because Arnold might become rather angry this afternoon, and I want you to be safe.'

'Oh don't worry about me, I'll be fine.'

Bessie was carrying Ella on one hip, but used her free hand to grip Mrs Evans quite forcefully. 'I mean it. Prepare lunch, and then disappear for a few hours. Walk into the village or something. I *promise* you the Roscoes will not be concerned by your absence.' She stared deep into her friend's eyes, where the message was received and understood.

'I'll be gone within the hour.'

Nodding her appreciation, Bessie then said a very difficult goodbye, aware that they would probably not be seeing each other for a long time. Indeed if she followed one particular route, they might never see each other again.

Of course the new cook at Erskine Avenue could well be very pleasant, and it would be hard for the housekeeper to be any worse than Mrs Muir, but when bidding farewell to an ally, it was always impossible to imagine that anybody in the future could ever be as much of a support.

Bessie tried to push out such negativity as she hurried off into town. There was a decision to make, just as in April, and she had to do a far better job of fixing her mind in advance. Being ready could make all the difference. If she had known for a few hours that she would be running away with Thomas, she could have used that time to think about how best to convey her decision. But if you were not even sure what you were going to do, you could not possibly start to think about how. She must not make that same mistake again.

Unfortunately as she neared Fulton Street, indecision still very much had the better of her, and now there were other things to occupy her mind – like finding Josiah. Putting Ella down, she tried to explain the situation:

'We're going to see a friend of mine. A dear friend. You'll like him. And he'll be looking after you for a bit. But you have to be really quiet. Understand? It's hush from now on.' Bessie put a finger to her lips. 'Can you do that for me?'

Ella imitated the action, and then started saying: 'Hoos, hoos,' with an excited shake of her head which made her pigtails dance.

'Oh Ella.' Bessie clung to her, overwhelmed with a love that was literally heart-breaking. 'Let's find Uncle Josiah, shall we? He'll make everything seem better.'

They crept in, and tried to sneak up to his room, but Mrs Jennet caught them, and Josiah was on the second floor anyway, so a maid needed to be dispatched. Mrs Jennet was obviously amazed at the fine clothes on display, but there had been no alternative for Bessie. She could not wear an Arabrook or work dress, because they did not exist any more. All she had left was the attire suitable for Mrs Arnold Bateford, and there was Ella to explain as well, but she was passed off as the child of a friend in need – while the dress was explained as a cast-off from a generous new employer.

When Josiah appeared, his eyes immediately glistened, but Bessie could not give in to emotion just yet. There was too much still to be resolved, so she took him aside and said simply that things were about to change. She was not sure how, but she should at least be able to see him more in the future. And could he possibly look after Ella, while she sorted things out?

'You aren't planning on doing anything dangerous, are you?' Josiah's heart began to pound. He had not come to terms with her being at Bateford Hall, not one bit, but no news was good news, and so he had assumed that she was getting through it. He had even begun to hope that she was settled, had adapted to life as a wife, and forgotten everything else. If that meant forgetting him too, it was fine, as long as she was safe. But now she had that worrying look in her eyes again, and it pitched him back into his initial despair. 'Why did you leave without saying goodbye Bessie? Why didn't you let me talk to you one more time? Why did you marry that awful man?'

Bessie winced. 'I'll explain everything later, if there's time. Forgive me Josiah. I love you, but I couldn't face that particular goodbye.'

He sighed as Isabel was placed onto a chair beside him, and Bessie prepared to leave. 'Just whatever you do, don't put your life at risk. Promise me.'

She struggled to do anything other than shrug at first, but when he would not let her go, she gave the promise that he sought, and then began the long walk back to the Hall. A decision had come to her in a flash last time, and would do so again. By the time she reached the bottom of that drive, she would know, and perhaps it would indeed have been the case if not for the distraction of seeing Charles ahead of her. He had gone out too. Had he been following her as once before? No, she would be ahead of him. But had he seen her? Would he report on her to Arnold? So many questions, when she already had far too many coursing around her head.

Hurrying in through the back entrance, she was relieved to find that Mrs Evans had now gone, and having heated up the food, it was time to enter Arnold's study – a nervous moment – but in fact he did not appear to be aware of the absence of any of his relatives.

'Would you like to eat lunch now?' she asked, and when he said yes, she returned to the kitchen to bring up their final meal.

The big table was still in the dining room, and other major pieces of furniture also remained in situ. The new place was partly furnished, so they did not need all these duplicates, and in return for some of the items being left behind, Drew had given an extra couple of hundred pounds. Things had in fact become very civilised indeed, and the meal was conducted in exactly the same vein. No ranting, no tears. Simply silence – and not because of any rules, but because that was how they all felt. Bessie in particular needed some quiet time.

If she ended up going with the flow of things because of a failure to reach any decision, then she would soon have to explain Isabel's absence. So she pondered that first, and came to the conclusion that she could claim an inability to part with the little one, who she had taken to be with a friend. Arnold would not mind. He would enjoy his daughter being thwarted for a while, and when Charles surprisingly asked whether Isabel was ready for the journey, she decided to get it said.

'What friend?' demanded Arnold, so she offered up the explanation previously used when caught out with Harris. That female friend in town with the thinning hair. It was clear that Arnold was bored after the first few words, and before she had even got anywhere near to finishing, he was flicking his wrist as if it did not matter.

'She'll have to be brought back here,' he announced gruffly, before a smirk played about his lips. 'Although a day or two won't hurt.' His eyes sparkled for a moment, and Bessie wondered whether that was her answer.

He had reacted exactly as anticipated – she knew him – and when he looked at her like that, it was if they shared a connection. As bizarre as it seemed, they really understood one another. They were becoming, for want of a better phrase, a proper couple.

'Would that be the friend with the younger brother?' chipped in Charles, and Bessie turned to him, half-distracted, but somehow instinctively on alert.

'Brother?' she repeated.

'Yes, I thought you said that this friend had a brother, a year younger, and then out of the blue they were both to have another sibling, because their mother was pregnant again after more than a decade.'

Bessie swallowed. That was an exact description of the Cullen family. 'I . . . I don't believe that I've discussed my friend at length with you.'

'No? Are you sure?'

Arnold grunted to convey even greater boredom, but Charles pressed on with the first of many games he was set to play.

'I could have sworn that you'd discussed them at *considerable* length.'

'But I haven't,' snapped Bessie, with an intense surge of concern.

'Must be my mistake,' concluded Charles. 'Unless of course I have the mother's name right. She isn't Margaret by any chance?'

'What does it matter?' growled Arnold, but Bessie knew exactly why it mattered. Charles had found out. God knows how, but presumably he was now about to expose her. She presumed wrong. In answer to his father, he merely leaned back in his chair, and let it drop. Why? Was he saving it for later? Was he ever going to say? Was he simply planning to hold it over her until time immemorial?

Without any sort of debate, Bessie knew in a flash that she could not let it happen. Her hatred for Charles was stronger than it had ever been for his father, and that was saying something.

'Arnold,' she declared, staring forthrightly at her husband's end of the table. 'There's a matter I need to discuss with you before we make a move.'

He looked at her enquiringly, while Charles frowned, and Harris pricked his ears.

'It will come as a surprise,' she added. 'In fact it will be really quite a shock, but today is the best day, isn't it? Because this is a new beginning for us all.'

'A new and hopefully profitable one,' he confirmed, while Charles' frown became even more pronounced. She was not about to confess, surely? He did not want her to. The look on his face developed into one of panic, and Harris felt sure that he knew the details of this announcement already. Elizabeth was pregnant. Charles must have already guessed it, hence those curious references to children, and was pushing her into a confession, although it was hard to understand why she should be at all reluctant.

Bessie glanced at each Bateford in turn, and as she did so she knew that there were still two avenues open to her. Admitting to her true identity did not necessarily have to mean the end. She could say that she had come for revenge, but had fallen in love, been tamed. She could drop to her knees, and beg Arnold to keep her secret, to keep her by his side.

There was a strong chance that he would do it. He would not want anybody knowing who she really was, and the truth would give him even greater power over her. She would be required to make up for her treachery on a daily, *hourly*, basis. But whereas she now had the satisfaction of knowing that she was playing him, in the future it would all be about her repaying a debt. She would become a glorified bedroom slave, demeaning herself and her family's name into the bargain.

Was it not time to say: "Enough is enough", and to regain some semblance of dignity? To stop this obsession with games, and live a normal, working-class life? To take the name of Cullen, and hurl it at Arnold with all the anger and venom that she had ever felt. Gloat over his downfall, rub salt into his wounds, and avenge the death of her baby brother. Was it not time at last for her to remember who she was, why she was here, and what the hell had happened to her family?

'The fact of the matter is that I won't be coming to our new lodgings on Erskine Avenue.'

'What? You're my wife, you go wherever I go.' There was no anger on Arnold's face, merely confusion. She wanted him, she needed him; she had made that perfectly clear. What was all this about?

Bessie knew that the confusion would soon turn to consternation, and so kept a close eye on the poker – while feeling glad that the cat-o'-nine-tails was the first thing which she had chosen to pack. 'You say I'm your wife,' she replied, rubbing her chin. 'But am I really? That's the question. Were we ever actually married?'

'Married? Have you gone mad or something?'

'No. In fact I'm just recovering from madness I think. It's curiosity, that's all. What exactly is the position if you marry somebody who doesn't exist?'

'What the hell are you on about?'

'I'm "on about" the fact that Elizabeth Arabrook is a figment of my imagination. Nice name, don't you think? Arabrook? I took great care in my selection.'

'If you think you're being funny, you're not.'

'I suppose it could be viewed as rather amusing,' she confirmed flippantly. 'It all depends on how you look at it.'

The colour in Arnold's cheeks was really beginning to deepen now.

'Do you recall a girl who was arrested a couple of years ago for housebreaking? More specifically *this* housebreaking.'

He was about to speak, but then stopped as his brows knitted together.

'Come on darling, cast your mind back. I'm sure you can give me her name if you try really hard.'

'And *I'm* sure that you need another lesson in respect.'

'No doubt you're right, but who exactly would be on the receiving end of that lesson? Charles, can you enlighten him?'

Her stepson shot up, and raised both hands in a defensive manner. 'I think she's deranged.' If his father were ever to discover that he had known, even if only for a day, then the consequences would be beyond dire.

'You surprise me Charles.' Bessie tipped her head in an apparent act of disappointment. 'I'll have to give you a clue then Arnold. You always like to say that you . . . *culled* them. You know? A particular family.'

'Cu . . .' began Arnold.

'That's right. Cu . . . Cull . . . Cullen.'

'What the hell are you on about?' demanded Charles, finding solace in repeating his father's exact words.

Bessie shrugged playfully, but kept a firm fix on Arnold's position. 'You aren't very quick, are you Charles? What about you Arnold? Is it starting to register? Is it even remotely possible that all these months you might have been sleeping with a Cullen?'

There was no response, just blank shock.

'I'll take that as a yes, shall I? Don't look so flabbergasted darling – your daughter couldn't resist the charms of a worker, so why should you be any different?'

Now there was a response. Arnold lunged down the table, but it was far too long for even him to reach her, and by the time he was on his feet, she had taken up position on the opposite side, helping herself to the poker along the way.

'You did your level best to destroy us, all of us, and although it pains me to admit it, I really must commend your efforts. In fact it could be said that I found your campaign rather . . .' She paused, searching for the appropriate word. '. . . an inspiration.'

Arnold was breathing heavily now, and Harris, who was on Bessie's side of the table, wisely vacated his chair and migrated towards the corner.

'Do you remember when Stewart came to dinner? Last October?' She peered at her husband until confident that he had the relevant occasion in mind. 'You couldn't understand why he went all unpleasant and refused to give you any money? Well that was me. And when he came just recently, that was me again – in the water-closet, using my . . . well . . . how can I put this? Charms to turn him against you.'

'Charms? You dirty slut.'

'Oh please, let's not resort to mud-slinging just yet, shall we? I've barely started. The incentive scheme – that wasn't me alone, that was a joint venture with Thomas, fiddling your books. I loved him, I was going to run away with him, but then I fell ill, and somehow ended up as your wife. Nice twist though, don't you think? You proposing. And it took me a while, but eventually I came to realise what a position of power I was in. Particularly if I could become a *good* little wifey.' She turned to Charles who was creeping around to her side of the table. Was he planning to attack? Raising the poker slightly, she attacked verbally before he could decide anything: 'Must have made you furious to see me so affectionate with dear Papa. But rest assured, it was all an act. No woman could ever possibly be stirred by your father's feeble attempts at love-making.'

She began to chuckle maliciously – until a chair came hurtling out of nowhere. They were heavy objects, but it was the only thing to hand, and Arnold had managed to make it airborne with a considerable amount of flight on it. The only problem was that his aim was slightly off.

'I think you might have killed him,' remarked Bessie, leaning over Charles who was now prostrate at her feet.

'Although I doubt it'll be any great loss. You never did like him, did you?'

She was certainly not about to shed any tears of her own, not after young Peter Whitson had been strapped repeatedly at his direction, and Luke pitched head-first into that cistern on more than one occasion.

'Where was I?' she asked. 'Oh yes, using my attributes to best advantage. Actually . . . I'm not sure I should say any more. Maybe I ought to leave it to Drew. After all, it was his man who pretended to be an inspector, and then endured a pounding to get you locked up. And what a sight that was, seeing you behind bars.'

She was about to add: "*My* bars", but thankfully recognised that getting carried away could get Mr Matthews into serious trouble. She was glad when Charles distracted everything by emitting a deep groan.

'Ah, so you're not dead. What a pity.' She walked over to Harris, whose jaw had now dropped so low that it was resting on his collar, and suggested that he might want to take his older brother upstairs to lie down. 'Help his head.'

Charles did not catch what she said. He had temporarily lost the use of his ears, and sight was a bit of a problem too. Leaning heavily on Harris, he staggered from the room, and Bessie focused once again upon their father:

'Well now, it's just you and me. Isn't that cosy?'

'I don't believe it. I don't believe any of it. Charles is right – you're deranged.'

'Am I? Then how do I know all this stuff?'

'You've been talking to people, worked it out. I don't know, but it's lies. All lies.'

'Oh Arnold, denial is such a pitiful state, particularly when I can prove the truth of everything I'm saying.'

'How? By getting Roscoe to back you up? Reinforce your nasty little pretence?'

'No,' she replied calmly. 'I was thinking more of a trip down memory lane. Or rather *up* . . . Ulmers Hill. You remember it, don't you?'

'Why should I?'

'Because everything that has happened since is linked to that hill. You came across Luke on the summit. You know Luke? The father of your grand-daughter? Of course you do. And when you tried to take him away, I said that if you so much as laid a finger on him, you'd live to regret it. Well *this* is you living to regret it.' Bessie raised her eyebrows in a conclusive act of triumph, and then the volcano really did erupt.

He ran around the table like a bull at a gate, and being as she did not fancy doing a few turns of the dining room, she stood her ground, and at the last minute deftly stuck out the poker – level with his knees. He went sprawling, and while he was incapacitated, she dropped the flippancy – along with the poker – and asked a very sombre question:

'Why Arnold? I can understand what you did to Luke, and even sending me to prison for being so obstructive, but why my parents? Why evict my mother when you knew it would mean the workhouse? Why have my father charged when he was only showing the same anger which you yourself had shown?'

Arnold's lip curled as he turned over to face her. 'Why do you think?'

'I don't know. That's why I'm asking.'

'Because I could.'

Bessie waited for him to say something else, something that might actually have a bit of meaning, but there *was* nothing else, so she licked her lips contemptuously, and moved towards the door. 'Oh I nearly forgot.'

Wrenching the wedding-ring down over her knuckle, she held it up for him to see. 'Whom God has joined together, let no man put asunder.' Balancing it upon her thumb, she flicked it, just like that masked man with his gold sovereign. 'I think you can now very much say that we've been put asunder, don't you?' As it ricochetted off the fender and into the fire, she smiled and waltzed out.

Pushing himself up off the carpet, Arnold then just stood there, eyes bulging, and slobber running down his chin. This could not be happening to him. It could not be HAPPENING! He sprang into the hall, down the front steps, and cried out:

'I'll keep her! Your dear little come-by-chance. I won't let the Roscoes have her. I'll keep her, and make her suffer every day for what you've done.'

'And how exactly are you planning on doing that? When you don't even know where she is.' Bessie did not bother to turn, but dismissed him with words over her shoulder – and that was the final straw. Snatching a handful of pebbles from his drive, he threw them at her – with a vastly improved aim. They rained down upon the back of her head, and then darting forward, he had her pinned to the ground – with his belt off – before she could even begin to react.

'Think you've clever, don't you? So bloody clever. Well how clever do you feel now?' He wrapped the belt around her neck, threaded it through the buckle, and began to pull. His hands were shaking, almost jerking with anger, but he managed to pull that belt tighter – and tighter still.

Bessie's own hands flailed, trying to scratch his face, but he held his head just far enough back, and although her fingernails dug into the flesh on his upper arms, he did not feel it. He did not feel anything until he was hauled onto his feet, and thrown to the side by a man half his age, and twice his strength. Thomas Bateford was back.

Quickly removing the noose from her throat, he helped her to sit up and breathe, and then gazed at her, not knowing what on earth to think – or to say. But he did not have to say a word, because as soon as she could draw in the air, she did it for him.

'I'm leaving him Thomas. It's over. It's all over. And I love you with all my heart.'

'Then why did you refuse me? How could you do that? How could you possibly accept the likes of him?'

'I didn't. You disappeared before I could explain. I was all set to run away with you, with Ella. We were going to be together.'

'Run away? You mean . . . you were willing to leave everything behind? To have nothing in this life except me?'

'I was willing to give you the whole of my life. If only you had stayed that one night.'

'Oh my God.' His head dropped, and his voice was full of the most gut-wrenching gloom, but hers was equally full of light as she whispered:

'Don't be sorry. It was written in the stars. Your father's lost everything. Everything that matters. The mill, this place, and none of it would have happened if we'd left. Justice Thomas. At last we have justice.' Gently she lifted up his chin, and as their enemy skulked back into his house for the final time, they shared their first embrace. A tender kiss which wiped away the past, and heralded the arrival of their future.

'Oh Bessie, I love you. I love you so much that I sometimes think I'm going to burst.' His brow was creased in earnest, but she eased the tension by passing her fingers across it.

'Please don't burst on me now,' she smiled, but he remained utterly serious.

'I thought I'd lost you. When I saw you enter that church, I thought it was over forever.'

'You saw me?' she repeated, and when he had fully explained, she wanted to say how much she had been waiting for him to rescue her, but knew that it would be too painful, so instead declared: 'It was never going to be permanent. I was never going to be with your father any longer than was absolutely necessary.'

'But five months was way too long. It felt like an eternity.' He closed his eyes, but quickly opened them again, stood up, whisked her off her feet, and whisked away all thought of those months with it. Carrying her into the wood, he placed her down upon their special mossy place, and Bessie tried to ignore the voice in her head arguing that Arnold might well have been for keeps if it had not been for Charles. Would she have left otherwise? And what was Arnold feeling right now?

'I never stopped loving you,' whispered Thomas as he saw a troubled look cross her eyes.

'And I never stopped loving you.'

'I've been such a fool.'

'Don't say that. Just kiss me again. Kiss me as if our very lives depend upon it.'

He did just that, and then held her in his arms until the Roscoe barouche pulled up, and they were forced once more out into the open. Bessie had brought Thomas up to speed, so he knew that he would be seeing his sister – for the first time in eighteen months. He expected her to seem older, embittered, but although there was still definitely anger directed towards him, she had somehow remained so very young.

'I heard you'd disappeared,' she remarked coldly, and Drew wondered who exactly he was meeting – until Bessie explained. Thomas was an ally, had always been an ally, and Arnold now knew everything.

Encouraging Drew and Thomas to talk as they wandered up towards the house, she then held back with Cynthia. It was important to have a word about Thomas, but Cynthia had other questions first:

'I can't understand why you'd marry my father, and then conspire against him like this. It doesn't make any sense.' She stared, wary and bemused, until remembering the many ways in which Arnold Bateford could bring a person to their knees, and incite pure hatred as a result. 'Has life with him really been that bad?'

'No, not really.' Bessie wanted to take her time, but they would soon encounter Arnold again, and she needed Cynthia to know in advance, so added: 'I did it because he hurt my family. My real name is Bessie Cullen. I'm Luke's sister.'

'Luke?' Cynthia's eyes dilated in one blink. 'As in my . . ?'

Bessie nodded. 'I came here as a nursemaid, to look after your daughter, and although I'd like to say that it was my only motive, I also came for revenge, and made a mess of it to begin with. But this time I think that it's working out much better.'

'D . . . do you know . . . where Luke is?' It was clear that Cynthia had not absorbed a word of what had just been said.

'I'm afraid that I don't.'

'And what about Isabel? She isn't here, is she? My father can't hurt her?'

'No, no.' Bessie laid a calming hand upon Cynthia's forearm. 'I took her to be with a friend in town. And I need you to know that Thomas is also a friend. He isn't just your brother, he's always been on your side. He's taken beatings for my sake, for Isabel's sake. He loves you both dearly.'

'You obviously know everything,' observed Cynthia, still with a hard edge to her words. 'So you'll know that he betrayed me.'

'No, he didn't.'

'But he did. He's the reason Luke had to flee.'

'No. Luke told a friend that he was leaving, and it was that friend – Daniel Eldridge – who told Arnold. Your brother couldn't do it to you. He's always been loyal. He's one of the few good men. And your forgiveness would absolutely mean the world to him.'

Cynthia swallowed. 'It doesn't sound as if there's anything to forgive. If what you say is true.'

'It *is*,' promised Bessie. 'I'm not saying it because I care for him, I'm saying it because it happened. I was with Luke the night that he fled. I was furious when he told me that Danny was involved. I knew we were walking into a trap, but he wouldn't believe me. All he cared about was seeing you one last time. Hoping that Danny could get a message through to you.' Bessie was about to say: "He loved you, very much", but that was entirely the wrong thing. Luke was the past; Drew was

Cynthia's future; and such thoughts were distinctly unhealthy. 'Please tell Thomas that everything is fine between you. He really does need to hear it.'

Cynthia finally managed to nod, pushing aside what she had thought was the truth, and preparing to mend bridges, when the sound of horses' hooves met them from behind. It was the hire-cab, ready to take the Batefords to their new home, and within the minute Arnold was stalking back down the front steps, following by Harris, Bellamy – and Charles, who was still holding his head.

Bessie managed to catch Harris' eye, and gave an apologetic frown. It would have been nice if she could have taken him aside and talked privately, but as it was, she had to content herself with the knowledge that at least he would be happier in town, and she had certainly given him some gossip to go on.

Arnold surely could not have thought that her look was intended for him, but he walked over anyway, and Thomas instinctively stood in front of Bessie as protector – with Drew doing the same for Cynthia.

'Yes, go on, guard your scheming little whores all you like, but that's all they'll ever be,' growled Arnold, before fixing the full glare upon his wife.

She stared straight back, aware that in certain regards she had possibly earned her title, but not caring in the slightest.

'You'll never be able to forget me,' he predicted, to which Bessie replied that she already had. But for some reason it did not provoke Arnold to lunge at her. His face instead became lit with a strange sort of satisfaction, as if he knew that she was lying, and was comforted by it. 'I had you first, and you enjoyed it, no matter what you might say to him now.' Arnold tossed a dismissive glance in his son's direction. 'And you'll enjoy it again. You're my wife, and you'll be a wife to me in the future. I'll make damn sure of it.'

'You'll never get near her,' vowed Thomas, pushing himself right up against his father, but Arnold again seemed to be pleased, perhaps by the element of challenge, and after one more lingering stare, he was gone.

Linking her arm inside Thomas', Cynthia then strode back into what had once been her home, and the first sight which met her was the eight-day clock in the hall smashed to pieces. 'What happened?' she asked, turning to Bessie, and suddenly noticing the marks around her neck. 'And what did he do to you?' Cynthia put both hands to her own neck in horror, but Bessie assured her that it did not hurt.

'As for the clock, I'm afraid I don't know.' Bessie moved into the dining room, and found that the huge table – which had looked like it would stand for a thousand years – was now devoid of legs, and in three pieces. It appeared that Arnold had taken an axe to it, although she had no idea where he had found one.

The Batefords and Roscoes proceeded from room to room, and discovered the same scene repeated over and over again. There was not a stick of furniture left. The upholstery on the chairs had been ripped, the beds were destroyed, mirrors smashed. It was like a storm had blown through. Bessie's remaining clothes had suffered the worst attack, shredded – except for the red ones, which were deliberately unmarked – and prompting her to remark wryly: 'My, my, somebody did take it badly.'

Drew thankfully managed to laugh, which was good since everything would now have to be thrown out, leaving him with an utterly unfurnished house.

'I'm sorry,' she added, and offered to clear up, but he told her not to worry.

'What about Isabel?' asked Cynthia. 'You say that she's with a friend in town. What friend? Can I collect her?'

'No, it's alright, I'll go. Give you and Thomas a chance to catch up.'

'Somebody should go with you,' said Thomas, worried for her safety after what his father had just said, but she pooh-poohed his concerns, and headed out on the journey which she had been dreading from the beginning. This was the build-up to the handover which mattered, and she asked for God to give her the strength to see it through.

When she entered the kitchen at Fulton Street, Josiah's smiling face was there to greet her, and as always it made her feel like she might just about be able to cope.

'I'm sorry that I couldn't explain earlier Josiah, but now we have some time to talk.'

'What happened to your throat?' he demanded, trying to turn her to the light so that he could properly examine the ridges, but she eased his fingers away, and assured him that it was nothing.

'Nothing that matters any more,' she added. 'It's so wonderful to look at you properly, and to see you so well.'

'All the better that you're here.' He was not about to admit that he had spent most of the day crying with relief.

'Where's Ella?'

'Spending time with Adam and Cora. They've rather taken to their new friend.'

'What about Mr and Mrs Palmer?'

'Mr Palmer is away on business, and Mrs Palmer heard a child laughing, so came down to investigate.'

'Oh dear.'

'Don't worry. Mrs Jennet claimed Ella as her great-niece, and Mrs Palmer was so enchanted that she promptly took her upstairs to play with her own children.'

Bessie smiled. 'She *is* adorable, isn't she?'

'Yes. Just like her auntie has always been.'

'Oh Josiah, you say such lovely things, but I fear you look at me through rose-coloured spectacles.'

'I see what's there Bessie Cullen. Always have done. Or should I be calling you Bessie Bateford now?'

'Cullen will do just fine. He's out of my life. Forever.' She proceeded to explain – from the moment she had left in April, to the events of that very day, up at the Hall.

'I'm glad that I didn't know anything about it,' said Josiah at the end. 'The fact that you married him was bad enough. But the rest? I wouldn't have been able to sleep a wink.'

'I haven't done much sleeping myself recently. I was so desperate for everything to work out, and for this day to come.'

'It must have been my prayers that did it.' Josiah folded his arms with resolute pride. 'I've said a good long prayer for you every single night. One hundred and fifty-two in all.'

'And I've felt them, every last one!' She laughed, and gave him yet another hug. 'I've missed you Josiah Deakes. More than any words can say.'

He smiled back, but then it was as if a cloud appeared on his horizon, blotting out the sun.

'What is it?'

He shuffled. 'It's your mother.'

'What about her?'

'Well . . . I took the money like you asked me to, and she was there, but . . .'

'She *was* alive, wasn't she?'

'Oh yes.'

'So what then?'

'It's . . . well . . . I think she may have been drunk.'

'Drunk!'

'She didn't actually say anything, so it was hard to tell, but I smelt it on her, and it was pretty strong.'

Bessie pursed her lips.

'I tried to get word to you by leaving a message in the holly bush, but obviously it didn't work.'

'No it didn't. But that's my fault, not yours.' All those months watching Harris and his drinking, and it had never occurred to her that the problem could be even closer to home. In fact she had not really given her mother much thought at all. 'Thank you for telling me. I'll know what to expect when I go back to Henningborough.' Bessie sat quietly for a moment, hoping against hope that Marge Cullen had used that money to pay the rent, rather than paying for drink.

'I'm sorry to spoil the day,' whispered Josiah, and Bessie brightened as soon as she saw his anguish.

'You haven't. You make any day perfect. But I'll have to say goodbye soon. I need to take Ella home.'

'Will she be meeting Cynthia?'

'Yes.'

'That's going to be difficult. For you, I mean.'

Bessie nodded, and tried to remind herself that she was doing the right thing. 'Actually I must see somebody else first. I'll be about . . . half an hour. Can you have Ella ready by then?'

'Of course,' he promised, and thirty minutes later, Bessie was back – having filled in the gaps for Mr Matthews.

That was it. That was the last person to whom she owed an explanation, and when she gave Ella to Cynthia, it would all be over. The whole thing done and dusted, and back to the simple business of living.

Ella was in the kitchen, having tremendous fun with a big bowl of flour, and Mrs Jennet had received an open invitation to bring her great-niece to play upstairs whenever she was next in town.

'In fact if truth be told, I think Mrs Palmer would rather like to keep her, and she's not the only one!' The cook had difficulty tearing herself away, as did Josiah, and much as she wanted to, Bessie knew that she no longer had the right to suggest that Ella could visit again some day.

Then it was time to walk back to the valley. So many miles covered that day, and dusk now descending, but weariness was impossible in the presence of Ella, who insisted on toddling along by herself – until her own legs grew tired, and she fell over.

'Up-a-daisy!' exclaimed Bessie, lifting her up, and kissing the two little hands which had cushioned the fall.

Ella had a funny expression on her face, as if she was giving serious thought to the concept of crying, because her hands really did hurt. But thankfully the kisses were enough to dissuade her, and she became sleepy instead.

'No no, you mustn't go to sleep yet Ella. I need to tell you something. You're going to meet two very special people soon. Thomas. You remember Thomas? He looked after you when you were a baby.'

There was no recognition in those big blue eyes, but Bessie felt sure that Ella would know Thomas when she saw him, absolutely and completely sure.

'And then there's Cynthia. She loves you very much. Just like I do.' Tears began to blur Bessie's vision. 'You must never forget that. I love you. I'll always love you. For as long as I'm alive, and then for all eternity to come.'

Ella's assurance came in the form of an affectionate giggle, and for a moment Bessie had to fight the urge to run away. It was a strong urge too, strong enough to make her drag her heels, but not enough to make her act on it. Ella belonged to Cynthia now. That was a fact which had to be faced, and all that remained was to savour these last precious moments, until the time came to place her into the arms of her mother.

That act itself ended up as difficult as Bessie had imagined – if not more so – and once the break was made, Cynthia took her daughter upstairs, cradling her tight, all to herself. Bessie instantly felt jealous and bitter and angry, and of course guilty, but Thomas was there – ready and eager to divert her. He had been invited to stay at the house, since it was now going to be the Roscoes' base for the foreseeable future.

'But I thought you were only planning to be here for a week or two.'

'That was the original idea,' confirmed Drew. 'But it will be better for the child if we stay.'

Bessie almost countered that Northcliff was the far more impressive and commodious home, but stopped herself just in time. Drew was sacrificing that for the sake of Cynthia, and it was something to be admired, not questioned.

'I'd like to invite you to come and stay here as well,' offered Drew. 'Thomas has explained the extent of his feelings for you, and it would be wonderful for my wife to have you both by her side. Although of course . . .' He coughed. 'There would have to be a certain degree of separation.'

Thomas peered at her, all excited, and Bessie was sorely tempted. She would be able to see Ella every day, but she would also have to see Cynthia with Ella, and all those months of Ella and Agatha had been agonising enough. Besides, this house was not right. Bessie knew that she did not belong inside, so refused.

'We'll go somewhere together then,' suggested Thomas. 'Thank you for your offer Drew, but it's probably best if we find our own way. Perhaps settle in the village.'

'No,' said Bessie. 'You stay here. I'll be nearby.' She turned to Drew. 'Can I possibly have one of the mill cottages? I know that there are a couple empty.'

'A cottage?'

'That's right.'

'Well . . . yes, if . . . you really want one?'

'But you don't,' interceded Thomas. 'They're awful places. Why would you want to live in one of them, when we can live in the village, or here?'

'I have my mother to think about. I need to bring her back to Somerden, and hopefully Father will be with us in a matter of months. They can't live in this Hall, and all they've ever known are cottages like the ones in the valley. I think it would be comforting to have something familiar. And I'd have difficulty explaining who you are, if you were to live with us. It's simply easier if you stay here, and I'm down there. We'll be close. I'll be able to see you every day. I couldn't bear not to. And I can see Ella every so often, can't I?'

'I'm sure that Cynthia will be extremely happy for you to maintain contact with her sister,' replied Drew.

'Is that still the position? Isabel being Arnold's child?'

'Definitely.' His face was as adamant as his words, and although Bessie found the thought of yet more lies unsettling, she had to agree. Sometimes secrets were necessary, and she also needed him to keep a secret of her own.

'Can you do something else for me?'

'Of course.'

'If anybody asks, can you tell them that Mr and Mrs Bateford moved out, and if there's talk that Mrs Bateford has disappeared, say you don't know why. As far as you're concerned, I will always be Elizabeth Arabrook who married Arnold.'

'Alright. If that's your wish.'

'It is. And there's just one more favour, if you don't mind?'

'Name it,' smiled Drew.

'Can you keep Mrs Evans on as cook?'

'Yes, I think I can manage that.' He paused, eyes twinkling. 'She is a *good* cook, isn't she?'

'Brilliant,' confirmed Bessie. 'And there were some other people here who've been dismissed of late. If they were to return, asking for work, would you consider taking them back too?'

'I don't see why not. I want to keep Northcliff fully-staffed, so a second set of servants will be required.

If you give me their names tomorrow, then I'll know who to look out for.'

Bessie promised to do just that, although was planning to omit Mrs Muir and Constance from the list. They were a negative influence, and best gone. Tess showed similar tendencies, but Bessie had faith that she might not be too bad once relieved of her accomplices.

Thomas let them finish their discussion, but then immediately made it perfectly clear that he was not happy. Not happy one bit. 'Why does it matter? That you remain as Elizabeth Bateford.'

'Because I want to live back down in that valley as plain old Bessie Cullen, and I can only do that if nobody connects me to the person up here.' More to the point, she did not want Edie and Seamus to ever know what she had become. 'I want to go back to the way things were before all this. Back to the beginning.'

'Back to before me you mean.'

'No, it isn't like that.'

'Yes it is,' snapped Thomas. 'You said so yourself. Me up here, you down there – it's for the best. That's exactly how it was at the start.'

'I know, but it's best because it's a *fresh* start. I don't want to be constantly reminded that I'm married to your father. And you don't want that either, do you?'

Drew tactfully moved away as Thomas hung his head very low indeed.

'Please don't be upset,' she begged. 'It's like we were talking about before – permanent and temporary. This is something that's merely necessary, in the short term.'

'But I don't like it.'

'I know, but we're free of Arnold, that's all that matters. Little details like the roof under which we sleep

– they aren't important, surely? *Please* Thomas, let's be happy.' Her voice was beseeching, and eyes even more so, and finally they forced him to give her something of a smile. But it was not accompanied by any smiling within his soul. He simply could not understand it. Why, when the worst barrier of all had just gone from between them, was she already erecting another one?

CHAPTER TEN

As September moved into October, the weather turned inevitably autumnal, but it was not enough to deter Thomas from leaving the comforts of Roscoe Hall, and meeting up with Bessie in the wood every day. Their old rug was turning mouldy now, so he bought them a new one, and it was a joy to carry it openly, not having to fear what Charles or Arnold might see. In fact it was difficult to get out of the habit of skulking around. He would often find himself in a certain part of the house, seized by a sense of trepidation, and indeed transfixed by it, until realising that he no longer had to suffer in that way. He was sure that Drew had caught him on more than one occasion, and wondered what on earth was wrong with his brother-in-law.

Bessie was experiencing similar emotions, revisiting feelings of familiarity, but unlike Thomas she was embracing every one of them. Whether it was in the cottage, walking through the valley, or heading up Ulmers Hill – every time that she was struck by an old sentiment, she savoured it, desperately trying to recapture the Bessie Cullen of 1837. She did, however, need to put all that aside and be careful when making her way to see Thomas. It was so far so good with her little secret, and she did not want there to be any change. Elizabeth Arabrook had disappeared, Bessie Cullen had reappeared, and nobody was any the wiser.

'I love you,' said Thomas as she nestled against him, and he drew the rug around her legs.

'You only said that a minute ago.'

'But I have to keep on saying it, for fear that you might forget.'

'I won't,' she promised, hand resting upon his chest. That strong, manly chest which had saved her from Arnold's grasp. Somehow in the flurry of events, Thomas' gallantry had been neglected, but she would not be here now if it were not for him. 'I love you too,' she whispered. 'With all my heart.'

'All of it?'

'Yes . . . well . . . I do have to save a bit for Ella.'

Thomas smiled.

'How is she?'

'As beautiful as ever.'

'And is she happy? I mean with Cynthia?' It was hard to admit it, but there was a part of Bessie looking for a very definite negative in response.

'Oh yes. It's as if they've never been apart, as if you and I have never really existed. In fact I don't exist much even now. But I creep in whenever I can.'

'What about Drew? Is he comfortable with everything?'

'Yes. He doesn't have much of a look-in either, but it seems as if he wants to. I think he's eager to accept Ella as his own.'

'That's good,' said Bessie, before adding with anxiety: 'Your sister will let Ella out for our picnic on Sunday, won't she? I can't go any longer without seeing her.'

'Why don't you come up to the Hall? Cynthia can't refuse you when you've made all this a reality.'

'You know why.'

Thomas sighed, and Bessie could feel every ounce of his irritation.

'Don't you like it here?' she asked palliatively. 'In our private place.'

'Of course,' he replied – under significant duress – but then all irritation ebbed away as he kissed her.

She kissed him back, surrendering herself completely to the sense of warm security, but when he tried to push things further, she had to hold him at bay – in order to talk about serious matters:

'I need to work Thomas, and I was wondering – do you think Drew will take me on at the mill? I have experience, and I don't mind the hours.'

'Experience? Yes, I should think so, but why?'

'Because a mill cottage comes with mill work, and I'm already facing questions. Besides, I can't keep living off you forever. You've paid for my clothes, my food, and also the rent, while I've just been sitting around doing nothing. It's no good. I have to find a way to be useful.'

'But I'll never see you,' he complained.

'Yes you will. I'll sneak out every lunchtime, and Sunday is now a full day of rest. That will always be our special day.'

'But lunchtimes aren't enough, and I *like* to support you.' Thomas eased himself up, compelling her to move. 'It would be so much easier if you simply lived at the Hall. I could protect you.'

'Protect me? From what?'

'My father of course.'

'But he's gone.'

'He threatened you Bessie.'

'That wasn't a threat. It was the only way he had left of venting his feelings. He knows that he can't hurt me now. Please Thomas, I need to do this. I need to work in the mill.'

'Alright, have it your way then, but it means I'll be starting too. Drew's already suggested that I become his manager, and I'll say yes!'

Bessie beamed. 'You see? It's perfect. I'll be able to see you every minute of every day. Even more than I do now.'

Thomas was still not happy, but eventually he was drawn in by her smile, kissing her again, and this time she could not simply brush him off. She had to be blunt and say no.

'Why?'

'Because I have my . . .' She looked away. '. . . bleeding.'

'Oh . . . I'm sorry.'

'Don't be sorry. It's wonderful. I was late. More than a little late. But now this means that I'm not pregnant by him. I'm not carrying your half-brother or sister.'

That was a thought which brightened Thomas considerably. He wrapped his arms around her waist as if she was already carrying his own child, and said: 'We *will* be together soon, won't we?'

Bessie was not quite sure what to say, or how to put it, and he could tell instantly that she was not in favour of his suggestion.

'Why not?' he snapped.

'Because . . . well . . . we aren't married.'

'So you can lie with my father, but not with me, and all because of a few silly vows.' Arnold's malicious claim jumped to the fore, and it made Thomas feel very angry indeed.

'It isn't like that,' said Bessie.

'Isn't it?'

'No. Don't be hurt. Please. I love you. Isn't that enough?'

He did not respond.

'As soon as I'm no longer his wife, I'll marry you the next day, and become the Bateford that I should always have been.' She tried to draw his face back towards her. 'I want to be close to you more than you can imagine.'

'But it could be years.'

'It might not be.'

'He'll never release you. You know that.' Thomas shook his face free, and stood up. 'We're simply left waiting for him to die, and I can't wait that long.'

'But we're together, that's what counts. We have so many more years than him.' She was doing her best to be comforting, but her words only seemed to aggravate him even further.

'I should never have let you marry that man. You're right – you should have been Mrs *Thomas* Bateford from the start. If only I hadn't been such a fool.'

She was about to reiterate that he had not been anything of the sort, to not be so hard on himself, so hard on *them*, but he walked off before she could even begin to say it, leaving a leaden atmosphere behind.

Sitting there, she began to question whether she was being cruel to frustrate him in such a manner. He wanted to be intimate, despite the fact that she had been with his father so many times. Surely she ought to be eternally grateful for that? What exactly was she trying to prove with her abstinence, and living back in one of those cottages? Was she really so afraid of the person she had become? Probably. And there was yet another issue troubling her as well. Namely Luke. She had used some of Thomas' money to put an advertisement in the newspapers. Not the Somerden Register, but the neighbouring towns as far as Tucknott and Henningborough.

In all probability her quest would not bear fruit. Luke had no idea how to read or write, and if he had gone as far as she had suggested, then he was way beyond reach. But if that were not the case, and a friend saw it, then perhaps he might be able to respond. She had put about his sister looking for him, and wanting him home, so that ought to draw him once more into the valley. And if he did return, it would be best if nobody at the Hall ever knew, and that meant keeping secrets from Thomas. It did not feel nice, not nice at all, especially as she was already keeping back so many other details about her mother.

On the Monday after the handover of Bateford Hall, Bessie had gone to Henningborough in search of Margaret Cullen. The weekend had been taken up with settling into the new environment and buying some ordinary clothes, but by Monday she had felt ready to tackle whatever might await her at Kearney Street.

Once more in front of the relevant row of houses, she had prepared to knock on the door of the first floor apartment, praying that her mother would still be there, but deep down knowing that it was unlikely. The funds from Josiah should have been enough to cover the rent, and pin money could have seen to provisions, but if Marge had indeed become consumed with alcohol, then sewing would have been the last thing on her mind. And it was therefore not a shock when a stranger answered the door in the late afternoon.

'Can you help me?' she asked. 'I'm looking for my mother, Margaret Cullen.'

'She don't live here no more.'

Bessie almost said: "Yes, that much is obvious", and wondered why his use of a double negative should jar so much. Too many opulent parties with the likes of Mrs Forrester no doubt. 'Do you know where she's gone?'

'No.'

'What about – when she left?'

'I'd say . . . four months back. That's how long we've been 'ere, ain't it love?' He held the door open to receive confirmation from a woman who was sitting at a table, surrounded by children.

'Do you know where my mother went?' asked Bessie, trying not to feel pained by the sight of foreign knick-knacks and unknown faces staring back at her.

'No. But you're best trying the workhouse.'

'Workhouse!' It came out as an exclamation, but really there was no cause for surprise.

'Yes, she didn't go voluntary-like, if you catch me drift.'

Bessie did indeed catch his drift. Mother had been thrown out for non-payment of rent, after only a month. Walking back down the street, submerged by a mixture of vexation and disappointment, she was forced again to ask for directions to one of those awful places.

It was not far. They were not exactly in the poorest part of town, but not a million miles away from it, and of course the workhouse was not likely to be planted anywhere near the rich folk. Thankfully the man who dealt with her enquiry this time was not as odious as the one in Somerden, and when she asked for a Cullen, he scanned down some scribbled records, found the name, and led the way. Everything was laid out in a similar manner to Somers House, and there were the same vacant, skeletal wrecks of humanity on display. All because of a lack of money. Pieces of paper and little bits of metal – that was all it boiled down to. If you had them, you were well-fed and powerful. If not, you were hungry and helpless.

They entered the laundry where women were pounding clothes in a rhythmical manner, half-asleep – or half-dead. It was like watching a collection of ghosts, and Bessie was taken up to one particular ghost in the far corner. Swallowing, she braced herself for the same aggressive response as last time, but it did not happen, because it was not actually her mother.

'This is the only Cullen here. If it isn't her, we haven't got her.'

Bessie studied the woman, a little older than Marge, but with kinder eyes, and a capacity to smile, even in this place. For a moment Bessie was tempted to take her home instead. She was a Cullen after all, so could well be some distant relative, but in the end they walked away, and Bessie scanned as many faces as possible on their return to the entrance.

'Can I look at the records?' she asked. 'See if my mother has ever been here?'

No.

Apparently the records were in a bad state, and he promptly saw her out.

She had no idea where to go next, but then it soon became clear that the men's prison was the best bet. Perhaps Marge had gone back to staring at the outer walls, waiting for Wilf to fly over to her? It was certainly more than possible, but there was no sign. Bessie talked to one of the guards, slipped into "slut mode" as Arnold would undoubtedly describe it, and managed to discover that Wilf Cullen was still alive inside. The information was only on the promise of meeting up later in the local tavern, but like Munroe, the guard would find himself disappointed.

After that, Bessie simply migrated back to Kearney Street, and stood staring up at the buildings. No wonder her mother had turned to drink. Anybody would do so in the same situation. Where to look – that was now the issue. There was no way that Marge would have left town, left Wilf, not even in a drunken mist, and it was unlikely that she could have found the money for a fare anyway. So it was simply a case of trudging every street, which was precisely what Bessie proceeded to do – although to no avail, and as night approached, she recognised that this search really had to be narrowed down.

With extreme discomfort, she asked a few pedestrians about where the homeless might go, and the majority directed her to a bridge near the ironworks. The warmest place in town. Or so they thought. It was probably a myth, but when the sky turned red at night with the smoke and flames of those blast-furnaces, it certainly felt like it.

Moving from person to person, she was glad that her clothes were those of a worker, helping her feel close to them as a result. Some looked up, hands outstretched, asking for money. Others were huddled, swamped in rags, and uninterested in who was passing by. It smelt like many of them had been wearing their rags for months, even through the summer, but presumably you needed many layers when those layers had to act as your bedclothes as well.

In order to check that she was not walking past her mother, it was necessary to lift some of the faces, and peer at them. So many mothers and daughters, fathers and sons. Like a whole second town, and it felt like such an intrusion, but in the end it bore fruit. Marge was there, living within a stone's throw of the ironworks. Thomas must have walked past her on many an occasion, dismissed her as a sottish stranger – but today she was sottish in a good way. Having been through the second stage of intoxication – that quarrelsome lion-drunk where she was liable to spit and hiss in a territorial fight for her spot – Marge was now really quite merry.

'Ah Bessie, is that you?' she cried, and even gave her daughter that much-longed-for embrace.

But it did not last. By the next morning conviviality had worn off, and cold resentment had rolled back in.

Unable to stay at the tavern, because of the prison guard lying in wait, and with the New Crown coaching inn only accommodating those in a "fit state", there had been nothing else for it but to sit it out under the bridge. And then at first light Bessie had taken them to Padgett Street, paid for the use of a bath – and also more than a few cups of tea. That had restored Marge to her normal, bitter and unbending self, and Bessie had felt herself hardening to the same degree. She had once questioned whether living with her mother could be worse than living with Arnold, and now definitely knew the answer to that one.

With Thomas' money she then bought some clothes and shoes – along with a little drink. Watching Harris had taught her that people could not stop wanting spirits just like that. It would be a case of trying to wean her mother off it, and indeed that would probably be the case for many months to come.

Having been back in the mill cottage for a couple of weeks now, Bessie had not yet seen her mother drunk to the point of merriment again, but the gin kept disappearing at a steady rate. She wanted to discuss it with Thomas, ask him whether she should cut off the supply completely, and how exactly you could persuade somebody to turn away from a damaging influence when they were barely willing to speak to you. But every time she came close to raising the issue, the words would get stuck in her throat, and she would leave it until the next time – worried that if she withdrew the gin, then her mother might resort to begging or even stealing. For the other families in the valley to witness such a thing would be utterly unbearable.

When Marge did speak, it was to question what they were doing back in this place. They were not in the same cottage as before. Bessie had made sure of that. Too many reminders of baby Pauly. But nevertheless why were they back here, where was Luke, where was Wilf? Bessie gave very short answers, the shortest being that a man called Mr Roscoe had bought the mill because Bateford had apparently encountered some difficulties. No way was she saying what those difficulties were, nor the identity of *Mrs* Roscoe, and so they persisted in the same strained state as before, sharing nothing, saying nothing, doing nothing other than existing under the same roof.

Usually after meeting with Thomas, she would head back down to the cottage, to endure yet more of it, but not today. There was something which she had been putting off, and now it needed to be addressed. She was not sure whether Thomas had stormed into the fields to burn off his frustration, or gone back into his room at the Hall, but either way he would be alone, and out of the way. That meant it was the perfect time to creep in for a quick word with Drew. There was no doubt in her mind about this particular deception. Thomas would be even more unhappy if he were to hear what she was doing. He simply *had* to be kept in the dark.

Drew had opted to use Arnold's study as his own, and Bessie could see him through the window, so when Duncan vacated the hall, she shot inside.

'Good afternoon,' he said with a smile of surprise.

'Good afternoon,' she replied, wondering why she should suddenly feel so excited about skulking around again. 'I'm sorry to interrupt you like this, but I've come to settle the final part of our agreement.'

Drew's face was blank.

'The . . . er . . . money?'

'Oh, you mean the twelve hundred and fifty. That was it, wasn't it?'

'Yes.'

Drew paused, and she was gripped with a fear that he was not going to give it to her, but he was only concerned about the volume in one go. 'Are you sure it's wise to keep quite that much under your bedstead? I can store it here in my cash-box if you like, and you can have it in instalments.'

'Thank you, but it isn't for me. I owe it to somebody.'

'Who? If you don't mind me asking.'

'I don't mind at all, but I'm afraid they might not like me to say. They were a great help at the turn of the year, and took substantial risks in providing that help.'

'I understand.'

'Thank you for increasing the wages at the mill by the way.'

'I merely put it back to somewhere reasonable,' replied Drew, and unlocked his cash-box.

'And thank you for taking Duncan back on.'

'He's a fine young man as you said, and although I wasn't sure whether he was ready to step up from his old position, he is in fact a very able butler indeed.'

Bessie glowed, before feeling sad that she could not congratulate him herself. 'Will you give him a message for me?'

'Of course.'

'Tell him that you've heard from me, and that I wish him all the best. And I thank him for his loyal service.'

'He'll be glad to hear it. He's been asking after you.'

'Has he?'

'Yes, on more than one occasion.'

Bessie now felt so sad that she had to fight back the tears. 'Could you convey the same to Mrs Evans as well please?'

'What about Tess and Agatha?'

'No.' Bessie shook her head. 'No message for them', and Drew smiled again.

'Not exactly your favourites?'

'Nowhere near it.'

He counted out the money, and then left the room to fetch a receptacle for her. Looking at all the notes on the desk, she scratched her head, wondering whether it was enough. Gil had given her just over a hundred pounds on four separate occasions, and then an increased amount for two more months. Plus there was all that money which she had lost to the masked man, coming to several hundred. Yes, one thousand two hundred and fifty ought to be there or thereabouts.

When Drew returned, she had a quick word about working in the mill, requested that he show no prior knowledge when Thomas mentioned it, and then had to ask for Duncan to be distracted – so that she could head off with her wallet of cash.

Scurrying past the mill, she was soon on the road to Somerden, and every time that somebody walked by, it gave her a jolt of fear that they might be able to smell the money – or smell her anxiety at the very least. She was an idiot, putting herself in these kinds of situations, when Drew would happily have let her use his barouche, but by some miracle she actually reached Carrow Square without incident. Her arms were aching, but the wallet was intact, and without delay she knocked on the door of number twenty-two. Reeve answered, showing her into the drawing room, and then Gil appeared a few moments later.

'Well Mrs Bateford, we meet again.'

'It's Miss Cullen,' she replied with an icy tone, still not having forgiven him for all that nastiness at the wedding.

'Would you care for a drink Miss Cullen?'

'No, I won't be staying long. I only came to give you this.' She tipped out her precious cargo, making sure it clattered defiantly onto his coffee-table. 'It's all there. The incentive money, those notes I cost you when I . . .' She coughed. '. . . stole from your safe. Every last shilling, according to my best estimate.'

'Well well,' said Gil, eyes wide and impressed. 'You are indeed a woman of your word.'

'Yes I am.'

'And would you mind telling me how exactly you . . .' He was about to say: "Got your hands on it", but instead chose a more delicate phrase. 'Came by it? Being as dear Arnold has apparently hit something of a bad patch.'

'That bad patch was of my making Mr Tremaine, and this money is merely part of the accompanying settlement.'

Gil tried to piece together what he had heard on the local grapevine with what she was telling him in that distinctly uninformative response. 'You mean that this has come from Mr Roscoe?'

'Indeed it has.'

'And you aren't at all tempted to keep it for yourself?'

'No, I am not.'

Walking forward, Gil studied her. 'From what I gather, Arnold's tribulations were prompted by a surprise inspection of his factory. Tell me – how exactly did you manufacture that particular little event?'

'By finding somebody to pose as that inspector. When Arnold attacked him, as I entirely expected he would, I then saw to it that he was arrested for it.' She gave her account as if it had all been a matter of such complete simplicity.

'Very clever,' said Gil. 'Particularly the arresting bit. And I presume Arnold was required to hand over some of the mill in order to shorten his stay in gaol?'

'Exactly.'

Gil tipped his head to one side. 'My congratulations Miss Cullen. Certainly nobody can accuse you of a lack of pluck.'

Bessie almost smiled, but just about stopped herself in time.

'And what about you? Arnold appears to be in town without his "scandalously young wife". What has happened to the upwardly mobile Miss Arabrook?'

'I am back in a mill cottage, where I belong.'

'And does he know who you really are?'

'Yes he does.'

Usually it was only Gil's left eyebrow which went up, but this time it was both, amazed that she was still in one piece.

'Your involvement remains a secret,' she assured him. 'From everybody except Thomas.'

'Thank you,' he replied, serious for a change. 'And where is Thomas nowadays?'

'Back at the Hall.'

'I see.'

Bessie was not sure exactly what he thought he saw, but it was time for her to leave.

'How much is there?' he asked, stopping her at the door.

'One thousand two hundred and fifty.'

'Quite a sum, and gratefully received, but I don't actually need it all.' More to the point he had no right to it all. 'How about I keep half, and you have the rest?'

'No.'

'Come on. I'm sure you could use it.' He began to collect some up, but she shook her head, flapped her hands, and said no again.

'Poor and proud of it eh? Working-class rebel once more.'

'Something like that,' she replied, and very quickly was gone.

Spending time with Josiah helped to confirm that she had done the right thing, and then when she absolutely could not leave it any longer, she ambled back to the cottage. Hopefully it would be to find her mother asleep, rather than sitting in that same chair as usual, possibly a little worse for wear, but always grim.

In fact when she strode back over the threshold, her mother was very much on her feet, in tears, and clutching the arm of a man who currently had his back towards Bessie.

'Who *are* you? What are you doing?' she demanded.

'What am I doing? I'm coming home of course.' The man turned, and Bessie peered at him.

'No! I don't believe it.'

A grin spread over Luke's face. 'Hello Sis.'

She clasped both hands to her mouth, and he leaned down to give her a kiss. 'I . . . I . . . I only put the advertisement out last week.'

'What advertisement?'

'In the newspapers.'

'I haven't seen any papers. I've kept an ear to the ground for what's been going on, and as soon as I heard that Bateford was out of the way, I knew it was time to come back. Although I didn't actually expect to find you here in the valley.'

Marge was now stroking the arm that she was refusing to relinquish, and with the growing realisation that her brother was indeed back, Bessie could not prevent a flicker of resentment surging once more to the fore.

'You've changed so much. I hardly recognise you,' she said, concentrating on Luke, and trying to remind herself that it was not his fault that he was loved more than her.

'You've changed rather a bit yourself. You sound kind of . . . swanky.'

'And you sound kind of broad,' she retorted with a laugh, swiftly moving on.

'I suppose I am. The men I work with are a fairly coarse lot. Good blokes though, one and all.'

'What exactly do you do?'

'I'm a navvy.' He did not say it apologetically, but with pride, and Bessie shared that pride as she had done so ever since Finn Deakes entered her world. She did not care what people said. They did back-breaking work, and some of them were the best of men.

'No wonder you're . . .' Bessie could not find the word.

'Big?' filled in Luke.

'Pretty much.' He had turned from a skinny little lad into a strapping young man.

'It took me a whole year to become as strong and fast as the others,' he explained. 'You have to keep you, or you're no use to them.'

'And where have you been?'

'As far as sixty miles away at one point. Shifting earth for a canal bed. That took a few months. But now I'm on the railway tracks, connecting Henningborough to Thurleigh.'

Marge remained speechless, staring up at her son in awe, and as Luke tried in vain to extract his arm, he asked about Father. Bessie knew that she had to tell him, but before she could even think where to start, there was a flash of something rancorous from Marge's direction.

'It's your sister's fault.'

'You can't help yourself, can you? Even today.'

Luke stared from one to the other, confused.

'Don't worry Mother, I'll give him your unique version, shall I?' Bessie lifted her chin, and blurted it out: 'I was sent to prison for a year, for breaking into the Hall. Which, I might add, I didn't do. But I said too much in court, which meant that they threw the book at Father for punching Arnold Bateford. Gave him three years. Mother then lost the baby. It would have been a boy, called Pauly. And that was my fault too. Shall I tell him the next bit Mother? Or would you like to pick up the story at this point?'

Marge snarled. She did not want her son knowing about the workhouse. 'There's nothing much more to tell,' she said, voice all softly-softly towards him. 'I've been living in Henningborough, waiting for you and your father.' The voice quickly turned nasty again. 'And your sister's been in Thurleigh, away for months on end. Until recently when she decided to move us back here for some reason. Although of course . . . it happens to have turned out for the best now.'

Luke steered his mother over to a chair, and sat her down, as if set to declare something which was truly a revelation. 'Bessie helped me to escape that night. I'd be dead if not for her.'

'You would have coped. Your sister made everything worse.'

Luke looked up at Bessie, full of regret, and poised to argue further on her behalf, but she pursed her lips, telling him not to bother. 'I'm sorry to hear about the baby Ma.' He stood up and addressed himself to Bessie, aware that she would offer the more accurate reflection of events. 'Do you know what happened to *my* baby?'

The one advantage of Mother's behaviour was that she had never shown the slightest interest in this particular subject, and having not expected Luke back yet, Bessie had no answer prepared. So she said simply: 'I don't know,' and quickly went onto suggesting that they needed something to eat. Mercifully Luke let it drop, and she ensured that the meal was taken up with talking about nothing but him, hearing about his work, and all the other navvies.

Marge certainly liked it, practically gazed at him throughout, until announcing at the end of the meal that she would be moving back to Henningborough to be by his side.

'But . . .' began Bessie, who needed to stay because of Thomas, and Ella, and Josiah. Not to mention the Whitsons. She was actually surrounded by several people who loved her, and did not want to leave them.

Marge responded with a look which said very clearly: "You don't have to come", and before things could descend back into nastiness, Luke nipped her suggestion in the bud:

'No Ma, you can't. I'm barracked with the men. It's just the way that it is. But I'll visit whenever I can. Besides, the railway is ultimately coming to Somerden, so I'm heading your way.'

'But . . .'

'Please Ma, this is home. I want you to be here.'

Of course Marge could not possibly argue with her precious son, and soon the effects of the day's earlier gin, along with the tears of joy, sent her into a peaceful sleep. Once Luke had taken her upstairs, he came back down to Bessie, and tackled the issue which had earlier been brushed aside:

'I know that Roscoe owns the mill now. And that Cynthia is his wife.'

'But . . . how?'

'Like I said, I've kept an ear to the ground.'

Bessie swallowed. Why did she suddenly have this horrid sense that his reasons for returning had nothing to do with his family at all? 'Cynthia's the past Luke. You do realise that, don't you?'

'Of course I do. Life's moved on. But I *need* to hear about my child.'

'I . . .' Bessie could not say it. Drew did not want anybody to learn the truth, and that would definitely apply to his wife's former lover. 'I don't know,' she said.

'There's a child up at the Hall, but it's Cynthia's sister Isabel. Arnold and Jane had another baby.'

'Isabel?' repeated Luke.

'Yes.' Bessie literally began to pray that he would not connect it with his own middle name, and wondered why on earth she had mentioned it at all.

'So what do you think happened to my baby?'

'I don't know,' said Bessie again. She did not want to leave him with the impression that his offspring might be dead, or lost to another couple, but she could not say any more. She absolutely could not do it.

Luke fell silent.

'You mustn't go up there Luke. Not ever.'

'I won't.'

'You mean it? Promise me.'

'I've said so, haven't I? I came back here for you, and for our parents. I was a boy back then. I'm now a man, and I know where my obligations lie. Whatever Ma says, you saved my life, and although she doesn't seem willing to admit it, I'm sure that she owes you a lot too.' He paused. 'She's a tippler, isn't she?' He had seen enough of it among the other navvies to know a drunkard when he saw one.

Bessie did not like the word, but she nodded.

'What have you been doing about it?'

'What *can* I do? She isn't likely to respond to any encouragement from me, now is she?'

'How long has it been going on?'

'A few months.'

'And is she getting better or worse?'

'A bit better,' replied Bessie, with a powerful feeling that her mother would in future be making a considerable effort to improve.

'I have to leave early in the morning,' said Luke. 'Will you say goodbye for me?'

'No I will not! I don't care if you get her up at four o'clock, I'm not facing that look again. "My son's gone, and it's all your fault". No way.'

'But she knows that I'll only be gone for a bit.'

'I don't care. I'm not dealing with it.'

Luke sighed. 'I'll stir her before I go then.' He gave Bessie his word, but just in case he changed his mind, she slept with one eye open – although it proved to be unnecessary. His word obviously stood for more than it had once done, and when he told Marge that he would soon be back again, that was indeed the case.

Considering that it was quite a distance from where he was based, and that he had very little time off, he began to visit with surprising regularity. It was nice. In fact it was wonderful, but it made Bessie uneasy. Was he really this different? This responsible? She felt compelled to follow him when he left, but he always took the short-cut into town, and when he joined the main road, he did not double-back. The relief was really quite immense, and she finally began to calm down, to actually look forward to his visits, rather than viewing them as the harbinger of potential doom.

One visit in November was particularly special, because he managed to be with them for Father's birthday. The last one which Wilf would have to endure in prison. All he had to do now was hold on, and they prayed for him to find the strength to do so. Bessie prayed particularly hard, because she knew it was often the last stretch – when the end was in sight – that proved to be the most difficult.

During November she also heard with sadness about a failed Chartist uprising in Newport. The Somerden Register talked about it, about how it "illustrated the dangers of insurrection", but she knew that their cause was a noble one, and refused to think any differently. Whatever the reasons which had led to volleys of musket fire, she mourned the loss of those who had died. Mourned the sense of a movement which might be fading. The Petition had also been rejected by Parliament, and that fact made her feel guilty as well as sad. Perhaps if she had signed it, rather than running after Gil Tremaine, things might have turned out better.

Of course it was crazy to imagine that one extra name could have held any such power, but nevertheless it felt like she had not contributed as she should have done. Although thankfully she had managed to produce change on a small scale instead. One of the worst oppressors had been brought down, and even if it were necessary to take them one by one, the workers would win out in the end. Of that she had absolutely no doubt.

The following month brought a much happier occasion. Ella's second birthday. It was of course celebrated up at the Hall, and because Bessie had effectively barred herself, she could not attend. The exclusion was unbearable, and with it being the turn of the year, it was naturally too cold for Ella to go outside to see the auntie who loved her so much. Whenever Cynthia went down into the village, Ella would be left in the care of Agatha, and that made Bessie feel even worse, because she could have done it so easily if not for the decisions she had made. But you could not have everything in life. She realised that, and at least she felt close to her niece at the mill.

The weather was so frosty that it was not even feasible to meet Thomas daily in the wood, but it was exciting to share stolen glances across the factory floor. And more than once a week she was called into the manager's office to be "reprimanded" for some defect or other in performance. She enjoyed the kisses which they shared in there, because there was no pressure to go any further, and no atmosphere as a result.

Her evenings were often spent at the Whitson cottage, reading with Peter, and looking after the younger children. They were no replacement for Ella, but each delightful in their own right, and a welcome diversion. She even took them home sometimes, to give Edie and Seamus a break. They said that it made them feel like they were courting again, just the two of them, but having children's laughter in the house did nothing to lift Marge's mood. The only thing which did that was Luke's appearance, but often when he turned up he was only fit for sleeping.

The Marquis of Rowbury was pushing ahead with his railway tracks despite the hostile working environment. It was hard, if not downright cruel, to expect men to move earth when it was frozen solid. But he was another fully-paid-up-member of the "gentry with no heart" brigade, and although it was a begrudging admission, she had to concede that Gil Tremaine was not one of them. He employed Seamus again in the off-season, and it was heartwarming to think that perhaps Seamus was being rewarded with the money which she had secured from Drew. Certainly it was wonderful to see the Whitsons relaxed for the first time in years.

Sunday was now the only day when Thomas and Bessie met up in the wood – come rain, hail or shine –

and she headed up on January the twelfth, feeling the same as usual. Eager to spend time with him, to hear of Ella's development, but worried that he might want to push things onto the next level. It was a very cold day; in fact there was still snow lying on the ground, so surely he would not be interested. She certainly hoped not. Because it spoilt things, and filled her with concern that one day she might not be able to resist. Then what would happen if she fell pregnant? How would she explain it to Mother? And why should she even care?

Having a quick scan around before diving into the wood, she found Thomas waiting for her as usual. No matter how early she arrived, he was always there first. 'I'm not late, am I?'

'Not at all.' He leaped from where he had been leaning against his favourite wizened oak, and grasped her by the hands.

'What is it?' she asked.

'What's what?'

'Something's happened to you.' Bessie peered at him. His eyes were alive, face flushed, hands clammy. It was not something bad, that was for sure.

'Can you feel it?'

'Feel what?'

'The lightness.'

'The light?' She looked around. It seemed to be much the same as ever.

'No, not the daylight. The feeling. In your body. As if you might be able to lift off, and fly.'

Bessie shrugged and tried to smile, beginning to fear that he might be feverish, while at the same time wanting to show that she shared his obvious joy.

'You're free Bessie Cullen. And I can call you that for real now, because it's what you are. Miss Elizabeth Mary Cullen.'

'Am I?' she frowned. 'Why is that?'

'Because you've been released. *We've* been released. From every chain, fetter and obstruction that my father could ever use against us. You're a widow Bessie Cullen. My father's gone and done the only decent thing that he's ever done with his life. He's dead Bessie. My father is DEAD!'

CHAPTER ELEVEN

'Dead?' she repeated.

'Yes. His heart no longer beats, his lungs no longer breathe. There is life no more!' Thomas gave the last word a loud gleeful emphasis, before Bessie's shocked face made him turn all sombre. 'My deepest condolences Mrs Bateford. My heart doth grieve for your loss.' He stared at her for a moment, but then burst back into laughter. 'Isn't it wonderful?'

Wonderful? How could death ever be that? 'What happened?'

'I don't know. Who cares? We can be together now. We can be married.' He still had hold of her hands, and began to dance around her, eventually forcing some movement in response. 'Maybe we can become man and wife the same day as Victoria and Albert? February the tenth. Now that would be special, wouldn't it? Although no, I can't wait that long.' He stopped, clasped her face, and gave her what could only be described as a smacking great kiss, but it was a kiss that was not reciprocated. 'What is it?' he asked, leaning back and studying her properly for the first time.

'I . . . just . . . he was your flesh and blood. I can't understand how you can be so . . .'

'Happy?'

'Yes.'

'But you should be able to understand my happiness better than anyone. After everything that he did to you, to your family. You can't have forgotten it all, surely?'

'I haven't, but . . .'

'But what?' he snapped.

'It doesn't feel right to dance on somebody's grave. Not even his.'

'Dance on his grave? Do you think that if I were dead, he'd do any differently? Do you think that he gave my mother even so much as a cursory thought after he'd driven her to a premature end? If he had, he'd never have married *you*.'

That sounded not only angry, but bitter, and Bessie quickly realised that if she were not careful, this bitterness would soon all be levelled in her direction. 'I'm sorry Thomas. It's such a shock, that's all. I don't know what I'm saying.'

'He was a ruthless man who destroyed more lives than I can count, and if you think I'm going to be a hypocrite now and sugar-coat him, then you're wrong.'

'I wouldn't expect any such thing, and I don't have any feelings of sadness or anything, I promise. It's just . . . I feel a bit sorry for Harris I suppose. He's lost everybody, apart from Charles.'

'Well he's always liked being in Charles' shadow, so he can simply get on with it.' Thomas was still rankled, and suspicious, and worried. 'Unless of course you never wanted to be free, you never wanted to marry me, and my father has just been developing into some convenient excuse.'

Bessie knew that she had to answer very convincingly, and pull herself together, before this got way out of hand. 'I'm not just happy to be free Thomas, I'm ecstatic. To think that in a matter of weeks I can now become your wife – it fills me with such contentment, and such longing Thomas. It fills me with longing.' She drew him towards her with an appalling sense that she was doing exactly the same as with Munroe and Arnold, that it was all an act. Had she been acting so much that she did not even know how she felt any more?

'Kiss me Thomas, and remember – when your lips release mine, it will be as if Arnold never existed. In my head he'll be banished forever. Never to return.'

Thomas breathed deep, beginning to feel hope once more, and kissed her with almost brutal force. But then at last he had to let go, and his eyes searched her soul, seeking out any signs that she would not be true to her word, but there were none. She asked about the funeral, about how soon it would all be over, and when they could start their new life together.

After only a few minutes, she managed to sweep away all memory of her initial response, buried deep beneath the snow which had blown into their special place, and when he was fully settled, she suggested that perhaps they should part for now – or risk catching pneumonia. He agreed, in a totally relaxed manner, and they happily went their separate ways – although Bessie did not turn towards the valley as usual. Instead she simply walked around once Thomas was out of sight, trying to analyse what exactly it was that she did feel.

Hollow was the word which probably best described it. Arnold had not really crossed her thoughts much in the last four months, but he had been her arch-enemy for such a long time. In some ways he had become her reason for living, and he was the only man who had ever known her. It really did feel like a chapter was closing, and once more she was visited by doubts about whether she had gone about it in the right way. He was dead so soon after their separation. Had she contributed to that? Was she the cause? Should she feel guilty? And was she ready to be married again so soon?

She loved Thomas, truly she did, and wanted to be with him, but it meant yet more change, and that was something which had already consumed too much of her life. Not to mention the fact that this marriage would be a far cry from the first. Being Arnold's wife had been part of a mission. Now she would simply be a wife for a wife's sake. Having children, settling down, acting like everybody else. Was she prepared? Or was it conceited to even ask such a question? What gave her the right to think that she was different to any other woman, and what was the point of entering into debate anyway? This was happening, she was going to become a bride once more, and there was nothing that anybody could do about it.

Monday's newspaper made it seem even more real. Arnold Bateford. The words stood out from that obituary column as if the only words on the page. He had died on Friday. The funeral was set for Tuesday at eleven o'clock, where he would be laid to rest alongside his first wife Jane. First wife. So people did realise that there had been a second. Albeit of very brief tenure.

The service was for family members only, and that put Bessie in something of a quandary. Did she constitute family? Should she go? Since hearing the news, her head had been playing through those five months with Arnold in a never-ending loop. Maybe watching his last rites would help put them to bed. Bury a few ghosts. Drew had given her some days off, so she was free to attend, and Thomas had already asked her to do so – although she had a feeling that it was out of a sense of spite.

Thomas wanted Arnold – from wherever he was – to see his eldest son and former wife united by his grave. But could she really blame him for that? He had endured more years of fear than her, and the desire for retribution was an inherent, sometimes overpowering, human instinct. Indeed she had succumbed to it more deeply than most, but ultimately she said no. It was best that she stayed away.

During Monday night, however, she began to slowly change her mind. More silly questions surged to the fore – like whether she owed it to Arnold to say goodbye. Perhaps she did, perhaps not, but having already said no to Thomas, it would have to be done privately – which was probably the more appropriate option anyway. Most of what had happened between her and Arnold had been private, so she would watch from among the trees, as Thomas had done on her wedding-day, and then go to the grave once everybody had left.

It was quite a walk from the mill cottage to Winscott parish church, so she set off early, and upon reaching the second-hand clothes shop on the edge of the village, she bought herself a black coat. Correctly attired, she then trudged on towards the church where she had been married less than a year ago, and arrived in plenty of time to see three carriages pull up within minutes of one another. Louise and Evan; Charles and Harris; Drew, Cynthia and Thomas. That was the extent of it. The obituary had said family members only, so of course there could be nobody else, but would anybody else have come anyway?

As far as she knew, there was no function planned for afterwards. It had always been her belief that a meal was imperative, give the departed a good send-off on their way to heaven, but maybe everybody realised that with Arnold Bateford there was not much of a point. Dead on the Friday. Buried, done and dusted by the following Tuesday. It all seemed so fast – and frankly heartless.

With two minutes to go before the service began, another carriage drew up, and a man followed the others in. She wondered who he was for a while, and then spent the next several minutes numbed by the cold, still as a statue, trying to work out what the right thoughts might be for an occasion like this. Until at last the coffin emerged, carried by Evan, Charles, Harris and Drew. They turned left into an area beyond her line of sight, so she moved forward, entered the grounds, and found herself a safe vantage point.

The vicar was saying a few words, but most of them were lost on the wind which was howling around the headstones. Howling. How apt. It was often said that the weather which accompanied your entry and exit signified your personality more than people might imagine. She knew for a fact that she had been born during a rare summer storm, and was often tempted to use it as an excuse – that she could not help being the way she was. It had been written in the stars.

Once the words stopped, and the vicar bowed his head, the small gathering began to move away. Charles was talking to the stranger, who had also taken a place with the family, and that left Harris hovering. He looked so lost – and desperately in need of a drink. She wanted to go and give him a hug, but of course it was impossible, and thankfully Louise soon crossed over to offer her support.

As they advanced, Bessie shuffled around to the other side of the church, keeping herself concealed, but was stopped in her tracks by a loud bellow.

'I know you're in here!' It was Charles.

He had not seen her, she was sure of it. Was he referring to her? He had to be. Should she run? Hide? Why?

Presenting herself with forthright defiance, she declared: 'Indeed I am,' and quickly approached Thomas. 'I thought you might need me by your side.'

Charles was daggers drawn. 'Couldn't be bothered to attend the service, but wanted to see him plunged into the ground eh?'

'No.'

'Yes! This is the ultimate, isn't it? The final product of all that handiwork of yours.' Charles turned to his aunt and uncle – the only people who were as yet unaware of the truth. 'She isn't real, you know? Lied about everything. Her background. Her name. She's nothing but a common little parlour-maid, with devil juice flowing through her veins.'

He turned back to the object of his loathing. 'My father had a decent reputation, a business, a future before you came along. You killed him. You killed him you devious bitch!'

'Please!' exclaimed the vicar. 'The people buried here are God-fearing souls, in consecrated ground, and such language is an utter abomination.'

'You want to know about abominations vicar, you look at her. And *him*.' Charles proceeded to commit yet another outrage, and spat in Thomas' direction. 'I don't know how you had the audacity to even think of coming here.'

Thomas ignored the spittle – and the abuse – and took hold of Bessie's hand instead. 'Uncle Evan, Aunt Louise, this is Bessie Cullen. She's a good person, far better than any of us Batefords could ever be, and I love her very deeply.'

'You make me sick.' Charles stormed forward, forcing them apart. 'You murdered him, the two of you. He never stood a chance, and you can be damn sure that he'll haunt you for it. In this life and the next.'

'I'm sorry about all this,' said Thomas as Charles and Harris finally left. 'My brother is aggrieved for himself only, that he no longer controls the mill, and that *I* shall soon inherit my father's estate.'

'You?' Bessie frowned.

'I didn't want to say anything until this was over, but it comes to me, doesn't it Mr Winchell? Every last penny.'

The stranger coughed. 'Official discussion of such matters is usually reserved until tomorrow, but I suppose the ceremony has been concluded, so yes, you are the sole beneficiary.'

'But . . .' Bessie was about to say why, but could not even get the word out.

'Because he had no choice. My dear father pretended to the contrary all these years, but some rule means that I have the automatic right as the eldest. And there was nothing he could ever do about it.'

'If you come to my office at a time of your convenience, we can discuss the arrangements more fully,' concluded Mr Winchell, who was finding all this really most unsettling.

'Certainly,' said Thomas, and shook the solicitor's hand as Cynthia approached, offering her congratulations – in a genuine manner.

'Thank you,' he replied. 'But money isn't important. *This* is.' He put his arm around Bessie, and led her towards the Roscoe vehicle, ready to convey her home in style, but she would not accept his offer, so he walked with her – all the way back to the Hall.

'You're coming in,' he announced.

'No, I can't.'

'I'll clear the coast for you, but you're coming in to warm through, and that's that. I won't have you falling ill before our wedding-day like you did before his.'

Bessie knew that arguing was futile, so she scurried up to his room, and was soon glad of his insistence. It was one of those days where no matter how many layers you wore, you would still be cold, and she was indeed freezing.

'What will happen to Harris?' she asked, thawing out by the fire. 'If you now own the house on Erskine Avenue, where will he go?'

'*We* own it,' reminded Thomas.

'But what will happen to him?'

'I don't know. I haven't thought that far ahead. What do you think of the twentieth?'

'The twentieth? You mean this coming Monday?'

'Yes. For our wedding.'

'I . . .' She did not want to say no, but that was far too soon.

'What?' said Thomas, snappy again, and she had to explain the main obstacle – her family, and the fact that Luke was back:

'He only visits, and I thought it was best to keep it from Cynthia and Drew, because of . . . you know? Everything.'

'Very wise.'

'But Luke doesn't know anything about Arnold, you see? Or about you. Nor my mother. They don't even know that I've had proposals of marriage, never mind accepted any. And now there's this inheritance. I need more time.'

'Sorry, but I can't wait.'

'Oh Thomas, I know I said I'd marry you the next day . . .'

'And I'd marry you tomorrow if I could, but Monday is the earliest that the vicar can fit us in.'

'The vicar? You mean in that same church?'

'Yes. Arnold doesn't exist in your head, you said so.'

'Of course . . . I just . . . it's as if I'm drowning.'

'There's no need to feel like that at all.'

'But everything is about to change.' She was beginning to look panic-stricken, so Thomas put his hands upon her shoulders, forced them to lower, and said simply:

'Calm down. Forget everything else. What matters is that we're married. The rest can be left until later.'

'No it can't. What happens *after* we're married? Where will we live? What will we do?'

'Stop panicking. I'll book us a room in town for Monday night, and then you can return to the valley if you like, to your mother, and I can come back here until we sort it all out.'

'You mean go back to the way we are now?'

'Yes.'

'Are you sure?'

'Yes!' Thomas kissed her furrowed brow. 'Do you really think that my father's money matters to me? Because it doesn't. Not one bit. Of course there's a certain satisfaction in knowing that he couldn't keep it from me, but other than that I couldn't care less about claiming my inheritance. All I need is for you to be my wife, and to be happy.'

'You mean it?'

'Absolutely. Drew and Cynthia can be our witnesses, and nobody else need know a thing until you're ready.'

'Oh thank you Thomas, thank you.' She began to relax for real, and kissed him with such relief that he encouraged her to lie down, his hands beginning to explore her body.

'No, no, no,' she giggled. 'You have to wait a few more days for that.'

'No, don't make me wait,' he groaned.

'I have to. I want this to be special. The most special night of our lives, and I know you want that too.' She kissed him again, before springing up from the bed. 'I'm leaving now, before you make me do something I'll regret.' Popping her head out of the door to see if anybody was about, she turned back and whispered: 'I'll see you in the mill tomorrow?'

'You're going back to work?'

'Of course. No changes until I'm ready, remember? And besides, I need to earn money for my dress.'

'No you don't. *I'm* buying that.'

'You can't.'

'Yes I can, and I will.' He stood up. 'I'm adamant.' And in fact on a few more things over the coming days he was equally adamant.

She was instructed to go to The Linton on Sunday evening, and stay there overnight. It was the only inn in town which merited the title of hotel, and Drew's barouche would convey her from there to the church on Monday morning. Then after the ceremony, it would transport the new husband and wife back to their honeymoon suite. Thomas had a perfect picture in mind, and she was soon swept along by it, especially when it dawned on her that Josiah could be there to give her away. He knew everything, and although it was sad that her own father was not free to do it, at least this time there would be somebody special on her side of the aisle.

The days began to pass quickly, and gradually she became more and more excited. Indeed nervous to the point where she was as tense as before her first night with Arnold. It was ridiculous, she was no longer new to it, but there were different concerns, and she simply could not shift them out of her head. Presumably Thomas was still a novice to the lover's game, and it was that thought which scared her most of all. She was afraid of coming across as too experienced, or of the chance that she might start comparing the father with the son. What if she did the ultimate, and actually said Arnold's name? She had become so used to muttering it, because he liked to hear it. That would be horrendous. And then there was the issue of her back. What if Thomas found the sight of it utterly revolting? She had not yet told him anything about the cat-o'-nine-tails.

So many things which might spoil the moment. So many issues which made it impossible for her to sit still for even a second. Edie had no doubt noticed, and Bessie knew that if she was not careful, Marge would too. It was time to regain some control. To keep things in perspective. Thomas loved her, and she loved him back. Everything else was immaterial. All she had to do now was start convincing herself, and as she sank into bed on Friday night, she found herself making good progress.

Mother already knew that she would be spending a few nights with Josiah in town, and Thomas was arranging the hotel and transport, so that meant she could simply concentrate on calming down. There was one more day in the mill, one more evening in the cottage, and then it would be time to head off on Sunday afternoon. Marge was only interested in Luke's upcoming visit, so there would be no awkward questions. No more hurdles to overcome. The date and time were set, this was actually happening, and Bessie now focused on trying to slow the beating of her heart, on thinking positively – and muttering Thomas' name. Three nights of practice ought to ensure that his was the only one anywhere near her lips, and indeed that was already the case as she woke the following morning – or rather was awoken.

She slept downstairs in the back room, while Marge was upstairs, and within a minute of being stirred, Bessie realised that her mother was talking to somebody at the front door, so clambered out to investigate. It was probably inappropriate, but during these bitter nights, she had taken to sleeping in her day clothes. Much warmer than changing and losing what little body heat she had built up. So she was in fact ready to present herself to company – although baffled as to why anybody would be calling at this hour. It was only just coming light. Indeed there was another hour until the factory bell was even due to ring out. Drew believed that better-rested workers were simply better workers, so those six-thirty starts were now a thing of the past.

'Mrs Elizabeth Bateford?' enquired a big fellow in a gruff voice as Bessie reached her mother at the door.

'Er . . . no . . . of course not. I'm Bessie Cullen. Elizabeth Cullen. Mr Bateford used to own these cottages. You seem to be confused.'

'No confusion ma'am. You're the one that we want. We are authorised by the magistrates of Somerden to take you into custody.'

'Custody?'

The man looked over his shoulder, and a second individual walked forward. 'Come nice and easy ma'am. It's always best.'

'Wh . . . wh . . . what?' She clasped a hand to her mouth as breath evaded her. This was a nightmare. A revisiting of that terrible day in 1837. It was not real. It could *not* be real.

'Come on,' he reiterated, and as she was drawn forward, the prison-van came into the view, and she finally found her voice:

'What's all this about? What on earth is the charge?'

'Murder ma'am. You're being charged with murder.'

'Murder? I can't be! This is ridiculous! Where's Mr Matthews? Talk to Mr Matthews.'

'Just get in, and mind your head.' The man steered her towards the van, exactly as Arnold had been steered – and then left to peer out through the bars like an animal.

Before they could inflict that same fate upon her, Bessie stared at her mother, begging her to do something, but should have known better. There was a blank, slightly curious, and ever so slightly pleased look on Marge Cullen's face – and it was not some trick of the dawn. Those eyes had a very real fire of vindication, and hell would freeze over before she even considered providing any assistance.

'Edie! Seamus! Peter!' Bessie began to scream their names because they were the only people who could help her, and mercifully as she was about to be pushed into that awful contraption, Seamus appeared.

'What are you doing? Leave her alone!' He prepared to man-handle one of the constables out of the way, but Bessie urged him not to. She did not want him in trouble as well, and there was nothing that either of them could do to stop this right now.

'Take a message to the Hall Seamus. Tell Mr Roscoe that I've been arrested for murder. Tell him that I need his help.' She did not say: "Tell Thomas", but Drew would see to that, and hopefully Thomas would see to Josiah.

By the time the van door was locked, and the men had climbed back into their seats, quite a crowd had gathered. Last time there had been nobody to hear her cries; now every cottage seemed to be emptying to provide a fully enthralled audience. Bessie stared up at the sky, and knew that Arnold was looking down, head tipped slightly to the side, with that smirk of satisfaction which he did so well. It was his death they were talking about, it had to be, and he was watching her. She could feel his eyes boring holes deep into her flesh, and as she was forced inexorably away from the valley, it was with the sudden certain knowledge that this time she would never be back.

Her journey to gaol took the best part of five hours, not including the various stops, and long before they arrived, she knew where they were going. Henningborough. All capital cases were heard in that town because the courthouse was connected to the men's prison on Ogdell Road, and in the quadrangle of that prison were the gallows, ready for the steady stream of guilty verdicts. So whether you were a man, woman or child, if you were on remand, you went to Ogdell Road.

The prospect of hanging was enough to make anybody's blood run cold, but Bessie was not actually seized by too many chills. According to the paper, Arnold had died on the Friday. She had been at work that day, with hundreds of alibi witnesses – although if his death was Friday night, then she might be in slightly more trouble. Mother had refused to speak, so there was no way that she would intervene positively at trial, but nevertheless Bessie had Thomas, Drew, Mr Matthews, perhaps even Gil Tremaine on her side. Mr Matthews surely knew nothing about this, and when he did, he would help her. Above all else, she was innocent. It did not always count for much, but it imbued her with enough confidence to walk tall as she was thrust into yet another cell.

This one had a very sturdy door. No need for a chain around the ankle in this place, and it was bare, with depressing walls, and that murky air which was all too familiar. No rodents though, so she had known worse, and was now close to her father, which gave her a great sense of comfort.

She saw nobody that day, nor the next, except a procession of different guards who quietly deposited food on a regular basis. But as Monday dawned, she felt hopeful that at last she might see a welcome face. It was supposed to be the day of her wedding, but as long as it was a day where she heard something of what lay ahead, then she would be relatively content. And indeed she did. Come mid-afternoon the door opened, and her good friend appeared.

'Oh Mr Matthews, thank heavens. I don't know what's been happening, but they have this all wrong.'

Fraser swallowed, and eased her onto the bedstead provided to those who were not yet convicted. Innocent until proven guilty did mean something at least.

'You do believe me, don't you? I haven't killed anybody.'

'Of course I believe you.'

'Then you can get me out? I know I've already asked too much of you, but I have the strongest of alibis, so it shouldn't be too difficult.'

'If it were the most Herculean of tasks, I would still undertake it – if I were able.'

'What do you mean?'

'I mean that I am no longer a magistrate.'

'No longer?'

'When you came to me last summer, I was in the process of being . . . well . . . sidelined by certain colleagues because of my unconventional methods, and I am afraid that . . .'

'Having the likes of Arnold arrested was the final straw,' completed Bessie.

Fraser looked down.

'I've cost you your position.'

'No, never think that. My new approach meant that it was only a matter of time before I was put out to pasture. But unfortunately I cannot now assist you as I would wish.'

Bessie's breathing became a little more shallow. 'But . . . it doesn't really matter, does it? Because I have . . . this . . . this alibi . . . so they can't convict me. Can they?'

'From what I gather, the authorities are fully aware of your alibi.'

'Aware?'

'Yes. They know that you are not the one who struck the fatal blow, but it is enough for a murder charge that you conspired with Thomas Bateford, who did.'

'Thomas!'

'Yes. He has also been charged. And unlike you, he has no alibi.'

'Oh dear God.' She put both hands to her throat, but instead of comforting her, Fraser stood up and away. 'Where is he?'

'Here, in the prison.'

'Thomas! Thomas!' She began to scream it, a truly blood-curdling shriek, but it was no good.

'He is being kept in a separate section,' explained Fraser. 'So you cannot converse. Cannot . . . manufacture any kind of story.'

'Manufacture? They're not being serious, are they?'

Fraser did not answer. She would soon be lost, just like his dear Poppy. He could feel it, and he could not stay to watch it. 'All I can do is arrange for you to have an attorney and defence counsel. They will be able to argue your case to best effect.'

Her prison door had been left open, guard outside, and Fraser promptly stepped back over the threshold.

'No, don't go,' she begged.

'I have to.'

'But . . . but my father . . .'

'I enquired after him before coming here. He is fine.' Fraser gritted his teeth. 'Good luck Miss Cullen. I am . . . truly sorry.'

He turned to leave, but she lunged forward and actually grabbed a hold of him. 'Can't you have a word anyway? They might listen, you never know.'

'I have already made entreaties on your behalf. The trial is set for this Wednesday. You will be tried together, and there is nothing else that I can do.' He pushed her away, as gently as possible, and then was gone.

For the next hour Bessie stood swaying in the middle of that room, as if somebody had punched the stuffing out of her, and left a shell not knowing which way to drop. But then at last some stuffing returned, and she paced the cell, thinking hard. Thomas had no alibi – was that correct? Friday . . . Friday . . . think back. He would usually be in the mill, but no, Drew had given him errands to run. What errands? And where was Drew? Why had he not come to see her? If only she could talk to one of them. But nobody else came that day, nor the next morning. It was only after lunch that she at last had another visitor.

'My name is Mr Knowles,' announced a business-like individual. 'I'm acting both for yourself and Mr Thomas Bateford, and it is my job to prepare the case for your counsel in open court.'

'Have you talked to Thomas?'

'Indeed I have.'

'And how is he?'

'He seems quite positive under the circumstances. Now I need to discuss your whereabouts on the morning of Friday the tenth of January. Am I right in thinking that you were working in the mill owned by a Mr Andrew Roscoe?'

'Yes. Can I speak to Drew? I need to speak to him.'

'No. Such contact is not allowed I'm afraid. You were married to the deceased, correct?'

'Yes.'

'And he believed that you were Elizabeth Arabrook, when you were in fact Elizabeth Cullen?'

'Yes.' It sounded bad, and it began to sound even worse as Mr Knowles pursued questions about the reasons for her deception, what had happened to cause the breakdown of her marriage, what her feelings were for Thomas.

'Is all this completely necessary?' she asked, knowing very well that it was, but afraid that if it screamed deceit in her own ears, it would scream even louder in those of a jury.

'If you're concerned about testifying, there is no need. Your counsel believes that in such cases it is wise to say as little as possible, so neither you nor Thomas will be taking to the stand.'

'But then how will we prove our innocence?'

'Mr Zeldack will attack the prosecution witnesses, and present rebuttal evidence, establishing your side of the story. He is a very able advocate, so the best thing you can do is to follow the advice which I gave to your co-defendant. Rest well, and be fresh for the morning. A new set of clothes will be delivered, specifically designed to convey the right impression.'

'But tomorrow is too soon. You haven't prepared anything yet.'

'There is seldom sufficient time in order to prepare properly. We simply do what we can with the time allotted to us. I shall see you in court.'

Bessie leaned against the door once it had shut again, and tried to think with some measure of clarity. This was dreadful. In fact she had a feeling that this was worse than anything that had ever happened before, and soon her options would dwindle to nought. She had to escape. That was the answer. Seduce a guard to make him look the other way. There was nobody around like Garrick, but there was one particular character who seemed potentially . . . persuadable. She could then go on the run. If she made it into the next county, surely they would not find her?

What about Thomas? There was no use in fleeing without him. Could she make the guard free him too? Possibly. She waited impatiently for the next meal to arrive, praying that it would be her chosen target, but it was not.

'Where is he?' She gave a description, but received no response from the man who had come instead.

Leaving it an hour, she called out for water. Another guard appeared, and again she gave the description, but nobody would tell her. Why not? Where had he gone? Should she try with one of the others? Or would it now look so obvious? Was all this a thoroughly stupid idea anyway?

She sat down. Why was she assuming that they were already dead and buried? They were innocent. They might win. Fleeing was an admission of guilt, and frankly was not really in her spirit. Stop and fight – that was the motto of Bessie Cullen. Fight to clear their names.

Straightening her posture, she began to resurrect glimmers of courage, but then Arnold's words jumped aggressively into her head. "The day you stop fearing me is the day you die". That was what he had said after Henderson, and he had meant it, but she had not listened, not properly. Was all this some sort of punishment for what she had done? Putting him in her old cell? Rubbing his nose in the dirt. They said that if you pursued revenge, you ought to dig two graves. Had she been digging her own these last few months, and not even realised it? Digging Thomas' too? She *had* stopped fearing Arnold, it was a fact. When goading him with her true identity, there had been no fear in her heart at all. She had enjoyed it. And now if he had his way, she would be sent to the gallows for it. She would be sent to the gallows – and possibly as soon as tomorrow.

Chapter Twelve

Bessie looked intently in Thomas' direction, and tried to convey something of what she was feeling. They were both in the dock, but chained at opposite ends, so unable to make contact, and whenever she spoke, a guard prodded her between the bars, so it all had to be done in a look. Her emotions were understandably still dominated by fear, but even stronger was a sense of love, and a strange surge of camaraderie. There might only be the two of them, but they were facing this together, just like the Tolpuddle martyrs, a band of brothers. Of course this was not about fighting for a living wage, but it always boiled down to the same thing. Little people against the establishment, and today Thomas and Bessie were the little people assigned with the task.

Unfortunately Thomas did not appear to share her desire to take on anybody. In fact having made visual contact for only a few seconds he then turned away. There were obviously nerves in evidence, and also considerable uncertainty because this was an environment that was all new to him. He had not even been in the witness area when she had faced court before. Plus they both knew what the punishment would be for a guilty verdict. Perhaps that was why he also had an air of penitence, regret that they had been brought to this pitiable state. But it was not his fault. She wanted to allay that thought completely, but he would not turn back and allow her to do so.

The one advantage to being chained to their dock was that the bars surrounding them were much lower as a result. Only waist height, which was far less demeaning, and less suffocating too. Indeed the whole set-up of the court was very different to Somerden. She and Thomas were at the back, facing the judge, and the witness stand was to the side, pointing directly at the jury. Like four sides of a square, with no doubt the lawyers due to prowl around in the middle. It felt ordered, which was comforting, but the positioning of the observers had the main impact. None of them were on the floor of the court; they were all in a gallery running around three sides. Naturally there was nobody over the top of the judge, but people were massed right behind her and Thomas, and on both flanks as well. Surely that incited the throwing of missiles down onto the defendants below? Certainly it gave the whole thing a very gladiatorial essence, and upped the sense of trepidation by a fair few degrees.

It was hard to twist around because of the shackles, but Bessie managed to scan the crowd, and identify who was there. Drew and Cynthia of course, and Luke sitting next to them, which made the day seem even more bizarre. Their faces shared the same expression, and although each of them were dear to her in their different ways, she soon moved on. Mother was not in the courtroom, and Bessie questioned what that might mean. Marge Cullen was clearly not interested in supporting her daughter, but maybe she was not enticed by the idea of watching her hang either. Did a weak flicker of sentiment still exist? Bessie chose not to depress herself by exploring an answer to that particular one, and instead concluded that absence obviously signified death during the daytime, and hence Marge was not required to testify.

Louise and Evan were not present, nor Fraser Matthews, but he had already done enough by providing Messrs Knowles and Zeldack, and she knew that he would find the helplessness unbearable. While at the opposite end of the spectrum, Charles looked set to enjoy the occasion immensely. Bessie wanted to snarl at him, but he would only draw extreme pleasure from it, and so she instead comforted herself with the thought that Harris had chosen to stay away. It must have meant defying a direct order from his brother, but she and Harris had shared a strange sort of bond, and it was nice to think that it might have meant as much to him as it did to her.

The positive swell evaporated, however, as she realised that Josiah was not in the room. Thomas had presumably been arrested on the Saturday too, so could not have sent a message, and Drew might not even be aware of Josiah. She hoped to goodness that he had not been waiting to be taken to the church on Monday, only for nobody to appear. Surely something as major as a murder trial would have featured in the Somerden Register? Word would have spread. Perhaps he simply could not make the trip, and perhaps it was for the best that he did not witness something like this again.

The good thing about being in Henningborough was that there were not too many Somerden residents here at all. Certainly not the lines of mill workers gawking as before. Just a couple of faces this time. Would they be testifying to her presence at the mill that day? Hopefully. Although why Mr Winchell was in attendance, she simply could not understand. And last but not least there was Gil Tremaine. Somehow he always gave her a sense of being able to solve anything – as long as he was in the right mood of course – but even he would be hard pressed to get them out of this one.

She was not sure about the time, but there seemed to be some delay, and that filled her with relief rather than impatience. Mr Knowles was talking earnestly to Mr Zeldack, and this extra time could be giving them the chance to polish their line of attack. The fate of two people lay completely in their hands, and she wondered whether they appreciated the significance of that austere position. Or took little interest if such souls were won or lost. It was simply the way that they had chosen to make a living.

As soon as she had begun to pray for the delay to persist, proceedings got underway with the arrival of Judge Ingram. He was appropriately formidable, and encouraged his attendant to kick-start affairs even before he had sat down. A judge in a hurry. Bessie swallowed. That did not feel good at all.

'The charge on the indictment records that on the tenth of January this year, Arnold Thomas Bateford and Elizabeth Mary Bateford did maliciously and feloniously conspire to assault Mr Bateford senior with such severity that he did die as a result of his injuries. First defendant, how do you plead?'

The attendant's voice was incisive, and it was strange to hear Thomas referred to as Arnold Thomas. In fact it almost felt like a horrid slur, but of more immediate concern was that neither she nor Thomas knew who the first defendant was supposed to be. Was it the person whose name had been read out first? Mr Zeldack nodded in Thomas' direction, which gave them the answer.

'Not guilty, my lord.'

'It's "your worship", not "my lord".'

'Sorry,' said Thomas, and mumbled a proper repeat.

'Second defendant, how do you plead?'

'Not guilty,' declared Bessie, and was loath to add "your worship". People's lives were at stake here. What did silly titles matter? But ultimately self-preservation prevailed, and compliance overtook defiance.

'Let's proceed then,' ordered Judge Ingram, and stared directly at Bessie. 'For the purposes of this trial, your marriage to the victim shall be viewed as lawful, and you shall be addressed as Mrs Bateford.' He flashed his focus across the dock. 'To avoid any confusion, you shall be referred to as Thomas, and the victim as Mr Bateford. Is that clear?'

Thomas said yes, and then with all that sorted, Judge Ingram flicked his wrist at a man who turned out to be prosecution counsel.

'Gentlemen of the jury,' began a dapper-looking individual with an extremely confident edge. 'Today you will be hearing accounts of lust, greed and manipulation. The prisoners at the bar stand accused of a crime which is one of the worst on our country's statute book. That of murder.' He boomed the word for dramatic effect. 'And once we have examined the evidence, you will be left in absolutely no doubt as to their guilt.' He usually said so much more – found opening addresses to be a wonderful opportunity to employ some delightfully powerful prose – but Judge Ingram would shoot it down in flames, so he proceeded expeditiously to the first witness: 'Mr Bellamy Jones.'

Bessie knew that name, but could not think where to place it, until a man rose from his seat behind her, and made his way down to the stand. It was Arnold's butler of course, the one who had gone with his master to Erskine Avenue.

'Do you swear that you shall present the truth, the whole truth, and nothing but the truth, so help you God?' The attendant rushed out the words, having said them a thousand times, and Bellamy replied:

'I do,' before being asked by the prosecutor to explain the nature of his relationship with the victim. 'I was his butler.'

'And for how many years did you hold this position?'

'Er . . . well . . .' Bellamy started to count.

'More years than you care to remember?'

'Yes.'

'And so you were in his service at both Erskine Avenue where the crime took place, and at his previous residence – Bateford Hall?'

'That's right.'

'It was September of last year when the victim left Bateford Hall, sold his business, and moved into the centre of town, is that correct?'

'Yes.'

'And why did he make such a move?'

Mr Zeldack stood up. 'How can the witness be expected to recount what was in the mind of his employer four months ago?'

'I shall rephrase,' sighed Mr Pennington. 'What did you observe during this time?'

'Well . . . there seemed to be a bit of trouble over an inspection of the factory, and then Mr Bateford was taken into custody for a few days.' He paused, anticipating that counsel would say something, but there was silence, so he carried on. 'Then when he was released, half of the mill was sold to Mr Roscoe, but . . . that arrangement didn't quite work out, so Mr Bateford signed over the rest . . . and left.'

It was a short account of events, but gave the prosecutor enough juicy morsels to get his teeth into.

'Trouble over an inspection you say? Are you aware that this "inspector" was not in fact an inspector at all, but masqueraded as one, under the direction of Mr Roscoe?'

'No. No, I wasn't aware.'

Bessie knew that unless Bellamy had overheard the events of the thirteenth of September, then he would be unaware of rather a lot of things, but that was not the point. The prosecution could introduce all this apparent treachery into evidence by playing through a series of Yes or No.

'But you observed the tactics which Mr Roscoe employed once he had a share of the mill?'

'Yes,' replied Bellamy, and counsel nodded to encourage him to elucidate. 'He closed down his half, and put men on guard so that Mr Bateford couldn't enter the mill.'

'He was looking to sever the victim's income, and force him to sell his remaining half?'

'Yes.'

'Which eventually he did?'

'Yes.'

Mr Pennington stared at the jury, and pursed his lips as if to say: "That sort of approach might just about be legal, but dirty tricks nevertheless".

'Now then,' he continued. 'Can you please recount for us the events of the tenth of January?'

'I rose at the usual hour, and . . . took up my post as expected. Breakfast was prepared, but none of the family attended, and I began to wonder whether I ought to knock on Mr Bateford's door, but . . .'

'You didn't?'

'No, I . . . I thought he might require some extra rest.'

'What happened next?'

'He came down at around eleven, and told me that I was not in fact needed. That I should return to my quarters below-stairs.'

'Did he make any enquiries as to food?'

'No.'

'And was this typical behaviour for Mr Bateford?'

Bellamy coughed. 'Not exactly . . . typical, but . . . more recently . . .' He ground to a halt.

'More recently the victim had been drinking heavily, and his normal daily routine had slipped.'

Mr Zeldack rose to his feet with a look of exasperated protest.

'Yes, yes,' said the judge, who did not need to hear the reason. 'Try not to put words into the mouth of your witness Mr Pennington.'

'Sorry your worship.' The prosecutor bowed in deferential submission, and then turned back to Bellamy. 'Had Mr Bateford been drinking heavily in the period leading up to his death?'

'Yes.'

'Probably little wonder after losing his mill in such a manner.'

That remark was unnecessary, but seemed to provoke a certain level of agreement from among the jury.

'When did you go back above-stairs?'

'Just after twelve thirty.'

'And why was that?'

'It was nearly time for lunch, and the cook needed to know whether to prepare anything specific.'

'What did you find above-stairs?'

'I found . . .' Bellamy put a hand to his mouth in discomfort. 'I found Mr Bateford dead.'

'Where was his body?'

'The drawing room.'

'Whereabouts in the drawing room?'

'On the floor.'

'Did you notice anything else?'

'I saw that there was a bottle by his side. Whisky I think.'

'So you can categorically tell this court that the victim was alive at eleven, but dead at twelve thirty?'

'That's correct.'

'Did you hear anything else during this period? Raised voices for instance?'

'No.'

'But presumably you wouldn't have done so from where you were situated anyway?'

'Really!' exclaimed Mr Zeldack, and knowing that he was about to be admonished, Mr Pennington quickly added:

'I only have one more question your worship. Upon finding the body Mr Jones, did you immediately send word to Doctor Driscoll, who lives at number seventy-three Erskine Avenue?'

'Yes I did.'

'Thank you, that is all.'

Now it was the turn of the defence to try and make that sound a whole lot better.

'Disregarding what Mr Pennington *thinks* you may or may not have been able to hear, I would like you to confirm that you were aware of nothing during that whole hour and a half. Nothing happening above you whatsoever.' Mr Zeldack set Bellamy, making it quite clear that he wanted the truth, not the prosecution's take on it. But there was no need. Bellamy had no idea what had befallen Mr Bateford, and was simply here to say what he did know, and then leave.

'I didn't hear anything, and neither did the rest of the staff.'

'Prosecuting counsel will be painting a picture of a victim struck over the head, perhaps with that whisky bottle, ultimately leading to death, but I contend that there is a perfectly rational alternative . . .'

'Is there a question on the way?' interrupted Mr Pennington, and Zeldack offered assurances that he was just coming to it:

'Could you describe the deceased's general condition when you saw him at eleven o'clock?'

'Yes, he was . . . er . . . slightly . . .'

It was as if the whole court was desperate to add: "The worse for wear", but Bellamy got there himself in the end.

'So he was drunk?' clarified Mr Zeldack.

'Yes.'

'And was whisky his usual tipple of choice?'

'For many years it had been port, but yes, he had recently turned to whisky.'

'Did anybody call during this hour and a half?'

'No.'

'Presumably if they had, you would have heard the doorbell, even below-stairs.' Mr Zeldack glanced at his opposite number, and Bessie received the first very palpable impression of how much these lawyers enjoyed sparring with one another, and how little it probably meant to them.

'The bell rings in the staff quarters, so yes I would have heard it.'

'And did you see either of the defendants that day?'

'No, I hadn't seen them for some months.'

'So to summarise . . .' Mr Zeldack made sure that he had the jury's full attention. 'The deceased enters his drawing room, drunk, and we can perhaps surmise that he pours himself yet another beverage. Nobody calls. There are no signs of an altercation or any commotion, and Mr Bateford is later found dead with a bottle of his favourite tipple by his side.' It was important to finish with a question. 'Is that the position according to your evidence?'

'Yes,' replied Bellamy.

'The sad and lonely death of a drunkard,' concluded Mr Zeldack, and when Mr Pennington stood up, he quickly made it clear that he had no further lines of enquiry. So the prosecution then proceeded to call Doctor Driscoll, and the man who had been sitting next to Gil, now took up Bellamy's place in the spotlight.

'Can you state your name and occupation please?'

'My name is Anthony Driscoll. I am a surgeon-apothecary, and also medical officer to the Somerden Poor Law Union.'

'You have a surgery at your home on Erskine Avenue, is that right?'

'Yes it is.'

'Can you now please detail for the court the events of Friday the tenth of January as you saw them?'

Doctor Driscoll swallowed and began. 'I was in my surgery, with my last patient before lunch, when a maid from Mr Bateford's house came running in, seeking medical assistance for her employer. I attended the scene, but there was nothing that could be done. Mr Bateford had been dead for at least half an hour before I arrived.'

'What did you observe as to the cause of death?'

'There was vomit around the deceased's mouth. Also coagulated blood on the back of his head, and the presence of petechial haemorrhaging caused by the extravasation of blood in the eyes.'

'In layman's terms please.' Mr Pennington could tell that almost every word of that had flown right over his jury's head.

The doctor nodded, spent a minute trying to work out how much simplification was required, and then announced: 'My original finding was that the deceased had fallen, knocked his head, and suffocated as a result of vomit blocking the airway.'

There were a few wrinkled noses in the court at that point.

'You say *original* finding?'

'Yes. It was only when the constables came to me on Thursday that I began to question whether the deceased might have received a blow to the back of the head.'

'Do you now believe that such a blow is indeed the case?'

'No. His body was found next to the fireplace, and there was blood on the surrounds, which suggests a fall with his head impacting upon the grate.'

'But you cannot discount the possibility that the fall was caused by a push?'

'No, I cannot discount it.'

'If . . .' Mr Pennington took pains to stress the word and avoid any potential objection. '. . . the victim had been pushed, would he have been conscious following the assault? In other words – would Mr Bateford have been awake when suffocating on that blockage of vomit?'

'Possibly. In fact . . . probably.'

Prosecution counsel turned to the jury. 'So Thomas might well have stood there, watching his father writhing in agony, helpless, haemorrhaging, choking, and ultimately dying?'

'Your worship, surely this is . . .'

Judge Ingram flicked his wrist again. He knew it was unacceptable. 'Watch your step Mr Pennington.'

'My apologies.' Another bowed head of false submission. 'One final question Doctor Driscoll. Is it true that the blow to the head, however caused, led to the victim's death?'

'Yes . . . I should say so. It is unlikely that he would have choked without it.'

'Thank you.'

Mr Zeldack then took over as Mr Pennington sat down. 'So Doctor Driscoll, your assessment of the scene, and of the body, did not lead you to suspect any foul play whatsoever?'

'That is correct.'

'And in your opinion, Mr Bateford was not hit across the head?'

'I believe the head-wound was caused by impacting on the edge of his fireplace.'

'Did the scene reveal any signs of a struggle?'

'No, the only thing out of place was the whisky bottle.'

'Which was not even broken?'

Doctor Driscoll provided confirmation, and Mr Zeldack glanced in the direction of the jury before deciding that he would make it crystal clear:

'Surely a confrontation would have led to it being smashed into a thousand little pieces, instead of merely dropping out of the deceased's hand as he fell?'

'I cannot really speculate,' replied the doctor, which saved Mr Pennington the trouble.

'The prosecution are seeking to establish that a push was involved, but you saw no evidence of that?'

'I saw no evidence either way.'

'So to conclude, as far as you're concerned, there is absolutely no basis for suggesting that anybody else was even in that room?'

'Yes, that is the position as I see it.'

'Mr Bateford was simply drunk, fell over, and died?'

'Correct.'

Mr Zeldack resumed his seat, satisfied. There were some good prosecution witnesses to come, so it was important to win over the ones like Doctor Driscoll, and medical men often held good sway with juries.

'The prosecution calls Mr Charles Bateford.'

Bessie and Thomas both took a deep breath. The best that they could hope for was that Charles went so over the top with personal animosity that he sounded vindictive, and hence unbalanced. But it soon became apparent that unbalanced was not in fact to be the case. Mr Pennington had already advised Charles that in terms of conviction, a cold outlining of the facts – accompanied by dignified grief – would work to best effect.

'Mr Bateford, is it alright if the court addresses you as Charles, in order to avoid any risk of confusion?'

'Yes, absolutely fine.'

'Thank you.' Mr Pennington cast his gaze down, as if to emphasise that there was now a lot of material that needed to be covered. 'I must first take you back to the September of 1838, which was when Mrs Bateford came to work for your father, correct?'

'Yes.'

'And she said that her name was Elizabeth Arabrook?'

'She did.'

'When it was in fact . . ?'

'Elizabeth Cullen. She had only just been released from prison after serving a year's sentence for breaking into our house.' Charles almost added more, but had been advised to let it out in short, damning statements.

'Why do you think then that she applied for the role of nursemaid?'

Mr Zeldack was forced onto his feet again. 'It is not for the witness to start guessing as to my client's state of mind.'

'I am not asking him to guess,' countered Pennington. 'Merely to offer us his opinion based upon intimate knowledge of the events over the last sixteen months.'

'Proceed,' ruled the judge.

'I think that she was fixed upon revenge right from the start,' announced Charles.

'And none of you recognised her?'

'No. She had altered her appearance most considerably.'

'Now as to your brother Thomas. How would you describe his relationship with your father?'

'Strained. In fact they were continually at odds, which is why my father put me in charge of the mill.'

'Your father did not feel that Thomas was trustworthy?'

'Not trustworthy at all.'

Bessie was sure that there should have been an objection at that point, but then again it would have been fairly futile. The power was in the prosecution's question.

'In April last year, your father married the accused, still believing that she was Miss Arabrook, is that correct?' Mr Pennington stood squarely in front of Bessie.

'Yes.'

'And . . .' He shifted along the front of the dock towards Thomas. '. . . your brother disappeared?'

'Yes.'

'Did you have any idea as to why?'

'Not at the time, no.'

'But the events of September the thirteenth gave you a greater understanding of this issue?'

'Yes they did.' Charles' eyes held a sudden gleam as if they had now reached the fun part, and the next several minutes were taken up with exploring that particular day – and the full glory of what it signified.

Bessie would have preferred to have blocked up her ears. Every conclusion was worse than the last. Thomas returned, which meant that he had known all along about the date set for his father's downfall. It was immediately obvious that she and Thomas were lovers, and had probably been so since long before her marriage. She had conspired with Drew Roscoe to deprive Arnold of his business, and Arnold had never suspected. She was a consummate liar, Thomas was enraptured, and having schemed to destroy Arnold, they had then gone the whole hog and killed him.

'But when your father was found dead, you didn't automatically assume that it was murder?' pointed out Mr Pennington.

'No,' conceded Charles. 'I was in shock. I didn't really know what to think.'

'Where were you when your father died?'

'I was in the house, on Erskine Avenue. Upstairs with my brother Harris.'

'You did not partake of breakfast that morning?'

'No. We all overslept. It had been a late night, but Harris and I were about to head down for lunch when the alarm was raised.'

'Do you accept that your father had been drinking to excess in the weeks before he died?'

'Yes. He had been having difficult coming to terms with what had been perpetrated against him.' Charles resisted the urge to glower in Bessie's direction.

'So what changed your mind about the cause of death?'

'The funeral,' he declared with an affronted sniff. 'They attended . . .'

'And by "they", you mean the two accused?'

'Yes, and they were frankly . . . flaunting themselves. Gloating over my father's grave. I found it intolerable, and immediately decided that I owed it to his memory to call in the constables.'

'And what did the constables discover?'

'Evidence that a window on the ground floor of our home had been forced open.'

That prompted a few murmurs from around the court, and more worryingly from among the jury.

'You hadn't noticed it before?'

'No, it was in the library, not the drawing room, and the glass in the window wasn't broken. Only the catch.'

'Do you believe that your brother Thomas bore such malice to your father that he could actually have killed him?'

Charles swallowed, stared directly at the jurors, and declared: 'I'm afraid that I do, which is awful as I feel terribly responsible. I really should have seen it coming. I should have done something to stop it, because I heard him threaten my father with this dreadful act on a previous occasion.'

'Threaten?'

'Yes, to kill him.'

'Kill him?' seized the prosecutor, as if it was the first time that he had heard such dramatic news.

'Yes.'

'And it was not an off-the-cuff remark, made say . . . in jest?'

'No. It was a very deliberate and serious statement. He said: "One day I'll kill you". I can remember it as if it was yesterday.'

'And when exactly was this?'

'Shortly after Miss Cullen joined the staff at Bateford Hall.'

'Thank you Charles.' Mr Pennington said it with almost sycophantic gratitude. Poor Charlie had been through such an ordeal, but had done it all for the sake of justice.

Mr Zeldack rose slowly, still debating how best to tackle this individual, and ultimately opting for the diplomatic approach. Too aggressive and it might alienate the jury, who appeared to have been drawn in. Better to simply pick at as many facts as possible.

'I know that this is distressing for you,' he began, trying not to tip into toadyism. 'But we now have to explore one or two details in greater depth. Firstly the issue of this window. You say the constables discovered the forced lock, but that you did not?'

'Correct.'

'Do you often spend time in the library?'

'Not very often.'

'It is therefore quite reasonable that you didn't notice anything wrong yourself?'

'Yes, perfectly reasonable,' replied Charles in a somewhat curt tone. 'In fact I doubt that anybody would have noticed unless they had actually come to open it.'

'And of course being winter, nobody is likely to do such a thing?'

'Precisely.'

"Good", thought Mr Zeldack. Just the answer that he had been looking for. 'You moved into the property last September?'

'Yes.'

'And do you recall having ever opened that window?'

'Well . . .' Charles hesitated.

'Being autumn and then winter, I think we would all find it rather strange if you had.' That ought to block out any thoughts of lying.

'I have no such recollection.'

'So this lock, which we are being led to believe was broken by Thomas in his murderous pursuit of your father, might actually have been broken since the day you moved in?'

'Well . . .' Charles looked to the prosecution bench, but Mr Pennington was unable to dream up any useful intervention. 'Possibly,' came the eventual reply.

'Did you see Thomas at Erskine Avenue that day or any other?'

'No, but . . .'

'And you have no evidence that Mrs Bateford betrayed her vows with Thomas or any other man?'

'No, but they plotted against my father, so what does that tell you?'

'*Mrs* Bateford did indeed plot against her husband,' clarified Zeldack. 'Assisted by Mr Roscoe, but there is no proof that Thomas was actually involved at all. Is there?'

'He came back on the very day that she revealed what she'd done!'

'But I put it to you that his return was mere coincidence.'

'Coincidence?' scoffed Charles.

'Yes, because it is the only explanation which makes any sense.'

The witness frowned.

'If, as you maintain, the two defendants were lovers plotting your father's demise, why did Thomas leave before the marriage even took place? Why did he not stay to assist Mrs Bateford in this "plotting"? To persist with their illicit relationship under your father's very nose?'

'I don't know. Maybe he wanted to distance himself from it all.'

'Distance himself? By living a few miles away, and biding his time?'

'Yes, probably.'

'So it would surprise you to know that during the five months that he was away, he was here in Henningborough, employed at the ironworks.' Mr Zeldack crossed over to the jury, and then peered at Charles expecting an answer.

'I didn't know.'

'No doubt you are also ignorant of what the ironworks really mean, but those of us who are residents of Henningborough understand exactly what it is like to live in its shadow, and very few of us would ever choose to work there unless utterly destitute.' Mr Zeldack tipped his head towards the jury, seeking confirmation from fellow Henningborough comrades, and many of them did indeed have knowing looks.

'So,' he continued. 'I would suggest that Thomas chose to work in such an inhospitable environment because he needed to earn a living, and never in fact envisaged a return to Bateford Hall. His return was indeed a coincidence, and he was in no way involved in any plotting whatsoever.'

'I don't agree,' was all Charles could say.

'There has long been bad blood between you and your older brother, isn't that correct?'

'We've never really . . . seen eye to eye.'

'You resent him for being older, don't you? The one person standing between you and that first-born status.' Mr Zeldack suddenly realised that he was being more forceful than planned, but decided to go with an increasingly effective flow.

'I resent his disloyalty to our father,' came the inflamed retort.

'So much so that you are now willing to ascribe him with murderous intentions which never actually existed.'

'He threatened to kill, and that's the truth of it!' Charles stood very tall, and very angry indeed.

'I don't doubt it,' countered Mr Zeldack, expertly deflecting the indignation. 'But if you cast your mind back, I think you'll recall that it was only said after Thomas had received multiple blows from your father who was kicking him in the ribs while down on the floor.'

That did not receive a comment.

'Isn't *that* the truth of it sir?'

'Yes, but . . .'

'Is there any man among us who wouldn't swear some sort of vengeance when reduced to that state?' Mr Zeldack spread his arms out, scanning the gallery, before pressing home his advantage: 'You've already testified that you were upstairs when your father died?'

'Yes.'

'And you didn't hear anything?'

'Well . . . I'm not sure. I may have heard . . . a thud.'

'You may have heard a thud? I see. And why haven't you mentioned this before?'

'I've only just remembered it.'

'Come sir, what really happened is that you and Harris were upstairs, all the staff were below-stairs, and nobody heard a single thing from anybody, because there was nothing to hear.'

'I . . . no . . .'

'You want the defendants to be convicted because you have your own axe to grind. You hate them both, but the evidence doesn't quite support your claims, does it? Mrs Bateford plotted against her husband because of the unjust misery he inflicted upon her family. She had cause to want him dead, but was working in a mill with hundreds of witnesses at the time. While as for Thomas – he has no such alibi, but wasn't responsible for any plotting, and had no such motive. So being as neither of them has all of the required elements – motive, means *and* opportunity – you are looking to connect them through some conspiracy which never existed, and force the law to view them as a pair.'

Mr Pennington had risen to his feet very early on in that speech, but Mr Zeldack had stuck to his guns, browbeaten the objection, and now said: 'Isn't that an accurate reflection of the state of things?'

'No!' slammed Charles, and went on to refute it with admirable passion, but Zeldack promptly sat down, leaving Pennington's star witness to appear rather desperate and on the back foot.

Bessie wanted to clap, but just about managed to control herself. And it was a good thing too, because such an action would not have gone down well with the male jury – who all continued to listen with an open mind – until the final prosecution witness took to the stand.

'Can you provide the court with your occupation please Mr Winchell?'

'I am a solicitor. Arnold Bateford's solicitor.'

'Can you please explain what happened at your office on the morning of January the tenth?'

'Yes.' He seemed unsettled again, but the more he focused on the law, the more relaxed he became, and was able to speak clearly:

'Thomas came to see me, to enquire as to whether or not there were grounds for annulment regarding the marriage of his father to Elizabeth Arabrook. On the basis that Arabrook isn't in fact her real name.'

'And what would annulment have meant?'

'The contract of marriage would have been rendered void. Legally it would no longer have held any force whatsoever.'

'Do you believe that such grounds existed?'

'That depends on whether you view the union as void or voidable.'

'Please explain.' Mr Pennington stood right next to the jury to ensure their attention did not stray. This might be dry stuff, but it was very, *very* important.

'If the contract is void, then it is regarded as having never taken place, and can be so treated by both parties, without the necessity for any decree of annulment.'

'And voidable?'

'The union is regarded as valid and subsisting until a decree annulling it has been pronounced.'

'In your learned opinion Mr Winchell, which term applied to the marriage in question?'

'Voidable.'

'So that means the need for a decree. And would this decree have happened if the victim had objected?'

'No, I consider that to be most unlikely.'

'I see.' Mr Pennington soon received the impression that he was one of only a few people who "saw", and prepared to paraphrase – after one more question: 'Did you convey this judgement to Thomas?'

'Yes I did.'

'So Thomas came to you, looking for annulment, and you told him in really quite blunt terms that it wouldn't happen unless his father agreed to it?'

'That's right.'

'How did he react?'

'He seemed particularly disappointed. Angry even.'

'Why?'

'Because he was convinced that his father's consent would never be secured.'

'And did you go on to discuss anything else during this meeting?'

'We moved onto the issue of inheritance, and I informed Thomas that he would automatically receive everything in the event of his father's death.'

'Informed?'

'Yes. He appeared to be unaware of this entitlement.'

'But why would the victim leave the entirety of his estate to a son with whom he was at considerable odds?'

'He had no choice in the matter,' explained Mr Winchell. 'In fact Arnold didn't even make a formal declaration of his wishes after death because he knew that primogeniture would apply.'

'Primogeniture being the right of succession belonging to the first-born.'

'That's correct. Arnold's father had modified the rule so that it would apply only to the male line, but Arnold knew that he could make no other changes.'

'This meeting with Thomas – it was at your office, wasn't it? In Somerden?'

'Yes it was.'

'Only a few streets away from Erskine Avenue in fact?'

'Yes.'

'And at what time?'

'Nine thirty until about . . . ten fifteen.'

'So he left your office at ten fifteen, only minutes away from the home of his father, with all this information ringing remorselessly in his ears?'

Mr Zeldack felt like making it clear to the court that his opposite number was about to enter one of his famous repetitive phases, but knew that he himself might need recourse to such a tactic before too long.

'That is when he left, yes,' confirmed Mr Winchell.

'Do you know where Thomas went afterwards?'

'No.'

'Or why he was interested in the annulment of his father's marriage?'

'I received the impression that he wished to marry her himself.'

'Marry her himself,' repeated Mr Pennington with a wry look towards the jury. 'Lovers indeed.'

'If the prosecution is suggesting that my clients have committed adultery, then I feel compelled to argue that it is neither a legitimate nor rational conclusion from the evidence of this witness.' Mr Zeldack was really quite indignant, and the judge supported him in that indignation, prompting Mr Pennington to pause – before pressing on regardless. Finishing with a flourish could well prove fatal to the opposition, and he was not going to pass it up purely because of one objection.

'Defence counsel would like us to believe that having walking all the way into town on a bitter January morning, Thomas took this news in his stride, and simply toddled off back home,' he began flippantly. 'That his father dying on this very day is nothing more than mere "coincidence", and that we should read absolutely nothing into it. Do you think that such a hypothesis is rational? Or ludicrously absurd?'

'I don't know. It isn't for me to say.'

That was bound to be the answer, but it did not bother Mr Pennington in the least. 'Surely it is more likely that Thomas stalked the streets of Somerden, churning over what he perceived to be the various injustices of life, becoming increasingly resentful, boiling with anger, and then making a bee-line for Erskine Avenue, to act upon that anger in the most heinous manner?'

'I cannot say which is more likely than the other,' replied Mr Winchell with unfaltering fairness.

'Can't you? Thomas discovered that not only would the love of his life be locked into marriage until Arnold died. He also discovered that Arnold's death would bring considerable riches. Two birds with one stone. Surely a motive for murder if ever there was one.'

Mr Winchell did not respond.

'Indeed not just the one motive, but two. Lust *and* greed. In the mind of a man who had previously threatened to kill.'

'Prosecution counsel is presenting a closing argument, not examining his witness,' sighed Mr Zeldack, but the damage had already been done, and he knew it. He also knew that it was going to be nigh on impossible to discredit a solicitor like Mr Winchell who had offered only facts, not speculation.

While he made an attempt, Bessie looked towards Thomas, but still he would not look back. Running errands for Drew – that was what he had been doing. That was what he *said* he had been doing. But it was all a lie. He had lied to her. Lied over something so very important, although she could hardly complain, could she? And none of this was his fault anyway. By visiting Mr Winchell on that day of all days, Thomas had given himself motive, means and opportunity; but he would never have even been there if she had not been so stubborn. If she had just consented to loving him, annulment would never have crossed his mind. If she had slept with him as she had slept with Arnold a hundred times before. But she had held back. For some utterly insane reason she had held back, and now they faced punishment because of it. Hanging by their necks until dead. How could that be? How could such consequences stem from such a small decision? And how on earth could she keep it from costing them both their lives?

CHAPTER THIRTEEN

Judge Ingram did not wish to hear any defence witnesses until he had taken time out for sustenance, and it ended up being a ridiculously long affair. Bessie and Thomas were given plenty of opportunity back in their cells to assess if the evidence against them was currently overwhelming, in their favour, or in the balance. Mr Winchell had been damaging, there was no getting away from it, but nobody had seen Thomas at the scene, and there remained substantial question-marks over whether the death even constituted a murder at all. In Bessie's mind that added up to reasonable doubt. Yes, as she was chained once more to her end of the dock, she had become convinced that the overall picture was one of too much doubt to convict.

'The defence calls Hazel Gibson.'

Bessie did not recognise the name, but recognised the face – a fellow worker from the mill, and Mr Zeldack only had one issue to explore:

'Was the second defendant in the mill on the day in question?'

'Yes.'

'All day?'

'Yes.'

'What about lunchtime?'

'I don't know.'

Bessie knew. She had spent the time with Edie and Peter, but Edie was not in court to testify to that fact.

Why not? Bessie became nervous – until Mr Zeldack made sure that it did not matter:

'How long is the lunch break Miss Gibson?'

'An hour.'

'And was anybody absent when work resumed?'

'No. Mr Roscoe rewards punctuality and good work, so usually we're all back before time.'

'A break of less than an hour then? Hardly enough time to reach Somerden, commit murder, and be ready once more at your machine.' Mr Zeldack addressed that comment towards the jury, before promptly taking a seat as Mr Pennington rose from his.

"Surely there isn't anything to challenge", groaned Bessie, and it seemed that she was right. He declared that he had no questions, and it gave her a further boost. But when they came to the final mill witness, prosecution counsel suddenly changed his mind.

'So Mrs Yardy, you say that the defendant was working alongside you on the tenth of January?'

'Yes.'

'And as far as you were concerned, she was Elizabeth Cullen?'

'Bessie Cullen, yes.'

'You had no idea whatsoever that your new colleague was in fact the victim's wife?'

'No . . . I mean yes.' Val Yardy was not confused as to her memory, it was merely the phrasing of the question. 'Yes, I had no idea.'

'So she lied to you?'

'Not really. She just didn't say.'

'What would you have done if she *had* said?'

'What do you mean?'

'Would you have treated her any differently?'

'I doubt it.' Val had the look of a woman who could not understand why she was facing an interrogation when nobody else had.

'What did you think about the victim, Mr Bateford?'

'I . . . nothing. He was the Master.'

'But was he a good Master?'

'Er . . . well . . .'

'Answer the question,' directed the judge.

'I don't know what you mean by good.'

'Was he well-liked?' clarified Mr Pennington, glad that this witness was beginning to appear evasive.

'Not really.'

'So everybody at the mill prefers Mr Roscoe at the helm?'

Mr Zeldack stood up with his usual objection. How could one individual be expected to answer for the opinions of another?

'I shall rephrase. Do you prefer Mr Roscoe as your employer?'

'Yes, and so does everybody else.' Mrs Yardy looked at the dock, convinced that she was saying exactly the right thing.

'You're now aware that Mrs Elizabeth Bateford played a part in the transfer of the business, is that correct?'

'Yes.'

'So you know that if not for her, you'd still be under Mr Bateford's employ?'

'Yes, that's been the talk.'

'Which means that effectively Mrs Bateford has acted as some sort of saviour?'

Mr Zeldack was not sure whether to object, and before he could decide, the witness had provided whole-hearted agreement.

'I see. So you expect this court to believe that if you had known of her "saviour status", you would not have treated her any differently?'

'Well . . .' Mrs Yardy swallowed.

'Surely you would have felt some sort of gratitude towards her, and wished to express that in some way?'

'I suppose a few of us might have given her a slap on the back.'

'A slap on the back? Of course. Or perhaps . . .' Mr Pennington wandered off towards the jury. '. . . you might have chosen to make a somewhat more dramatic gesture?'

Val looked blank.

'Have you and your colleagues decided that the best possible expression of gratitude is to provide her with a false alibi?'

'No! She was at the mill, I swear it.'

'Was she? Are you sure that it was the day in question?'

'Yes.'

'You aren't confused with the previous Thursday when she was off sick?'

'Previous Thursday?' repeated Mrs Yardy with a frazzled shake of the head, but before she could even give it any thought, Mr Pennington chose to keep her in that state by switching to a different issue entirely:

'The first defendant, Thomas Bateford – he has recently been acting as manager at the mill, hasn't he?'

'Yes.'

'And how would you assess his conduct towards the second defendant?'

'I don't know, I . . .'

'Is he believed to have been giving her preferential treatment?'

'No.'

'What about talking to her?'

'He's called her into the office a few times.'

'Called her into the office?' Mr Pennington repeated that phrase very slowly indeed. 'I wonder why.'

'Is that a question?' demanded Mr Zeldack, worried that this was fast getting out of hand.

'Do you know what would prompt him to call her in?' paraphrased the prosecutor, before raising his eyebrows as if to ask: "Is that enough of a question for you?"

'No.'

'So you don't know whether it was for an amorous liaison or not?'

'No.'

'Or perhaps to plot a murder?'

'The witness has already said that she doesn't know!' protested the defence, and Judge Ingram pressed Mr Pennington to move on – which was not something that distressed him, since he had squeezed all he could out of that particular theme.

'Has Mrs Bateford's attitude altered at all recently? Has she seemed excited? Nervous? Agitated?'

'Perhaps a little . . . distracted.'

'Distracted? And is that because of her impending nuptials?'

'Nuptials?' came the surprised repeat, which led Pennington nicely onto introducing the fact that a wedding had been arranged for two days ago. Or as he put it: 'Having rid herself of one Arnold Bateford, Bessie Cullen was about to embrace another.'

'I didn't know,' said Mrs Yardy, which led to another choice remark about how the accused obviously wished to keep it a secret, as with so many things.

Mr Zeldack was again given cause to exercise his legs. 'Counsel are here to investigate through enquiry, not provide running commentary,' he argued, but it had already been said, and all he could do now was to call up Andrew Roscoe, and hope against hope that he had not chosen the wrong person as a character witness.

'How well do you know Thomas?'

'Very well,' replied Drew confidently. 'He lives with me and my wife.'

'And your wife is his sister, correct?'

'Yes.'

'On the day of Mr Bateford's death, were you aware that Thomas was absent from the mill?'

'Yes. He asked to have some time to himself.'

'He asked?' repeated Mr Zeldack, wanting to make it perfectly clear that his client had not skulked off, but had been completely open about his intentions.

'That's right.'

'Did you know why he needed the free time?'

'No.'

'But you knew about his upcoming marriage?'

'Yes, of course. I was invited.'

'Not quite the illicit secret which the prosecution would have us believe,' observed Mr Zeldack, before quickly moving on as Pennington became fidgety. 'It has already been raised in evidence that Mrs Bateford provided you with assistance in procuring Bateford Mill. Can you confirm that this is the case?'

'Yes I can.'

'And were you mindful of her motives?'

Usually Mr Pennington would find fault with such a question, but decided that on balance, talk of motives was probably in his favour.

'Arnold was responsible for treating her family in an unjust manner,' replied Drew. 'Indeed persecution would probably be the more apt description, and I believe that she simply wished to redress the balance.'

'You mean revenge?' clarified Zeldack, knowing that if he did not say it, the prosecution would.

'Yes, and in my opinion, it was a more than legitimate course of action.'

'During your discussions with Mrs Bateford, did she ever mention Thomas?'

'No.'

'Not once?'

'Not once.'

'But she did explain about her motives, her intentions, her true identity?'

'That's correct.'

'So the fact that Thomas was never mentioned – would it suggest to you that he was in no way involved?'

'That's exactly what it suggests,' replied Drew. 'In fact I saw him the day of his return, and he was clearly ignorant of all that had been taking place.'

'Was Mrs Bateford in the mill on the day of her husband's death?'

'Yes. There were no reports of absenteeism.'

'And when Thomas arrived back home that day, how did he seem to you?'

'If I had to use one word, it would be . . . dispirited.'

'Dispirited?' Mr Zeldack raised an eyebrow in the jury's direction. 'Understandable I suppose, having heard from Mr Winchell that annulment would not in fact be the solution which he had imagined.'

'Indeed,' endorsed Drew before the prosecution could intervene. This was a case of life – or death, and he realised the absolute importance of keeping one step ahead of all prosecution ploys.

'When did Thomas return that day?' Mr Zeldack already knew that this particular answer would be far from propitious, but needed to neutralise the impact – leave Pennington with few lines to pursue. He also needed to put in as many concluding statements as possible, because this was his final witness, and when all other questions had been asked, they would proceed straight onto Judge Ingram's summary. There would be no more opportunity for him to undo anything damaging.

'I saw him in the early evening, and then he attended dinner.'

'So he was out all day?'

'Not necessarily,' replied Drew. 'I wasn't aware of when he left that morning, any more than when he returned. My home is an open one, not a prison.'

'How would you describe Thomas as a person?'

Mr Pennington protested about relevance, and Zeldack countered:

'The prosecution considered the opinion of Charles Bateford to be relevant. Why not Mr Roscoe, who is after all a fellow member of the family?'

The judge allowed it, and Drew answered: 'I believe him to be a man of distinguished repute, who is utterly incapable of any acts of violence.'

'But according to the testimony of his brother, he had previously threatened his father with the most extreme violence.'

'If swearing vengeance against Arnold Bateford is enough to merit an indictment, then half of Somerden should be in the dock, including both myself and my wife.'

'Your wife?'

'Yes,' declared Drew. 'I'm sure she won't mind me saying that her father was an unfeeling tyrant.'

'An unfeeling tyrant who gave many people a reason to kill him?'

'A very many people, yes.'

'And the prosecution believe that greed and lust were enough to push Thomas into doing just that.'

'I don't believe it for a minute. There's no evidence that Thomas was anywhere near Erskine Avenue, and I'm not completely sure that he was even aware of his father's new address.'

Mr Zeldack nearly smiled. Drew was doing his closing argument for him.

'You say that Thomas was deflated that night?'

'Yes. Quiet. Unresponsive. I'd never seen him in such a state.'

'Surely that would not have been the case if he had murdered his father, and hence secured everything that his heart desired?'

Mr Pennington objected on the grounds of speculation, and this time the judge supported him. In fact defence counsel was encouraged to sit down if he did not have anything new and concrete to explore, but Mr Zeldack knew that it was important to reiterate the doctor's evidence. Bring it back to the fore. Now he simply needed to work out how.

'Were you aware that the deceased had been drinking heavily of late?' He was expecting a negative, but to his surprise, caught a break:

'Yes.'

'You were?'

'Yes. It was beginning to circulate around town.'

'A result of the loss of his mill?'

'I believe that he was not taking it too well,' confirmed Drew.

'So in some ways it might be said that *you* are as responsible for Mr Bateford's death as anyone?'

'Absolutely,' replied Drew, who knew exactly what the defence needed. 'I was somewhat . . . ruthless in my dealings with him, but he had been more than ruthless when conducting business with my late father. The difference, however, between Mark Roscoe and Arnold Bateford is that Mr Bateford turned to drink to such an extent that he was in his cups long before mid-morning.'

'Which as Doctor Driscoll suggests, makes a finding of accidental death perfectly reasonable?'

Before Drew could say: 'Indeed,' Mr Pennington jumped up and declared:

'Really Judge, I beg of you to bring this double-act to an end,' and Mr Zeldack promptly sat down before the attack could reverberate too deeply.

'Mr Roscoe,' sighed the prosecution, as if now they would finally be cutting through the prosaic prattle, and getting to the truth. 'Why exactly did you wish to take Bateford Mill from the victim?'

'Because it has potential, and . . . because my wife suffered at her father's hands, and I was seeking retribution on her behalf.'

'But that isn't quite accurate, is it?'

'What isn't?'

'That your wife suffered at her father's hands. It is in fact *you* who have suffered, most grievously, for being tricked into marrying a young woman who was already carrying another man's child.'

It would have been possible to hear a pin drop at that moment – for a few seconds anyway – until shock began to flood the gallery. Drew glanced up at his wife, looking for her forgiveness, but Cynthia's expression was blank. In fact it was practically frozen, and the same could be said for Luke's beside her.

'I don't see how anything about my marriage is relevant,' growled Drew.

'But you're the one who has made it very relevant indeed,' countered Mr Pennington, which was true, and on the point of law he should have been allowed to proceed, but the judge had respect for men of property, and did not appreciate seeing them baited in such a manner.

'Next question,' came the order, and Pennington did as he was told.

'Mrs Bateford approached you with the plot to topple her husband, yes?'

'I wouldn't say topple. I paid him a considerable sum for the mill *and* for the land, in a perfectly legal transfer.'

'If you could simply answer yes or no.'

'Life isn't as simple as yes or no,' retorted Drew, but when Judge Ingram endorsed the need for clarity, he was forced to add: 'Yes.'

'And it was she who suggested using a counterfeit inspector?'

'We . . . talked it through . . . together.'

'Yes or no Mr Roscoe, and remember that you are under oath.'

'Yes.'

'She foresaw that this would ultimately lead to her husband's arrest?'

'Yes.'

'So in order to obtain what she wanted, Mrs Bateford was perfectly willing to have her husband thrown into gaol on the basis of a man who did not even exist.'

There was no response.

'Well Mr Roscoe?'

'I wasn't sure whether you were asking a question or not.'

'You've come into this courtroom with a very definite agenda, haven't you?'

'No.'

'You hated Mr Bateford, and as a result of that hatred you wish to see his murder go unpunished.'

'There's no evidence that it even *is* a murder.'

'On the contrary, there is more than sufficient evidence for this prosecution, but you're looking to twist it otherwise.'

'I'm not the one twisting anything, I'm simply not telling you what you want to hear.'

'Tread carefully Mr Pennington.' The judge issued a warning glare, but the prosecutor knew that this could win him the case – his sixth in a row – and was about to go for it:

'You cannot account for Thomas' whereabouts after he left Mr Winchell's office, no more than anybody else, and yet you seek to maintain that he "might" have been at home.'

'That's because he might have been.'

'You describe Thomas as dispirited, and yet somebody in a silent mood may just as much be beset by guilt as by disappointment. Or indeed concerned about the authorities catching up with him.'

'I was asked for my opinion on his demeanour, and I gave it,' replied Drew, remaining calm.

'As for the whereabouts of Mrs Bateford, you say that no absenteeism was reported that day, but you didn't actually lay eyes on her yourself, did you?'

'No, I wasn't in the mill. But there were nearly four hundred others who were.'

'Of course.' Mr Pennington gave his response with an air of thinly-veiled contempt. 'Four hundred witnesses of which three have testified in support of Mrs Bateford. Or in relatively convincing support I should say. Although when one considers the indebtedness of these women both to yourself *and* to the accused, one does have to question whether their testimony should be given any credence by this court whatsoever.'

Mr Zeldack did not merely stand up this time, he sprang forth. 'If you're suggesting that my witnesses have perjured themselves, you'd better have some jolly good evidence to back it up.'

'I am not only suggesting it, I am arguing that Mr Roscoe is the mastermind behind it!'

'Your worship!' shrieked Zeldack, and Judge Ingram scratched his head in irritation.

'Mr Pennington, if you wish to pursue this particular possibility, then please put it in the form of a question, and when you have received your answer, I advise you to let it drop.'

Prosecution counsel nodded and promptly turned back to Drew, who answered without the need for a question:

'I have in no way influenced the testimony of anybody in this courtroom today. Not even in the smallest, most insignificant degree!' Drew locked his jaws, and Mr Pennington responded by breathing deeply in and out.

'You say that you were ruthless in your dealings with the victim?'

'Yes, that is what I said.'

'And you freely admit to conspiring against him with Mrs Bateford?'

'Yes.'

'Which involved not only fabrication, but frankly dirty tricks?'

'We aren't here to assess Mr Roscoe's approach to business,' reminded Mr Zeldack, and received support from the Bench.

'I'm just trying to investigate the witness' character,' argued Pennington. 'When he contends that Thomas Bateford is a man of such high repute, how can we believe it if he himself is an individual of rather ill repute?'

'I have ruled against you on this issue,' snapped Judge Ingram, 'and I won't have you circumventing me in this manner. Now finish your questions, or I'll finish them for you.'

Mr Pennington nodded more obediently this time. There would be many other cases in front of this same judge, so it was important not to burn all his bridges at once. 'You knew of the victim's drinking, correct?'

'Yes.'

'Knew that since he was regularly incapacitated by drink, he would be easy to overpower?'

'I knew of his drinking,' repeated Drew, now becoming tired of such nonsense. 'Nothing more.'

'Was Thomas similarly well-informed?'

'I have no idea. You'll have to ask him.'

'I would, except that he isn't taking to the stand.' Mr Pennington glanced at the jury as if to say: "So what do you think about *that*?"

'I can't imagine Thomas knew anything about it at all,' added Drew quickly. 'I heard while I was in town, and Thomas rarely went to town, too busy in the mill.'

'Except on the day in question of course.'

Drew pursed his lips.

'Quite a coincidence that, don't you think?'

'I've found that life's full of them.'

Judge Ingram was looking stern again, so Pennington wisely used the all-important word:

'*Finally*, to recap then Mr Roscoe. Mrs Bateford conspired with you in order to transfer property from her husband, but according to your testimony, Thomas wasn't involved. Thomas then returned by utter chance, discovered that the victim's death would profit him in more than one regard, made preparations to marry Mrs Bateford within a week of the funeral, but we aren't supposed to see some sort of continuing conspiracy there?'

'My dealings with Mrs Bateford are entirely separate to her relationship with Thomas.'

'Are they? I put it to you that a conspiracy persisted throughout, and that not only did the defendants have motive and means, at least one of them had a gold-plated opportunity.'

'I don't agree.'

'Don't agree? Is that because you're a fellow conspirator yourself?'

'You what?' The exclamation blurted out before Mr Zeldack could conjure up slightly more elegant legal terminology.

'You've told us under oath that your father-in-law was a tyrant. You hated him as much as the defendants, so surely it is perfectly logical to suggest that all three of you conspired together to kill him.'

'You're mad Mr Pennington.'

'I'm merely reminding you of your own testimony Mr Roscoe. You hated the victim for the way in which he treated your father, for everything that he stood for, and most importantly for palming you off with another man's whore.'

'Now wait a minute you little . . .'

'You're glad that he's dead, aren't you? You're glad that he choked on his own vomit. That it was a slow, terrifying, demeaning death. And more than anything you're glad that they did it!'

'Yes I'm glad, and I wish to God I'd done it for them! You should give them a medal, not the noose!'

It took Drew a few seconds to appreciate exactly what he had just said there, and then he tried to backtrack, but it was all too late. Mr Pennington sat down, the picture of mock contrition, and since there were no more witnesses to call, Judge Ingram decided to pass over the distinctly unorthodox methods of his prosecutor, and proceed swiftly to summary.

When Bessie realised what he was doing, that the trial was nearly over, and soon no more words would be allowed, she had to say something: 'Please your worship, can I speak?'

'Speak? But you have elected not to testify.'

'I know, but this isn't right.'

Mr Pennington stood up. 'If she intends to speak, then I must have recourse to cross-examination.'

'Oh must you?' retorted the judge, who saw the perfect opening to teach this pretentious little upstart a lesson. 'I disagree. If you wish to make a short statement to the court Mrs Bateford, I am willing to allow it. But it will be only that – a statement.'

Mr Pennington was all set to protest – until thinking better of it – and then Bessie stared imploringly at the jury:

'We didn't do it. Neither of us. Not individually, and not plotting together. We had no idea that Arnold was drinking, and we certainly didn't break into his house. Yes, there was something of a feud, but just because a man has enemies, it doesn't mean that his death is a murder. Even the doctor thinks that it was an accident, and as for testifying – neither of us are afraid to take to the stand. You have to understand that. We'll stay here and answer any question you like, for as long as you like, because we're innocent. As God is my witness, we're innocent.'

Thomas studied each juror's face in turn as she uttered every desperate word, and he knew that it was no good. They were not convinced. At least not completely. And doubt was dangerous. "They might have done it. Best convict. We'll all be safer in our beds". That was the way of things, and with that in mind, there was only one possible way to guard against it.

'May I also issue a brief statement?' he asked, and Bessie gazed across with such immense pride. They were going down fighting – well begging – but begging together.

'I'll allow it,' declared Judge Ingram. 'As long as you ensure that it is indeed brief.'

'I will.' Thomas coughed, and began. 'You've heard about how I was with Mr Winchell, and that nobody can then account for my whereabouts until early evening. But *I* of course can account for them, and it is time that I did so.' He paused, cleared his throat once more, and took a shallow breath. 'I went around to Erskine

Avenue. It was only a short walk, and I was aware of the new address. I didn't wish to be presented officially, so I forced a window open, and located my father in the drawing room. All I wanted to do was to talk. That was my only intention – to request that he annul the marriage, but he was too drunk to even listen to me.'

'No Thomas, this isn't true.' Bessie shook her head frantically from side to side. 'Don't admit to something you haven't done. For God's sake, don't do it.'

He stopped, finally looked at her for several seconds – and then carried on. 'My father became abusive . . . aggressive . . . he pushed me, I pushed back, and he fell. It wasn't murder. In fact I didn't even realise that he'd knocked his head. I definitely did *not* stand there watching him choke, but left what I thought was an inebriated, obstinate man to sleep off his stupor on the floor. It was an accident, nothing more. An act of self-defence following a visit motivated by frustration. But nevertheless I am responsible for my father's death, and that is something which I must now accept.'

'Stop it Thomas, please stop it!'

'I must also stress that I am the only one who should bear this responsibility. Bessie was at the mill, as four hundred honest citizens are willing to corroborate. She had no idea that I was visiting a solicitor, and certainly no idea of what he said. My visit to Erskine Avenue was a solitary attempt to enter into some sort of dialogue, and Bessie is completely innocent of all involvement.'

That was it, the end of his statement, and it left the judge bemused – until Bessie gave him even more cause for bemusement:

'It isn't true, none of it! He's trying to protect me, like everybody else before him. I *did* it. I was the one who hated Arnold, who suffered the most at his hands. I plotted with Drew to take away his business, and then I made up my mind to kill him. *My* mind. It was all me, I . . .'

'No don't,' snapped Thomas, before the judge snapped even louder.

'But I need to explain how I . . .'

'You've had your chance to speak Mrs Bateford . . .'

'But I . . .'

'Not another word from anybody!' Judge Ingram banged his mallet down repeatedly, finally managed to restore order to his courtroom, and then addressed the jury – voice loud and fast to combat any interruption. 'Before you consider your verdicts, it is my duty to review the important points of evidence and law. You must remember that the burden of proof lies with the prosecution, and for each defendant, you must assess whether such a burden has been met. As regards the second defendant, she has people who have testified to her presence at the mill. If you believe these people, and believe that she was not complicit in any plot to kill her husband, then you must acquit her. The fact that she previously conspired against her husband is irrelevant if she did not conspire in this particular regard.'

'But I did it all,' she wailed, and the judge gave an infuriated glare before moving on. Never before had he come across two prisoners tripping over themselves to be hung.

'As for the first defendant, you must weigh up the evidence. It is a great crime to lust after another man's wife, and it is clear that Thomas Bateford lusted unrelentingly after the wife of his very own father. He also received rather significant news on that day, and nobody can account for his whereabouts. You have to ask yourselves whether he is simply falling on his sword now out of concern for his lover, or whether he did indeed visit his father's new address. Once there, you must then decide whether his actions are enough to constitute murder. You have heard from the parish constables about the state of the window, but there is no evidence as to when that lock was actually broken. Nobody inside the house heard anything, and there were no signs of any struggle. Does this point against murder? Or is it inconclusive? And what about those who have testified? Taken as a whole, what do they tell you about the tragic events at Erskine Avenue? With all that in mind, I must now ask you to consider your verdicts.'

The witnesses had played their part, the judge his, and suddenly it was over to the jury to fill in the conclusion. Twelve good men and true – who wasted no time in forming into a tight huddle. Most of them had already made up their minds, and finding that those minds were in agreement, they were able to announce within only a couple of minutes that they had reached a verdict on the second defendant.

Bessie knew what they were going to say. Innocent. A glorious word under normal circumstances, but not any more.

'On the single count of the indictment, how do you find the defendant Elizabeth Mary Bateford. Guilty or not guilty?'

'Not guilty.'

'And you need more time for the first defendant?'

'Yes.'

'Then proceed.'

The huddle reformed as Judge Ingram directed Bessie to be released from her chains.

'I deserve to die, not him. I've deserved it for a long time,' she whimpered, while being encouraged to exit from her end of the dock. If she had been found guilty, they would have used force. Not guilty, and it was like they were guiding a small child. The power of three little letters. But forceful or otherwise, Bessie was not about to be led away from Thomas, not while she still had breath in her body. Taking the guards by surprise, she darted back along the dock, and immediately held his face between her hands. 'You didn't have to do this. The evidence wasn't that bad. We could have got through it.'

'I couldn't take the risk,' he whispered. 'If it weren't for my family, you would never have seen the inside of a courtroom. It was time for all this to end.'

'But not with you.'

'I'm not afraid of dying Bessie. I've made my peace with Cynthia, and you're safe now. For the first time in my life I feel strong and free of doubt.'

'Oh Thomas.' She began to cry, and before those cries could turn into sobs, the guards made a second attempt to extract her from the dock – and this time it was with much greater force.

'You can't take me,' she resisted. 'I have to make them understand. Thomas loves me, you see? And that's the only reason he's saying these things. He didn't hurt anybody, he couldn't. He's a wonderful man. Surely you can see that? He's selfless, kind, considerate. All that's good. It's obvious, isn't it? *Please* just open your eyes!'

She had now fully captured the attentions of the jury, and that made Judge Ingram's irritation soar. The longer they were interrupted, the longer he would have to wait for his dinner.

'Mrs Bateford,' he declared with a cold, commanding air. 'As far as you're concerned, this trial is over. You have no further contribution to make, and so I am therefore going to demand that you leave.'

'But Thomas wants to take back what he said, don't you Thomas? It's all wrong.'

'Wrong or otherwise, I won't tolerate any more outbursts in my court. You either watch in silence from the gallery, or be removed from this building completely.'

Bessie opened her mouth again.

'And if you aggravate me any further, I'll have you put back in a cell.'

He meant it, and without another word she allowed herself to be pushed out. Thomas needed her. She at least had to be able to see him, but as she scrambled up the stairs, others were on their way down.

'What are you doing?'

'I . . . I . . . can't watch,' stammered Cynthia.

'But he needs us.'

'I just . . . I can't.' She hurried on down, Luke with his arm around her, and Drew held back for a moment so that he could say he was sorry.

Bessie had no idea how to respond, and anyway her only thought was about being with Thomas. Racing on up to the gallery, she practically flung herself against the railing, and leaned out as far as physically possible in order to make him look at her. Except he would not do it. He was not paying any attention to the jury either, but staring straight ahead of him, into the empty space, preparing for what was to come.

Less than five minutes later, the jury felt that they had devoted enough of their lives to deliberating, and the verdict was in. A quick chat, that was all it had been, and now they were ready to pass judgement on a man. Hang him or save him. It seemed to make little difference. 'Save him, save him, oh God save him.' Bessie kept on whispering the words over and over as the judge asked for that verdict, and the foreman prepared to give it.

'Guilty.'

The word seemed to be hurled through the air like a spear through her chest, and the only thing Bessie could do was to hurl it right back with a scream. A scream that kept on growing in intensity – until a hand clamped itself over her mouth.

Gil had made his way down to her, knowing what she would do, and what the consequences might be as a result.

The judge – who had nearly suffered a perforated eardrum – snarled up at the gallery, but seeing that she had now been brought under control, decided to ignore her and move straight onto sentencing. The familiar Black-cap was produced, and once in place, Judge Ingram stared directly at the prisoner.

'By your own admission you are responsible for your father's death, and the jury has decided that such responsibility amounts to murder. You have been convicted of the most deplorable of crimes. That of patricide. Unable to wait for a dead man's shoes, you chose to deprive your father of life prematurely, and it now falls to me to deprive you of the same. There is no other sentence which I can pass. You will be put to death by hanging, and your body then buried in unconsecrated ground. I advise you that in the short time left, you pray to God that he may have mercy upon your soul.' The judge was about to leave it at that, but then decided that perhaps the circumstances merited a certain latitude. 'Is there anything else you wish to say before being led from court?'

'Yes.' Thomas looked up. 'I want you to know that I've always loved you Bessie. From the very first day that I met you, and I'll go on loving you forever. We'll never be apart. Nothing can break a love as strong as ours. Not my father, not this court. Not even death.'

She needed to reply, more than anything in the world she needed it, but Gil's hand was still fixed firmly over her mouth, and his other arm was wrapped around her body, keeping both arms down. She was as trapped as Thomas, who was now being removed from the shackles of the dock, only to have his wrists locked behind his back instead. That was even worse, made him seem even more hopeless – and ever so close to the end.

Wriggling and fighting, and jerking her head like a wild horse, she finally managed to free her face. 'Let go of me!'

'You can't help him now.'

'I don't care.' She wriggled some more, thrusting her elbows back into Gil's ribs, and ultimately a stamp on the foot was enough. Tearing towards the stairs, she almost threw herself down them, but there was such a crush of people. She had to push and shove a way through, and near the bottom, somebody shoved back. Her head struck the wall, and for a minute everything went blank, but then the daylight flooded back. Hauling herself up, she followed the noise, and was soon out with the crowd as it moved towards the gallows.

'They can't hang him today. They can't, they can't!'

'I think you'll find that they can,' replied a burly middle-aged woman. 'They don't hang around.' She began to titter at the little play on words, and Bessie shunted her away in disgust. So many people. Where had they all come from? For every tier she managed to separate, an even more impenetrable one lay ahead. Why on earth would they want to join such a procession? And why were they keeping her from Thomas? She could not see him. Even when they entered the quadrangle, he was not in sight. It was only as he began to ascend the steps of the scaffold that he rose above everybody else.

The baying crowd spread out and encircled him, as if paying homage to that thing, set there in the centre so regally, proud of the service it provided to the district. Bessie hated it, every beam, every splinter, every person who had ever contributed to its construction. What gave one human being the right to do this to another? State-sponsored slaughter – there was no other term for it – and all designed to satisfy the bloodthirsty masses.

'Tell them you're innocent Thomas, *please*.' She begged it, screamed it, and somehow over the jeers and the laughter, he managed to hear it. His eyes searched for her, darting here and there, and as they found her, they found no peace. She knew that now at last he was scared, and her heart felt like it flipped over in her chest. There had to be something she could do. 'A priest! Shouldn't there be a priest?' she screamed, but nobody took any notice. The executioner and guards were getting on with it by themselves. There was no order, no last rites. And no delay.

Bessie tried again to forge a way through, but the vultures kept holding her back. Even crawling on the floor, searching for a route between their legs, it was no good. She gripped her head, and closed her eyes, pleading for help from somewhere, but all she heard was that same woman saying:

'You can't close your eyes love. This is the best bit. What do you reckon Avril? A snap? Or shall we get ourselves a kicker?'

'You evil witch! Get away from me, you hear? Get away!' Bessie staggered up, eyes open once more because she knew that they had to be. She had to look in case Thomas needed to see her. But it was already too late. A hood had been placed over his head, and the noose was being secured around his neck. He was blind, and all alone, and there was nothing she could do about it.

'Thomas!' she cried. 'Thomas I love you, I love you.' Surely he would hear her again. It was vital that he heard her, because he would not be alone for long. All she needed was a knife, something sharp. Life was short. What did it matter if it was shortened still further? As long as they were not kept apart. She rummaged feverishly through the pockets around her. If she died at exactly the same moment, then they would move into the next world together. Hopefully to heaven. As one. Oh how she prayed that it would be to heaven, and that they could fly there on the wings of the same angel.

Everybody was oblivious, so enthralled, that they did not even feel her probing hands, but neither did she feel anything sharp. Did nobody have anything sharp! She stared back at the scaffold. The hangman had put his hand upon the lever of the trap-door.

'No!' She wailed it, and then held her breath, praying that time would then also be held, and she could find what she was looking for. 'Just wait!' she begged, but the hangman waited for nobody. He pressed the lever with relish, Thomas dropped, the wood creaked, and the strangest thing of all was that nothing hit her except the powerful smell of ammonia.

'Ah, so you're back,' said Gil as he rather unceremoniously propped her up.

'Wh . . . what . . ?' She was back in the courthouse, at the bottom of the stairs. 'He's dead. Thomas is dead!'

'No he isn't. At least not yet. They never hang anybody this late.'

'I . . . but . . .'

'If the trial finishes after three, it always has to wait until the next morning.'

'But I saw it, I was there.'

'You were unconscious, so I don't know exactly where you've been, but you haven't left this building.'

'But all those people . . . they . . .'

'If you're referring to the ones on the stairs, they've gone home. Important to get an early bed before the real action tomorrow. You know you were lucky not to be trampled.'

'You mean it?' Bessie gripped his shirt. 'You're not just saying it? Thomas is still alive?'

'Yes, he's still alive, and will continue to be so until first thing tomorrow.'

'Then we have a chance to get him out. We have to get him out Gil!'

'I didn't come here to watch either of you swing,' he replied, keeping as calm as she was frantic, and then helped her onto her feet.

'Oh my head hurts.' She put a hand to her temple, and tried to focus. 'What was that stuff?'

'Smelling-salts. I always keep a bottle to hand. Damsels have an alarming habit of fainting in my presence.' Gil smiled, but Bessie was most definitely not in the mood.

'What are we going to do?'

'Well first of all we're going to make tracks for the local tavern, and book ourselves a room.' It was nearly dark now, and once she had her legs working properly, he hurried them along, one eye over his shoulder, until safely at their destination – where he promptly announced that he had to go out. While *she* had to stay put.

'Why?'

'Because a rescue needs to be organised, and you can't become involved.'

'Why not?'

'Because it's too dangerous.'

'I don't care about danger! And I can help. Distract one of the guards or something. Seduce him even.'

'As seductive as I'm sure you can be, I fear we may need something slightly more persuasive than the enthralling sight of your cleavage.'

'Don't you start patronising me again Gil Tremaine. And don't you *dare* think of leaving me behind.'

'Miss Cullen.' Gil's bottom jaw was suddenly set resolutely forward. 'For once in your life, you're going to have to grasp this concept of doing as you're told, and leaving it to somebody who has far more experience with these matters than you do.'

'Who?'

'A man that I've heard about. If anybody can help Thomas, he can. Which means that all you have to do is to wait near the Ash forest on the north edge of town at first light.'

'But . . .'

'Listen! First light! Ash forest! North! I'll bring Thomas to you.'

'But I can't just sit here all night doing nothing.'

'You'll have to. If you interfere, not only Thomas will die, but others too. Do you want that on your conscience?'

'Of course I don't.'

'Then promise me you'll do as I say. It is absolutely, completely and utterly imperative that you stop meddling, and DO AS I SAY!'

Bessie grimaced, groaned, sighed, and literally wrung her hands, but ultimately promised – and meant every word of it. She would not move. 'How will this man get into the prison?' she asked tensely. 'Please tell me.'

'I don't know, but do I know that you can help him by telling me where in the prison Thomas is being kept.'

'Kept? I have no idea.' She began to shake with a fresh surge of panic, but then pulled herself together, telling him what little she *did* know – about where she had been, and how Thomas was not within calling distance of the east wing.

'That's the remand section?'

'Yes.'

'I see.'

'I'm sorry that I can't tell you any more.'

'Don't worry. It ought to be enough.'

'Are you sure that this is possible?'

'Everything's possible,' grinned Gil. 'Just you be waiting near the Ash forest like I said. Before that death-bell tolls, Thomas will not only be out of prison, he'll be out of Henningborough. Trust me!'

CHAPTER FOURTEEN

Trust me. 'Is that wise?' pondered Gil a few hours later as he returned to the prison and stood observing from a safe distance.

He had been here last night too, and enjoyed a most illuminating conversation with a local landlady who had enjoyed many a hanging in her time. He was therefore fully acquainted with the exterior, the gallows quadrangle, and now the east wing. It was just the rest that was a bit of a problem, and since nobody was likely to offer him a guided tour, he would have to settle for the next best thing. An aerial overview. And he knew precisely the place which would give it to him.

A couple of minutes away, down a rather forbidding back-street, there was a door set in the side of a nondescript building. Believed derelict, it had escaped the recent spate of raids, and continued to provide a much-appreciated service to its loyal clientele. Gil rang the bell, which had deliberately been allowed to rust over, and stood back so that his face was irradiated by a lone gas lamp at the end of the alley. He knew that an eye would soon be pressed against the peep-hole, and if it did not behold a familiar face – or somebody on referral – then the door would not be opened.

'Ah hello sir. Haven't seen you in an awfully long time. Come on in.' The door was drawn back by a stooped old man, and Gil crossed the threshold.

'Good to see you Rogers. How has life been treating you?'

'Not so bad, not so bad. All things considered. Apart from my joints that is. They've been playing me up a bit.'

'You want to get out of here occasionally. Catch some sun.'

'Oh no sir. I'm sure I'll have more than enough heat in the next world.'

Gil grinned. 'There are people who do far worse with their lives than you Rogers.'

'That's a comfort,' he replied, and proceeded to lead them down a distinctly dingy staircase. It was the sort of staircase which usually led to a murky old cellar where the only life-forms were the ones growing on the walls. But this was a cellar with a difference. A few years ago it had been rescued and renovated – into a warm and very welcoming hostelry. Opening the door at the bottom was like stepping from a prehistoric cave into a playhouse. Full of gaiety and colour, drink and women – and one woman in particular could not believe her eyes.

'Gil!' cried a thirty-something female with cascades of curly golden hair. She rushed over, and would have wrapped her arms around his neck if not for the fact that he was so tall, and she so small.

'Hello Tara,' smiled Gil, and leaned down so that she could give him the intended greeting. 'How have you been?'

'Fine, absolutely fine.' Her reply was dismissive as if it did not matter if things had been dire of late, because everything had suddenly been transformed by his appearance.

'And how is the business?'

'That's pretty good too.' She steered him across to the bar, and ordered him a double-whisky, followed by a single for herself. Usually she never drank with customers, but Gil was different. 'We've had a couple of new clients in the last month, and they seem to be working out well.'

Gil had a look around to see if he recognised anybody, and formed the strongest suspicion that it might be Mr Underwood in the far corner. Although it was hard to see past the woman on his lap, and of course he would not be known as Mr Underwood in here. It was first names only, and many of those were false. The last King seemed to be a popular choice, so no doubt there was a Bill and a Will in the room, along with a Willis, Wilkes and Wiley.

His observations meant that he was oblivious to the substantial volume of whisky being pressed into his hand until the glass was actually thrust up towards his lips, and then he considered it churlish not to take a sip or two.

'So where have you been? We thought we'd never see you again.' Tara knew that it was dangerous to appear too clingy, but had to make some sort of reference to the fact that she had been neglected for seventeen months.

'Oh you needn't have worried,' sighed Gil in that adorably good-natured manner of his. 'I'm like a bad penny. Always turn up in the end.'

'Well I wish you'd turn up a bit more often,' she joked, before deciding that she had better not push it. 'So what brings you to town this time?'

'A mission of mercy as it happens.'

'A girl?'

'Not exactly.'

'Anything that I can help you with?'

'Yes, as it happens. I could do with gaining access to your roof.'

'Roof?'

'It's a long story,' said Gil, with an eyebrow raise and a shrug.

'Of course . . . if that's what you need, the roof's all yours. But you don't have to rush off right away, do you?'

Her question was rather forlorn, and he gave it some serious thought. The guards at the prison worked in twelve-hour shifts, changing on the stroke of twelve, and that was why he was planning to go in at around four – when eyes were becoming tired, and minds inattentive. He would need at least a couple of hours to prepare beforehand, and that did not include finalising the ultimate stratagem, but he could afford a bit of a chin-wag first.

'So how are all your girls?' he asked, wanting to make sure that he kept this conversation well away from himself.

'Fine, yes, as you can see. You know Sandie?'

Gil's look was vacant.

'The Londoner?'

'Oh yes.'

'Well she found a nice young man, an accountant's clerk, and married him last summer.'

'Married?' repeated Gil, trying not to appear too surprised. 'Did she meet him through here?'

'No, no. None of this lot would ever be interested in settling down. Besides, as you know, most of them are already married.'

'Yes.' He glanced around again. Most of the gentlemen in attendance did indeed have that ball-and-chain look.

'But as I always say,' declared Tara. 'My girls provide a service which makes the life of many a wife much more tolerable.'

Gil grinned. He was not sure how many wives in Henningborough would be in agreement with that, but perhaps the proposition did have some merit. He was about to enter into a little light repartee on the subject, when a flash of sadness crossed Tara's eyes.

'What's wrong?' he asked, and she did not even attempt to keep it from him.

'It's Olivia. You remember . . .'

'I remember her,' said Gil, and as Tara breathed deep, he filled in the gaping big hole. 'She's dead, isn't she?'

A slow blink of the eyes was his answer.

'What happened?'

'She started taking some work on the side, that's what happened.' Tara's voice was instantly snappy – with anger, sadness and deep frustration. 'I told her not to. I tell them *all* not to, but would she listen? Said she'd found the man of her dreams. The man to take her out of this place. All too good to be true of course. The poor girl did something to annoy him, and he blew up, just like that, without any warning. I don't know how she managed it, but she staggered back here, and for a while we thought we might be able to save her, but . . .'

'But what?'

'The burns were too severe.' Tara swallowed and gritted her teeth, guilty that she had not done more to stop it from ever reaching that horrible point.

'Has anything happened to the man?'

'What do *you* think?'

What he thought was currently unfit for annunciation, but what he began to think over the next few minutes was that life was on its head. Thomas Bateford set to hang, while a whole host of deviants were free and walking the streets. Where was the justice? Nowhere. That was the truth of it. Nowhere to be seen. So if you did want justice in this world, you had to seize it for yourself. Seize it through whatever means necessary.

'Who is he?' demanded Gil. 'I want his name. I want everything about him.'

Tara complied, outlining all the background information which she had discovered even before her friend had come across him. She made it her number one priority to keep abreast of all such individuals in the area, in case they should ever come a-knocking at her door.

'Don't you think you ought to increase security around here?' he asked once she had finished.

'No need. I take care of things so that everybody's safe.'

'I know you do. But what if your trusty veto lets you down one of these days?'

'Then Rogers and I will deal appropriately with the threat.'

Gil scratched his head for a moment. 'I don't mean to be rude, but I think Rogers might have difficulty in standing up straight, never mind repelling any such invaders.'

A small gleam came back into Tara's eyes as she retorted: 'Rogers might not be blessed with your straight back, but what he lacks in posture, he makes up for in precision. He can shoot a gun far better than *you*.'

'Can he now?'

'Look – I'll show you.' Tara dragged Gil around to a table set at the side of the bar, almost out of view, and with a heavy brass statue in the middle. When that statue was made to lie down, the panelling behind the table opened – by just an inch.

'I was impressed the first time, but that just gets better and better,' remarked Gil as Tara pushed the panelling back, drew him through, and closed it firmly behind them. They were now in the underworld beyond the underworld. If the authorities were ever to become aware of this place, they would find an unlicensed bar, and would never suspect anything else. Even if they did, they would never know how to get through to it.

Directly in front of them was a spiral staircase, leading you up to the ground floor, and then to many more flights of stairs – and many more rooms. The building had once been a mill, before Marshall & Taylor had taken all Henningborough's business, so there had only ever been small windows in place, and now most of those were bricked up. Secret? Sordid? It was a matter of opinion. Or as Rogers would say during one of his philosophical moments: 'You pays your money, you takes your choice.'

To the left, still in the basement, were Tara's living quarters – an elaborately furnished affair, with a sumptuous central sofa, which she now began to take apart, until revealing what frankly constituted an arsenal beneath the seats. Gil placed one hand upon her shoulder, and the other upon his hip, conveying that he was now positively flabbergasted. Indeed it was even enough to make him question whether to ask about borrowing something, but then he quickly decided against it. He was not really an admirer of armaments. A little too crude for his tastes.

'Well I'd better be going then,' he announced, having already put his glass down.

'You didn't really want that, did you?'

'Not tonight. But thank you anyway.'

'Are you sure that I can't tempt you into staying? We have a new girl who's just started, you'll like her, she's . . .'

'Now now Tara, you know me. I prefer my women a little bit harder to come by.'

'I'm not convinced that you like women at all,' she countered, but was secretly glad. If he ever said yes to anyone, she wanted it to be her. 'How about some company up there then? We could watch the stars together.'

'Nice idea, but it was clouding over as I came in.'

'Oh.'

'Maybe next time,' he suggested as she looked so downcast.

'When?'

'When the days draw out a bit. Around the time of your birthday.'

'You know when it is.'

'Of course I do.'

Tara was filled with a sense of joy that was quite literally overwhelming. If he remembered a detail such as that, then it meant . . ? Well it was probably best not to explore exactly what it meant, but knowing that she would see him before the end of June made it much easier to let him go.

'I'll probably come down the back way, so I'll say goodbye now.'

'Make sure that you don't take the really fast route,' she quipped, but there was genuine concern in her words.

'You mean jumping? Landing smack on the pavement on a cold winter's night? That isn't my idea of fun Tara. Anyway there'd be nobody watching, and that wouldn't be any good, now would it? When I exit this world, it's going to be in a blaze of glory.' He tipped her a wink, before taking his leave, little realising that she was watching him all the way up the spiral staircase, and then trying to listen to him for as long as she could after that.

Once he reached the first floor landing, the stairs became rather disordered. Three up here, and a couple more rooms; another five and then yet more. The place had been gutted with the departure of the mill machinery, and when Tara had moved in, she had designed it specifically so as to provide a cosy atmosphere. Not a long passageway with closed doors as far as the eye could see. Something more subtle, and hence more inviting. But nevertheless there were plenty of closed doors, and Gil had an almost irresistible urge to open a few, frighten some of the regulars. His hand even crept close to one of the handles for a moment, but ultimately he held off for Tara's sake, made it to the attic, and clambered out onto the roof. It was unsafe – in fact downright perilous – but completely necessary, and gave him the perfect vantage point over Henningborough's sprawling prison.

East wing was something of a misnomer, because there was not actually any corresponding west wing. It simply described the old structure wedged between the courthouse and the quadrangle. Beyond the quadrangle was then the bulk of the prison population, housed in a huge, relatively rectangular building – but with a northern bulge. Thomas had not been in the east wing to date, so it would be strange if they had moved him there now. That left the quadrangle or main building.

Surely it would have been cruel to put him in sight of the gallows when not even convicted, but of course it was a possibility, and also logical to assume that if he had been with the general population, then he could now have been taken out pending execution of the sentence. Gil certainly hoped so. By his reckoning, there were about fifty cells in the quadrangle, but probably hundreds in the main building, and the prisoners were not all herded together like in the women's version. This was a modern set-up – the magistrates' pride and joy – with everybody having their own cell. Solitary confinement and hard labour through the crank, which had to be turned so many times a day. More than enough to make you think twice about getting caught again in the future.

Gil was not sure how he would go about locating Thomas if faced with hundreds of blank doors, so preferred to assume for the time being that the quadrangle was the place. Of course fifty people were not sent to their death on a daily basis, so some of the cells were occupied by men completing lesser sentences. Indeed it was often said that those inside for a long stay were accorded a gallows view in order to provide them with a little entertainment. Gil was not sure whether to laugh or feel sick, but actually there was no opportunity for either, because time was gathering apace – and he needed to give consideration to his way in.

The main entrance was obviously not viable, so that left only one other traditional access-point.

The quadrangle gate. It was sturdy and well fortified, opening only to admit the masses for "showtime", but was not otherwise patrolled as far as he knew. That gave it significant advantages, but there was also one major disadvantage – it was on a street with an awful lot of foot-traffic. Even in the middle of the night, there was a risk that he might be seen entering, and that was far too much of a risk to take.

The walls of the main prison were too high, as were those of the east wing, so that meant scaling either the quadrangle or the courthouse. The quadrangle buildings were lower, so feasible, and the south-facing ones backed onto the canal, which would be dark and devoid of life at this time of night. Attacking it from that angle would certainly have the advantage of concealment, but once over the top, he would still need to find a way to break in, whereas entering through the courthouse would mean that he was already "in". Since he had also taken the precaution of attaching a piece of string to one of the ground floor window locks in that place, then his mind was made up. The courthouse it would be.

Climbing back into the attic, he waited within its slightly warmer surrounds until midnight, and then watched the changing of the guard, to give himself an idea of how many men he would be dealing with. Surprisingly few in fact. It was amazing how such a small number could exert control over so many – with the help of some iron and steel of course. Trying not to dwell on thoughts of the latter, he made his way down to the rear exit of Tara's place, known only to a few people, and even less obvious than that entrance, before coming out at the end of the street. Time to get going. Time to turn these fantasies into reality – and quite frankly he could not wait. He had expected to feel nerves at this point, but there were none in his body whatsoever. Even as he walked past the prison which seemed so much bigger from street level, he did not feel intimidated or fearful. This was a challenge, nothing more, and the only issue that mattered was: Could he rise to it?

As the town clock chimed four times, he was ready to find out. Head to toe in black, cloak in place, hood up, equipment to hand, and holding a bag of belongings. He had taken lodgings in a poor part of town – perfect because working people had long days, and generally slept at night, so there ought to be nobody about when he came to open the door. He had also packed everything because he would not be back once this deed was done.

The only thing not yet in place was his face-mask, because he needed to appear relatively normal – just in case he did meet someone. But as it happened he neared the very prison itself without encountering a soul. The tavern was not far away at this point, and as he stared in the relevant direction, he hoped against hope that Bessie Cullen had done as she was told. He also reminded himself of the need to employ the masked man's accent. No matter how good his outfit, it would all be to nought if he spoke as normal.

Having deposited the bag of belongings behind a wall several streets away, he now moved towards the back of the courthouse, scanned around, pulled on his piece of string, and was inside in a flash. Of course there were no lamps lit, and the moon was still blanketed in cloud, but Gil had the eyes of a cat, and as he vacated the back he could see through into court. For a moment he was tempted to go and sit in the judge's chair, just to see what it felt like, but again managed to restrain himself, and instead entered the dock, following the route of the prisoners, and reaching the basement. There he came upon the door which took you into the east wing, and naturally it was locked, but easy enough to overcome. The authorities had complete faith in their control over the prison, and nobody had escaped since it was built, so they did not envisage that anybody would get near to this point. Unfortunately they had overlooked just one small detail – that one day somebody might wish to break *in*.

Fixing the face-mask in place, he then felt properly in character, and was soon on the other side of the door, drawing his sword. It was important to be prepared, but hopefully he would have no cause to use it. The longer that his presence went undetected in here, the better. And that meant listening – for every footfall, jangle, echo and breath. He had to keep a step ahead, which also involved keeping one eye over his shoulder. Not only for nasty surprises coming up from the rear, but so that he always had a good hideout to scurry back to. Together the two elements of the strategy worked brilliantly, enabling him to creep past one guard who was asleep, melt into the shadows as another walked by, and hurry down a different corridor entirely when he heard the faint approach of a third.

"This is easy", thought Gil after a few minutes, although a critic in his head did point out that such comments were usually followed by the onset of catastrophe.

Catastrophe, however, was not the word which best described what happened next. Vexation was a far more accurate description. He had reached the other end of the east wing, and was ready to enter the quadrangle, when he encountered an obstruction. A door to be precise. Of course it was to be expected, but the problem was that it was the only door connecting the east wing with the quadrangle, and there was a guard sitting on the other side of it. Gil could see him quite clearly through the grate, and that created an issue about what to do next. Make the guard open the door for some reason, or wait for him to move off? Bodily functions dictated that the latter would happen eventually, but it could take hours, and Gil did not have hours.

Slinking away, he found a recess in the wall, and began to think. Perhaps it would have been better if he had indeed brought Bessie along. Her face at the grate would be enough to open that door immediately, and followed by enough drink the guard might even be convinced in the morning that she was nothing more than some delightful dream.

'But she isn't here,' said Gil. 'So you'll have to think of something else. Or turn yourself into . . .'

His eyes sparkled at the thought. Was it possible? A lot would have to be done with the voice, but he was more than able to manipulate it as required – although had never actually manipulated it in a feminine way. Could he sound high-pitched enough? Or was any attempt to be high-pitched the wrong way to go about things? Women did not in fact spend their days shrieking – although it did feel like it sometimes. But even if he could strike the right tone, what could he do about his build? At over six feet tall, with broad shoulders, there was no way that he could pass for a woman, even in this light.

Perhaps . . .

'Yes!' Gil almost clapped his hands as he accepted that a woman might be out, but ghosts were most definitely in. After quickly glancing around, he hurried back and pressed his face right up against the grate. "Look who's here!" was the blunt message he was after. Except the guard was not looking. In fact he was looking everywhere else *except* the door.

What now? Start knocking at regular intervals? Murmur in a ghoulish manner? Gil nearly retreated to give it some thought, but was already bored of thinking, so went instinctively for what appeared to be the most sensible option. A single knock. The noise would not carry too far, but ought to alert this guard's attention. It did. Eyes instantly became fixed onto the grate, but still there was no reaction.

"What the hell's wrong with you?" thought Gil before realising that the set-up of the lights was effectively rendering him invisible – especially in a jet-black mask. Backing away, he seized his own lamp, and returned, boldly holding it up exactly where his face had just been. Now *that* ought to do the trick.

'Who's there?' snapped the guard immediately, but Gil did not respond. He wanted to provoke interest, not scare the man away, and during the long pause which followed he became convinced that the lock was about to turn. But he was wrong.

'I said who's there?'

"Oh for God's sake!" Gil almost said that out loud, but instead managed to come out with something sultry – suddenly having the sense to appreciate that if this guard was afraid of a light, he would run a mile if he thought it was being carried by some spooky apparition.

'How do you do sir?' he purred.

'Who *are* you? How did you get in here?'

'I'm the answer to all your little prayers.'

'What are you talking about? Show yourself.'

Gil smiled. Those last two words were promising, so he stepped forward and did exactly that. With knees bent to make himself appear shorter, and tilting his stance so that his shoulders were not apparent, he had a chance of pulling this off.

'What are you doing here?'

'I'm here because you called for me.'

'Called for you?'

'Yes. I'm Asteria, the lady of the night, and it is my role in life to answer to lonely souls such as yourself, who cry out to me in the darkest hours.'

'Who says I'm lonely?'

'You did. I've heard your thoughts, remember?' Gil was not only whispering so as not to attract attention, but also because it was the only way that his voice could be dulcet enough; and even though the guard remained suspicious, he was also intrigued – which meant that it was working.

'Take that mask off. Let me see your face.'

'But I don't have a face. Only a body sent to serve the needs of men like you.'

That was enough. From feeling the part of suave crusader, Gil now felt completely embarrassed, so drew himself away, hoping to draw the guard with him. But this guard was not yet willing to move – despite the fact that "Asteria" had left a seductive finger trailing in her wake.

'Give me your hand then.'

'My hand?'

'Yes.'

Gil hesitated. He had thin fingers, which were ideal for intricate work like fiddling with locks, and possibly ideal for this purpose too. Surely they could pass as the slender digits of a female? He had not done hard work in many a year, so they would certainly be soft enough, which was presumably the main thing about to be examined.

Slowly and provocatively, he removed a glove, and dangled his fingers through the grate, wondering whether other women had this much difficulty when offering themselves up so unashamedly.

'How did you get in here?'

'I have ways.'

'You mean you can walk through bolted doors?'

'As I say, I have ways.' Gil now had his hand back, and was out of sight again, pounding the side of his head against the wall in frustration.

'So why can't you come through this door then?'

'Because *you* have to come to me. I've done as much as I can, but now you have to decide whether or not you want me.' He closed his eyes, trying to block out the truth of exactly what he was saying, and refusing to utter another sound.

He was pressed, multiple times, but did not even concede a syllable, and eventually – having reached the conclusion that such offers did not pass his way every day – the guard put a key in the lock, and turned it. The moment that the door opened, he was hit over the head, dragged into a dark recess, and arranged in a suitable pose with gin bottle in hand. No doubt he would be dismissed in the morning for being drunk on duty, so Gil pushed a few pounds into his pocket by way of compensation, relieved him of his key, and finally shot through the door.

The key was a significant bonus, but Gil did not wish to use it in checking every cell. Too noisy, too risky, it would take far too long, and he would end up disturbing a whole host of prisoners who could well start pleading for release. Thankfully the first cell suggested that there was in fact no need for a key. The door was different to those in the east wing. This was made of seven thick parallel bars. With everybody having been convicted – or sentenced to death – it was to convey a greater sense that you were caged, and deserving to be caged. Not nice, but perfect for Gil because all he had to do was hold up his lamp, and peer through.

Most of the prisoners simply assumed that he was a guard doing the rounds, and it was easy to identify whether or not they were familiar. A few were stubbornly reluctant to move over, and one even needed to be prodded, but eventually Gil had examined every cell – and found that they were all occupied, but *not* by Thomas Bateford.

He sank down on his haunches, and then let his head drop. Not only was this proving to be more trying than he had imagined, it was also decidedly more boring. Fifty-odd cells. An hour and a half wasted, and now he had to tackle the main prison anyway. What if there were too many cells? What if he ran out of time, and Thomas hanged? And why should that be a concern anyway. Thomas was not a friend; was barely more than an acquaintance. All this hassle for an acquaintance!

Gil tolerated only a couple more thoughts like that, before abruptly cutting them out. Responsibility was not the issue. Nobody deserved to swing for Arnold Bateford, and when Gil Tremaine set out to do something, he saw it through. That was the fundamental fact, and fixing it firmly to the fore, he pushed himself back up, and advanced.

The situation was exactly the same as before, one door, one guard, but now Gil had one key. There was no need for further exploration of his female side; he simply unlocked the door, walked through, and presented himself on the other side. Guard number two stood up, initially relaxed, but then saw a man with a black velvet face, and his mouth dropped open. Preparing to scream – but not quite quick enough – Gil whisked his burnouse around so fast that the man was slammed against the wall, and slithered slowly to the ground. As he did so, a tinge of regret surged up. These were ordinary men, being paid a pittance to do mind-numbing work, but there was no other way around it. Simple as that.

Tying the man to his chair with a nice thick piece of rope, Gil then began his search. The cell doors were the same as in the quadrangle, but the whole building was much more ordered. Designed along rigid lines, with fewer places to hide, he had to listen intently because there was a lot further to run in order to hurry out of sight, and it made his search slower as a result. So slow in fact that by the time he had covered the ground floor he knew that he had to do something different. With three more stories, and the chance that he might not strike it lucky until the very last cell, time was going to run out. Each cell had a corresponding number on the wall, so there had to be some sort of log-book, and it was that book which he now needed to see.

The office was bound to be by the front entrance, but there was yet another door in between him and it, and this one was of truly immense proportions. There was no way to get through without creating an almighty disturbance, and his key was not a fit either, so all he could do was wait. Wait for it to open, and keep on waiting, and waiting.

Checking his timepiece, Gil actually began to panic at one point, and panic was not an emotion with which he was particularly familiar. Neither was relief. Usually he felt so in control that relief did not come into it, but when guard number three approached, the relief was frankly overwhelming.

Pouncing forward, he tried to be a little less rough about it this time, and not actually cause the blood to flow. The way he was going, there would be no guards left soon. Having dragged him to the side, and taken his key, Gil then opened the door, and by some miracle found that the office was unattended. Locating the book was therefore fairly straightforward, and it did not take long before that name popped out. The physical description matched too, so there was no mistake. On the second floor. Cell two hundred and eighty-nine. At last. Were things finally set to go his way?

Preparing to retrace his steps, Gil closed the book, but then the outer door caught his eye. Would this new key work? Should he try it? Yes, and yes. He now had possession of an easy way to exit the entire building, and that could come in very handy in a few minutes time. Flying up the stairs, he raced down one corridor, just about managed to evade an oncoming guard, made it to the end of a second, and then found the right cell. He still had the lamp from earlier, and through the bars could see Thomas sitting up, staring forward, expression blank – until blinded by the light, and forced to turn away. Gil tried both keys in the lock, but already had a feeling that neither of them would work, and he was right. Time for some tools.

As he set to work, Thomas turned back, and with eyes steadily growing accustomed, he was able to see the hood and cloak, and wondered if he had begun to dream. 'What's happening?'

'Shush,' said Gil, filing the lock with furious intent, and head fixed to the left for any signs of trouble.

There was no need to concern himself with anything to the right because there was a wall beyond the next cell, meaning that he was squarely trapped in a dead-end, and it was a most disagreeable position.

'What are you doing?' asked Thomas, creeping forward.

'Trying to contrive your escape.'

'But why?'

'This really isn't the time for questions Mr Bateford.'

'But . . . I don't want to escape. I'm resigned to my fate.'

'Well apparently there's a young woman out there who isn't quite as resigned as you are.'

'Bessie!'

'For heaven's sake shut up or lower your voice!' Gil just about managed to maintain his thick Scottish accent despite the stress, and kept on filing.

'I'm sorry,' said Thomas, regretful but stern. 'But I want you to leave. I have been a coward once before. Please do not make me one again.'

Gil abruptly stopped what he was doing, put a hand through the bars, grabbed Thomas by the right wrist, and pressed painfully into the flesh. 'Reaching this point has involved a considerable feat of ingenuity, and getting out will involve an even greater one, so do *not* tell me that I have bothered unnecessarily. If you want to die, by all means die, but save it for when you're on the outside.'

Thomas could not think what to say, which was good enough for Gil, who let go, and put the file away. It was having no effect whatsoever. This needed something powerful, and he had just the answer. Pulling out one thing after another, Thomas watched it all in a sort of horrified awe, before finally asking:

'What *is* all that?'

'Tricks of the trade sir. Tricks of the trade.' It was important to chuck in the odd sir, appear like a servile man-for-hire, and it was also important to get some tinder going, which Gil successfully managed to do after dismantling the lamp.

'Why do we need a fire?' demanded Thomas as Gil put the lamp back together, and poured something into the lock.

'Because gunpowder generally doesn't burn by itself.'

'Gunpowder! What the hell are you going to do?'

'Blow this door off.'

'But the guards will hear.'

'Strange as it seems, I've actually thought of that one. But we don't really have much choice. It's rapidly heading for seven o'clock, which means that it won't be long before the birds are a-tweeting, and you're a-hanging. Is that really what you want?'

Thomas gulped.

'No? Thought not. Here.' Gil pushed his sword through the bars. 'As soon as this door's open, we'll be running for it to the end of the corridor. Then we turn left, reach the stairs as fast as you can move, and if anybody gets in our way, they'll simply have to be dealt with.'

'I won't kill in cold blood,' declared Thomas immediately. 'So you might as well have this back.'

'You don't need to kill, just look as if you *can*. Wave it around. And wave this in the other hand.' Gil gave him some money. 'It usually means that you won't have to do anything.'

Now devoid of a weapon, Gil drew out the poniard that was stored down the inside of his trousers. What it lacked in length, it made up for in muscle, with a very thick steel blade. 'Perfect for pressing none too gently against somebody's ribs,' he quipped, before noticing for the first time that Thomas was wearing prison garb. 'What happened to your clothes?'

'The guards took them. Said they can't bear to see a man hanged in a good suit.'

'Fortunate that I've come prepared then.'

'You mean that you have clothes in there as well?'

'Yes.' Producing them on cue, Gil instructed Thomas to change – and quickly.

'Is there anything you *don't* have hidden under that thing?'

'That *thing*,' retorted Gil indignantly, 'is a burnouse, and the answer is no.' It was amazing what you could store about your person in concealed pockets, flaps, double-linings and such-like. It was also very empowering to know that you had absolutely everything to hand. 'Brace yourself, and hands over the ears if you value your ability to hear.'

The tinder had now successfully ignited the end of a nice long stick, and having pasted himself against the wall, Gil made contact with the gunpowder at arm's length. A second later, the lock was gone – and without too much surrounding damage. It had actually been quite a small, neat explosion, although had made a considerably loud noise.

'Come on!' He pulled the cell door open, and Thomas staggered forward.

'I'm not . . . really sure . . .' He could smell whisky-breath through the mask, and was suddenly questioning whether it was wise to follow the instructions of a drunken Scotsman.

'There's *definitely* no choice now,' snapped Gil, wondering what Bessie could possibly see in this ditherer.

Racing along the corridor, they covered it without any trouble, and were almost at the end of the next, but then a guard appeared. Using his burnouse again, Gil soon had the fellow in a spin, but also inadvertently sent him crashing down the flight of stairs.

'Is he dead?' asked Thomas as Gil went down to find out.

'No. But he's just joined a growing company of men who are going to have sore heads tomorrow. Help me get him up.'

Thomas took hold of one arm, and together they hauled him back up the stairs, before putting him somewhere out of the way. Then it was back down themselves, but as they reached the first floor, Gil met a familiar face. The third guard was standing in front of him, hand to his temple, but awake, and poised to raise the alarm.

'Utter a sound, and I'll run you through,' vowed Gil, poniard held out about four feet from the guard's chest. Close enough so that one dart would be enough.

Aware of that particular fact, the man promptly closed his mouth.

'Turn and face the wall.'

The man did so, and Gil prepared to tie him up, but the sound of several approaching footsteps changed all that.

Grabbing hold of him, Gil pushed them all back up to the second floor, and prepared to send these reinforcements on a wild goose chase. 'Tell them it's happening on the top level,' he ordered, thrusting the forlorn guard out into the stairway, but keeping the poniard pointing at him from behind a nice piece of jutting wall. Thomas was hidden as well, and valuing his life, the guard did as he was told – before again submitting to being tied up.

'Very sensible,' said Gil, putting a gag in his mouth, patting him on top of the head, and leaving him with the other man. Nicely tucked out of the way.

Carrying on down the stairs, they finally arrived at the ground floor, and that door leading to the office – to freedom – but Gil did not stop. He propelled Thomas past it, blew out his lamp, and pressed them into the shadows as more guards rushed past. Such a minor lock, but such a great rumpus. Gil would have to find a far more efficient way of doing things in future.

'Here.' He handed Thomas the exit key. 'When I give you the signal, open that door, walk forward about twenty strides, open another door, and walk out. Oh and remember to stoop – because only a small section of the door opens.'

'Walk out? You mean through the front entrance? But there's a gate. *Two* gates!'

'Yes, and they'll automatically be opened for you.'

'Why?'

'Because you have the right look, and will have the right speech too. If anybody confronts you, sound authoritative, say that you've been here on the orders of the magistrates, and are investigating security. Say that you entered with the last shift, and that the place is a disgrace. You've seen a man fast asleep, another absent from his post, and that you'll be reporting it all to their superiors. Then keep on walking.'

'But I . . .'

'Don't doubt yourself Mr Bateford. Just do it.'

'And what are *you* going to do?'

Gil pulled out yet more rope. 'I'm taking the scenic route.'

'Why can't I . . ?'

'Because this is where we part. When you get out, head for the ironworks, but turn left just before the bridge. Walk for about five hundred yards, and you'll find two disused lots. Apparently there'll be a gentleman waiting for you in the first one.'

'Who?'

Gil shrugged. 'All I know is that there was a job needed doing, and money to pay me to do it.' He seized back his sword, stepped out, checked up the stairs, and then said: 'Go!'

As nervous as he was, Thomas obeyed, and Gil watched his back for a moment – in case any of those guards returned a bit too prompt – before making his way to the quadrangle. The man on the chair was still out cold, although Gil could detect signs of breathing, and the blood was drying up. Taking advantage of the key one last time, he accessed the gallows area, and then slipped it into his pocket as a souvenir. The scaffold was right in the middle, and he went around rather than running across it. Making contact with that wood would be just too much like tempting fate.

Using the rope, he clambered up onto the roof, shuffled along for a short distance, and lowered himself down on the other side. The cells backed right onto the canal, and he only just avoided pitching himself into the icy depths before setting off like the wind. With cloak, coverall and mask removed in flight, he made it back to where he had left his bag, changed, packed everything away, and re-emerged dressed as the Gil Tremaine from court. He then walked the streets sedately – because running would attract attention, and also because he was out of puff – and made it to the abandoned lots just as it was starting to come light.

'What are you doing?' he demanded as he entered the first building with timepiece in hand, and an accompanying look of irritation.

'Gil!' exclaimed Thomas.

'I said the second building. How long have you been here?'

'About ten minutes. I was beginning to wonder what to do.'

'And I was beginning to think you'd been caught. Come on.' He bundled Thomas out, and they scooted off towards the Ash forest – where Bessie was waiting anxiously, peering into the gloom. The Carrion crows were cawing away in the trees, as if preparing for a feast, and the light was rising so rapidly on the horizon. They were bad signs. She knew it. Things were going badly.

'Bessie!' hissed a voice from behind, and she swung round.

'Thomas!' She ran to him, clasping him so tight that she could feel his heart beating through her own chest, and actually be sure that he was for real.

'Bessie, you're freezing.' He kissed warmth back into her hands, but she assured him that she was not cold. Not any more. She had been standing there since five o'clock, but now all of a sudden it felt like a beautiful summer's day.

'Oh Thomas, I thought I'd lost you!' She clasped his face between her hands, and then they kissed as if nobody else was there – until Gil coughed, reminding them otherwise. 'Gil, you did it. Oh thank you, thank you.' She gazed at him, eyes glistening with gratitude. 'How did it happen? How did you . . ?'

'There's no time to go into it,' he interrupted as a man approached.

Bessie and Thomas both turned around in fear, but it was friend, not foe, and despite the fact that he was now sporting a beard, she recognised him. He was the one who had tried to bar her from entering the house on Market Square. That day when she had met the Chartists.

'Thomas, this is Medwin,' introduced Gil. 'He's an ex-middy, knows the docks, and he's going to have you on a sailing-ship before teatime.'

'Sailing-ship?'

'Yes. To the New World. You can't stay in this one for much longer.'

'And Bessie too?' reminded Thomas, which caused her to look at both of them with blank confusion.

'I didn't . . . I don't . . .' Her brain had not ventured beyond the hope of his escape. 'My . . . my father, I promised I'd be waiting with Ella when he's released, I . . .'

'Your brother can do that.'

'But . . .'

'If this is going to be an argument, can you keep it short?' requested Gil. 'In my experience the authorities tend to take the absconding of convicted felons rather seriously.'

'You have to come with me,' said Thomas adamantly.

'I want to. It's just that there's . . . there's Luke, and . . . my mother. She can't support herself, and Luke doesn't earn enough, and I gave Father my word. I just feel that I . . . I have to be there.'

'But I can't leave you.'

'It isn't leaving,' she explained desperately. 'It's a delay, that's all. The moment that Father is out, I'll come, and it's only July. It will pass in a flash. We'll be together forever after that.' She was staring beseechingly, as if begging for his consent, but Thomas could see that her mind was made up, and he had never been able to alter it before.

'Why? Why must there always be this barrier between us?' He punched his right fist into his left palm, and Gil saved her from having to answer that one by producing some money.

'Take this.' It was a huge wad of notes.

'No I can't.'

'Yes you can.'

'But the man in the mask – he gave me some.'

'How much?'

Thomas emptied his pockets, and before he could start to count, Gil declared:

'Not enough. You need to set yourself up with everything in a strange country. You can't ever come back here, you know?'

'Can't I hide somewhere in England? Just until July.'

'Not if you value your neck. And if you value ours, you'll go. Like *now*.'

'Please,' cajoled Bessie. 'I love you, and I need you to be safe.' She clung to him again, but when she tried to ease him away, he would not let go.

'Join me Bessie, *please*.'

'I will, I will. Six little months, I promise.'

Gil nodded at Medwin, who took a firm hold of the convict's right forearm, and with Bessie's desperate persuasion, Thomas was slowly led away. His eyes were fixed upon her with every step, and hers fixed on him, but then at last the tears and early morning mist meant that they disappeared from one another's view.

'I don't know why I'm crying. It's wonderful,' she said, finally focusing on Gil when sure that there was no more chance of Thomas returning to her sight. 'Thank you.' She seized his hand, and gave it a shake to add force to her words. 'Thomas would be hanging this minute if not for you.'

'I didn't do anything,' said Gil, shrugging to suggest that he was unworthy of such praise.

'But you found somebody who could. I must thank him. Who is he? You have to tell me.'

'It's best that I don't. Mercenaries aren't generally appreciative of attention. And I'm sure he feels my money was sufficient thanks.'

'Has this cost you an awful lot?'

Gil tipped his head dismissively.

'It seems that I'm in your debt yet again. And so soon.'

'Don't worry about it.'

But she did worry about such things. And she soon had a lot more to worry about – when a group of men appeared in the distance, armed with clubs and pikes. 'Oh no!' She put a hand to her mouth, and glanced in the direction which Thomas and Medwin had taken, before hating herself for having given the enemy any indication of their route.

'Don't panic,' said Gil. 'They're Chartist sentinels, not prison guards.'

'Chartists? You mean they're on our side?'

'Yes.'

'Then what are they doing?'

'Making their presence felt.'

'Won't they be arrested?'

'Unlikely. The authorities know that it will only stir up feeling, so they're largely ignoring them. Although there are some cavalry stationed a few streets away.'

'Cavalry?' The word conjured up fear for Bessie, and she could not really understand it. Probably hearing too many tales about Peterloo from Josiah. Sabres drawn. Innocent people slashed. But that was twenty years ago. Surely it would never happen again.

'Come on. We'd better get out of here,' said Gil, absorbing her sense of concern.

Half an hour later, they were back at the tavern, and Gil had left her there while he fetched his horse and Tilbury. The owner of the coaching inn was looking after them, and on the way he retrieved that special bag of belongings too. It was rather reckless to be carrying such a collection so casually down the street, but it was amazing how far nonchalance could get you, and nobody accosted him. In fact there were no signs that the pandemonium at the prison had yet emanated out into the town at all. Presumably they were still in shock, and debating what to do next. Gil smiled at the thought, and then once he had fixed his sword and bag into a secret place underneath the seat, he went to collect Bessie.

'The sooner I see the back of this town forever, the better,' she declared, climbing aboard. 'I hate it here.'

'Yes, I can't imagine it's left you with many fond memories.'

'None whatsoever,' she confirmed, before addressing something urgent. 'I know that this is an imposition, and I want you to understand how grateful I am for everything that you've done so far. I'll never be able to convey the full extent of my gratitude.'

'As I've said before, please don't try. Copious thanks does become very irksome very quickly.'

'I remember.' Bessie smiled only briefly. 'The thing is – I need to know whether this man might be willing to help my father as well. I should have asked you before you left last night. I don't know why I didn't. It all just happened in such a rush, but I've gone and left him in that place when I could have got him out. I've left him to rot.'

'Don't talk like that,' said Gil as her voice became increasingly distraught. 'How long has he been in there now?'

'Two and a half years.'

'And obviously he gets out in July?'

'Yes.'

'Then perhaps it might be best to leave him in there anyway. You have to keep in mind that Thomas is now an outlaw. He no longer has the right to live openly in this country, which is a small price to pay when you're about to hang, but your father has nearly served the whole of his sentence, and is so much older. He might not want to leave England, leave his home.'

Bessie did not respond.

'Isn't that true?'

'Possibly,' she conceded.

'And is he coping in there?'

'Yes. I've been told that he's alright.'

'Well then he's come this far, I suggest you give him the chance to see it through to the end.'

'You make it sound like a challenge. That he'll be proud of his achievement.'

'I think he probably will be. Wouldn't you?'

It took a few more statements to convince her, but at last she dropped the idea, and Gil was extremely grateful for that. His escapades might ultimately have been quite exciting, but he had now lost that element of surprise, and some of those corridors were extremely narrow and confined. It would be easy to end up cornered, and he had no desire to embrace that particular possibility again just yet.

'You didn't ask by the way,' said Gil, changing the subject as they left Henningborough, and headed out into the countryside.

'Ask who?'

'Thomas.'

'What?'

'Whether he did it. Whether he killed his father.'

'Of course he didn't do it! Why? Do *you* think he did it?'

'I don't know.' Gil had not really given it much thought, and riding hell-for-leather on a wobbly road was not the time for analysis.

'Aren't we going rather fast?' asked Bessie as they began to eat up the miles at alarming speed.

'It isn't me, it's the horse. He seems to want to get home.' Gil looked across and grinned – and it was almost the last thing he did, because seconds later, they hit a rut in the road – and the wheel on his side lifted up.

Bessie instantly felt herself tipping towards the edge, and launched herself across him, while he pulled on the reins for all he was worth.

'Hold onto your hat!' he cried as his wheel mercifully came back down again, and it was now simply a case of trying to bring the horse to a stop – a task which was much easier said than done – but eventually achieved on the outskirts of Thurleigh. The gallop turned back to a canter, then to a trot, and finally they were stationary – with Bessie still prostrate across his lap. A situation which she was very quick to remedy.

'Sorry about that,' said Gil, and his matter of fact expression instantly gave her the giggles.

'I think somebody's trying to tell me something.'

'What? Like never take a lift from a mad aristo?'

'No. Like I'm long overdue in this world. I could have been dead at least three times in the past year.'

'*Three*? Good gracious.' Gil rubbed his head, questioning whether his life was really as thrilling as it ought to be. 'That would have been quite ironic, wouldn't it? Manage to evade the hangman, and then my Tilbury does for you.'

'I think probably tragic would be the far better word.'

Gil stepped down. 'Time to assess the damage,' he declared, rolling up his sleeves, and getting on his hands and knees to investigate the under-carriage.

Bessie wanted to help, but did not know the first thing about carriage mechanics, so instead retrieved Gil's bag, which had come out between her legs. His things were spilling out, so she pressed them back in, and cut herself on something sharp.

'Ow.' The nick made her flinch, and having gingerly pushed his clothes aside, the poniard became apparent.

"I suppose he likes to be prepared", she concluded. The dagger by his bed was testament to that much.

Storing it back at the bottom of his bag, with some other rather curious items, she then placed the black velvety material on top. It was ever so delightfully soft . . . and vaguely familiar, although she could not understand why, because Gil never wore black. Frowning, she pulled it out to discover that it was a cloak – and there was another piece too. Same colour, but with two very distinct holes.

Two holes . . . "Wait a minute". Bessie held it up. She could see through them. They were eye-holes. Just like that man last April. The man who had seized Gil's money, and carried it off into the night. But why did Gil have . . ? No . . . that was ridiculous. The man had been taller, with an accent, and when he had flicked that gold sovereign at her from the town wall, it had been with his left hand. Gil was right-handed.

'I'm afraid the king-bolt on the axle's gone,' announced Gil, standing up, and flapping soil off his hands. 'Which means that unfortunately we're walking the rest of the way.'

Bessie stared at him, face still locked into a frown, and then suddenly noticed his trousers for the first time. He was wearing *black*, and shoes to match. 'Oh my God,' she whispered, and as Gil saw the material in her hands, he could have said exactly the same thing. 'It was you last April. It was you!'

CHAPTER FIFTEEN

Stepping down from the Tilbury, Bessie moved a few strides away, still clutching his bag, and with her brain flashing through the images of that fateful night. She had left Josiah's in the early hours, seized by the sudden mad belief that a solution was presenting itself to her. Reaching Carrow Square, she had then stolen Gil's money, only to be accosted by the night-watchman on the way out, and pitched into the canal. With the money on the waterside, a masked man had picked it up with ease, leading to a chase halfway across Somerden. A futile chase, followed by an agonising return to Carrow Square, and a grovelling apology in Gil's bedroom.

But none of it was true. None of it. It had been *him* all along. She had been arguing with him on the rooftops, and not even known it. How could that be? How could he adopt an accent so well that his own voice became literally unrecognisable? And how could he have found the time to put on all this stuff? The cloak, the mask. If he had spied her in the act of escape, there would only have been time to put on some shoes before she was led out of sight towards the canal, and that . . .

'You knew I was coming, didn't you? When you went back to your guests earlier in the evening, and left me in that cloakroom, you *knew* I'd return.'

'I had my suspicions, yes.'

'That was why the window was so easy to open . . . the lights on . . . the safe! You laid it all out for me!'

Gil raised his eyebrows in what was meant to be an expression of chastened acceptance, but to Bessie it was an arrogant act of provocation. Her blood began to boil, the colour in her cheeks rose, and Gil moved forward to calm her down, but she was not having any of it.

'Don't you come near me.'

He kept on coming.'

'I'm telling you – stay back!' She drew out the poniard, and jabbed it at him, which managed to secure the desired effect.

'Aren't you getting all this just a little bit out of proportion?'

'Out of proportion! You were watching me! The entire time that I was in your house!'

Gil did not confirm the truth of that, because frankly there was no need.

'Where?'

'Where what?'

'Where were you watching me from? Where were you hiding?'

'Does it matter?'

'Yes it does. Tell me.'

'Alright, I was "hiding" behind the curtains.'

'The curtains? You mean in the study?'

'That is correct.'

"Oh my God". She could picture herself knelt beneath his desk, head practically inside his safe, and all the time he had only been a breath away.

'Who else was involved?'

'Involved?'

'Yes, you know what involved means, don't you?'

'Nobody.'

'Are you sure? Not Reeve? Not Sylvia?'

'Sylvia?'

'Don't act the innocent with me Tremaine. There was some female around that night, and I know it for a fact, because her things were in the room right next to yours.'

Gil tipped his head, as if shocked to discover that there was something about her movements of that night of which he still remained ignorant. 'No,' he replied uninformatively. 'There was no other woman involved.'

'Well the night-watchman must have been.'

'I can assure you that he was not.'

'Not?' Bessie could not believe her ears.

'Yes,' said Gil as if he could not understand why she was having a problem with this particular issue.

'So let me get this straight. You encouraged me . . . no, that isn't quite strong enough . . . you *incited* me to take your money, presumably for the perverse enjoyment of taking it back, and the watchman simply got in the way, is that it?'

'Pretty much.'

'Which means that he was genuinely trying to drown me, and you just bloody well stood there!'

'Trying being the operative word. I was confident that you'd prevail in the end.'

'Oh you were confident, were you?' Bessie repeated him through gritted teeth. 'You really are a perfidious wretch.'

'Whoa!' Gil held his hands up, the attack all too much for him.

'What? Surprised that I know such a big word? Well I do, and when you called me truculent once, you were right. I was born savage, and if you hadn't just been responsible for saving Thomas' life, I'd be slashing you to pieces with this thing.'

'But I have, as you say, just saved the life of your one true-love, which means that really you should be showering me with considerable gratitude.'

'Gratitude!'

'Well . . . maybe not quite that far, but at the very least you have no cause to be aggrieved. Surely you realise that whatever I did that night, it doesn't alter what you did. Not one bit. You still broke into my house.'

'Yes, because I was desperate, and you knew it! All you had to do was bolt that window, and lock your safe. Save me from myself. But you couldn't do it, could you? You have to leave it all open for me. Draw me in, and then lie in wait, like a cat waiting to pounce.'

'It wasn't quite like that,' countered Gil with a relaxed air of control.

'What was it like then? When you pinned me against the wall as if I was some intruder, and put a dagger to my throat. What was that exactly?'

'That was . . . well . . . high spirits? I had to maintain the act, you understand.'

'Oh and you did Gil. So very well. Especially on the town wall. What a nice touch.' She hated it, but tears pricked her eyes, and in turn they pricked his conscience.

'Perhaps that gesture was a little . . . over the top?'

'Oh no, no, no Gil, it was utterly perfect. The aristo flicking crumbs across to the beggar.'

'You aren't a beggar.'

'But of course I am. That's all I've ever been to you. Gil and his games with the gutter girl. You've had yourself no end of fun.'

'Don't you think you ought to calm down now?'

'I very much doubt I'll be calming down this side of 1850!'

'So you're planning on scolding me at the limit of your lungs for the rest of the decade, are you?'

'No, I think I've had enough of scolding. How about I start cutting? Remember? Like you did, to emphasise how I'd *bled* you dry.'

Gil did indeed remember. His palm had stung for a week.

'How about it?' She placed the blade against her own hand. 'Or how about here?' She moved it quickly up to the side of her neck.

'I'd rather you didn't.'

'Why? Are you the only one allowed to make such theatrical gestures? All the rest of us have to act sensibly, is that it?'

'I doubt your conduct can ever have been described as sensible.'

'And no doubt you're right, but at least my motives occasionally have an element of merit. What's your excuse?'

'I don't need an excuse for my behaviour.'

'Of course you don't, but I think that outfit deserves *something* of an explanation, don't you?'

'I'm permitted to dress as I wish, and as you've presumably now gathered, it has enabled me to enter Henningborough prison tonight.'

'But why against *me*? That's what I don't understand. Why make me feel guilty about money that had never even been lost?'

There was no immediate response, because Gil had no immediate answer.

'I know we're not exactly . . . friends.' Her eyes began to glisten some more. 'But I thought at least we shared . . . I don't know . . . common ground. I never thought you'd want to laugh at me like this.'

'It wasn't about laughing at you.'

'What was it then? Have you done it to anybody else?'

'No, but then nobody else has tried stealing from me.'

It was impossible to argue with that.

'Look.' Gil clasped his hands in an act of resolution. 'How about we forget that any of this ever happened? You did something foolish, and perhaps I did something foolish in return. Simple as that.'

'It isn't as simple as that.' Bessie dropped his bag unceremoniously onto the seat. 'And we can't just pretend that it didn't happen.'

'Why not? This outfit is entirely responsible for the fact that Thomas Bateford isn't dead, so why don't you just view last April as some sort of . . . valuable trial run?'

'Because if you hadn't done what you did last April, there wouldn't have been any *need* to save him now! The only reason I ever married Arnold was because I caught a chill, and the only reason I caught that chill is because I was pitched headfirst into the Somerden canal. If none of that had happened, Thomas would never have left before I could talk to him, he would never have felt betrayed, never have gone to Mr Winchell. There wouldn't have been any court, any fleeing to the far ends of the earth, and quite frankly Arnold would probably never have even died!'

Gil stared for a moment as if she was in some way possessed, and then shook his head most forcefully, refusing to accept that so much could have stemmed from so little.

'You don't believe it, do you? Of course you don't. In that cosy little world of yours, you can't even begin to imagine how one act by one person can have such an effect. Because you always think you can fix things, don't you? One click of those fingers and everything's alright again, but that isn't how it happens in the real world. In *my* world. Actions impact on life and death – yes, life and death, and then there's nothing you can do except try and learn to live with the consequences.' She thrust his belongings back across the seat towards him, stared coldly into his eyes, and then walked away.

'What are you doing?'

'What does it look like?'

'It looks like you're walking all the way back to Somerden.'

'Got it in one.'

'But that's another twelve miles. You can't do it on foot. Not by yourself.'

'I've done it before. I can do it again.'

'It isn't safe.' Gil ran after her, and placed himself slap-bang in the middle of her path.

'My God Gil, if I didn't know any better, I might have thought you cared.'

'Of course I care! I wouldn't have turned up at the trial if I didn't.'

'You turned up at the trial because you've got nothing better to do, and because you were hoping to play at dressing up. Clearly one of your favourite pursuits.' She stepped to the side, but he blocked her immediately.

'And your favourite pursuit is obviously indulging in hysteria, which comes as rather a surprise, because I assumed that histrionics were the province of other women, not the mighty Bessie Cullen.'

'Well that makes two of us facing nasty surprises today, because I thought that beneath this thick layer of flippancy, you might actually have a heart of gold, but actually you don't have a heart at all. You're an unscrupulous, unprincipled, unbelievably objectionable man who . . .'

'Nice long adjectives there again,' praised Gil. 'I particularly admire your sense of alliteration.'

'Oh go to hell!'

'Don't forget to add parasite,' he reminded her when she had stalked about ten yards – and which immediately incited her to stalk back.

'Don't worry, I haven't forgotten. You feed off others for your feather-bedded existence, and you've been feeding off me for your fun. But not any more. It's over Gil Tremaine, and I hope more than anything that I never lay eyes on you again as long as I live.'

'Being as you've now plummeted somewhat down the social ladder, there's a very good chance that your wish will be granted.' He shrugged his shoulders as if to say: "That's how the cookie doth crumble".

'Do you know something Gil? As long as I don't have to encounter you any more, I wouldn't mind plummeting as low as pondlife!'

'What a delightfully dramatic statement. I really must use that one myself some day.'

'I hate you.'

'No you don't. You wouldn't even know how to go about it.'

'Wouldn't I? Well just you wait and see.'

'You'll never manage it,' he predicted as she turned and flounced off once more. 'You'll be knocking on my door again before too long. I'll bet a gold sovereign on it.'

'I won't, you know, I won't, I won't, I won't!' repeated Bessie for the best part of six miles before she finally began to stop chanting it. Yet even six miles on from that, as her legs neared Somerden, her brain was still with Gil Tremaine – and she was still boiling with indignation.

What gave that man the right to treat her in such a manner? The patronising self-righteous . . . yes, parasite! Parasite above all else. He might not be as cruel as Arnold, or exploit to the same extent, but he still toyed with people, still considered himself entitled to manipulate them, because he was richer, more powerful, more intelligent.

Intelligence – that was the worst of it. He felt he was better than her, knew more words, more about life, more everything, and that night he had even known what was going through her head. When she thought of how she had been watched, dangled on a string, ridiculed. Her face flushed crimson, and her whole body wanted to shrink deep inside itself. For anybody to get the better of a Cullen was offensive, but that man of all men? It was *beyond* offensive. It was intolerable. And it was also totally impossible to shift it from out of her mind. She saw the coaching inn, the courthouse, so many visions which ought to plant more important issues in there, but *still* he was at the forefront. Even when she saw Dolly – or Freya McNeill – or whatever her name was, it was not enough of a distraction. In that moment Bessie did not care whether the laundry-maid was alright, or whether Mr Emerson had caught up with her; she cared about nothing except Gil Tremaine. Gil Tremaine and his boundless superiority – and in the end it took the sight of Erskine Avenue itself to at last begin to push him to the side.

She knew the relevant number, knew where she was supposed to have taken up residence, and where her husband had died. It was identical to the rest of them, a Georgian terrace, impressive, quite forbidding, but this one had an extra something hanging over it – because a murder had been committed within its bounds. Of that she had absolutely no doubt.

Crossing the street, she rang the bell, and within a minute Bellamy answered. If he was shocked to see her, he did not show it. His expression conveyed sadness if anything, and he appeared tired. She wondered whether the sadness was for Thomas, but since he did not ask, she chose not to offer up any information just yet.

'Can I speak to Harris please?'

'I'll see if he's available,' came the reply, deferentially executing his role as always, and showing her into the drawing room.

It was probably unintentional, merely a force of habit, but she would have preferred not to be shown into that room of all rooms, not to have to look at the fireplace where Arnold had breathed his last. Or choked his last. Even if he had only been semi-conscious, panic must have coursed through his veins, and that was an awful thought. Nobody deserved to die like that, and it was as if Arnold knew it, as if he was hovering here, haunting all those who had ever done him wrong. She could picture him so vividly. Standing by the near-empty decanters, ranting at life, and what it had done to him. Vowing to exact some dastardly revenge. When in fact he was the one who had set all of this misery in motion.

It seemed a curious truth that those who dished it out on such a regular basis were always the ones least well-equipped to take it. They would rail and bellow, and indulge in self-pity, when those who had been on the receiving-end for years were merely supposed to suffer in subdued silence. But some wilful girl by the name of Cullen had bitten back, and she could feel his aggrieved frustration in every feature of this room. The layout, the style of furniture, the clash of garish colours which had surely not been left by the previous occupants. It had all the hallmarks of Arnold's touch, and that was why it looked so very much like one of the rooms down Holliston Road. Or what she had long imagined those rooms to look like, and presumably he had become fully acquainted with them in his final weeks. She might have been the one who killed their marriage, but she had honoured her troth to the end, which was more than could be said for him.

'You wanted to see me,' said a meek voice from behind her, and Bessie turned to face a traumatised Harris – followed by a less-than-traumatised Charles.

'I'm surprised you aren't still in Henningborough,' she remarked coldly.

'Same here,' retorted the older sibling. 'Although it's probably best for Thomas that you aren't. Your face as his parting image would surely have been most unpleasant.'

'You did it, didn't you?' she declared, in control of herself, but brutally direct. 'You killed Arnold, and you set it up to point right at Thomas.'

'No I didn't.'

'Come on Charles, there's no need to be shy any more. I thought you'd be bursting with pride, eager to tell me how you've pulled it off.'

'Oh I *am* proud, don't you worry about that.' He took a symbolically dominant position in front of that fireplace. 'It's a bit like role-reversal, isn't it? You standing in the dining room, listing all your little achievements. "The Munroe dinner – that was me. Oh and the incentive scheme – that was me and Thomas". Remember?' Charles copied her voice contemptuously, before laughing. 'Well now it's my turn. Dear father's death? No, that wasn't me, but the window lock? Yes, that was me, and informing the constables – well as you know, that was me too. Do you want to know why?'

'The funeral. You've said.'

'Yes, but it wasn't the sight of you and Thomas. As repulsive as that has always been. It was actually the rather enlightening talk I had with Mr Winchell.'

'Enquiring as to what you were likely to get?'

'How perceptive. Yes I was, and when I heard all that primo nonsense, I have to admit that I wasn't best pleased. But then I heard of how Thomas had been informed on the very day of my father's death. The very morning. But most importantly, not quite the very hour. Well I ask you – how could I possibly look such a Gift-horse in the mouth?'

'And by Gift-horse you mean inciting the authorities to murder your brother on your behalf?'

'I consider that to be an overly melodramatic way to put it, but yes. I didn't have to kill my father, and I didn't have to kill Thomas either. I merely had to fiddle with a lock.'

'Don't talk like that, it's bad,' said Harris.

'Oh do shut up.' Charles hissed the retort, and there was something in that hiss which made Bessie turn to the younger brother, who was curled up in a chair furthest from the fire – and literally shaking.

'I'm sorry,' he cried as she stared at him. 'We shouldn't have done it.'

'*We*? You mean . . . I don't believe it.'

'I was afraid. I'm sorry.'

'You don't owe her any apology,' condemned Charles. 'Thomas had means, motive and opportunity, just like the lawyer said. All we did was point it out, but you can't accept that, can you Elizabeth? That dear departed Thomas might just have hung for a crime which he actually committed.'

'He's certainly very dear, and unfortunately departed, but he hasn't hung.'

Charles looked up at the clock. 'I think you'll find that by now he has.'

'No he hasn't. He's escaped.'

'What?'

'Escaped. As of seven o'clock this morning. Thomas is a free man.'

Harris leaped up from his seat. 'Really?'

'Yes.'

'You mean it? You're telling the truth?'

'Yes.'

'And he's already far away? There's no danger of him ever being caught?'

'None whatsoever,' she confirmed, smirking at the now glowering Charles.

'Oh thank you, thank you. When you see him, you must tell him that I'm sorry. You will, won't you? I'm sorry. So very sorry.' Harris clasped Bessie by the arm. 'You have to make him understand that I didn't know about the window and the constables until it was too late. That I should have spoken out, but I was scared.'

He peered at her so desperately, his eyes so beseeching, that she felt compelled to say something comforting. 'It might not have made much difference Harris. It was the evidence that Thomas was here in

Somerden, and what Mr Winchell said – those things did more damage than the window lock.'

'But I knew he was innocent. I could have told them. I could have told them that . . .'

'Hold your tongue,' ordered Charles.

'I can't! I have to say it. I did it, I did it! I killed him.'

'What?' Bessie frowned for a moment before realising that Harris had just got himself into such a state that he needed a bit more reassurance. 'You haven't killed anyone Harris. Thomas is free. He's alive. If you don't believe me, read the papers tomorrow. It will all be in there.'

'I'm not talking about Thomas. I'm talking about my father. I killed him Elizabeth. I killed him!'

Bessie swallowed, stared at him, and then asked for a repeat – which Harris gave, again with the same level of panic, and adding the words: 'I didn't mean to. It was an accident.'

She was certainly not about to dispute him on that one. He was no murderer. Leading him back to his chair before his legs could give way, she swallowed once more, and then encouraged him to explain.

'It was late. We were all out together, but when it reached the early hours, Father didn't come home with us. He went to . . . you know . . ?'

Bessie knew.

'When he finally got back, it was almost light, and I could hear him along the landing, shouting and bawling. Mostly . . . about you.'

'I can imagine.' Words to the effect that she was the same as those women down Holliston Road, only *far* worse.

'Then it all went quiet, and when I got up later, I thought that he wouldn't be around for a bit. So

I tiptoed down for a . . . well for a little drink. Except I'd got it wrong. He was in here, and he . . .'

'Became aggressive,' filled in Bessie.

'Yes. Said that I was a total waste of space. That he wished I'd never been born. I didn't say anything back. I didn't aggravate him. All I wanted was a drink, but he wouldn't let me have any. He thrust the whisky at me, taunted me, said horrible things, and I didn't mean to push him, really I didn't, but all of a sudden he was on the ground, and he wasn't moving.'

'Then why not just say that?' demanded Bessie. 'Why on earth cover it up?'

'I didn't. I mean . . . it wasn't intentional. I told Charles, and when we came back down, there was all this nasty stuff around Father's mouth, and Charles said that we needed to keep quiet, because otherwise there might be trouble. And at first it seemed like the right thing to do. The doctor thought that it was natural causes. Everything was going fine, until . . .'

'Your brother manipulated an accident into a murder.' She turned away from Harris, and focused venomously on the second son. 'Thomas might have done it eh?'

'He wanted to,' came the defiant retort.

'That isn't quite the same though, is it?' She prowled towards him. 'You sent your own flesh and blood to the gallows, full well knowing that he was innocent. I didn't think even you could stoop *that* low.'

'Low? I'll tell you about low. Low is what I would have been forced to tolerate if I'd let Thomas steal my inheritance. And it *would* have been stealing because it belonged to me! After everything I've had to put up with, I was just supposed to let him waltz off with all this money in one hand, and the likes of *you* in the other? Well no way! Not Charles Bateford!'

'You know something Charles? I may not exactly be the person I set out to be, but no matter what I do, I'll never be as despicable as you.'

He licked his lips, as if set to spit again, but this time managed to keep it in his mouth, buoyed by the knowledge that he had still won. 'Dead or alive, it doesn't make any difference. Thomas forfeits, case closed, and it all comes to me. Although of course when I say all, I mean what's left after you finished with him. You, and the cards, and all those other bloody women. If he hadn't died when he did, I've have *had* to kill him, before there was nothing left.'

'Ah, you poor thing,' sneered Bessie. 'You really have suffered, haven't you? Well go on – enjoy it. Enjoy every last penny of it. Because once it's gone, it's gone, and the one thing it won't buy you is the one thing you've craved since birth.'

She stepped very close to her stepson.

'You're small Charles. You're small and inadequate, and everybody knows it. Thomas might be out of the picture, Arnold might be dead, but you'll never be anything other than you've always been. A pathetic number two.'

Charles put his hand up to slap her, but she had learnt to be quick on her toes, and her dart out of the way caused him to almost topple to the floor.

'Sermon over for the day, is it?' he growled. 'Then get the hell out of my house.'

'With pleasure.' Bessie walked commandingly towards the exit, but Harris lurched up, stopping her.

'I really am sorry. You do believe me, don't you? Please forgive me.'

'It isn't my forgiveness that you need Harris. You were willing to sit by and let Thomas hang for your mistake.'

'I know, I . . . I . . .' His lip quivered, and although she was so full of anger, she still could not direct much of it at him. They were the same age, and yet he seemed so very much younger. Lost. Deprived. Of love, attention, guidance; and perhaps during her time at Bateford Hall she could have done a bit more to address that.

'I'm sure Thomas will understand that you were afraid,' she conceded softly.

'Do you think so?'

'Yes.'

'Will you come back and see me one day?'

'No.' She did not want to hurt him, but he had to know the truth. 'I'll never be back here.'

Harris sank down again, before glancing towards the drink.

'Try and stop using that as a support,' she advised him. 'And stand up for yourself.' She stared at Charles, knowing how he was going to treat Harris in the future, and it made her wonder whether her advice was all wrong. Harris was set to be suppressed by one male or another for the whole of his life, and maybe it would indeed be better if he drank himself to death. Get it over with quickly.

What a family. Of the four children born, one had rebelled against Arnold's every word, one had fallen pregnant, one was a miscreant, and one now a killer. If anybody were to hear it, they would feel heartily sorry for the man, consider him entitled to be disappointed in his offspring, but she knew that they were equally entitled to be disappointed in him. That even applied to

Charles, although there were malignant forces at work there which would have found an outlet regardless of his upbringing. And what had Jane done about it all? Absolutely nothing. Just sat back in fear. Did that make her the most blameworthy of them all?

As Bessie walked out of Somerden, she came to the conclusion that not a single one of them could escape the blame, and while Arnold had lost his life, and of course Jane, the rest of them had all lost two and a half years. Lies, plots, resentment, revenge. What the hell was it all about? They would each be rotting in a box like Arnold before too long.

She dwelt on that for quite some time, before finally being struck by the realisation that such thoughts themselves were a waste, and that if you were alive for any particular purpose, it was to be happy, and to try and bring that happiness to others. Which thankfully she could now do right away by giving Cynthia and Drew the wonderful news about Thomas. She could not wait to see their faces, and even began to run as she neared the Hall, so eager to share in something joyful.

'You'll never believe what's happened!' she exclaimed, bursting into the study unannounced, but being checked by the sight of three tense faces.

Drew, Cynthia and Luke.

'Ah, another Cullen. How delightful,' observed Drew with uncharacteristic sarcasm.

'What's going on?' asked Bessie, which was rather a strange statement on the day of Thomas' intended execution, but she knew instinctively that this had nothing to do with Thomas.

'Good question. Why don't you answer for us Cynthia?' Drew strode abruptly forward, forcing Bessie to step aside, and as he closed the door, she caught a look which passed between his wife and her brother – a look which said everything.

'Oh God Luke, what have you done?'

The words were whispered, but Drew heard them, and found them really quite amusing.

'Brilliant!' He clapped his hands. 'You know him so well.'

'Tell me you haven't . . .' Bessie shook her head, wincing, imploring somebody to tell her that this was not happening.

'Oh yes he has,' declared Drew. 'Go on, enlighten your sister as to when it started. Or should I say – when it started again.'

Faced with the glare of not only Drew, but now Bessie, Luke could do nothing other than stare down at the floor, leaving Cynthia to reply:

'The beginning of October.'

'My, you even manage to sound smug,' condemned Drew, before crossing over to his desk.

Beginning of October? Bessie tried to think what that meant, but first she had to remember what year she was in. 1840 . . . yes, that was it . . . they had entered a new decade, and three months ago had been . . . exactly when Luke arrived back. On the third! Back for his family, not for Cynthia Bateford. "I know where my obligations lie. No I won't go up to the Hall. No I won't do anything stupid again".

'You lying little toe-rag,' she hissed, and that brought Luke's eyes quickly up off the floor.

'Don't talk to him like that,' snapped Cynthia. 'We have nothing to be ashamed of. We love each other, that's all.'

'I must have been brought up all wrong then,' declared Drew. 'Because I thought adultery was an affront to most people's sense of morals. And letting yourself get pregnant was even worse.'

'Pregnant?'

'Yes, you're going to be an auntie again. Isn't that nice?'

Bessie's legs suddenly felt like they had nothing in them at all. 'I'm so sorry Drew.'

'And don't start apologising for me either,' retaliated Cynthia. 'I'm glad of our love, and I'm glad of our babies, and if Thomas were still here, he'd be the same. He believed in love, and following your heart, and when somebody captures your soul, there's no use in trying to fight it. You have to . . .'

'Shush,' said Bessie as Cynthia seemed set to embrace some sort of love anthem, and Drew's anger began to look even more intense. She had spent enough time with Arnold to know when a man was being pushed to the edge, and Drew was getting very close indeed.

'No, no,' he retorted. 'Let her speak. Let's have it all out in the open, shall we? Thomas and Bessie. Cynthia and Luke. Brother and sister with brother and sister. What a glorious symmetry. Only now of course Thomas is dead, and I think I might send you to join him.' He lunged at Luke, took him unawares, and had an arm locked around his neck before any of them knew what was happening.

'Leave him alone!' shrieked Cynthia, and tried to intervene, but Drew had such control that he was able to swing her lover's body around effortlessly, and it was Luke's legs that in fact sent Cynthia flying back onto the sofa.

It was a forceful landing, but on a soft surface, so she suffered no twinge, but in that moment Drew would not have cared less if she had.

'Please stop it,' implored Bessie.

'Stop? Sure, I'll stop Miss Cullen. When I've broken your brother's bleeding neck.'

'No don't!' She knew that she ought to grab something, attack Drew with it, but he was the victim here, and hopefully she could distract him in some other way.

'Thomas isn't dead.'

'What?'

'He's alive. Escaped this morning. He's out on the run. Miles away by now. Free, and safe.' Bessie looked across to Cynthia, expecting some sort of reaction, possibly tears, but the girl only had eyes for Luke – who successfully managed to use the moment to his advantage, bringing an elbow up into the bottom of Drew's stomach, and breaking free.

As Drew bent over, Luke staggered away, and Bessie was afraid that her sibling was now about to turn aggressor, but in fact he said that he was sorry.

'I know we've done wrong, but it doesn't have to be like this.'

'You expect me to give you my blessing, do you?' Drew straightened up in spite of the pain. 'Accept it? Carry on as normal?'

Luke was not quite sure what he expected. He loved Cynthie, more than life itself, but he had not actually imagined them living together. At least not yet. 'We didn't set out to hurt you,' he added lamely.

'Oh how comforting. You've ruined my life. You and your curse of a sister, but hey all's well, because you didn't mean it!'

'We're sorry Drew, really we are,' said Bessie, following Luke's lead, but doing more harm than good.

'Everything was fine until you darkened my door. You do realise that, don't you? Why eh? What is it with you Cullens? Always feeling the need to meddle with people who are none of your flaming concern.'

'Luke isn't meddling with anyone. We love each other.' Cynthia stood up, and moved towards the father of her children.

'Don't even *think* of placing a finger on him,' warned Drew, and it actually made her stop. 'You're still in my house, and you're still my wife.'

'I'm not your anything, and I never was.' She said it with considerable spite, and then very deliberately took up her position by Luke's side.

Drew could not think of anything else to do, except pick up a vase from the side, and smash it against his desk. The remaining fragment was not much of a weapon, and indeed Cynthia laughed, but the jagged edge looked pretty nasty from where Bessie was standing.

'I told you not to touch him,' repeated Drew, brandishing the glass, but Cynthia proceeded to do precisely that, stroking Luke's arm, before announcing:

'We're leaving. And we're taking Isabel with us.'

She led Luke across to the door, but then they were halted in their defiant exit by the fact that it was locked.

'Oh dear,' said Drew, holding up the key, and tipping it from side to side like a pendulum for all to see.

'Open this door.'

'No.'

'Open it!'

'Or what? Are you going to scream? Go ahead, scream as much as you like, but nobody leaves until

I say so.' Drew promptly deposited the key back into his pocket.

'You can't keep us here forever.'

'I wasn't thinking about forever Cynthia. Perhaps just . . . until the baby's born. Because of course it might, just might, be mine.'

'It isn't.'

'Oh come, come, you can't actually say that, now can you? You may have convinced this sap here to the contrary, but we both know that we've been intimate these last few months.'

'I haven't convinced Luke of anything. He's well aware that we sleep together, but he's also aware that it means nothing. Two years of sleeping together, and nothing's happened, because my body only responds to love, and I've only ever known love with one man.'

Her voice was now so smug that each word was literally dripping with self-conceit, but Drew did not react. He just stood there, transfixed by a hurt that was starting to blind him.

'Get us out of here Luke.' Cynthia directed him towards a chair, and he dutifully began to bash at the panelling as Arnold had once done. But that old wood had been replaced with solid oak, and it stood strong in the face of this particular onslaught.

'I can give you everything,' said Drew, creeping forward. 'Whereas him? All he can offer you is poverty, and a family full of convicts.'

'I don't care.'

'You don't care? I went to a colossal amount of trouble to get you back into this house. To get you back with the daughter who meant so much to you, and you don't even care!'

'No I don't.' There was not one ounce of remorse, pity or concern in Cynthia's voice. 'Because I love Luke.'

'So you keep on saying.'

'Drew, please put that down.' Bessie had kept a close eye on that glass, and the worry in her words caused Luke to stop his assault, and turn around.

As soon as he realised that Drew was practically upon them, he tried to push Cynthia behind him, but she was not in the mood to be protected.

'We're leaving Andrew, and there's nothing you can do to stop us.'

'Andrew? Andrew! What on earth makes you think that you have the right to take that sort of tone with me? Eh? What the bloody hell have I done that's so wrong?'

'You're keeping us imprisoned for a start, like Thomas in a cell, and just like Thomas, we're now going to escape.'

It was probably uncalled for, but in that instant Bessie almost felt as hateful towards Cynthia as Drew did. What was she playing at? Why be so remorselessly aggressive? And how dare she bring Thomas up whenever it suited her, while showing little or no interest at all in the fact that he was actually still alive.

'Let's move away from the door, and talk this through.' Bessie put her anger aside, and spoke cajolingly as the tension built – and nobody budged.

'Yes, let's talk. It's always good to talk, isn't it?' Drew's eyes were locked onto Cynthia, and hers were now locked onto him.

'There's nothing to talk about. I'm leaving with Luke, and you'll just have to put up with it.'

'Oh for Christ's sake.' Bessie sprang in front of them, so that she was right in Drew's face. 'Ignore her, she's confused. A few days away from here, and she'll soon come to her senses. Mark my words.'

'No I *won't*!' retorted Cynthia, before deciding to cement that statement by stepping to the fore, and threading her arm through Luke's.

'Can't you see what you're doing, you stupid cow?'

Cynthia did not manage to find any words this time. She had never been called a name like that before. But in fact it was lucky for her that she was pregnant, because otherwise she might have felt the full force of Bessie's hand smacking her across the face as well.

'She's telling the truth,' announced Drew calmly. 'That's what she's doing. There won't be any change, not today, not tomorrow, not ever. Because she loves him. Isn't that marvellous? All the world rejoice!' He flung his arms out. 'Well she can go ahead and love him. She can love him and be damned.' Thrusting forward, glass to the fore, he was going to make sure he pierced some flesh – and they all saw it, like in a kind of slow motion. Cynthia instinctively clasped both hands to her stomach, Luke began to turn his back as a shield, and Bessie lunged across. But the one thing none of them could do was to stop the motion of that glass, and when it reached its target, a peaceful tranquillity at last visited the room. Silence descended, breathing was put on hold, and nobody uttered a sound – until of course that all changed in an instant as the first drops of blood began to fall.

Chapter Sixteen

'They're arguing again,' announced the housekeeper as she swept back into the kitchen.

'When aren't they?' sighed the butler. 'This family must surely be the most discordant in Somerden.'

It was seven thirty in the morning on Monday the second of March, and the staff at number seventy-three Erskine Avenue were partaking of their usual chatter while attending to the family's breakfast.

'Once more unto the breach dear friends,' was the quip as the housekeeper breezed back out. Breezy was the right word for Miss Hawkins. Always on the go, with skirts billowing out behind her, she created quite a swish whenever she passed by, and usually brought up any dust that might be lying around the place as well. With cheeks aglow, and formidable hips, she regularly busied herself with things that were actually none of her business, but everybody loved her. Even the butler – although he would not be giving her the satisfaction of ever admitting to it.

He sat quietly for a few minutes once she had gone, and then finished his tea in one gulp, and strutted out as well. There was no need to be up for another half an hour, but he rose early in order to talk to her for a bit. He always thought that she was at her best in the mornings, somehow youthful again, reminding him of the years when they had both been fresh-faced – and an awful lot thinner.

They had served here together for the best part of twenty years now. First for Mr Bainbridge, and more recently Doctor Driscoll, both moving gradually through the ranks to their present positions of power. They had courted once, but it had not worked out, so now they spent their lives in a contented state of companionship.

Heading up the back stairs, he walked towards his customary position in the hall, and again rued the design of this particular townhouse. Too much space by the stairs, and nowhere near enough where he needed it by the front door. Indeed the hall funnelled itself into a sort of bottleneck, making it impossible for any two people to walk abreast through the entrance. It was a case of being forced into single file – or the embarrassing option of advancing like crabs, stomach to stomach. Apart from that, the rest of the house was pretty much the same as any other in the area, apart from the fact that it seemed to have been squeezed from either side, so that if you studied it in isolation, it would have the look of a rather squashed rectangle.

The butler was used to standing a little way back from this narrow section, but today curiosity got the better of him, and he edged closer to the dining room. For the housekeeper to mention a dispute, it was surely worth investigating, but unfortunately the voices through the door were too muffled, so he took another step closer, and then at last they came into range.

'I don't see what the problem is,' bewailed Robbie's injured tone.

'You don't see? I brought you up to have some sense, and still you don't see!'

That was his father.

'It's only a bit of fun. Not like serious money or anything.'

'Serious?' Anthony Driscoll clenched his teeth, pursed his lips, and promptly marched over to the door – just as an enquiring ear had decided to lean right up against the panelling.

'Ah hello sir.' The butler straightened up fast. 'How are you this fine morning?'

'I'm . . . in adequate health, thank you. And yourself? Are you well?' His staff were not generally this cheery first thing. There was obviously something wrong.

'Yes, I can't complain sir, can't complain at all.'

'You're looking a little flush. I think you should go back to bed.'

'Oh no, really, I'm fine.'

'I would beg to differ. Now do as I say.'

'Certainly sir.' There was no arguing when your master was a medical man. You could hardly tell him that his diagnosis was wrong.

Having dispatched the butler, Doctor Driscoll then entered his drawing room for a moment, but was soon back.

'Please Father, just this one night.'

'No. You won't be attending any more card-parties, and that's my final word on the matter.'

'But I'm about to hit a winning streak, I can feel it.'

'It doesn't matter whether you win or not,' he snapped, before realising the utter stupidity of such a statement. 'Of course it would be better if you won, because then I wouldn't have to bail you out all the time. Where do you think money comes from Robert? Trees in the back garden?'

'Well I didn't think those near the house were called Silver Birch for nothing.' Robbie grinned, but his father did not.

'I've given you my decision, and if I find you've gone behind my back, I'll make sure that you never wring another penny out of me for as long as you live. Is that clear?'

There would have been no need for the butler to stand too close to hear the end of that particular sentence.

'What a dreadfully harsh attitude,' lamented Robbie, adopting the hurt expression which generally worked to such good effect on his mother. 'You'd see your only son starving in the street simply because he sought refuge from his exceedingly dull life.'

'Oh you poor darling!' chipped in sister Ivy.

'If you starve, it will be your own fault for disobeying me. And I most definitely *will* see you out on the streets before I hand over another pound to those vagabonds you call friends.' Anthony almost bared his teeth in frustration, but Robbie would still have persisted with a fresh line of appeal if not for his other sister.

'Do you think we could return to what we were discussing originally?' Leah spoke with an element of fatigue, not sarcasm.

'Good idea. I've said all there is to say on your brother's escapades. Now let's discuss your mother.'

'I think she should stay where she is,' came Ivy's quick contribution. 'She's better off there, and more to the point, she'll drive me mad if she comes back.'

'How can you say such a thing?'

'Because it's true Leah. We all know what she's like when she's ill. It's: "Get me this. Get me that. You're not leaving me in this state, are you? I'm so ill, I don't know how I bear the burdens of such torment". I can't stand it!'

Leah stared with an expression of utter horror, and said simply: '*I'll* look after her. I want to.'

'You say that now, but just you wait until you've had a few weeks of to-ing and fro-ing to every beck and call. Then you won't be so condescending.'

'That's enough Ivy! We all know your views loud and clear.' Anthony sighed. If only his children knew when to bite their tongues a bit more often. Except Leah of course. She was the only one who had never forced him to feel ashamed. A sensible child – perhaps rather too sensible – she occasionally did come across as somewhat holier-than-thou, but he could rely on her, and that was a comfort to him.

'If you think you can care for your mother with only Miss Hawkins to help, then that is fine by me.' He tried to smile, but was all too aware that Ivy's brutal declarations were terrifyingly accurate. Mrs Driscoll was a difficult woman. Perfectly amiable sometimes, and the life and soul of any party, but demanding and difficult nevertheless.

'So what are you doing today Father?' Robbie issued this question with an extremely innocent expression, but Anthony was not fooled in the least.

'I have patients to see, and then I am interviewing for the chambermaid's post. Which you already knew.'

'Did I? But I thought that was the housekeeper's domain.'

'It is, but I need to take charge this time. Secure somebody appropriate.'

'Oh good.' Robbie's eyes lit up. 'I'll assist you.'

'No you won't. You're the reason I'm doing these interviews in the first place! You badger poor Miss

Hawkins into appointing whoever takes your fancy, and then when they're here, you pester them until they run out in floods of tears. Well *I'm* making the selection this time, and it won't be anybody you find remotely appealing.'

'Really Father, I don't know what you mean.'

'Oh just go away Robert, I've had far too much of you already today. And keep your distance from those applicants, or there'll be trouble.'

Anthony sneezed perfectly on cue, as if his body was equally eager to be rid of these irritants, and when all of his children had left the room, he again questioned why mealtimes had become so wearisome. It was not as if his son was a minor any more, but reaching maturity had made him even *more* of a bother, and Ivy was a worry at times. Lack of discipline in the formative years – that was the cause, and the blame lay squarely with his wife. "You're too busy dear. Leave the child-rearing to me", she had said, before proceeding to do absolutely nothing. And now it was all too late.

That depressing thought hovered around Anthony for the best part of the morning, and then having finally gone away, it resurrected itself as he began the first interviews in the afternoon. He just knew for a fact that his son would be appearing out of the woodwork at some point. In fact telling him to do otherwise had been about as much use as talking to a brick wall. And of course that proved to be the case.

Robbie had so far been watching the arrivals from his bedroom window, but had recently begun to ponder when to make his move.

'Seen anything you like?' asked Ivy, twisting a lock of hair mischievously through her fingers.

'Perhaps.'

'What is she? Red-head?'

'Possibly.'

'Those green eyes do it for you every time, don't they? Or is it the fact that their passions are so easily ignited?'

'Please don't encourage him,' implored Leah. 'He's bad enough as it is.'

'Oh he's nowhere near bad enough yet,' retorted Ivy, who had still not forgiven her sister for winning that discussion at breakfast.

'Right, I do believe I'm ready now,' announced Robbie. 'Ready, willing and able – and determined to save those poor dears from their enforced ennui.'

'They don't know how lucky they are,' observed Ivy, and her supportive cackle followed him all the way down to the kitchen door, which he flung open as if truly the master of their fate.

'Ah hello ladies, I believe you're all here for the vacant position – yes?'

They stared back in silence, unnerved by the brash individual in front of them, and a few wondering whether he was the one they had heard murmurings about.

After a long pause during which Robbie began to feel just the slightest bit uncomfortable, an answer finally came from the back.

'Yes, we're all hoping to find work.'

'Good.' Robbie breathed out. He was used to getting quick responses, and so anything else disturbed him. 'I just thought you'd like to know that I shall be assessing you along with my father. And I prefer to make acquaintances *before* the formal interview. It's so much cosier that way.'

He beamed a smile, and was still beaming it when another applicant entered, gave a nod to the brunette sitting closest, and then left via the back entrance. Robbie scrutinised her with a sense of intense perturbation. Surely acknowledgement would not have been too much to ask for. But he could not wallow for long as the brunette stood up.

'Please, let me do the honours,' he said, seizing her arm, and taking her upstairs. 'Don't want you getting lost, now do we?'

Within less than ten seconds, they had gone as far as they needed to go – and reached the Driscoll drawing room.

'I thought I'd be their escort for the day Father. You don't mind, do you?'

Anthony gave an icy stare. 'Thank you. You may now leave us to it.'

'Oh no, since I'm here, I really ought to stay. Might be able to add a different dimension to things.' He took up a chair in the corner, and made very sure that his eyes did not stray towards his father again. If he caught one of those "Get out of here" looks, it might be hard to ignore.

Anthony had no choice but to start with his son present, but was determined to issue some very stern words once this interview was over. Robbie did not say anything during the process, partly because he thought that he would have more chance of staying if he was good for a while, but mostly because this applicant was frankly rather on the plain side, and so not worthy of his attention.

As soon as she stood up to leave, he stood up with her, knowing that it was the only way to avoid his father's wrath. Then a minute later, he returned with the next offering, and Anthony observed it all with a burning desire to throw his son out of the nearest window, but instead simply chose to get on with it.

The next girl was the red-head, and red-heads pleased Robbie immensely, so he began his usual line of questioning:

'You're not married then?' He could tell through the corner of one eye that Father was staring at him. 'It's a question of whether or not you would live in.' But clarification did not help. Anthony had long been concerned about his son's interest in the staff sleeping arrangements.

'No, I am not married.'

'How old are you?'

'Sixteen.'

'Sixteen? A good age. I remember sixteen . . .'

Robbie was quickly interrupted by his father, who knew perfectly well how this particular line went.

'Do you have any previous experience,' he asked.

'Yes, and I have references too.' She rose to present them, but Robbie intercepted, placing one hand upon her wrist, and removing them slowly with the other. Anthony then grabbed them from his son, and concluded the interview. This girl might be better than the first three, but they were not having her. No way.

Robbie continued the same ritual with many of those that followed, knowing exactly the effect that it would have, until finally they came to the one who had answered his question earlier, and then he remained quiet.

'Do you have any experience Miss Scanlon?'

'Yes, I have done this kind of work before.'

'But you don't have a reference?'

'No. Unfortunately my employer died without leaving any assessment of my work, but I can say with confidence that she would not have faulted my commitment. I was always punctual, and dedicated to the efficient completion of my tasks.'

'I see.'

'And I am also happy to work on an unpaid basis at first. If that is what you prefer? In order to prove my commitment.'

'No,' said Anthony, deep in thought. 'I believe that everybody is entitled to remuneration for their labour.'

'Oh . . . I see.' Elizia Scanlon swallowed, unsure of whether to say anything else. To put her case was one thing. To beg was probably too much.

'And would you be looking to live in?'

'No.'

'You do realise that you have to be here at six every morning. Six until four.'

'Yes. That won't be a problem.'

'Right.' Anthony turned to his son. 'Go and see if there are any more applicants.'

'There aren't.'

'Do as you're told. And if not, then wait for me in the surgery.' This time he managed to convey a very severe visual message, and a reluctant Robbie obeyed.

'Miss Scanlon, or should I say, Mrs Bateford?'

Bessie lowered her gaze. 'I thought perhaps you might not recognise me.'

'I wouldn't have done, except your voice is unmistakably not that of a servant any more. Neither, I might add, was your explanation.'

'I'm sorry to have wasted your time.'

'Why did you come here? Why would you want to work down the street from where your husband was murdered?'

And where Charles presumably still lived. 'Because I have found it hard to gain employment elsewhere.'

'People know you?'

'They know the name Cullen. My maiden name.'

'Hence the change to Scanlon.'

'Yes.' It was so horribly – or appropriately – close to scandal, but at least it held an element of truth. Marge Cullen had been Marge Scanlon before she married. 'And there's something else.' Bessie moved her left hand from behind her back, and held it out for inspection.

'What happened to it?'

'An accident.'

'What kind of accident?'

'Some glass slipped.'

He turned it over, and tried to straighten one of the fingers, but they were all fixed, like a claw. 'You can't move them?'

'No sir.'

'Does it pain you?'

'It did at first, but now it is much better.'

He turned the palm upwards again, and studied the cicatrix. It had healed well, but there was nothing he could do. Movement might come back one day, but it was unlikely, and until then, this hand was not much use to her.

'I'll be going then,' said Bessie, drawing it back self-consciously.

'Where are you living?'

'Nevin Street.'

'Which number?'

'Eighteen.'

'Right, well thank you for your application Miss Scanlon, I shall consider it carefully.'

Bessie knew what that meant. He pitied her, but would not be employing her.

When she had left, Anthony sat down again, and completely forgot about talking to his son – so his son came to him.

'Well my vote goes to the red-head,' declared Robbie boldly.

'No, I've already rejected her.'

'Well what about that girl with the northern accent then?'

'Perhaps. Or perhaps the last one.'

'Last one? But there's something funny going on with her hand.'

'I'm aware of that.'

'When I say funny, I mean deformed.' Robbie pulled a face. 'It fair gave me the shivers.'

'Her fingers are simply paralysed. Nothing more.'

'But we can't have a paralysed maid, can we? She won't be able to do anything.'

'I think she will manage adequately. In fact I know she will. And she's about to be given the chance.'

'You aren't being serious?'

'I am deadly serious.'

'But Father!' Robbie proceeded to moan for the next five minutes, but it made absolutely no difference.

'We're having her Robert, and that's that!'

CHAPTER SEVENTEEN

A week later, number seventy-three Erskine Avenue was all set for the return of Millicent Driscoll. The doctor had left first thing to collect her, Leah was busy ensuring that all the rooms smelt sweet and inviting, and the butler was standing ready to offer greetings with a beaming smile. He had developed the very useful ability of putting on a beaming smile wherever necessary, even if totally false, and although it was an uncharitable thing to say, life had been significantly more peaceful since Mrs Driscoll's departure for rest and recuperation at her sister's house. But every good thing must come to an end eventually, and after another ten minutes of tranquillity, the front door opened and the doctor appeared. Alone.

'Isn't Mrs Driscoll with you?' enquired the butler, experiencing a guilty surge of hope.

'Yes, she's here,' sighed Anthony, stepping aside to allow a direct view of the carriage – if you could call it that. His wife was always quick to remind him that *other people* had a carriage, whereas they merely owned a conveyance, and not a very comfortable one at that. Perhaps she was right. He did have to admit that it was looking rather shabby, but carriages – like money – did not grow on trees, and whatever word you could ascribe to it, Millicent was in the back, with seemingly no intentions of getting out.

'Is anything wrong sir?'

'My wife . . .' announced Anthony, eyebrows knitted in a frown. '. . . requires that she be carried in.' He stared apologetically, as his butler gazed around the bottleneck.

'Mother!' exclaimed Leah from the top of the stairs, hurrying down excitedly, until realising that Mother was not in fact present.

The same explanation was offered, and then Leah hurried off outside, leaving Robbie to sum up the situation.

'I know what that look's all about,' he declared, grinning provocatively at his father. 'You're thinking: "She's a bit big, this entrance is a bit small, and how on God's earth are we going to equate the two?" I'm right, aren't I?'

'Really Robert, do you have to be so terribly blunt?'

'There's not much point being anything else.'

'Well you're wrong,' condemned Anthony in the face of that infuriatingly persistent grin. 'I was thinking that although your mother's ankle is now healing well, it is still weak, and she is perfectly entitled to request assistance.'

'I don't believe a word of it,' retorted Robbie, before deciding that he knew precisely the thing.

Dragging the butler off, they then reappeared three minutes later with the chaise-longue. It was from Millicent's bedroom – her favourite seat – despite the fact that her bottom had never actually taken up residence on it. She liked the effect that it gave to a room – effortless elegance – just like herself, although Robbie really could not follow the reasoning. To him it looked like a sofa that had never quite reached its potential. Indeed he found it rather ugly, but nevertheless today could be its day.

When Anthony saw the cumbersome green object being manoeuvred haphazardly down his stairs, all he could do at first was blink, but then came to the conclusion that he could not think of anything better, and so sent them on outside. Goodness knows what the neighbours would make of it, but when it was placed down in front of the carriage, his wife could apparently see nothing wrong with it. Not a thing. Millicent Driscoll turned Egyptian Goddess for the day – it was perfect, and her outfit was even a match!

In as ladylike a manner as possible she deposited herself, folded her arms, and indicated readiness for the off, while her son and butler took a very deep breath. Millicent's convalescence did not seem to have helped much at all in her long-standing quest to lose weight, and it took one almighty heave to lift her up. The chaise-longue creaked, as if telling them that it was not used to such challenges, and their own backs creaked telling them exactly the same, but somehow they managed to keep Millicent upright, and shuffled her towards the front door.

"Please God, don't let anybody see this", prayed the butler, face glowing red, and a line of perspiration massing on his brow as they began the difficult manoeuvre of crossing the threshold. It was possible to fit the chaise-longue through the door – they had discovered that much on the way out – but there was little room left for anybody's legs hanging over the side, and of course Millicent was not willing to move those legs, or accommodate their distress in any regard whatsoever. In fact the only thing she did was to bark instructions, telling them how bad a job they were doing, and Robbie became convinced that if there were a whip

to hand, she would have used it on him. But finally –
with a large helping of Divine intervention – they laid her
down in the hall, and Robbie sank onto the end, panting.
The butler was tempted to do the same, but had learnt
never to fully relax, even with an amiable family like the
Driscolls, and so merely sagged unassisted.

'Why have we stopped?' demanded Millicent.
'You don't really think that I can manage those stairs,
do you?'

Robbie looked desolate, and the butler looked half-
dead, so Leah declared positively: 'We can do it. Come
on, I'll help in the middle.'

'Get a move on. It's draughty. I'll catch a chill.'

That comment successfully kick-started things again.
The thought of Millicent Driscoll complaining of a chest
infection for the next month was enough to stir even the
weariest of legs.

Approaching that mountain of a first step, the
butler put in a superb effort, and actually succeeded in
clearing it, followed by the second and third – before it
was Robbie's turn. Anthony stood with arms folded,
observing it all with a powerful sense of regret. Was this
really what he had envisaged for himself when he was
twenty years of age? Why had he not put more thought
into his decisions? Nobody in their twenties should ever
be allowed to make a decision until having accepted a
six-month cooling-off period. Maybe if he had enjoyed
just such a period, he would not be standing in this hall
now, watching a scene which distressed him greatly, and
a wife who frankly irritated him to distraction.

While Anthony dwelt on what might have been, and
Ivy monitored progress from above, Robbie put all his
concentration into trying to raise a leg, while also

maintaining the strength in his arms. They were throbbing, and aching, and paining him in every possible regard – probably because the most strenuous thing that he usually did with his arms was to hold a pack of cards – but somehow, from somewhere, he found the strength to plant a foot onto the bottom step. It was his right foot, and the left then followed suit and matched the achievement. So far so good, and thus it continued for three more stairs, until that right leg was once again called upon to act – and promptly decided that enough was enough. The knee buckled, the seat tipped violently, and Millicent tipped with it. Latching onto the back in a desperate attempt to save herself, she discovered that despite declarations to the contrary, she was actually quite hot, her hands sweaty, and the plush promptly slid from her grasp.

The sight of his wife literally bounding down the stairs like some ball towards his feet, was all too much for Anthony Driscoll. Stuffing a handkerchief in his mouth, he turned and immediately ran back into his surgery – supposedly in need of medical equipment, while Leah let go of the chaise-longue, and bent down to offer assistance. But Millicent was no longer in the mood for assistance.

'Let go of me!' She shot up like a Jack-in-the-box, and straightened her disordered clothes. 'If this is the best you can do, I'm better off taking care of myself.' She abruptly marched up the stairs, with no signs of apparent injury or weakness, and indeed managed to ascend with such alacrity that she was up in her bedroom before her husband could even resurface.

'Presumably she found the sudden use of her legs,' he concluded, and as Ivy cackled from above, he let out a heavy sigh.

Half an hour later, Robbie had apologised on the minute, every minute, in a desperate attempt to convince Mother that her fall from grace had not been deliberate, and that none of her dignity had in fact been dented. But unfortunately she was refusing to listen, so he had decided to leave her wallowing in the presence of handmaiden Leah, and now went off in search of Elizia.

Oblivious to most of what had been going on, Bessie was busy with her list of tasks, making beds, lighting fires, and cleaning anything and everything. It was a step down from her work at Mrs Langley's. She did not wait at table, and it was certainly a step down from where she had been this time twelve months ago. A governess with a middle-class family. But beggars could not be choosers, and at least her life was simple now. That was the one thing you could say about it, and mercifully Doctor Driscoll was ensuring that it would stay that way. Her name was Elizia Scanlon, and no other name would be passing his lips.

She had not quite been able to believe it when the messenger came to call at Nevin Street, and told her that she was being offered the position. It had been like a wonderful gift from heaven, and she was determined to repay his kindness in full, working better than any other maid before her, with every room so spick-and-span that you could eat your dinner off the surfaces. Of course that would be slightly easier if she did not have to face constant interruption, but two of the doctor's children seemed to enjoy causing something of a disturbance, and indeed as she set about cleaning the son's bedroom, her focus was once again tested.

'Ah, so you've reached me already,' declared Robbie. 'You do realise that if you whip through this work any quicker, we'll have to find some more chores for you to do.' He grinned, and although Bessie was not rude, she was clearly not amused. 'You're far too severe for one so young Elizia. How old are you by the way?'

'Nineteen.'

'Gosh, that's even younger than Leah. I'm twenty-four, in case you're interested.'

The lack of a response suggested that she was not.

'*Please*,' he implored. 'You have to stop and talk to me. I've just faced an episode of significant trauma.' He proceeded to explain, and then concluded with a statement reflecting considerably hurt feelings: 'Nobody seems to care that I could have been crushed. If Mother had landed on me, I'd have been squashed flat. In the hall, right now. You'd be scraping me off the floor, and there wasn't much in it, I can tell you. Yet she refuses point-blank to accept that I didn't do it on purpose. For some bizarre reason, she actually believes that I've just made an attempt on her life!'

He sat on the end of the bed that Elizia was trying to make, and gazed at her. 'Do I look like a murderer to you?'

'I'm glad that nobody appears to have suffered any serious injury,' she replied, and moved onto dusting the window-sill.

A lull followed, during which Robbie stared at her back, wondering what sort of strategy might work best. 'I'm bored. Show me some mercy Elizia.' He said it just as she turned around, and caught a very definite look of censure from her. 'Something flashed across your mind, I can tell,' he seized. 'What was it?'

In exact words it would have been: "If you're that bored, why don't you clean your own room?"

But she kept control of herself, and instead replied: 'I was thinking . . . that beds don't make themselves,' which was still rather caustic, although Robbie took it in good heart.

'God damn it Elizia, you're right.' He rolled up his sleeves. 'I'll make my own bed.'

'No Mr Driscoll, that isn't necessary.'

'Yes it is.' Flinging the duvet off, he deliberately made a complete shambles of it all – in order to look like a helpless young man in need of assistance – but it was not enough to make her smile. He reminded her a lot of Harris, but was different in one key respect – for all his smiles, he left her feeling uneasy, and that was rather curious when Harris was the one responsible for a man's death. Perhaps it was the fact that Robert Driscoll's eyes were set just a bit too close together. Or perhaps it was simply that she now viewed all males in a very bleak light. Ever since that day when she had discovered three things about three of them which had shocked her to the very core. Each one continued to fill her with deep sadness, and as a result she had vowed that nobody would ever get close enough to make her feel like that again. From now on she was assuming the worst of absolutely everybody, and that included Doctor Driscoll's only son.

'Don't you go redoing it,' he ordered with a laugh as she saw the product of his "work". 'It might be a mess, but it's *my* mess.'

Bessie had no intentions of redoing anything. She merely wanted to get out of this room as fast as possible, complete her other tasks, and go home.

Home. Could it really be called that in all honesty? The residents themselves called it the rookery. Nevin, and a couple of other streets, which constituted the Somerden Slum. It was not far from Holliston, although of course the places along that road looked a great deal better, because clients did not wish to embrace squalor, and the rookery offered nothing except squalor and filth. It was a crowded, wretched, dangerous area, but it was the best that they could do since Drew had cut Cynthia off completely. If she wished to leave, then she would be leaving with nothing. So Marge, Cynthia, Ella, Bessie and Luke were now squeezed into a small dwelling that made the mill cottage look like a palace.

One drunk, one pregnant, one child, one challenged by an injury, and one Luke. A rum bunch indeed, although as predicted, Marge was now making a considerable effort to battle the gin. There was the odd lapse, but generally she was managing to keep to Adam's ale, and usually in the form of a cup of tea. She had also taken on some seamstressing work, because there were suddenly people around her that she loved, people to work for, and another baby on the way too.

Luke was still navvying, but it paid very little, and as a family they were struggling to find the rent. Doctor Driscoll was neither mean nor generous. He paid the average, and Bessie knew she could expect no more. If she needed more, it would entail a visit to Gil, but there was no way that she was doing any such thing. She had vowed to stay away, and she was sticking to that vow. Besides, they only had to cope on a temporary basis until Wilf's release. Then a new life would beckon with Thomas.

She sometimes felt bad when thinking about it. The doctor had taken a chance on her, and she was set to leave so soon, but she could not tell him any of her plans just yet. He had hired her when nobody else would listen, when she had made so many enquiries that she had lost count, and had even turned to making match-boxes from home. Rising at five in the morning, collecting the materials from the factory, and taking four hundred back in the evening. Four hundred was not a bad figure, but it was nowhere near enough. Her hand meant that she was far too slow, and for her endeavours in seeking to prove her worth, she had not even been paid.

That had been a disheartening day, and frankly returning home was now a regularly disheartening experience. Ella was coping fine, and that was a joy, but it was all Mammy and Daddy, and whenever Bessie so much as looked at her niece, Marge would say:

'Come on Isabel, come to Grandmamma.'

It hurt. More than words could say. But she was not the only one hurting. Cynthia was having issues with the poverty and the deprivation, and even after July, life would still be a struggle, so there was no great salvation on the horizon. It was simply a case of rolling up your sleeves and getting on with it, and Bessie prepared to once again hide her irritation in the face of Cynthia's never-ending stream of complaints.

'Where have you been?' demanded Luke the moment that she walked through the door.

'At work. Where do you think?' Bessie had meandered a little on the way, but that was entirely her prerogative.

'Here, read this.' Luke thrust a letter into her hand, but she first returned with a question of her own:

'Why?'

'Cynthia's gone,' snapped Marge, as tense as her son. 'Or hadn't you noticed?'

Bessie stared at Cynthia's chair, and at Ella's empty play area, and then proceeded to take her time enjoying an unexpected moment of power. After all the years of being criticised for reading the wrong type of literature, and here was her mother, in need of that knowledge of letters. Well, well, well, how life doth pan out. It was so very tempting to pass comment, but instead Bessie took a cruel satisfaction in relaying the letter's contents:

'Cynthia has returned to Drew. Apparently not because she wants to, but because of Isabel and the baby. She can't bring a new life into the "type of surroundings that they we are currently forced to endure". Her heart is aching to do differently, but she has to look at it from every angle, and there is simply no other option.' A sickly expression of love followed, and at the end Cynthia begged Luke not to come after her, but to know that his children would have a better life, and to be contented by that knowledge.

'You're lying,' growled Marge.

'Excuse me?'

'You're lying. You aren't reading what's there.'

'Then take it outside, and ask somebody else. Here, have it.' Bessie shoved the letter brutally forward, and Marge was all set to do exactly that, but Luke stopped her.

'No Ma, it's true. I know she's been having difficulties.'

'Yes, but it'll get easier. We need to support her more, that's all. We can't let this happen.'

'It's already happened,' declared Luke dolefully.

'No it hasn't. If you go after her, you'll catch up before she even reaches the Hall. Go on, get moving.'

Marge literally pushed Luke towards the door, but Bessie spoke out, and stopped him.

'Look at our life Luke. Do you really want this for your children? Day-in, day-out. When they could have so much better.'

'This is fine,' retorted Marge. 'Although I dare say that after the finery of Bateford Hall, it doesn't seem quite good enough any more.'

That was the first ever reference to her daughter's secret life. There had not even been a mention of the trial, not in all these weeks, and Bessie chose to ignore it now. 'Ella could fall ill if she stays here much longer. It's damp, cold and unsuitable – and you know it.'

'But it won't be long before it's summer,' argued Luke. 'It'll be better then, and Ma's right – Cynthie just needs some more time.'

'It isn't time she needs, it's being left where she is.'

'You don't understand Bessie.'

'I understand perfectly. She can't live our way. She's been brought up differently, and there's no way to adapt.'

'Yes there is,' slammed Marge. 'If you give her a chance, but you've never wanted her here, have you? All because Isabel loves her more than you. You're jealous, and you can't deal with it.'

'That has nothing to do with anything.'

'Hasn't it? You've wanted to keep Isabel to yourself all along. That's why you never told me. Months and months up at that Hall, with *my* grand-daughter, and not even a word.'

'You weren't exactly receptive Mother, and anyway I couldn't trust you. I was risking my life in that house, and since you don't consider that life to be worth very much, I'd have been a fool to tell you a thing.'

'And why exactly is that? Why do I wish you'd never been born?' Marge's expression was fierce, but those words which would once have stung so badly, now washed over Bessie like water off a duck's back. 'Because you destroy everything, time and again. Cynthia brings love, and light, and children into my home. Whereas you? All you've ever done is take them away.'

'There wouldn't be a home to put anybody *in* if it wasn't for me,' reminded Bessie. 'Did Cynthia pay the rent in Henningborough? Did she? Was she the one who rescued you from living under a bridge? Got you out of the workhouse?'

'Workhouse?' repeated Luke.

'Yes, the mother who thinks the world of you has actually spent several months in one of them *because* of you. Because of your incessant inability to keep your damn trousers buttoned.'

'Don't you talk to him like that,' warned Marge. 'Don't you dare!'

'Why not? Everything fell apart the first time because of him, and now we're living in this street rather than the valley, and all BECAUSE OF HIM!'

'I can't help being in love,' muttered Luke, and from such a strong, fit young man, that seemed such a truly pathetic statement.

'No,' said Bessie. 'But you could do something to avoid acting on it.'

'And so speaks the voice of chastity. How many men have *you* slept with? Arnold? Thomas? Countless others no doubt.'

'I have never slept with Thomas!'

'Why were you always sneaking off to the wood to be with him then? Thought I didn't know? Me and Cynthie knew about you long before the trial.'

'I was "sneaking" as you put it, in order to spend time with him. Companionship.'

'Oh yes?' challenged Luke.

'Yes! But you wouldn't have the first idea what that means, would you? Meeting up with Cynthia all those times before you even came to see us. No wonder you were visiting with such bleeding regularity. And her with those "trips down to the village". You're like a pair of animals!'

'And *you're* just as bad. You and Thomas were lovers, and I won't believe otherwise.'

'You don't have to Luke. The proof is right here.' Bessie stalked towards him, jabbing at her stomach. 'I'm not pregnant!'

'No, but Cynthia is, and I won't have two of my children being raised by another man. I can't take it.'

'Well you should have thought of that, shouldn't you? Like you should have thought of a lot of things.'

'Leave him alone.'

'Oh of course Mother, we mustn't upset dear Luke, must we? I've suffered, you've suffered, this entire bloody family's suffered, but as long as it doesn't impact on dear Lukey-boy!'

'It *has* impacted on me,' he declared resentfully.

'How exactly?'

'I had to leave. I had to take up navvying.'

'So you think that teaming up with a few mates equates to what you left behind, do you? To the prison, and the workhouse, and the full fury of Bateford retribution.'

'I think we've all had it tough.'

'No Luke. You ran away, and I helped you to do it. I helped to save you, so that you wouldn't have to witness any of the consequences of your unutterable madness. But there was no such escaping for the rest of us. We had to stay and face it all.' She was now right up close to him, and aggressively wedged her scarred hand between the two of them. 'Look at it Luke. This is a direct product of your selfish, self-gratifying madness.'

'It isn't madness to love Cynthia, and Drew did that anyway. It had nothing to do with me.'

'No, nothing ever does.' Bessie swung away, and sneered. 'Go on then, go and make another mistake. Might as well. Why stop at two? Run after Cynthia right this minute. Do as Mother says.'

Luke hesitated.

'What are you waiting for?' demanded Marge before Bessie could utter it.

'I'm just trying to think.'

'There's nothing to think about. You love her. You have to go and get her.'

'Maybe . . . maybe I ought to give it just a few months.' He could secure work that paid better, and a nice place to live. He always knew where to find Cynthia and his children. It would be possible to retrieve them at any time, and have his family back.

'She's playing games with you,' hissed Marge, standing right in front of Bessie. 'Don't listen to her. Cynthia needs rescuing. And Isabel too. They rely on you. Don't let them down.'

'But I think . . .'

'Don't think at all Luke. Just do it.'

'But shouldn't I respect her decision? That's what she asked for, isn't it? She has to do what she believes is right, and I . . . I think I have to let her.'

'No Luke, you don't.'

'I do.'

'No!' Marge attempted to seize his arm, but he shook her away.

'I need to be by myself,' he snapped, and that was it. He was out of the house, and beyond her reach.

'Oh dear,' remarked Bessie. 'Your precious baby boy has gone and ignored you. That's a dangerous new precedent, now isn't it?'

'You . . !' Marge swung round with a vicious snarl. 'You evil, you manipulative . . . I hate you, I hate you!'

'Oh have a gin, and get over it.' Bessie took out the bottle hidden in the far corner of the room. 'Come on. Do us all a favour, and drink yourself into oblivion. You're always at your best then.'

It was an appalling thing to do to an alcoholic, but Bessie did not care any more. In fact she was glad that Marge was furious, that Luke was distraught, and that Cynthia had given up. None of them deserved to be any different.

Waltzing out in a happier frame of mind than she had enjoyed in an awfully long time, and imbued by that sense of reckoning, Bessie decided that today was the day to visit Josiah. She had been putting it off, fearful of having to show him what had happened to her hand, and explain yet again what a disaster the Cullens had managed to heap upon themselves. But now suddenly she felt in the mood to cope with anything, and strode positively towards that familiar house on Fulton Street.

Mrs Jennet was in the kitchen, and before Bessie could even enquire as to Josiah's whereabouts, a host of questions came flying at her – about the trial, about life as Mrs Bateford, the fine dresses, the parties. It was understandable, and Bessie had plenty of time to explain, so gave as much information as she could, and left no question unanswered until the cook was finally satisfied.

'I knew the idea of you killing anybody was absolute riddlemeree. Never believed a word of it, *and* I told people so.'

Bessie smiled. 'Thank you very much.'

'Do you know where Thomas is now? Some people say he's holed up in the forest like Robin Hood.'

'I'm afraid I have no idea.' It was surely safe to say America, but Bessie liked to err on the side of caution as far as he was concerned. 'I suppose Josiah's upstairs?'

'No.' For the first time Mrs Jennet appeared a little pensive.

'Then . . . in his room? He isn't ill, is he?'

'No, he isn't here at all.'

'Isn't here?'

'No. He left.'

'Left? Why?'

'Something about a reference? It caused rather a lot of bother.'

Bessie was about to come out with yet another repeat, but instead took a deep breath, and asked the cook to explain from the very beginning.

'It was one of your husband's sons. He paid a visit, and asked to talk to Mr Palmer.' She stopped almost as soon as she had started. 'You do know dear, you could have told me what was happening in your life.'

'I know,' said Bessie, slightly abrupt because she was desperate to hear about Josiah, but also uncomfortable because she had lied to so many people. 'I wanted to protect you if possible. From the truth.'

'Which was kind of you, and . . . yes, I suppose . . . for the best, but . . .'

'What about this son?'

'I don't know which one it was, but he was after some details about a reference, and Mr Palmer called us all into his study one by one. Asked us most deliberately whether we knew anything, and I didn't have the faintest clue what he was even talking about, but Josiah obviously did. Because the next morning he packed his bag and was gone.'

'When did all this happen?'

'About the time of your trial.'

Bessie groaned, before lowering her head. Why had Josiah not simply denied its existence? She had told him that she would destroy it. Perhaps he had feared that she had not kept her word. Probably because she had failed to confirm it. "Oh Charles Bateford, I hope you rot in hell for this".

'Where's Josiah now?'

'A place along . . . Vaughn Street.'

'Vaughn Street? But there aren't any big houses along there. In fact it's . . .'

'Not exactly the best part of town,' completed Mrs Jennet. 'Sadly that's true, but it's where he's living now.'

'Where is he working?'

'I'm not really sure.'

'He *is* working, isn't he?'

Mrs Jennet pursed her lips, and as soon as Bessie was able, she hurried away to find out for herself. The street was not actually too bad. In comparison to Nevin Street anyway. But it was painful to think that she had made him move at all.

Knocking on the relevant door with a sense of trepidation, she received no answer, and that filled her with even greater trepidation. Was he at work? She assumed that she would have to wait – and worry some more – but then a woman entered a neighbouring house, and saved her from it all. Josiah was at The King George.

The King George. Bessie tried to think. Yes, now it came back to her. She had tried nearly all of the public houses herself during the search for employment, and although The George was decidedly down-market, it had been far too good for the likes of her.

'You've a nice enough face an' all, but that hand'll be putting them off their ale.'

Such had been the put-down, and one of the kinder ones at that.

'What exactly is he doing there?' she asked.

'I don't know. Barman I think.'

"Oh dear God". Bessie raced off down the street. Josiah was not the sort of age, nor the sort of man, to be working in a bar. She could not get her legs there fast enough, but then as soon as she arrived, her biggest wish in life was to be a million miles away. Josiah was there, which was wonderful, but so were a whole host of customers, and one big bully of a man in particular seemed to be drawing enjoyment from running Josiah ragged.

'Faster old man. I said faster, or I'll pour it down your neck.'

"Leave him alone, or I'll break *yours*", thought Bessie, before realising how ridiculous it was in the face of an adversary twice her size and weight.

'Bessie!' cried Josiah when he eventually caught sight of her. 'I . . .' His eyes flooded with tears. 'I can't talk right now.'

'Don't worry. I'll wait.'

'But I'll be hours.'

'It doesn't matter. You'll find me outside.' And when he came out three hours later, she had kept to her word.

'Oh Bessie, I'm so sorry I wasn't there for you in Henningborough. I didn't hear about it until it was all over, and then . . .' Tears fell down his face like she had never seen before, and wrapping her arms around him, she offered him her shoulder to soak up the sadness.

'No, *I'm* sorry Josiah. For everything that I've put you through.'

'You haven't put me through anything.'

'I have. I should have known that the reference would come back to haunt us one day. I destroyed it, I *did*, but I should have made sure that you knew it.'

'I would have left anyway. The others might have got into trouble otherwise.' He stepped back, and tried to stem the flow of emotion by appreciating how lucky he was. 'As long as you're alive Bessie. I don't know what I would have done if they'd . . .'

'But they didn't.'

'No, but you must have been so scared.' He gripped her hands, to show that he was now there for her, and that was when he noticed her injury. Horror instantly sprang into his face, and although she knew that it was not intended, the reaction did hurt because she had encountered it many times before. Brushing it aside, she explained what had taken place, where she was working now, and that Thomas had escaped – of which Josiah was already aware – but she said nothing about the New World, nor her plans to go there.

'Back where we both began then,' he concluded with a wry smile. Bessie once more as a maid, and he had done a variety of odd jobs before finally securing that coveted role of footman at Fulton Street many moons ago.

'It's all my fault.'

'No it isn't.'

'Please Josiah, stop denying the obvious. I'm the reason you lost your position, and I'm the reason that you can't find a better replacement than this.'

He swallowed and looked down. 'Mr Palmer won't write me a reference, and Mrs Langley is dead, so . . .' All his good work, building a fine reputation over the course of the years – it had ultimately been to nothing. Lost in an instant. 'I need you to forge one for *me* now,' he laughed, but she knew that it was not funny, and that more than ever, she ought to go cap-in-hand to Gil.

He could fix this. He could fix anything. Out of generosity? Possibly. Out of the glee of seeing her crawling back to him? Most definitely. But still she could not do it, and perhaps there was no need. There might just yet be another way.

Telling Josiah that she had better be getting home, she instead returned to Erskine Avenue, and went up the back stairs. The surgery acted as Doctor Driscoll's study as well, and the housekeeper had just told her that he liked to retire there each evening after his meal.

'What a pleasant surprise,' exclaimed Robbie, catching sight of her as he left the dining room. 'Can't keep away from us eh?'

'I need to speak to your father.' She knocked on the door, was admitted, and left Robbie hovering in a most affronted manner outside – debating whether to press his ear to the door, intrude openly, or skulk out to another card party which his father had forbidden him from attending.

'Please forgive me for disturbing you,' said Bessie as the doctor rose to his feet.

'Not at all. I wasn't doing anything very much. What can I do for you?' He invited her to pull up a chair, and then resumed his own.

'I was wondering . . . well . . . I know how kind you've been to me, so very kind, giving me a position here, and I think you've found that I'm a good worker in return? Even though I've only been here such a short while.'

'Yes, I've already received some excellent reports.'

'Well . . . it's just . . . there's somebody else who's a really excellent worker, with the best of temperaments, but he's recently experienced a bit of bad luck – entirely not of his own making – and I was thinking that perhaps you might . . . well . . . need somebody else to work here? Part-time possibly, as a second butler? Or perhaps a valet? Or . . . or even a footman?' She did not really want to suggest the latter, but any role inside a nice house would be better than where he was now.

Anthony drew heavily on some snuff, wishing that he could say yes, but knowing absolutely that he could not. This house ran on a very small number of staff, so there was certainly capacity, but what was not available was money. He tried to make that clear, without being too specific, and thankfully Bessie did not ask more than twice, before leaving.

Alone once more, he then leaned back in his chair, and revisited an issue which seemed to dominate his thoughts all too often. He frankly could not afford the costs as they now stood, never mind taking on anything extra. Food, staff, maintaining a house, carriage – it all sucked up cash like it was going out of fashion. Far too *much* cash, and while Millicent thought that patients' fees and the dispensing of medicines paid for everything, he knew different. She had married him for love all those years ago, and probably regretted it ever since, but not as much as he was regretting it now. A poor apprentice doctor, she had believed that he would rise high, and he had. He could have enjoyed a comfortable life as a bachelor, but a family unfortunately stretched the finances, and a wife like Millicent stretched them to the limit. The problem was that he was not a university man tending to the wealthy as she liked to pretend; he was little more than a tradesman tending to those who only had limited funds to pay him, and he had reached the point where income was yet again being dwarfed by outgoings. Something drastic would have to be done, and it would have to be done very soon indeed.

CHAPTER EIGHTEEN

Standing in the half-open doorway of Leah's bedroom, Robbie peered through. Elizia was in there, dusting a bookcase, and doing a very efficient job indeed. In fact efficient would be the perfect word for Elizia. Busy as a bee, flitting here and there, no time to talk – whereas he had all the time in the world, and he was determined to fill it with this particular female.

'Good afternoon,' he said as she stood up to stretch her back.

'Good afternoon,' she replied, no longer startled by his sudden vexatious appearances.

'How about doing something exciting with me tonight?' he asked, walking forward and leaning against the bookcase so that she could not ignore him. 'Tomorrow is your day off, so surely you can afford to live a little.'

'No thank you.'

'But what else are you going to do? Sit around at home for hours on end?'

'Yes.'

'Isn't that rather dull?'

'I like my home Mr Driscoll.'

'So do I, but it's important to broaden one's horizons every so often. And I've told you before, it's Robbie.'

'Your father is Doctor Driscoll, your mother is Mrs Driscoll, your sisters are the Misses Driscoll, and *you* are Mr Driscoll.'

Robbie grinned. 'You do know I'll wear you down in the end, don't you?'

Bessie did not reply, but went next door to retrieve some polish, and lingered for five minutes, buffing up a table which had already been buffed enough. When she returned it was with the expectation that he would have left, but she was wrong, and it filled her with concern. They were now into April, and there were a couple of things floating around her mind in need of attention – with this bored young man being one of them.

'I need you to understand something Mr Driscoll. I am *not* playing games, and I am *not* being coy. I simply wish to come here in the morning, leave in the afternoon, and do my work in between.'

'How about coming here in the afternoon, leaving in the morning, and having some fun in between?' He twinkled, but she was not the slightest bit impressed. 'You do realise that you probably wouldn't be here at all if not for me. I had considerable influence over my father's decision.'

'I am sure your father knows his own mind, and he has a loyal, dedicated servant as a result. I owe nobody any more than that.'

'It isn't about owing. In fact that's such a dreadfully cold concept.' Conjured up thoughts of outstanding debts, of which Robbie still had several. 'It's more about wishing to repay a good turn.'

'I'm leaving now Mr Driscoll.'

'But your shift doesn't finish for another ten minutes.'

'I have things to attend to downstairs.' She abruptly crossed the room, but a noise stopped her near the door. 'What was that?'

'What was what?'

'That noise.'

'I didn't hear anything.' Robbie approached her with a beam of satisfaction. 'Unless of course you're trying to find some excuse for staying with me?'

'No I am not,' she retorted, hastily moving off before he could reach her, and soon escaping out into the sunshine.

It was a long day from six o'clock in the morning, but it still felt depressingly early. Too many hours stretching out ahead of her. *Far* too many to think about going home. The atmosphere was as bad as ever. In fact Marge's hatred had plumbed new depths. With Cynthia and Ella gone, and Luke the victim as always, that left only one person on the receiving end. Bessie could not deal with it, so had taken to heading home only when it was time to eat a little food and go to sleep. The intervening period was spent walking the streets, watching other people pass by, basking in some spring warmth, and then sitting in The King George. Josiah's employer watched over him constantly, and the customers barked their orders, so it was hard to talk, but they each drew comfort from the other's presence, and it gave Bessie time to think about that remaining issue on her mind.

Robert Driscoll was right. It was her free day tomorrow, and hence the perfect time to address matters. In fact when she came to think about it, why wait until tomorrow? Why not seize the day? After sitting for another thirty minutes, she finally concluded that she would, and as darkness gathered, her feet once again pointed in the direction of Carrow Square.

It felt most uncomfortable. Indeed it rendered her quite nauseous, but it was an unavoidable evil, and as she neared the property, feelings of resentment were temporarily overtaken by the need for vigilance. The watch-box was occupied. Was it that man who had done his best to drown her? She could not tell, so had to creep further forward, and at last was able to distinguish a different face. Thank heavens for that. Hopefully his perverted colleague had died, or left, or at the very least stopped trying to pitch people into watery graves.

With her new station in life, she knew she really ought to take the tradesman's entrance, but was not even entertaining the idea as far as Gil Tremaine was concerned. Marching forthrightly up to his door, she knocked boldly, but soon began to feel slightly less bold as the night-watchman approached.

"Come on Reeve, open up", she hissed, and at last the door was pulled back – at the very moment that the rich-man's-guard was set to accost her.

'Tell this individual that I'm entitled to be here,' she directed, and although Reeve did not quite do that, he did send the man on his way. 'Thank you,' she added, losing a little of the attitude on the other side of the threshold. 'I need to speak to Mr Tremaine. Please inform him that I am here.'

'But he has just sat down to dinner,' explained Reeve. 'This very minute. I'm not sure that it's the right time to disturb him.'

'Why don't we give him the option?' she replied, and ultimately Reeve shuffled his way over to the dining room door, only to return with news that she would indeed have to come back another day.

'Come back?' repeated Bessie, instantly beginning to boil, but then remembering the trick used to such good effect with Arnold – bury your emotions beneath a thick veil of compliance. 'Yes, I suppose it isn't appropriate to keep a man from his food, now is it? Do you think tomorrow afternoon might be more convenient?'

'I cannot speak for Mr Tremaine, but there is certainly a much better chance of him being available.' Reeve prepared to reopen the front door, but Bessie made it clear that she would be going via the rear.

'Is the alley gate open?'

'Yes.'

'Good. Then I need not put you to any more trouble. I can find my own way out.' She headed off down the back stairs, dived into the cloakroom, and then when Reeve went past to check that she had closed the back door properly, she shot up towards the dining room, knocked, and entered before Gil even had a chance to answer.

'Ah Miss Cullen, won't you join us? We're having partridge followed by plum pudding.'

'No thank you. I only need a word.'

'A seat you may gladly have, but I'm afraid a word is absolutely impossible.'

'But it will only take five minutes.'

'Five seconds is far too long when one is about to tuck into such a fine spread. Surely you're already aware of how I can never refuse the allure of a good bird.'

Bessie tried to stop herself, but simply could not avoid scowling, and Gil looked stern.

'You aren't going to compel me into calling the first footman, are you?'

'I think you should Gil, and without delay,' chipped in a familiar voice. 'We don't want trash like *that* spoiling our meal.'

Bessie turned to Sylvia Chaloner. 'Who do you think you're calling trash?'

'I'd say that's rather obvious, wouldn't you? I don't know how you have the temerity to foist yourself upon polite society.'

'Why?' whispered another voice from across the table, which unbeknown to Bessie belonged to Mrs Ashby, the comrade-in-arms when it came to Sylvia's quest to hook Gil Tremaine.

'*Why* is none of your business,' retorted Bessie, before refocusing on Gil. 'A word. That's all. And then you'll be back with your bird . . . or mutton . . . in no time.'

Sylvia was too engaged to notice the personal reference. 'She's the one I was telling you about. Arnold Bateford's widow. Up in court for his murder, and only a maid to begin with. Tricked her way into the poor man's house.'

'Why isn't she in prison?'

'Because she's innocent,' snapped Bessie.

'That's a matter for debate,' countered Sylvia. 'But either way, you're still trash.'

'Oh you do love that word, don't you? Maybe because it's so strikingly familiar from whenever you take a look at yourself in the mirror.'

'*Excuse* me!'

'Don't act so shocked Mrs Chaloner. Surely you realise that there's nothing more trashy than throwing yourself at a fellow who absolutely has no intention of marrying you.'

'I really must insist that you leave,' said Gil, but Bessie now had no desire to go anywhere.

'And I really must insist that you tell Mrs Chaloner what you told me.'

Gil glared, and Sylvia demanded an explanation.

'Go on Gil. Tell her how you made it perfectly clear that the thought of marrying her was laughable. In fact *beyond* laughable. Which, I must admit, is rather tragic when you think about all the years she's been putting in trying to secure that very end.'

'Lies!' squealed Sylvia, rising as fast as the blood had risen to her cheeks. 'Isn't it Gil?'

The master of the house rubbed his neck. 'Miss Cullen has long been known to have . . . how can I put this? Etiquette issues? I think it's best if we simply ignore her.'

'That doesn't answer my question. Did you tell this devious little strumpet that you have no wish to marry me?'

Since Sylvia seemed to be fixed upon remaining standing, Gil decided that now was the time for him to stand up too. 'Miss Cullen is indeed a singularly irritating young woman. And I'm sure that devious can be chalked up as one of her many attributes, but she has never actually been a strumpet.' He looked down at Bessie. 'She is, however, about to be forcibly removed from this house, so please everyone – pile up your plates, and I shall be back very shortly.'

Strong-arming her across to his study, Gil successfully managed to resist all attempts at extrication until they were safely inside.

'I am *not* devious!' she declared, rubbing her wrist, and feeling even more nauseous at the sight of those curtains which had kept him so concealed.

'Forgive me, but when I reflect upon an image of you stuffing the contents of my safe into that oversized sack of yours, I must beg to differ.'

Bessie was all set to retaliate, reminding him how he had in fact incited her into that act of theft, but the slamming of his front door distracted her. 'I think your lady-friend has just exited the building.'

Gil sat down, stretched out his legs, crossed one over the other, and clasped both hands behind his head. 'Yes, I must indeed thank you for your delightfully direct intervention. All my hints have been falling on decidedly deaf ears.'

'Thank me? You mean . . .' Bessie paused. 'You mean you're glad?'

'Oh absolutely.'

'So . . . you . . . wait a minute. You refused to see me on purpose? Wound me up like some sort of clock, knowing that I'd barge in and cause a scene?'

'A very effective clock, and a captivating scene. I can't imagine that Sylvia will be inviting herself to any more of my gatherings in future. Mind you, what I'm now going to do for a whist partner is anybody's guess.'

'You . . .'

'What?'

'You really don't care about a thing, do you?'

'On the contrary, I care about many things, but I generally feel that the world is a much better place if you try and smile through it all.'

'It's nice to have something to smile about. Not everybody is so fortunate.'

'Oh come now, it can't be that bad.' Gil sat forward, propping his chin on the back of his hands in a mock act of sympathy. 'How can I help you?'

'I don't need your help.'

'Don't you? Well you're here for something, which I think is exactly as I predicted, isn't it?'

'The only reason I'm here is because of the money you're dishonestly withholding from Drew Roscoe.'

'Dishonestly?'

'Yes. I gave you hundreds of pounds to compensate for losses that you never actually incurred.'

'But you gave those hundreds voluntarily.'

'It doesn't make any difference. You're still six hundred pounds better off than you should be.'

'Six hundred?' Gil's eyes widened. 'I did lose some notes and all my coinage in that canal if you remember, and I was forced to go to considerable lengths to get the rest back.'

'Lengths which you enjoyed to the full,' she growled. 'Five hundred and fifty then.'

'That's exactly what *I* thought.' Gil leaned underneath his desk, opened the safe, and produced the wallet – all ready to go.

'You knew that I was coming for it?'

'I knew you'd be along eventually, yes.'

'A step ahead eh? Well done Gil. You must love dealing with me. Boosts your sense of invincibility, does it?'

'You certainly have the capacity to enliven an otherwise dull affair,' he conceded, before holding up the wallet, which she took with one hand. 'What's happened to the other one?'

'Nothing.'

'Nothing? That, Miss Cullen, is one of the most ridiculous answers you've ever given me.'

'Well it's the only one you're getting.' She turned to leave, but he was not ready to see her go just yet.

'Tell me – has the colour of money regained its lustre for you? Or are you planning on giving it all back to its rightful owner?'

'Giving it back of course.'

'Really? Every last little penny?'

'Yes.' She was going to take it to Roscoe Hall, and hand it over – although hopefully without Cynthia ever becoming aware of it.

'But there's no need. Roscoe isn't even aware that there's any issue of overpayment. If you give him half, he'll be perfectly satisfied.'

'No doubt he will be, but I won't.'

'So you like living in a mill cottage then?'

'I'm not. Not any more.'

'Another change of circumstances.'

'Something like that.'

'So where *are* you living now?'

'That's none of your . . .'

'Business,' completed Gil. 'Yes, yes, I know. But it's simply an expression of interest, nothing more. And indeed I am not the only one who's interested. Stewart Munroe seems particularly distressed about where you might have ended up.'

'Well he'll just have to stay distressed, won't he?' The retort was a particularly caustic one as she tried not to dwell on that unsavoury conduct in the water-closet.

'Are you absolutely sure that I can't be of any assistance?'

'Positive.'

'But you've had such a powerful effect on the Sylvia issue, it seems only fair that I return the favour.'

'You don't owe me any favours, and I don't owe you any. I have what I came for, and now we're finished.'

'Until the next time.'

'There won't be any next time.'

'Oh yes there will be. I'm utterly convinced of it.'

'Well you can take your conviction, and your plum pudding, and shove them . . .' She stopped as Gil grinned at her.

'Go on,' he directed. 'You know you want to say something outrageously coarse.'

'Yes I do, and what does that say about *you?*'

'That I bring out your dark side. But don't worry, you do the same with me. Fabulous, isn't it?'

'Oh . . . go away!' she snarled, and flounced out before he could say another word.

It was only upon reaching the end of the street that she realised how often she flounced away from Gil Tremaine, and how pathetic it probably looked. "Bessie, when are you going to learn?" she groaned, before trying to focus on the more pressing need to appear casual. Clutching the wallet to her chest would be a dangerously possessive act, so she held it down by her side, and as the enormity of all that wealth began to make her knees weak, she could not help but reflect on Gil's suggestion.

Her family were living in a slum, while Drew had not one manor house, but two! Was it crazy to even think of making him any richer? Especially when he was indeed totally oblivious to the debt. But what if Gil ever talked to Drew? He might find some sneaky way to probe the existence of a recent windfall, and then know that she had kept the cash for herself. That would be awful. He would hold it over her, think her weak, be amused as always. Be proved right. She hated that thought. Although was dented pride really a good enough motive for giving all this money back to Drew? Or should she focus on the fact that he deserved it. He had been through an ordeal over the last year, and every bit of it had stemmed from her first visit to Northcliff.

As she approached Nevin Street both sides of the argument were battling for supremacy, but for once she did not let that distress her. It had been a long day, and with confronting Mr Driscoll *and* Gil – her emotions were bound to be at sixes and sevens. The best thing to do was to sleep on it, and if there were any questions about the wallet, she would say that Josiah had let her borrow a couple of books. That ought to deter Marge and Luke from probing any further. But as it turned out, it was not only her mother and brother she needed to worry about. It was Cynthia and Ella too.

'Wh . . . what . . ?' stammered Bessie, entering the front room to see them sitting there – so casually – by the fire.

'They're back!' exclaimed Luke. 'I knew they would be. I told you, didn't I?'

Bessie had no such recollection, although in that moment it was hard to recollect anything. 'What . . . er . . . Drew . . ?'

'Did he throw me out?' completed Cynthia, with just a hint of sarcasm. 'No he didn't. I left of my own accord because I realised that there was no point in living at all if I don't live with Luke.' She turned and stroked his face, but Bessie did not see love's young dream; she saw selfishness, and it made her angry.

'Did Drew . . . do anything?'

'No, he simply let me go.' Cynthia answered without turning away from Luke, and then Marge chipped in with her two pennies worth:

'Knew there was nothing he *could* do. He's no match for my Luke.' Marge joined her son by the fire, put Ella on her knee, and made a very definite statement. Cynthia was not merely revered for bringing baby Ella into the world, but because she was the daughter that Marge had always wanted. Fine-boned and feminine, rather than sturdy and stubborn. And in Marge's eyes there were now three generations of Cullen girls in this house, with one very definite outsider.

In that instant Bessie hated them, every one, and the venom was even strong enough to include her beloved niece. No longer did Ella gaze up at Auntie Bessie as if she was the only person of importance in the world. It was Cynthia who now enjoyed that privilege, Cynthia who had given up the child, and done nothing to get her back. Indeed none of them had done anything. Not Luke, not Marge. They had all sat back and allowed the situation to drift. And yet here they were together, and in possession of everything they could ever ask for. Well almost everything anyway.

'I have to go out again,' she announced, and received barely a murmur of acknowledgement. If she were to be absent for days, they would show few signs of concern – unless of course it reached pay-day, which was a different matter entirely. Then all of a sudden Bessie Cullen became important. The resident cash-cow. Well so be it. She would keep on giving them the Driscoll wages, and tolerate being ignored the rest of the time. But she was not giving them Drew's money. No way. To hell with them. To hell with the lot of them.

Stalking around Somerden, she repeated that phrase practically a hundred times over before her brain finally became less inflamed, and more clinical. Time to see Josiah again, but first a little reorganisation was required. Melting away from the main thoroughfare, she used the seclusion of a narrow alley to remove fifty pounds from her hoard, placed it in her pocket, and then entered The King George.

It was rowdier than before, mainly because the navvies were in, and one navvy in particular was making his presence felt. Talking louder than everybody else. Laughing louder. Why was it that some men were like that? Was it all about deflecting from a deficiency in some other area? Probably, and when Bessie realised that it was the bully from last month, she was in just the mood to give him a piece of her mind – and would have done so if not for the fact that Josiah caught her eye, reminding her of other priorities.

As she walked up, he frowned, which was unusual because his eyes tended to sparkle at her approach.

'What are you doing back here?'

'I've come to tell you that you don't need to work in this place any more.'

'Of course I do.'

'No you don't. I have some money. I can help you.'

'Don't be silly Bessie. You're poorer than I am. Now get yourself off home. It isn't safe for you to be out at this time of night.'

'I'm perfectly safe, and this is important.' She took him aside, and drew the notes towards the edge of her pocket, just far enough so that he alone could see.

'How much is there?'

'Fifty pounds.'

Thankfully he did not repeat that with an accompanying shriek. His eyes simply bulged instead.

'And it's all yours Josiah.'

'Mine!'

'Yes. So you can stop working in conditions like these.'

He swallowed, and then peered into her pocket again, before adopting a very severe expression.

'You think I've stolen it, don't you? Well you can cut that right out, because I haven't.'

'So where did you get it?' he demanded.

'That doesn't matter. It's yours.'

'It *does* matter. Where?'

'Arnold Bateford.'

'Bateford!'

'Yes.' She knew the importance of giving a really convincing explanation, and ironically the trial had provided her with just the thing. 'His money was meant to go to Thomas, under this rule called primo-something-or-other. Means that all the assets keep going down through the line of the first-born. But because Thomas was convicted, and sentenced to hang, then the law treats him as if he's now dead.'

She paused, hoping to goodness that the law was not right in its assumption. There had been no reports of any ships lost in the Atlantic, which was a merciful relief, but the loss of an individual would presumably not be reported, and whenever she considered that possibility, her legs became hollow, and her stomach churned into knots.

'So the money has come to you instead?' prompted Josiah.

'Some, yes. It's mostly gone to Charles and Harris, but as his wife I am entitled to a certain share.'

'What sort of a share?'

'Enough that I can give you this.'

'I don't believe you.'

'What do you mean?'

'I think that this is the whole amount, and that you're giving it all to me, and I won't take it.'

'That isn't it one bit. This is just a part, and you *must* take it.'

'No.'

'Josiah!' She was about to drag him outside, and show him the contents of the wallet, but was stopped in her tracks by the approach of the bully.

'What do you call this?'

A tankard was held out in Josiah's direction, and having examined it, Bessie replied: 'Looks like ale to me.'

'I wasn't asking you. I'm asking him.'

'I . . .'

'It's sludge from where I'm standing.' The bully grabbed hold of Josiah's hand, thrust the tankard into it, and ordered a replacement.

Josiah duly hurried away, and once he was out of earshot, Bessie calmly said: 'If you lay a hand on my friend again, you'll see a side of me that is decidedly unpleasant.'

The man scanned her up and down, as if she was some annoying bug which had crawled onto his boot. 'Looks to me like there's no side of you that's particularly pleasant.'

Bessie smiled with a perverse air of satisfaction. 'You're right. There are many around here who would make such a contention. Indeed I'm quite notorious in these parts.'

'For what? Being a pest.'

'No. For murdering my husband.'

'Murdering?'

'Yes. You might have heard of him. Arnold Bateford?'

The expression was blank.

'He choked on his own vomit. Just a few streets away in fact, and I was put on trial. Along with my lover that is.'

The onset of recognition began to show, so she pressed on: 'Everybody assumed that he choked after drinking too much whisky, and indeed that was the jury's conclusion – acquitting me of all the charges, and convicting my lover of an unlawful push. But of course the truth is very different.'

'What makes you think I'm interested in your truth?'

'Because you look to me like a man for whom it could prove quite enlightening.'

The bully sniffed a couple of times, before eventually encouraging her to proceed.

Bessie leaned up and whispered a trumped-up word in his ear, left it to register, and then explained how it worked. 'A few drops in my husband's whisky, that was all it took. At first he would have felt drowsy, and then his limbs would have become a little numb, followed quickly by the failure of internal organs, including most importantly his heart. Five minutes from start to finish, and without so much as a single trace of evidence left in its wake.'

'Where did you get this stuff?'

'Oh I couldn't possibly reveal my sources, could I? But suffice to say – I have more than enough to hand should I ever be tempted to take such an action again in the future.' She smiled up at him, making sure that she looked as akin to a mad witch as possible.

The bully stood very tall, and suddenly very menacing. 'Are you threatening me?'

'Me? A mere slip of a thing, threaten a man like yourself? How could I possibly do that?' She turned away as Josiah approached, clasped the tankard that he was carrying, and then – after a short delay – presented it to the loud-mouthed navvy. 'Here you are. The replacement, just as you ordered.'

He peered suspiciously at the liquid. 'I don't want it.'

'But it's precisely what you want. A nice tankard, full of ale.' She pushed it right up under his nostrils, and he reacted like your average woman presented with a squealing rat.

'Get it away from me!' His hands went up in instinctive defence, catching Bessie's face in the process, and the red mist suddenly enveloped Josiah. It was all the weeks of upheaval that did it. The abuse of this place, the knowledge of how far he had fallen, and now seeing the girl he cherished as a daughter struck by some lout – it was all too much for him. Seizing the tankard from Bessie's hand, he poured the contents right over the top of the man's head, and then threw it audaciously to the floor.

There was no violent blow involved – the tankard did not actually make contact with the bully – but he keeled over nevertheless, and it was only as he stared up, eyes bloodshot with fury, that Josiah's own red mist quickly began to depart, and he feared what on earth he had done. Pushing Bessie behind him, he prepared to defend them by some means or another, and braced for impact, but it did not come. The bully did not charge; he simply waved his hands about as if being attacked by a swarm of bees. Having done that for a full minute, he then shot up, ran towards his friends at the corner table, yanked one of them onto their feet, and set about wiping his face furiously on the man's shirt.

'What's he doing?' whispered Josiah, to which Bessie replied that she had absolutely no idea.

'Come on,' she added as the publican glared. 'It's time to go.' Leading the way out, she took Josiah to the alley previously vacated, and the street-lamp helped in her bid to show him the rest of the money. '*Now* do you believe me?'

'I've never seen so many notes in all my life.'

'Yes, it is a tidy sum, isn't it? Which is why you should accept fifty pounds without argument. In fact I don't think it's enough. You should have more.'

'No, no, no, and I won't be having fifty. I'll take . . . well, I don't know . . . twenty-five perhaps? I really don't think I ought to have even that. Your family need this. It could alter their lives so completely.'

'It won't be altering anything. They don't even know about it.'

'Don't even know?'

'No. I'll be producing a bit when and if they need it.'

'Why?'

'Because if Mother ever gets to hear about it, she'll drink her way through it all in no time.'

'Oh I see.' Josiah paused, and Bessie tried not to be overwhelmed by yet another volume of lies. 'Nevertheless, the more you have, the better-placed you'll be. You shouldn't be giving your money to me or anybody else.'

'It isn't my money, it's yours.'

'That isn't true.'

'It *is*!' she snapped. 'If it weren't for me and my escapades with the Bateford family, you'd still be working at Fulton Street, in the comfort of your own room, in the security of a good position. Your entire life has been turned upside down because of me, and this goes only a very small way towards compensating you for that.'

Josiah was silent.

'You see? There's no way to counter it, is there? Because it's a fact. I've ruined your life . . . and I'm going to give you a hundred pounds in order to make amends.'

'No! Twenty-five. That's it. That's all I'll take.'

Bessie pursed her lips, but it made absolutely no difference. 'I really don't like this stubborn side of you Josiah. I wish you'd stop it.'

'Don't you go talking to me about stubbornness Missy. I love you to pieces, you know that, but once you get an idea into your head, there's no reasoning with you.'

'Exactly, so why start now?' She forced the fifty pounds into his hands, and then began to draw some more out of the wallet.

'Leave it Bessie.'

'No.'

'But I can't accept it. I can't.'

'You don't have any choice in the matter.' She thrust more of Drew's money at him, and when Josiah realised that her will was stronger than his, he looked at it almost sorrowfully.

'You're too good to me Bessie.'

'No I'm not. I'm not a good person at all.'

'Yes you are, and if I *am* going to take this, then it has to be on condition that you cut out rubbish talk like that.'

'It isn't rubbish.'

'Yes it is. And will you please stop pushing money at me?' He glanced around nervously. 'I'll take what you originally offered. If you insist. But no more.'

'Sorry. That offer has been taken off the table. You'll have a hundred, and that's that.'

'No I won't.'

'A hundred!'

'Seventy-five Bessie, seventy-five, but THAT IS IT!' He grunted, really quite aggressively, but then once it was in his pocket, and her wallet was shut again, he could not help but give in to a laugh. 'Anybody would think that we were a couple of stray dogs fighting over the last scrap of food.'

'Fighting not to eat it,' added Bessie. 'It does seem rather odd, doesn't it? But I don't care.'

'Neither do I.' He smiled, and breathed out as if the weight of the world was being lifted from off his shoulders. 'Thank you,' he said simply. 'I'm not sure I could have put up with much more of that place.'

'Well you don't have to now. You can think about what you want to do, and if you ever need a reference Josiah, you go to Carrow Square. Number twenty-two. The man who lives there is a Mr Tremaine. Say that Bessie Cullen sent you. He owes me one.'

Almost the last thing she had said to Gil was that neither of them owed the other anything, but this was an important exception.

'Twenty-two. Carrow Square. I'll remember,' promised Josiah, and then prepared to walk her home.

'No, I'm fine.'

'You are *not* fine, and there is no way that I'm letting you walk the streets with this amount of money all by yourself.'

The situation could rapidly have descended into another argument, but she knew that it was quicker to simply comply, and then double-back.

'Do you have somewhere in mind? Where you can store all this?'

'Yes. Don't worry,' she said.

'But I *do* worry. That's what I do.' He put her arm through his, and led the way to Nevin Street, following her directions towards the end, and helpfully refusing to come in. Marge Cullen was not a great admirer of his, and he had no desire to embrace that piercingly cold stare. He was also unaware of which number along the row was actually occupied by the Cullens, so when he saw Bessie pass through a door and close it behind her, he was confident that she was home, and walked back to his own with a sense of peace.

She had in fact entered number thirty-four, and immediately apologised to the occupants. 'Sorry. I seem to be in the wrong house.'

'One too many eh?' chuckled the man at the table, while his wife kept stirring the pot, and paid no attention.

With a sheepish shrug of admission, Bessie backed out, checked that Josiah was not around, and then soon well on her way towards the valley.

Time to see the Whitsons. Or rather – time to see Peter. It had been hard enough convincing Josiah to take the money, but Seamus would be even worse. His views on charity were entrenched, and he might not want to deal with the likes of her at all. She had only seen him and Edie once since the trial – and that accompanying revelation of her behaviour. The look in their eyes had conveyed three very definite emotions. Sadness, betrayal and shame. Shame most of all, and Bessie could not face that again. At least not yet.

It was dark before she even set off for the valley, which made the walk a distinctly uncomfortable affair. Leaving the road meant risking the loss of her footing, but taking the normal route made her feel really very vulnerable indeed. With every step she became more and more convinced that somebody was about to leap out from behind the bushes. Interested in plunder, or pillage, or both. It was therefore rather a surprise to her when she actually reached the mill cottages in one piece, and also a surprise to find that the Whitson home showed no signs of life.

She had expected Peter and the other children to be in bed, but time must have really got away from her because their parents had also gone to sleep – which was of course a good thing. Her aim was to attract only Peter's attention, and get him to come outside. Pulling up a few blades of grass, she rolled them into a ball, and threw them at his window, but they collapsed and flopped down before getting anywhere near their target. She tried a couple more times before finally accepting defeat, and looking for an alternative. Stones were no good. There was a danger that she might actually break the pane, so ultimately she had to claw at the ground for some grains of soil. The light patter of it against the window eventually stirred Peter, and a tired little face appeared.

Putting a finger up to her mouth, she managed to stop him from making any loud exclamations, and then pointed downwards, indicating the front door in order to avoid waking his parents.

Thankfully he picked up on what she was trying to communicate, and the front door opened only a minute later.

'What's wrong?' he asked, and Bessie could not help wondering whether that was a purely working-class trait – to always assume the worst.

'Nothing. I'm sorry to wake you, but I need to give you something.' She held out a hundred pounds, and as if to bestow its blessing, the moon appeared from behind a cloud, shining down for Peter to see.

His lips began to part, and Bessie immediately clamped her hand over them, in order to keep him quiet.

'You have to whisper Peter. Like me. Can you do that?'

His eyes at first simply kept staring, but eventually a little sense returned, and he nodded.

'You must listen very carefully now, because I need you to do something else.'

He nodded again, eyes fixed upon the money, but ears open.

'I need you to go out first thing tomorrow, and return with this in your pocket. When your father demands an explanation, say that a man on horseback handed it to you. You'll presumably then be told to hand it back, and when you've walked around for a bit, you must return again and say that you can't find the man, that you tried to refuse it initially, but he wouldn't hear of it. That he was talking about God, and how it was necessary to give generously of your wealth in order to enter the Kingdom of Heaven.'

'But there won't be any man?' whispered Peter.

'No.'

'So it will be a lie?'

'Yes.'

'But aren't lies bad?'

'Yes, usually, but this is my lie not yours, so you don't have to worry about it, and it's all for a good cause.'

'Why don't you just come in and . . .'

'I can't, and nobody can ever know that I've been here. You must keep it quiet, just like you must keep quiet about the money. Your father will tell you the same tomorrow. When you find some luck in this life, it's always best not to broadcast it. Don't go telling any of the other families around here.'

Peter put his fingers out to touch the money, and his mouth now spread into a grin. 'How much is there?'

'You know your numbers and your letters Peter. You tell me.'

He took the notes, held them up, and worked it out.

'Good lad. I see you've been keeping up with your lessons.'

'Yes. Every day, before bed. I never miss them.'

'I'm so proud of you,' she said, and kissed him on the forehead as if he was her very own son.

'When will I see you again?'

'I don't know. Hopefully soon.'

'Sooner than last time?'

The last time that she had seen him properly had been three months ago, and in three months time she would be close to boarding a ship for America. But she could not possibly tell him that. 'Yes,' she said. 'Sooner than that.' There was no way that she would be leaving without saying goodbye. 'Now you must go back inside, and hop into bed. Remember what I said. Man on a horse, giving away his wealth, and my visit – that's our little secret.'

Peter grinned some more, and when she had ushered him reluctantly back inside, she turned her attention to the Hall for her final call of the evening.

It was now that she felt the first real nerves, and that feeling became more intense as she reached the drive. Her feet had not trodden this path since the accident, since the day that one of her hands had been rendered useless, and made life a whole lot more difficult. Dwelling on it was not something that she indulged in, but it did occasionally fill her with regret – when doing simple tasks like tying up her hair, or attempting to buckle a belt. That was when she felt it the most. But at least she still *had* her hand, so counted herself lucky, and Drew was not likely to attack her a second time. Surely? He considered her responsible for the misery that he had suffered, and Cynthia had just left – yet again. This was probably the worst possible day to be paying a visit, but the alternative was to accept that walk back to Somerden. All that way, with all this money. Not a prospect which was particularly appealing, but she had managed it one way, so there was a fair chance she would manage it a second time. Weighing up the two, however, she decided that Drew was the better option by a whisker, so strode up the steps and prepared to say good evening to Duncan.

'Mrs Bateford! I mean . . . Cullen . . . or Elizabeth . . . isn't it?'

'Bessie will do just fine,' she smiled, walking forward.

'I . . . I . . . don't know what to say. When I heard . . . I . . . couldn't believe it, I . . .'

'Yes, I'm sure it came as something of a shock.'

'Is it all true? What people have been saying about you?'

'I don't know, but if you're asking whether I came here under false pretences, then yes I did. Did I work against Arnold? Yes, but did I kill him? No I didn't, and neither did Thomas.'

'How is he? Mr Thomas I mean.'

'Unfortunately I can't answer that for you Duncan, but I know the hangman will never get a hold of him. And for that I will give thanks to the Lord every day of my life.'

'I'm glad too,' he said. 'I always liked Mr Thomas.'

Bessie smiled again, before an air of penitence came over her. 'I'm sorry that I couldn't tell you the truth. I wanted to, but I also wanted to protect you as much as possible when living here.'

'Oh don't worry, I understand that. I'm just glad that I was able to help.' He paused. 'I . . . I *did* help just a bit, didn't I?'

'Your assistance was invaluable. I couldn't have done any of it without you Duncan.'

He beamed.

'How is everything? At the mill and the cottages.'

'Fine from what I hear. People much prefer Mr Roscoe, I know that much.'

'And that's entirely down to you Duncan. The mill would still be in Arnold's hands if not for the help you gave me. Their happiness is a direct result of your selfless acts of courage.'

Duncan's beam now almost stretched from ear to ear.

'And congratulations on your new position. I don't think I've ever encountered a butler as young as you before.'

He straightened his uniform, and then modestly replied: 'There isn't much to it really.'

'Don't you do yourself down. I'm sure that you're a great support to Mr Roscoe. In fact is it possible that I could speak to him, do you think?'

Doubt instantly flashed across Duncan's face. 'I'll ask, but I'm not sure . . .' Rather than finishing that sentence, he hurried upstairs, and Bessie saw that he turned right – towards her old room, and to the nursery.

Within the minute he was back, and the answer was not a positive one. 'Perhaps you could come back another day,' suggested Duncan in his official voice, before adding: 'Mr Roscoe's in a bit of a state.'

'I see.' It was probably a bad idea anyway. 'I'll be going then.'

'Are you heading back into town?'

'Yes.'

'Isn't it . . . rather late?'

'Don't worry, I'll be fine, and I think you can safely retire too. Drew won't be expecting any other guests at this time of night.'

Duncan looked at the new clock. 'Yes. Good idea.'

'Is Mrs Evans still up and about?'

'No I don't think so. But I can wake her if you like.'

'Oh no, I wouldn't dream of it. If you can just give her my best wishes, and say that I'll see her when I'm next around.'

'I will.'

'Well good night then Duncan.'

'Good night . . . Bessie.'

She set off down the drive, but as soon as the front door was out of sight, her legs scooted around to the back entrance, up the staff stairs, and then she hovered on the landing until Duncan vacated the hall. This was probably a very bad idea indeed, but as usual she was doing it nevertheless.

Standing in front of the nursery door, she knocked gently, and then a second time – equally gentle – before turning the handle. He was in there, sitting cross-legged on the floor, surrounded by some of Ella's things. A little hairbrush, one of her napkins, a pair of mittens. There was also a framed tapestry in front of him, and he was stroking his left wrist with the blade of a knife.

Bessie took one look and prepared to run for it, but when Drew turned his head, he did not lunge at her, or make any sudden movement at all. He simply turned back, and focused upon the tapestry.

'Amor vincit omnia,' he declared with the flourish of a court announcer, emphasising each word with deliberate bitterness.

'What does it mean?' whispered Bessie.

'It means that love conquers all things. Nice sentiment, don't you think? Love conquers all things. My mother made it. Only it isn't true, is it? Not for me anyway. Not when love is so one-sided.'

'It's a beautiful tapestry,' she muttered, not knowing what else to say. How could you refute a statement like that? It was the truth. Unrequited love was the worst love of all, and usually all attempts to come to terms with it were ineffectual. 'I . . .' She was about to add: "I'm sorry", but was that the right thing either? Probably not. She crept forward a little, closing the door behind her to show that she was not afraid. To make it clear that she had come as a friend, because it was obvious that in this moment his own life was more in peril than hers.

What else should she do? Move right up to him? Try and choose a soothing platitude? Just as she was deliberating the options, he uttered the words which captured exactly how she was feeling:

'I don't know what to do.' He stared up with tears in his eyes. 'I can't live without them.'

It was then that Bessie lost all hesitation, and joined him on the floor. 'Please give me the knife,' she said, hand outstretched.

He gazed down, oblivious to the fact that the sharp edge had been quite so close to his vein, and proceeded to keep it hovering there, as if at a crossroads in his life.

'*Please*.' She almost only breathed the word, staring deep into his eyes, and the softness of her petition eventually encouraged him to pass it over. Putting it on the floor, she then pushed it well away, and placed the wallet down too.

'Am I an ogre, do you think?'

'Of course you aren't.'

'Then why won't she love me?'

'I . . . I don't know Drew.'

'I thought that when she came back things would work out this time. I was willing to do anything for her. To give her anything that she could ever ask for. To *be* everything she ever wanted.'

'With some people you can give them the earth, and they'll still want the moon.'

'Then how do I get her the moon?'

'You can't.'

'But I must. There has to be something I can do.'

'There isn't. She met Luke first, that's all. Her heart was already lost before you clapped eyes on her.'

'So I never stood a chance?'

'No, I'm afraid you didn't. Arnold forced her to marry you, so you were always the enemy in her mind. And even though she knows that you aren't the enemy any more, she can't change how she feels towards my brother.'

'But if I change how *I* am. Become more . . . well . . . more like the man she wants. I've tried to be a father to Ella, but perhaps I haven't done enough. I love her so much. I just need to try and show it a bit better.'

'And I love her too,' said Bessie. 'But she isn't actually ours, and no matter what you do, it won't make any difference because frankly this has nothing to do with you. I know that might sound like a strange thing to say, but this is about Cynthia and Luke. It's always been about Cynthia and Luke, and the rest of us are merely . . .'

'Victims of circumstance?'

'Yes, I suppose that about sums it up.'

He looked down at the hands on her lap, and forced her to expose the one which he had injured. 'I'm sorry. So very sorry.'

She tried to cover it again, but he would not let her. He lifted it up, examined it closely, and then put the very scar to his lips.

'Please Drew, don't do that.'

'Perhaps I can make it better. Somehow.'

'You don't need to. I've never blamed you.'

'But you should.'

'No Drew. You were angry that day, and you were entitled.'

'But you suffered for it. The last person in the world who should have suffered.' He eased up, and knelt forward, facing her. 'Forgive me for what I've done. Please.'

'As I've said, there's nothing to forgive.'

'But there is, you know that there is.' He peered at her, eyes so sunken and troubled, and in that moment she did not care about her hand. Her heart was overwhelmed with sadness for him, and when he touched her face, she reciprocated the action in order to try and offer come comfort.

Subconsciously she should have known what was coming next, but it was still a shock when he tried to kiss her. Such a shock that she did not say anything, so he cupped her face between his hands, and kissed her as a man would kiss his wife.

'No,' she said, finally twisting away. 'You don't want to do that.'

'Yes I do. More than anything.' He kissed her on the cheek, and then on the neck.

'Drew, this isn't the answer.'

'I'm not looking for an answer.' He wrapped his arms around her, and a warm sensation surged right through her. It was powerful, and safe, and comforting – and it made her feel so very much like crying.

'No Drew,' she whispered, turning her head down as he tried to kiss her once more. 'It's wrong.'

'Why is it wrong?'

'You know why. For a thousand different reasons that will all come back to haunt us in the morning.'

'But I don't care about the morning.' He lifted her chin, stared at her once more, and this time there was a spark in his eyes, and his breathing was shallow. 'Don't refuse me. For God's sake, please don't do it to me.'

"But you must", screamed a voice from deep inside. "You must, you must, you must!"

Chapter Nineteen

Shifting her gaze from the ceiling to the window, she saw Drew standing there, returning the knife to its casing, and for a moment every ounce of her yearned for him to pierce her through the heart with it.

'Good morning,' he said as she sat up and began an attempt to make herself decent again.

Good morning? How could he possibly say that? 'What have I done?'

'The question is: "What have *we* done?" But don't even ask that.' He came across, and crouched down beside her. 'You helped me through a night that might otherwise have claimed my life.'

'That isn't true.'

'Yes it is.'

'Either way, it was wrong. It was bad.'

'Please, don't talk like that. I'm glad it happened.'

'Glad? Are you out of your mind?'

'No, I'm feeling rather more "in my mind" than usual actually.'

'But I don't love you.'

Drew smiled. 'I don't love you either, but I needed you, and you came to me.'

Yes, but how she wished now more than anything that she had stayed away. 'I only came to return some money.'

'What money?'

'The notes that you gave me last October. To repay somebody? I paid them too much.' She hunted around for the wallet, and found it under the wardrobe. 'Three hundred and seventy-five pounds.' She pressed it back into Drew's hand, but he just as forcefully pressed it back into her lap.

'Keep it.'

'No! That would make things even worse.'

'Worse?' Drew frowned. 'It isn't some sort of reward you know?'

'I know, it's just . . .' There was no possible way of expressing how she felt in any words that might make sense, so she did not even attempt it. 'I've already taken out a hundred and seventy-five – for some really good people – and I was wondering if you could possibly provide Mrs Evans and Duncan with a bonus as well? They were such a support to me when I was here.'

'Of course. But I need you to have the rest. I don't want you to be struggling.'

Bessie knew that he was referring to Cynthia. 'We'll be fine,' she assured him, but still he persisted.

Putting his hand inside the wallet, he separated off a wad of notes, and forced her to take them. 'For Isabel, and . . . and for the baby. When they're older. I don't want it going to anybody else.'

In other words – Luke. 'Alright, I'll accept it on their behalf,' she agreed. 'But *only* on their behalf.'

He nodded his appreciation, and Bessie swallowed as an uneasy silence fell upon them.

'Do you have a wash-basin that I can use? To freshen up?'

'Yes.' Drew opened the door, but she held back until it was clear that nobody else was around, and then darted into his bedroom.

'There's everything you need.'

'Thank you,' she said, and he mercifully left her to it.

Above the wash-stand was a mirror, and the first thing she did was to stare at it, but she found herself unable to recognise the woman staring back. So many things had happened over the years, some she would gladly repeat, some where she cringed at the very thought, but never anything quite like this. She had never completely "let go" before. Her hair was tousled, face flushed. Oh dear Lord, what on earth had possessed her?

Fixing her hair back up, she slapped some water around her face, rubbed her lips until they began to sting, and then washed the soil from beneath her fingernails. If only she could go back to the moment when she had dug her hand into that earth outside Peter's cottage. If only she could undo the last twelve hours. Twelve little hours. That was all. It was not too much to ask, surely?

"Yes it is", screamed the voice of self-reproach planted firmly to the fore. "And now you'll just have to learn to live with it".

Returning to the nursery, she saw Drew by the window again, arms folded as if surrounded by a sudden sense of calm, and in that instant she felt resentment like never before.

'I'll go now,' she announced.

'Let me escort you downstairs.'

'No. If you can simply distract Duncan while I . . .'

'There's no reason to be ashamed you know?'

'I don't want to debate it. Just let me get out of here, will you?'

'As you wish. But there's something downstairs which I need to give to you first.'

'No . . . no!' Bessie almost wailed the words at him.

'It's merely a whirligig toy for Ella. She always liked it. And I want to make a small gift of some writing materials, so that you can respond to Thomas.'

'Thomas?'

'Yes. A letter arrived from him a couple of days ago. It's addressed to me, but I know it's for you.' Drew went downstairs, retrieved the items, and returned to her. 'Take care Bessie Cullen. I *can* call you Bessie now, can't I?'

'Of course.' She winced the response, before focusing all her attention upon the handwriting of the man who had literally been willing to die for her.

'When any more come, I'll send them on to you. Where are you living now?'

She was forced to provide their lowly address, and then when the coast was clear, she ran out of the house, into the wood, and slumped down upon their special spot.

With fingers trembling, she took a deep breath, and tried even harder to pretend that last night had been nothing more than a terrible nightmare. This should be a moment of such joyful release; she had been looking forward to it for all these weeks and months.

'Oh Thomas,' she groaned, heart in her mouth, and self-loathing in her veins. But she knew she had to do it. She had to read his words. And almost with a sense of fear, she forced herself to break the seal – and entered his world once more.

Saturday 25th January 1840
My dearest Bessie,

It was so terrible to part in the way that we did. There was so much more that I wanted to say. Most especially that I love you, and that every day apart from you will be an unbearable torture. When Medwin led me from your sight, it was like my heart was breaking in two, and many times I turned back, all set to retrace my steps, but your words have kept me on the path to freedom. We have to accept separation now in order to be together in the future – I understand that, but the future seems so very far away, and time has begun to move at such a slow pace, as if determined to compound my agony.

You say that it is only a delay until July, but then you have the voyage to undertake, and although this ship has made a good start, it is said that the journey can sometimes take fifty, or even sixty days. I might not see you until September. September! How distant a month. But of course you do not need to hear me lamenting a situation that is the same for you as it is for me. We must both find the strength and patience to endure. Somehow.

I know that it is a painful subject, but am I right in thinking that your father was convicted on the very day after you? If so, he ought to be released on the fourteenth, and if your crossing is a speedy one, I may yet see you in August. I shall cling to that possibility, and pray that your birthday at the start of that month is the last one I ever miss.

Please forgive the scrawly nature of my script Bessie. I am shaken by emotion, and the movements of this vessel are enough to disorder even the steadiest of hands. I should probably have waited until reaching dry land, but writing helps me to feel close to you, and I want to send this as soon as we dock. So I shall persist in the hope that my words are legible – although in future I shall definitely pick a time when the weather is slightly less tempestuous. The wind is blowing a gale, and the rigging is starting to rattle in a most alarming manner. In fact

My apologies for the interruption Bessie. That was one of the sails being ripped by the storm, and sparking quite a level of pandemonium. I will have to leave this now, and continue it in the morning. Rest well my love. I hope that things are more peaceful where you are set to lay your lovely head tonight.

Sunday 26th January

Good morning! The winds have eased, and I am able to resume in a state of relative tranquillity. I know that it will seem strange when you read this – as if I am pretending that you are actually here with me – but as I sit with pen in hand, I do feel that I am talking directly to you. That somehow you can sense it, despite the miles – or leagues – which lie between us.

The storm abated quickly last night. Once it had caused some damage, it was happy to move on, and leave our captain unhappy about his torn sail. Repairs have been ongoing this morning, and I offered to help, but he was uninterested. I can now understand why you were so keen to work in the mill. I have also become used to a life of occupation, and these unfilled hours are already beginning to drag.

Presumably you are in the factory right now. Oh how I wish I was there with you, poised to summon you in for one of our "meetings". Can you feel me smiling Bessie? Because I am. Smiling at the memory of your soft lips and tender embrace. You must look after yourself in that place without me. There are so many dangers, and I need you to take the greatest of care – as I am endeavouring to do here.

One of the passengers fell ill overnight, and some of the others are concerned, but I am completely free of anxiety. God saved us both from the hangman's noose – when the odds were stacked rather heavily against us – and that is proof enough that we are destined to be together. If we can survive such a trial, we can survive anything. I am sure that you feel it too, although I must confess that I nearly jeopardised our chances with my own stupidity. When that remarkable Scotsman entered my cell, I initially refused his offer of rescue. I had resigned myself to dying, and was not afraid since I knew that in death I would still be with you. But now that I have this second chance at life, I am desperate to share our time on earth together first, before moving on.

I have so many plans whirling around in my mind, of places that we can go, people that we can see, adventures to share. The only thing which keeps me in the present is the constant rolling of this ship on the surgent seas. It seems that we are cursed never to be still! And the wind is whipping up yet again. At least you should not have to endure this turmoil yourself, able to travel when the winter storms are but a distant memory, and the calm of summer has arrived to envelop you.

Monday 3rd February

I cannot believe that it is over a week now since I last put pen to paper. You have been in my thoughts throughout, but there has been so much going on, and I find it hard to inhabit our private world against the backdrop of such disruption. The storm which I thought had abated was actually the forerunner of an even greater menace. Howling around us for a full twenty-four hours, it was enough to wake the dead – and indeed nearly succeeded in pitching us all into early graves.

Water came pouring down the hatchways in what can only be described as a torrent, and when we had overcome the risk of drowning by scrambling our way out, we were faced with an even greater calamity – that the ship might actually sink. It was all hands on deck, using every available receptacle to scoop water out quicker than it was streaming in. A rag-bag assortment of men and women against the mighty swell of the Atlantic Ocean. How could we prevail? But by some miracle we did – although sadly not without a cost in human lives.

When dawn broke we realised that three passengers were missing, presumed washed overboard, and understandably the grief of those left behind has been like a searing pain echoing all around us. During those brief periods when the bereaved are visited by a little peace, there are the cries of the sick to be faced instead. Not to mention the quarrelling, praying, drinking. Every conceivable expression of emotion in never-ending rotation until all I want is to scream for silence! And I would do it, I really would – except then of course I would be adding to the noisome torture which I loathe so much.

I know that you have suffered many a dark hour yourself, and can appreciate what it is like to spend every waking moment in an airless, cheerless, even hopeless place, where the rats offer the best hope of company. At least they keep their squeaking to a minimum. And I know that I am luckier than most, with no real cause for complaint, but I cannot take this any longer. I need some sleep. That is all. Just some sleep!!

Wednesday 5th February

I must start by apologising for every single word that I wrote last time. It was unnecessary, and disproportionately bleak, and this morning I am feeling so much more positive. I trust that you are the same. Eleven days have now passed since our separation; eleven days closer to being reunited, and February is such a short month – albeit with an extra twenty-four hours this year. If you are able to embark on the very day that your father is released, then there could be less than two hundred to go, and once I am free of this ship, I shall put every one of them to good use. I shall not rest until I drop to my knees with exhaustion, and then the moment that I am revived, my limbs will press on with the building of our future.

At least there are some positives to draw from all this – most importantly that we no longer have to keep our love a secret. We can shout it aloud to anybody willing to hear. In fact I ought to go and shout it up on deck right now! I hope that you are equally proud of the love we share, although I understand if you have not yet quite reached that stage. Recent events must have come as a great shock to your family, but do not let them sow any seeds of doubt in your mind. Tell them that I have never been a Bateford, nor ever shall be, not where it counts, not in my heart. I have even been thinking that in our new country it might be nice to take my mother's maiden name. God rest her soul. What do you think to becoming Mrs Kellett? Filling our own Kellett Hall with lots of Kellett children? I hope that sounds as appealing to you as it is to me, and I hope also that you will not mind if we put our travelling days behind us once we are settled in the United States.

I am not much of a seaman unfortunately. Indeed I have been plagued by seasickness ever since boarding, and the Atlantic is a truly unforgiving Mistress. Even when it is calm, we are in constant motion, to the point where I yearn for that dead calm when absolutely nothing moves. But then I feel guilty because it will mean a longer journey, and less time in America to prepare for the moment of your arrival.

Thursday 20th February

Another two weeks have passed. At least I think it is two weeks. I have lost track, but one of my fellow passengers assures me that he has kept an accurate record regarding the passing of the days.

My seasickness turned into something worse I am afraid. Much worse. There are words bandied about, but I do not wish to know which particular plague has had a grip of me. It is enough to know that it was too strong. Too strong by far, although mercifully not too strong for you. In my delirium I called out your name, and you came. I saw you here, standing right next to me, leaning over me, your cool hand upon my forehead, like an angel sent from heaven. If not for you, I would now surely be buried in the deep. You saved me Bessie Cullen, and when we are finally back together, I shall be your saviour in return. Every day in so many ways I shall love, honour, protect and defend you as you have protected me. I have been left weakened, but you are already restoring me to health. I can feel a power beginning to grow inside me, preparing me for the New World, and I need it to grow fast because we ought to be there in less than a week now. Just one more week, and the work can begin.

Monday 24th February

Land is in sight Bessie! It is really in sight! The captain said it would happen. He made us scrub our sleeping berths yesterday, and even entered our dark underworld to inspect the work, yet still I did not believe him. But it is true. I have made it, and in a matter of a few months now you shall too.

Please do not let these self-pitying ramblings put you off. I have been happy to inhabit the steerage in order to keep back as much money as possible for our new life. Whereas you shall have the best berth that money can buy, clean and utterly free of disease. It will be an adventure, not an ordeal, and it is worth it. If I had to do this another thousand times, it would still be worth it.

I will send this at the earliest opportunity, and address it to Drew, safe in the knowledge that he will place it into your hands. And I shall write again as soon as I can. In the meantime, tell Cynthia that I love her, and give Ella a great big hug from Uncle Thomas. I pray that they are well, and that the same applies to all of your family. OUR family I should say. I have not really been giving it much thought, but I am now of course an orphan, and Cynthia is settled with Drew, which means that without you I have nobody. I am adrift! So it would mean the world to me if your parents could one day accept me as their own. But if not, as long as I have you, all will be well.

It is nearly March now. We are creeping ever closer to the day when I can hold you in my arms again. God keep you my beloved. Stay safe, and remember that I am thinking of you constantly. You have all my love, today, tomorrow and forever.

Your devoted husband-to-be,
Thomas

Bessie let the letter slip slowly from her fingers, and tried to breathe properly. With every word, every paragraph, her guilt had begun to suffocate her, like a tightening noose, until now . . . now . . .

What was she going to do? How could she *un*do what had already been done? And how could she ever look Thomas in the eyes again? Thomas – who was so loyal, and loving, and totally undeserving of the crime which she had committed against him.

Pulling her knees right up under her chin, she wrapped her arms around them, and buried her head so low that the daylight was blocked out completely. She needed that. Needed to hide, and then she began to rock herself back and forth, again and again, to a dark monotonous rhythm.

'I didn't mean it Thomas. Believe me, I didn't. Oh God, forgive me. *Please* Thomas, forgive me.'

Chapter Twenty

Sunday 1st March 1840

My dearest Bessie,

This is just a quick note to confirm that I have safely reached the shore, and am now in the process of finding my land legs once again. It is actually rather more troublesome than it sounds. When my feet finally touched terra firma, it felt awfully strange. Indeed some of us have been wobbling about all over the place, and when I settled down last night, I found myself restless because it was so still! Having complained for the whole of the last month, I am now in a state where I yearn for motion. How ridiculous. You will be pleased to know that I promptly gave myself a few slaps around the face, and a stiff talking-to!

I hope that my first letter is already speeding its way towards you. It could have covered nearly a quarter of the distance by now, which is wonderful, but still such a pity that it cannot fly as fast as my thoughts. I am so eager to hear from you, and when you do send a message, you must post it to Trevor Quinn at the port. He will forward the letter to a passenger, who will carry it on board for a modest fee, and then leave it somewhere on this side of the ocean for me to collect. I gave Mr Quinn a decent sum of money before sailing, so he should be able to accommodate us for the foreseeable future. Indeed for as long as we need, because of course we are inching ever closer to your own journey.

Yesterday it was February. Today it is March. Only one day, but it feels like you have taken such a giant stride towards me, and believe me when I say that you will not regret a single one of those strides. This new country is absolutely amazing. It feels so open, so full of opportunity that I have already become a new man. I am going under the name of Kellett, and some of my fellow passengers have chosen to shorten Thomas to Tam. So that is the new me. Tam Kellett. Although if you wish, I shall always be your Thomas.

When I think about how close I came to hanging, to now experience this second beginning . . . words cannot really describe it. I am so determined to make the most of every second, to work, and to build, and to strive . . .

I have run out of verbs! And I must not ramble on anyway. You know what my dreams have always been. Now I must set about the hard work of putting them into practice. God keep you safe. I love you.

Your devoted husband-to-be,
Thomas

Tuesday 10th March 1840

My dearest Bessie,

These last ten days have been filled with hunting. Non-stop hunting – for the perfect home, and exercising a great deal of care because if all goes well it will not only be our homestead, but also that of our children and grandchildren too. What a scary thought, but yet so magical at the same time. The more I think about it, the more I am relieved that your first child will be mine. I am not sure how I would have coped if I had returned to Bateford Hall to find you pregnant, but I do not have to dwell on such a dire thought. All we have to focus on now is our own marriage, and starting our big family of Kelletts!

There is plenty of land available here, and I have become extremely enthused on a couple of occasions, but unfortunately they both turned out to be false dawns. Scratch the surface, and sometimes it becomes apparent that good land is not what it seems. You have to be careful not to be exploited, and also not to become the victim of theft. I am keeping my money pressed very closely to my chest. Or should I say – Mr Tremaine's money, but that will not be the case for very long. I plan to repay him as soon as possible Bessie. Do not worry – we will not be persisting in debt for a day longer than we have to.

I wonder what the weather is like with you. Are the spring flowers in bloom? They have not yet made it out of bud on this side of the ocean. I used to think that the winters in England were cold, but this last fortnight has been quite a revelation. The locals tell me that it is a regular occurrence, but also assure me that when spring does burst onto the scene, it is with a magnificence that is utterly unparalleled. Of course there will always be things that we miss about home, but this is a glorious land, and I am not just saying that because I need you here. It really is spectacular, and will provide us with more than enough by way of compensation.

I have moved inland now, and should have exciting developments to report next time, but I must hold off from saying too much just yet. I do not wish to make a promise that I cannot keep. And every promise that I do make, will be kept in full.

May time speed up Bessie Cullen. It is still creeping by far too slowly. I left my heart with you in England, and I need you to bring it back to me.

All my love forever,
Your devoted husband-to-be,
Thomas

Wednesday 18th March 1840
My dearest Bessie,

It seems such a long time since I first wrote, and I must confess that I am becoming impatient for your news. It is silly of me, because I know that my letters cannot yet have reached England, but perhaps I may hear something back before the end of next month? Oh how I do hope so, and even though our correspondence will always be a month out of date, at least I now have the satisfaction of announcing that I have found us a home!

When I say home, I mean land, but it will become a home, and it is in the most beautiful of locations. Imagine the perfect picture of paradise, and you will know exactly the scene set to greet you; and now you can also picture me working the ground, chopping logs, clearing the brush. Spring has sprung, and I am a farmer! Never in my wildest dreams did I foresee such a word to describe myself, but I already find it hard to conceive of anything better in the world than tilling the soil, building a home, and watching things grow. Of course I have absolutely no knowledge of farming, but some of the other travellers have accompanied me inland, and generously shared their knowledge on the way.

One particular man has bought the land neighbouring mine along the river. He is here with his daughter and baby grandson, having decided to move from England when his wife and son-in-law both died in quick succession. He has farmed all his life, is brimming over with knowledge, and indeed is the one who advised me to purchase this particular plot. Says that it is good fertile ground, which will generate a fine return. So we are helping one another in our endeavours. He is giving me the benefit of his wisdom, while I am doing the work which his ageing limbs cannot manage, and together we are building our futures.

I wish that you could have an input, tell me exactly what you want your home to look like, but if I were to ask now, then two months will pass before I receive your response, and I want everything to be ready by the time you arrive. So I shall hope that your dreams match my own, and if I err in any way, then it is simple enough to start all over again! You will indeed live in paradise Bessie, and I shall not rest until that is the case. And at least there is one thing that I can leave entirely up to you – the most important job of all – finding a name for our new place. It is now less than four months until your father's release. Perhaps only five until you can be with me, and it would be so lovely if the first word to fall from your lips is that very name. Followed, I hope, by "I love you".

I love you as much as ever Bessie. Still to the point where I fear that I am going to burst at times. But instead of bursting, I must work productively, and sow the seeds of a bountiful harvest. So I shall bid you yet another sad, but only temporary, farewell.

Your devoted husband-to-be,
Thomas

Bessie read all three letters a second time, and then put them aside. She should have written back upon receipt of the first one, but if something was now sent promptly, there was a chance that it might reach him before his birthday. She owed him that much at least.

It was a Sunday. Once every fortnight this day was her own, and she had taken herself out of town – with Drew's writing set – to find a quiet spot.

First for the date. It was April the twenty-sixth. Should she put that? No. She was going to pretend that only the first letter had arrived, so it was probably best to set it back by a week. 'My dearest Thomas.' Yes, that was the right way to start. And now for the hard part. The recounting of everything that had happened.

After a couple of minutes of deep thought, she decided that the only approach was to simply explain it all from the moment of his leaving, and tackle each separate event in order. Obviously leaving out those which she did not wish to discuss, like Gil Tremaine, so she breezed straight over him, and went onto Erskine Avenue. Arnold's death had been an accident – involving Harris – but Charles was guilty of the crime of using it to his advantage, and would now inherit. She begged Thomas not to dwell on that particular fact. 'You're free, which is all that matters,' she wrote, before addressing the issue of Roscoe Hall, and the revelation that Cynthia was pregnant again. 'It's Luke's, and Drew was furious, forcing us all to leave. So our new address is now eighteen, Nevin Street.'

'He only just gave me your letter,' she added. 'And it couldn't have come a day too soon. I was becoming desperate for your news.'

She chose not to say anything about her hand, and swiftly moved onto a discussion of the new role she had secured, working for Doctor Driscoll of all people. Back to life as a maid – and a busy life at that. She took pains to stress that an awful lot was happening. Cynthia and Ella living at Nevin Street too. Mother and Luke. That second baby on the way. But they were all getting by somehow. 'Missing you terribly,' she added, before signing off with appropriate words of love and best wishes for his birthday.

She hoped that they were appropriate anyway. This was the most difficult thing that she had ever done. Was the tone right? Did she sound loyal and honest enough? Did she sound like she was hiding something? Certainly his letters hid nothing, and they kept on coming, and coming, crammed full of hope, until at the end of June came the one in response to hers.

My dearest Bessie,

I have just this morning received your letter, and I am immediately putting pen to paper. It was such a joy to finally hear from you, to know that my letters are making it across the big divide. Little did I realise that when they had navigated the Atlantic Ocean, there might be an issue as to whether Drew actually gave them to you or not.

It was a shock to hear what has happened between him and Cynthia, but you must not blame yourself for bringing Luke back. You were right to set up home in one of the cottages, and he is entirely responsible for his own actions. As is Cynthia. I love her dearly, but I feel heartily sorry for Drew. Especially when he has been so good to us all. But I suppose that when you love somebody, you cannot stop loving them, even though you know that the consequences of that love might be utterly disastrous.

Your new address does not sound like a very good part of town, but do not despair. Every day that passes is a day less for you, and I continue to build the most enchanting of homes – although I wonder now whether it might need a few more rooms. Presumably there is a chance that Luke, Cynthia, Ella, the new baby – everybody might come, and I am sure that you would love it as much as I.

As for Harris, I bear him no ill will. Fear has seized his mouth often on occasion, and I cannot criticise anybody for fearing the noose. While as for Charles – he can keep the money. I never wanted any part of Arnold, and I say "Arnold" because it already feels as if that man never had any connection to me whatsoever. And I am heartily glad that he can no longer have any impact upon our lives.

I know that it must be awful to have to work as a domestic again, and maintaining a home here will of course involve similar chores, but at least it will be your own home. You will be paid in passion rather than pennies, and for every good year you can treat yourself to whatever you like. Although for now I must insist that all spare cash is set aside for our wedding. I already have a beautiful little church in mind. Near the Potomac River. In fact when I think about it I become even more impatient, and God understands this, because I have some extremely good news.

In the exact same month that your father is released, there will be a steamship crossing the Atlantic from Liverpool on what is set to be the first of many scheduled voyages over the coming years. It is going to travel twice a month, and should take half the time that I took. Half! Can you believe it? Everything is beginning to move in our direction Bessie. The ship is called the Britannia, and although fares may cost some tens of pounds, it is a small price to pay. You will, however, need to ask Mr Tremaine for his assistance. I wish that it were otherwise, but your journey will be so much better, and this ground will yield great profits in the future, so paying him back should not cause us any problems whatsoever.

It is such a relief for me to know that by the time you receive this letter, there will probably only be two weeks left of your father's imprisonment. He is no doubt waiting desperately for that time to pass, as I am waiting impatiently here.

Keep going my love. I know it is hard, but we are almost there.

Your devoted husband-to-be,

Thomas

Two weeks. Why did that make her feel so completely overwhelmed? She wrote back at once, reiterating that Cynthia's baby was due soon – indeed set to coincide with the end of Father's sentence, so there would have to be something of a delay in making the voyage. That was reasonable, surely? He would understand.

'Cynthia sends her love,' she added. 'And says that if it's a boy, he's going to be named Tommy.'

That ought to lift his spirits. Bessie then filled up the space by talking about how Ella was excited at the prospect of a baby brother or sister. That Luke was nervous, and tired; and when she had worked her way around to the trip again, she said that they would have to see who would be coming after the baby was born. But it would certainly be lovely if they could all sail the high seas together. 'Over to Uncle Sam. That's right, isn't it?' she asked, desperate to sound involved in his American life.

She was about to write that the delay would not be for too long, but could not say that with any certainty, so instead focused on how the new steamship would mean their letters crossing the sea so much faster. 'I will write again soon,' she promised. 'But I'd better get to sleep now. It has been such a long day, and I want to dream about our fairy-tale wedding. Everybody is thinking of you. Look after yourself Thomas. Don't work too hard. All my love.'

"Bessie" had been the ending last time, but ought she to put "Your devoted wife-to-be"? Yes she should, but . . . no, maybe next time.

Reading through her effort twice, she debated whether to make a second attempt, but then ultimately decided that it would do. So putting it in her pocket, she set off for Doctor Driscoll's, preparing to send it on her way home from work. The sooner Thomas realised that she would not be coming as anticipated, the better. Although she hoped to goodness that it did not sound to him like the beginning of a long line of excuses.

'You're in a hurry,' observed Robbie as he saw her disappearing towards the back stairs at exactly four o'clock.

'I have things to do,' she replied, and then was gone, leaving him to stare at an empty space yet again – and to purse his lips.

She seemed determined to keep scurrying off somewhere, and now appeared to be giving him the silent treatment as well, which he found completely intolerable. He had never been able to bear it from anybody. In fact he really could not bear silence in any regard, and talking to her during the day was becoming increasingly difficult – since Father had repeatedly made it clear that he was forbidden from interfering with her during working hours. So when exactly *was* he supposed to interfere with her?

'Don't be too downcast Robbie dear. I know how to help with your wee servant girl.' Ivy radiated mischief at him from the top of the stairs.

'But you know that I do the first part by myself. We agreed on that, remember?'

'Oh come now. It isn't a reflection that your powers are slipping. She's just a particularly obstructive one. Although I do have to question whether you actually picked the right girl in the first place.'

'I picked just fine thank you. She's a plucky little creature, and you know how we prefer it that way.'

'True.'

'Besides, I played Father like a fiddle in order to get her here, so I'm not giving up now.'

'Certainly not!' endorsed Ivy as if the concept was anathema to her. 'I'm just getting rather bored of waiting, that's all.'

'You and me both,' grumbled Robbie. 'But I'll get there in the end, don't you worry. I've never failed before.'

'No, I can't say as you have.'

'Well then, try having a bit of faith. And some patience while you're at it.'

'But if I can give you some utterly brilliant way of speeding things up, surely that's in your interests as much as mine? Provided of course that your male pride will allow you to even consider it.'

Robbie chewed on his lip. Pride had indeed become the predominant issue here, but after nearly four months it would just have to *stop* being the issue. 'Alright,' he sighed, joining her with an irritated air of frustration. 'What exactly have you got in mind then?'

'Just a little party Robbie. Liven us all up a bit, draw Mother out of this ridiculous depression of hers, and ensure that your little Elizia has to stay on late to help.' Ivy twinkled at him, and her brother's mood rapidly began to lift.

'That *is* rather a good idea.'

'I told you, didn't I? Sister Ivy to the rescue yet again!'

'And presumably Sister Ivy will be making sure that a certain individual is on the guest list?'

'Why of course', she replied unashamedly. 'Fingers in pies Robbie. Fingers in as many pies as possible.'

'But how do we know Elizia will actually be needed?'

'Because one of the usual serving-maids will be ill.'

'Will they?'

'I'll make sure of it!' Ivy linked her arm through his. 'Come on, let's plant this party idea into Mother's head. Once it takes root, Father won't have the slightest hope of stopping it.' They strode up towards Millicent's door, but before they could enter, Leah exited.

'It's probably best not to disturb her,' advised their younger sister. 'She's convinced that she's at death's door.'

'She's *always* at death's door,' dismissed Ivy. 'Sometimes I wish she'd pull herself together, and knock a bit harder.'

'Ivy!'

'Well I wouldn't mind but it's been going on forever, and it's all so ridiculously false as well. You watch – one mention of a party, and she'll be running around here like a three-year-old.' Ivy let go of Robbie's arm, and breezed in uninvited. 'Oh Mother, how *are* you?' She rushed over, and gave a perfunctory kiss on both cheeks.

'Can't you learn to knock Ivy? Have I taught you no manners at all?'

Her eldest child avoided the obvious opening to say something malicious. 'So sorry Mother, but Leah told me that you were in distress, and I was just so eager to alleviate that if at all possible.'

'I don't see how you can. With one relapse after another, I am left confined to this bed, to this room, and there doesn't appear to be any end in sight.'

For somebody who was practically immersed in pillows, lounging on a sumptuous mattress, with absolutely everything to hand, her claims of martyrish sacrifice were resting on decidedly shaky ground.

'Oh how dreadful Mother,' lamented Ivy. 'I was hoping that you might soon feel well enough to host one of your glorious parties. But since you are still too afflicted . . .'

'A party!' seized Millicent, and Robbie found the sudden burst into life so amusing that he began to choke.

'Yes,' pursued Ivy. 'To celebrate your return to health, although of course I didn't realise that you'd suffered another dreadful setback.'

'Well I wouldn't exactly describe it as a setback, and . . . perhaps the company of others might just be the tonic that I need. In fact . . . I don't know why I didn't think of it before.' Her eyes were wide as if she had just been struck by a remarkable wave of enlightenment.

Robbie was still choking, so Leah hurried off downstairs to fetch some water, but when she returned, it had gone all quiet.

'He stopped coughing the moment that you left,' rebuked Millicent, before turning the focus squarely back onto herself. 'Now where were we? Oh yes, naturally it would be a considerable effort on my behalf to raise myself from my convalescence, but I think that I can possibly draw the strength from somewhere, particularly when's in a good cause.'

Robbie was about to ask: 'What cause?' but Leah handed him the water. Most of it had swilled out of the glass en route up the stairs, but he gratefully gulped down what was on offer, before supporting Ivy with various words of admiration, praising Mother for her resilient attitude in the face of such adversity.

It all had the desired effect of not only securing a party, but one for that coming Friday.

'No need for formal invitations,' declared Millicent. 'I shall send the footman around with a personal message for a very personal celebration. Of my return to health, as you say.'

'Splendid!' Ivy gave the endorsement, and soon she and her siblings were dismissed – each with a list of tasks to be completed before day's-end.

'I'm not sure that I really want to attend,' groaned Leah as they headed back downstairs. 'Do you think Mother would notice if I chose to stay in my room?'

'Notice? She'd combust!' retorted Robbie. 'You'd be throwing her table arrangements all out of kilter.'

'Perhaps Father will be able to change her mind.'

'He'll try, but he won't succeed,' declared Ivy confidently. 'You and Father simply aren't strong enough. It's three against two, and as usual you're going to lose.'

Leah did not often do sulky, but she did it now. 'But Mother's always at her most annoying when arranging a party. I can't bear it.'

'My dear sister, I do believe you've just given us an unabashed example of spiteful ill-temper,' announced Robbie, which instantly made her feel awful.

'I don't mean it, really I don't. It's just that she never puts me with anybody decent. I always end up having the most atrocious time, and it drags on for hours and hours.'

'Sorry. You'll simply have to sacrifice yourself to the cause,' said Robbie. 'Ivy and I need a party, and a party we shall have.'

'But *why* do you need one?'

'Never you mind,' dismissed Ivy. 'Just hold your tongue, look sweet, and put up with it.'

'I will *not* look sweet!' declared Leah indignantly.

'Yes you will. You always do. It's your look.'

'I have other looks – including angry – and I might . . .'

'Oh do shut up Leah, you're getting on my nerves now.' And with that, the debate was concluded. A party was to be held at the Driscoll residence, and on Thursday Bessie was informed of the need for her presence.

'I don't understand,' she said when Miss Hawkins had announced it to her.

'They need you serving at table tomorrow evening.'

'But I . . . I . . . I don't do evenings.'

'Well apparently you are tomorrow.'

'But my hand. It will be putting people off their meal.'

'You mustn't say such things about yourself Elizia.' The housekeeper looked really quite sad for a moment. 'I know that it's out of the blue, but those are the instructions that I've been given.'

Instructions? From whom? Surely not Doctor Driscoll. He understood her position, and Bessie went to him in the hope that he might be able to save her from it all.

'Sorry,' he sighed. 'Nothing I can do. Dee has come down sick, so you'll just have to assist.'

'What about my hand?'

'It doesn't look as bad as you think,' he assured her before sneezing three times. 'Excuse me. Your hand is fine. There's no need to keep on hiding it.'

'But how can I possibly serve with it like this?'

'You won't have to. You'll simply be bringing things in and out, while Kerry and Abigail do the serving. You can hold a tray with your right hand, can't you? And balance it on your left if need be.'

Everybody seemed to have it all worked out. 'But you know who I am Doctor Driscoll. What if I'm recognised?'

'You're Miss Scanlon as far as I'm concerned, and the same will apply to the guests. Indeed it is a sad fact that people of a certain class seldom make eye-contact with their own staff, never mind anybody else's, so you ought to be fine.'

Bessie was not sure about the last bit, but she did have to concede that his argument was true. In fact when she had been "of a certain class", the exact same thought had crossed her mind on occasion.

'It isn't ideal, I know, but it can't be helped,' concluded the doctor, more pained for himself than for anybody else. He had not wanted this party, and had made that perfectly clear, but Millicent had proceeded to ignore his wishes in their entirety. She thought that he was always upsetting himself with mere trifles, complaining about costs unnecessarily, but he had the responsibility not her, and nobody seemed to appreciate that fact. Far from it. People actually tittered at him behind his back. "We all know who wears the breeches in *that* household", they would say, and as much as he wanted to get angry, he could not do it – because unfortunately it was true.

'It shouldn't happen again,' he promised as a palliative afterthought. 'And even if you *are* recognised, you must remember that you were found innocent of the charges against you.'

That did absolutely nothing to calm Bessie's nerves. She knew that she could not refuse – or report in sick herself – because he had been so good to her, but she worried all night, and was still worried while preparing to return to the Driscoll house for six o'clock. Having already been to work, she had been given permission to leave early, and was now in the front room at Nevin Street, standing before the mirror, trying to arrange her hair in the best way possible. It had been growing unchecked since last September, and was usually looped up, but today she was having it framing her face. In fact she would gladly have had it covering both eyes if still able to maintain the ability to see.

'Will that do?' she asked.

'What? Yes . . . fine,' came Cynthia's distracted reply. 'Have you read this yet?'

Bessie felt like retorting: "When would I have had *time* to read anything?" but instead simply shook her head.

'It's Wednesday's Somerden Register. I borrowed it from three doors down. Listen to this:

"Marquis accosted on highway.

The Marquis of Rowbury was nearing Somerden on Sunday evening when his four-in-hand was forcibly brought to a halt by a masked assailant. At the point of a sword, he was then ordered to step out, relieved of his jewellery, and made to part with a substantial volume of cash. The assailant is reported to have been dressed in black, and authorities are investigating whether this brazen daylight attack has any connection to the individual who earlier this year broke Thomas Bateford out of Henningborough gaol. Mr Bateford was sentenced to death in January for the murder of his father Arnold, but walked out through the main entrance just hours before he was due to go to the gallows, and currently remains at large.

A thousand-guinea reward is now being offered for information leading to the capture of this dangerous assailant, who is said to have a thick Scottish accent, and be approximately six feet five inches tall. The Marquis, who owns a number of mines and sawmills across the Midlands, is keen that no lawless individuals should be allowed to derail Somerden's burgeoning prosperity. Indeed he plans to open a sawmill here in town when the final stage of his Thurleigh to Somerden railway is complete. As previously reported in the Register, there have been some delays in laying this line, but it should now be operational towards the end of the year".

What about that then?' exclaimed Cynthia with absorbed reverence. 'They think it's the same man who saved Thomas!'

Bessie did not reply, but simply raised her eyebrows to suggest that she had been rendered momentarily speechless.

'Are you sure you didn't see him?'

'Who?'

'The man!'

'No I didn't. When Thomas came to me, he was all alone.'

'What exactly did he say?' probed Cynthia.

'Not much. He had to leave immediately.'

'Do you think it's the same person?'

'I shouldn't think so. Black is the favoured colour of highwaymen, isn't it?'

'But the paper says that there's a connection, and this man is certainly audacious. The Marquis must be furious to offer such a big reward. Makes you wonder how much was taken.'

'You mustn't let yourself become overexcited,' reminded Marge, and for once Bessie was glad of the intervention.

'I have to go,' she announced, promptly heading for the door.

'Who would you say it is?' pursued Cynthia. 'If you had to guess.'

'How can I *possibly* guess? It could be anybody. In town, out of town, in the next district!' Bessie shrugged as if it was such a ridiculous question. 'I really have to go. I'm running late.' And with that, she escaped.

CHAPTER TWENTY-ONE

Leah stared at the mirror, and the sight staring back was really quite frightful. It was a strong word, but nevertheless accurate, and not at all formulated out of any sense of self-pity. At her best she was not exactly a beauty, did not stand out like Ivy, but at least she could hold her own, and somebody had once said that she had the most perfect Cupid's-bow lips. In this horrid dress, however, she would only be standing out in one very negative sense, and that literally made her want to cry.

Why was Mother so insistent? What did she see in the thing? What could *anybody* see in the thing, and what could be done about it? Nothing. Absolutely nothing. That was the truth of it, and so Leah was forced to concentrate on the only area over which she had any control left – her face. A cup of tea was already to hand, and pressing her lips forward as if taking a sip, she held them there until the pain of the hot china began to penetrate. Yes, they were turning red. Well that was something anyway, although they would struggle to deflect from the frilled collar which appeared to be suffocating her. Oh if only she could take a pair of scissors to it. Now that would do the trick nicely.

As the guilty glory of rebellious thoughts began to grow, she barely heard the knock on her door, and since Robbie never left it very long before intruding, he had entered before there was any chance to respond.

'I never would have believed it, but I swear that Mother has now maintained a grudge for the best part of four months!' He presented himself in a tight grey offering, which might have been "a la mode" for all of a week five years ago, but was certainly not the case any more. 'Although then again . . .' He took one look at Leah, and qualified his conclusion. 'You look worse than I do.'

'I know. I wish I could change.'

'Then why don't you?'

'Because Mother is adamant. She wants me wearing this, and won't hear of anything else.'

'Same with me. Do you think we've done something despicable, and don't even know about it?'

'Probably.' Leah turned away from the mirror, and sank into a heap of misery on the end of the bed. 'I'd really like to wear my pink dress.'

'And I'd really like to be able to breathe. I'm sure this waistcoat is cutting off my circulation. Which – I might add – Father generally advises against.' He tried to stretch out his chest, but failed, and joined Leah on the bed. 'Why pink anyway? I thought you didn't want to attend this evening at all.'

'I didn't, but . . . being as I have to, I think . . . well . . . I don't look too bad in pink.'

'You mean you want to attract somebody's attention?'

'No.'

'Yes you do. Who is it? Not Lester Doubleday by any chance.'

'No!'

'Are you sure?'

'Absolutely!'

'Well I wouldn't sound so indignant if I were you. It's clear that Mother thinks he's a perfect pick, and you wouldn't even have to change the initials on your handkerchiefs.'

'Oh don't Robbie.'

'Who then?'

'Nobody.'

'Please don't lie to me Leah. You're not very good at it. Is he already spoken for, is that it?'

'No.'

'Does he have bad habits?'

'No! None whatsoever.'

'Then why the need for secrecy?'

'I . . . I'm just . . . not sure that he even regards me in that way.'

'Well he isn't going to start regarding you in any way if you go down dressed like that. No matter what you do to your lips.' Robbie pursed his own, trying to figure out an identity for himself, but having great difficulty. Apart from Lester, and Ivy's usual partner, he had no idea who was coming. Mother was being ridiculously enigmatic. 'Don't tell me then,' he concluded gruffly. 'But you *are* going to change.'

'I can't.'

'Yes you can, and I'll join you.'

'But Mother will only send us back upstairs.'

'Then if she does, I'll stop and undress right there in front of her. It will be what she wants after all.'

'Oh no!' Leah put a hand to her mouth in horror, and Robbie stood up quite abruptly.

'Please try not to act as if the sight of my body is worse than walking the plank.' He studied his profile, and came to the conclusion that he actually cut rather a dashing figure, although did wonder whether Elizia would even notice if he ended up stripped down to the buff.

'Do you really think that we can get away with it?' whispered Leah, the first stirrings of hope resurrecting themselves.

'I don't see why not. Let's put it this way – I'm game if you are.' It was meant to be a rallying cry, but he instantly appreciated that his sister was incapable of taking such a plunge. 'I'll rephrase – since I'm doing it, *you're* doing it.' He strode purposefully over to the door. 'And don't you go having any second thoughts while I'm away. I'll be back in fifteen minutes, and I want to see pink. An explosion of pink!'

'You will,' she promised, and set to work even before he had closed the door.

It was actually rather difficult to change without the aid of Abigail, but if you did not care about stretching some stitching here, or tearing a bit of lacing there, then a few sharp tugs soon produced extrication. And within less than ten minutes the job was done.

Once more in front of the mirror, she gazed at the line of roses running along the neckline, down the centre of the bodice, and right around her waist. They were so delicate, so exquisite, so totally beautiful, but the best feature of all was the skirt. It kept on flowing long after she had stopped, rippling gently around her, and making her feel like she was about to be whisked off her feet. She loved it, everything about it, and felt a positive swell of sibling love when Robbie returned and immediately declared:

'Well that's a vast improvement.'

It was a little deflating seconds later to realise that he was referring to his own ability to breathe, but nevertheless she did look better, and needed to have faith in that, without the need for any reassurance.

This rather stern internal order to adopt some self-confidence held strong for all of a minute – until Ivy entered, and put a significant dent in it.

'My, aren't we the picture of radiance,' commented Robbie, and it was no exaggeration. Ivy looked stunning. 'Did Mother tell you to wear that? Or have you broken rank, and picked your own like us?'

'No, this is all Mother's doing. She even had it rushed to the tailors yesterday for last-minute alterations. I can't quite believe it.'

'Neither can I,' returned her brother with a deep frown. 'Although I'm sure you aren't complaining. Not with your gentleman-friend in attendance.'

Ivy gave a contented smirk.

'I wonder why Mother wants you looking so good, and us looking so bad.'

'Probably because she realises that with you there's no hope of anything better.'

'Oh very funny,' sneered Robbie as Kerry knocked to tell them that they were needed downstairs. 'Seriously though, a few minutes ago we were dressed like a couple of frumps, and all on Mother's express instructions.'

'Well you certainly aren't frumpish any more,' observed Ivy coldly. She had elected to have her own hair fixed up – in order to show off the natural beauty-spot otherwise concealed – and did not appreciate seeing that selection now being copied by Leah. 'Why the drink of tea?' she asked, eager to find fault with something.

'I was thirsty.'

'But you haven't touched any of it.'

'Maybe she wanted to play Love Me Not,' suggested Robbie, taking the cup over to the window, and tipping its contents into a flowerpot. The Llewellyns were just arriving, and he wondered for a moment whether husband Llewellyn could be the object of Leah's attentions. Brash and rich, he might well hold a certain charm for a girl of a reserved nature, and despite denying that her love-interest was spoken for, they had not actually covered the issue of already married.

'That's a stupid game,' condemned Ivy, and when Robbie had used the side of one fist to slap tea-leaves onto the back of his other hand, he quickly reached the same conclusion. She Loves Me, She Loves Me Not. It almost always ended up as Not!

'Why do you suddenly look like the cat who's got the cream?' he demanded as Ivy licked her lips.

'Ten in a row. I've had ten in a row!'

'That's only because you tap on the Nots, and smack it down on the Loves. You'll give yourself a bruise.'

'You're only jealous,' she retorted, and he had to concede that she was right.

'What about you Leah?'

His other sister was sitting with a perplexed expression, having produced an exact mix, and wondering what that might mean.

'Who are you thinking about?'

'Nobody in particular.'

'Tell me!' snapped Ivy.

'It's Doubleday of course,' said Robbie. 'You might deny it Leah, but we know that beneath that meek exterior you're a positive flutter of emotion, and all as a result of Lester Doubleday.'

Leah was set to protest to the contrary, but realised that she was being saved from the piercing rigour of an Ivy interrogation. So she held her tongue, and even managed to smile when he embarked on a chant of: 'Leah loves Lester, Leah loves Lester!'

'Ah,' he sighed eventually. 'I shouldn't tease really. You're far too young for these affairs of the heart, whereas you and I Ivy dear – we're very much at risk of being left on the shelf, aren't we? And of course you more than me old maid.'

'There's only a year between us brother dear, and at least I have a chance of improving my prospects tonight, which is more than can be said for you. Unless of course you wish to pursue the delights of dear Nora.'

'Nora! Crikey, I like them young, but not *that* young.'

'Well what about my friend Melinda then?'

'No thanks.'

'Don't you go dismissing her in that sort of tone. She's much too good for the likes of you.' Ivy accompanied her appraisal with the hurling of a pillow in his direction.

'If you say so,' he returned, hurling it straight back.

'It will have to be your wee servant girl then. Do make some progress this evening for pity's sake.'

'Don't you worry. I've got a few more tactics up my sleeve just yet. She may be a tough nut to crack, but she isn't too tough for Robbie Driscoll.'

'Why do you want to crack her?' enquired Leah.

'Never you mind.'

'I think she's nice. In fact I think you ought to leave her alone.'

'Oh go back to fiddling with your hair,' dismissed Ivy, before focusing fervently upon her brother. 'Remember what we talked about . . .'

'There's no need for a lecture. I told you I'm not a quitter.' It was six out of six so far, but all of them combined had not been as much trouble as this seventh one.

'Do tell me if you need any more assistance, and . . .' She now spoke for Robbie's ears only. 'Give me the nod when things reach that critical stage.'

Robbie grinned. 'You're a poisonous one Ivy Driscoll. Sugar and spice, and all things vice, that's what our little Ivy's made of.'

'And don't you just love it?' Their eyes twinkled in unison, before she leaped up and declared: 'Right, let's meet my public.'

'No we can't,' objected Leah immediately.

'Why not?'

'Because we're leaving it until it's too late for Mother to send us back upstairs,' explained Robbie.

'Tough. I want to go now.'

'But there's two of us, and only one of you, so you're outnumbered.'

Ivy stared at Leah, utterly amazed that her own argument was being used against her, and in such a dogmatic fashion.

'Wouldn't you prefer to keep your public waiting for just a little longer?' chipped in Robbie.

'No I wouldn't!' Ivy stamped her foot, before actually giving that idea some thought. The more her partner had to hover, the more he ought to appreciate her when she did appear. 'Alright, I'll wait until Kerry knocks again, but that's all.'

'Can't you make it the third knock? Just to be on the safe side?'

Ivy exhaled air through her nostrils, but ultimately conceded, confident that if Mother had been ignored twice, then the third summons would follow quickly on the heels of the second. 'But not another minute,' she declared sharply. 'At the third call we move. And fast!'

By the time that call came, nine of the thirteen guests had arrived, and one of them had finally just managed to escape the clutches of Millicent in order to pursue a certain disappearing maid. A maid who only in fact became aware of his presence halfway down the back stairs.

'What are you doing here?' she growled.

'Preparing to indulge in a delightful dinner of course.'

'No you aren't. You're following me, aren't you? Come to see how low I've fallen.'

'I'm sorry to burst your inflated sense of self-importance. Not to mention self-pity. But I've known Anthony and his family far longer than I've known you.'

'I don't believe you.'

'Then cast your mind back to the trial. He was sitting right next to me if you recall.'

Bessie proceeded to cast her mind back, and seeing the glimmer of recognition upon her face, Gil added:

'Besides, ever since you dealt with Sylvia so efficiently, I'm now being viewed as somewhat "on the market" again. In fact I've been inundated with more invitations than I know what to do with.'

'I wonder if you'd still be quite so "inundated" were they to discover the true nature of your blackened soul.'

'Whatever do you mean Miss Cullen?'

'It's Scanlon. Elizia Scanlon.'

Gil's eyes opened wide. 'Elizia? You do realise that you'll soon run out of variations, don't you? And tell me – is this your third alias? Or your fourth? I lose track.'

'I think you'd be better employed keeping track of your own affairs. Been holding up any carriages lately?'

'Carriages? What a curious question.'

'It was *you*, wasn't it?'

'Was me what?'

'Accosting the Marquis of Rowbury.'

'The Marquis of Rowbury?' repeated Gil airily. 'Is he in town?'

'You know full well that he is.'

'Do I?'

'Why do it? You're rich. Only desperate people are driven to such things.'

'I'm afraid you'll have to tell me what this "thing" is.'

'Stealing of course, and acting as a highwayman in order to do it.'

'Oh I do think highwayman is such a coarse term.' Gil almost shuddered with the disagreeability of it all. 'I much prefer "Gentleman of the road", and many of them are indeed very gentlemanly. Some have even been known to dance with the lady companions of their victims. Now how refined is that?'

'Refined or otherwise, it's still theft, and you've never pulled your punches about how sinful it is when *I'm* doing it.'

'Yes, but you were caught red-handed, whereas I am merely the victim of an unsubstantiated allegation.'

'Unsubstantiated my foot. The paper says it's the same man who broke Thomas out of gaol, and we both know who that was!'

'But the paper also says that the dastardly individual is six feet and five inches tall,' reminded Gil. 'Whereas I am a mere six one.'

'Yes, but you were six feet five when I chased you all over Somerden! I don't know how you do it, but that costume adds four inches, and we both know it.'

'Pray tell me – why exactly would I wish to accost a nobleman anyway? A peer of the realm no less, and a man set to become an upstanding pillar of our very own community.'

'I don't know. You tell me.'

'Perhaps I was left feeling somewhat short after returning all those hundreds to you. Did you give them to Mr Roscoe by the way?'

'Yes I did.'

'All of it?'

'I wouldn't be working here otherwise, would I?'

'Oh I'm not so sure about that. Maybe you like the uniform.'

'You can be flippant all you like Gil Tremaine, and you can try and change the subject, but this time I'm one step ahead of you because I *know* that you were on that Somerden highway on Sunday evening, and I know . . .'

'Sunday?' he interrupted. 'I think you'll find that I was in Henningborough.'

'Henningborough? I don't believe it.'

'I'm afraid there really isn't much that I can do about your lack of faith on this particular occasion.'

'What were you doing?'

'Minding my own business, as you've so often encouraged me to do.'

'That doesn't answer my question.'

'Why exactly do you need an answer?'

'Because I want to work out who you are. Or rather what you are. Landowner, Chartist, Thief?'

Gil took each in turn. 'Yes, no, and . . . we've already discussed the latter.'

'So you're no longer a Chartist?'

'Correct. They don't know whether they're coming or going.'

'They know exactly where they're going,' defended Bessie. 'Straight to Parliament, to elect ordinary men as members of the House.'

'When you still need income from property worth three hundred pounds a year in order to qualify, I very much doubt it.'

Such a quick and apparently well-informed response put her temporarily on the back foot, and all she could manage in reply was a rather tame reference to the Chartist Petition.

'But what do you do when that petition is thrown out before it's even properly been considered?' countered Gil. 'Carry on as before, and hope for better things in the future? Or increase the stakes a little? Stick with persuasion or take up arms? Moral or physical? This is the thorny little issue on which they have absolutely no hope of resolution.'

'Well it's obvious that you favour physical,' attacked Bessie.

'I certainly don't believe that you can drive a nail with a feather.'

'Maybe you're simply not a believer at all. No longer wish to see us plebs with the vote, but prefer to do things purely for yourself.'

'Perhaps.'

'And perhaps I ought to do the same.'

'In what regard?'

'Report on you. Claim that nice big fat reward for myself.'

Gil grinned. 'You've surprised me in many ways Miss Cullen, but the one thing I know for sure is that you will never betray me.'

'I betrayed you over Sylvia. Right in front of all your swanky guests.'

'Yes, I'll have to grant you that one, but you'll never betray me on anything . . . important.'

'I wouldn't be so sure if I were you. You're clearly a dangerous man. It's my duty to protect other citizens from your . . . nefarious activities.'

'My, you really have swallowed a dictionary of late.'

'And you really are a thief!'

'I am whatever I fancy being at the time, and right now I'm a dinner guest, who is presumably being missed by the many ladies in attendance.'

'You love all that, don't you? Female attention with no intention of ever reciprocating.'

Gil leaned forward. 'Oh I don't know. I might reciprocate one day.'

'No you won't. You like toying with people too much.'

'A player *and* a thief?' He leaned back. 'What a devilish fellow I am. And if you were the subject of debate, what do you think people would call you?'

'A fighter!'

As Gil smiled, folded his arms, and prepared to listen to a fresh declaration of defiance, Robbie entered the drawing room, beaming broadly, and with a sister on each arm.

Unfortunately the beam did not last for very long because Millicent immediately stormed over, took Ivy aside, and demanded an account of Gil's whereabouts.

'I don't know. Hasn't he arrived yet?'

Yes, but he left the room a few minutes ago. I thought he was with you.'

'No, I've only just come down.'

'Then what have you been doing you silly girl?'

Ivy had very much enjoyed her entrance, majestic and yet sultry, but to have it now trampled underfoot, with insults to boot, was really quite aggravating. 'Whatever is the problem Mother?'

'The problem is that you're in danger of wrecking this evening before it's even begun.'

'What? You mean with Gil?'

'Yes!' Millicent issued the word as a high-pitched hiss, convinced that surely the penny would now drop, but it quickly became clear that dropped pennies was not the case. 'You've heard the rumours, haven't you? About Gil?'

'I've heard that Chaloner's now out of the picture.'

'So . . ?'

'So what?'

'So he's in the market for a quick bride!'

'Bride?' frowned Ivy. 'You think . . . no . . . he's not . . . you don't think he's looking towards us?'

'I don't just think it, I know it. When he heard about this party, he had a word with your father before I could even send the footman around with an invitation!'

'You mean he invited himself!'

'Exactly, and there can only be one reason for that.'

'Oh dear God!' Ivy clasped a hand to her mouth as at last they were both singing from the same hymn-sheet.

'Play your cards right girl, and we could have a Tremaine in the family. Now . . .' Millicent was about to say: "Go and get him", but Ivy shot off anyway, leaving her siblings to wonder what on earth that heated discussion had all been about.

Wonder quickly turned to retreat, however, as Millicent stalked over.

'What on earth do you think you're wearing?'

'Clothes by the look of things,' replied Robbie.

'Yes, but not what I selected. You're all wrong. Especially you Leah. You clash dreadfully with Ivy.'

'But she matches so much better with me.'

'Oh do shut up Robert. I want you both to change, this instant, and no dawdling. I'm warning you . . .'

'Good evening,' said a voice, cutting right across the hostess, and for the first time in her life Leah was glad to welcome the arrival of Mr Doubleday.

'Great to see you Lester,' declared Robbie. 'Mother was just saying – she wants the whole world to appreciate how beautiful Leah looks tonight. Don't you agree?'

'Oh yes, one hundred percent. She's absolutely . . . delicious.' Lester had a fondness for using excessive adjectives in entirely the wrong circumstances, and when he had offered up another half dozen, Millicent was forced to abandon any attempt to command her children's attention.

The moment that she moved away, Robbie smirked, and set about tackling the vexed question of Leah. There was no way that she was about to reveal the object of her desires with Lester hanging around. She needed to be left alone, free to send lingering looks in her chosen direction, so he steered the three of them over to a sofa, and as soon as she was down, he whipped Lester away. Leah was left completely on her own, which was not very nice on the face of it, but utterly necessary. If Robbie knew the identity of this mysterious individual, then he could help to ignite the fires of passion. There was no doubt that she would be utterly incapable of it by herself. He was being cruel to be kind. Simple as that. Although he did have to concede that there was a singularly selfish advantage to having Lester by his side – namely in keeping Melinda at bay. She was not an unattractive specimen, and from a good family, but dallied far too much in idle small talk, which he disliked on principle. In fact since he often did things himself which could become the subject of such talk, he found her positively unsettling.

So with Leah alone, and Lester firmly alongside him, everything was arranged to perfection – until Leah went and joined Melinda's brother on the chairs in the far corner. The parents were also in attendance. Mr and Mrs Kendrick. Apparently it was a Gaelic name meaning Son of Henry, so of course they had been particularly inventive and named their own son . . . Henry. A sulky individual in his early teens, the Kendrick son was doing absolutely nothing to mask the fact that he was currently very sulky indeed. Of course from Leah's perspective he was a lost soul in need of friendship, so she went to offer herself up – little realising that she was irritating her own brother into the bargain. But the irritation did not last long, because after two minutes of monosyllabic dialogue, Leah was left just as isolated as before, only now with a companion. Two forlorn individuals banished to the sidelines. "That would make rather a good painting", thought Robbie, while again regretting the fact that he was not more gifted in that regard.

When the Trumbles had arrived, followed by the O'Dwyers, he began to wonder whether the whole of Somerden were due to turn up, and crossed over to Mother to make enquiries. But she blanked him in a most unmaternal manner, forcing him to try his father instead.

'No, I believe that's everybody now,' sighed Anthony, keeping an eye on the number of beverages being consumed, and trying to assess how much damage this evening was likely to inflict in the end.

'What's going on with Mother? She's all of a flap, and it seems to have something to do with Ivy.'

'I don't know.'

'Please Father, don't say that. I've heard it already this evening, and it really is aggravating when so blatantly untrue.'

'Are you calling me a liar Robert?'

'Well . . .' Robbie shrugged as if to say: "If the cap fits".

'You do realise how offensive that is?'

'Oh come on Father, I never offend anybody. I just hate being out of the loop. It drives me to say and do things which are most unacceptable, but I simply can't help myself.'

Anthony fully understood that he was being blackmailed into an explanation, but gave it nonetheless. 'Your mother thinks Gil's on the hunt for a bride, and Ivy is it.'

There was an awful lot of significance in that hastily ushered statement, and it took Robbie a moment to absorb the full impact. 'My God, no wonder she's in a state. Having a Tremaine in the family would be the coup of the century!'

It could also solve a fair few financial concerns, but Anthony refused to view it in such a light. It was for every man to sort out his own affairs, not leech off the generosity of others. 'I doubt anything will come of it,' he concluded negatively.

'Why? Don't you think Ivy's attractive enough?'

'I'm really not in the mood for you Robert. I merely feel that having held out for this long, Gil is most unlikely to rush headlong into a marriage with anybody.'

'It's certainly to be hoped so,' said his son, staring at Leah, and chiding himself for being as thick as two short planks. Of course she was not mooning in any particular direction, because the man of her choice was not yet even in the room! Gil Tremaine. Two sisters in love with the same man. That was bad, very bad, especially as it looked like one sister was hell-bent on nailing down her man.

When Ivy entered, she did not just have her arm liked through Gil's, but was using her free hand to stroke his shoulder, and tipping her head towards him like lovers walking down a lane. "Stamping her mark like a cat against a tree", observed Robbie, while realising that he could not have organised things much better if he had tried. With Leah all solitary, Gil was bound to go across, and it would drive Ivy crazy. Not that he really wished for her to be crazy. She had been his partner-in-crime for many a year now, but with Millicent behind her all guns blazing, he felt it only fair to even things up a bit. Give both sisters an equal shot at the eligible bachelor.

'Good evening Gil,' he declared, sauntering forward, and gathering Lester up along the way.

'Good evening Robbie. Been keeping out of mischief of late?'

'Oh you know me. Pure as the driven snow.'

Gil raised his eyebrows knowingly, before turning to Lester. 'It's Mr Doubleday, isn't it?'

Lester suddenly had the look of a man who was chewing on a wasp. The family name might be spelt Doubleday, but it was pronounced Dubdy, as Tremaine knew full well, and since one snub deserved another, he refused the outstretched hand.

'Well nice to see you anyway,' concluded Gil, and then having exchanged a few words with Anthony, he headed over to formally greet the final Driscoll.

'Good evening Leah. Master Kendrick, could you see to a drink for the young lady? A Bristol-milk I think, and I'll have one too.'

Henry was encouraged to slope off, and when he had done so, Gil took over the vacant seat.

'You look absolutely heavenly this evening. In fact you're making it rather difficult for a man to keep his eyes off you.'

Leah smiled shyly, and fidgeted. For years he had been so easy to talk to, almost as easy as Robbie, but in these last few months everything had changed, and now her words were muddled before they even made it anywhere near her mouth. 'Your land – how is it . . . I mean . . . is everything going well?'

'Yes thank you. More than adequate for my modest requirements,' he replied, and prepared to open up a proper conversation, but Millicent came over – and immediately put a stop to it:

'Go and fetch Gil a drink Leah. He must be parched.'

'But . . .'

'No dallying dear.' Leah was practically hauled up and sent on her way. 'Gil, I was meaning to ask you – do you think you could possibly secure us an invite to Mrs Forrester's next party? I fear that since my husband is so busy, she feels she must overlook us.'

Gil stared apologetically at the departing daughter, and then diplomatically explained that Mrs Forrester arranged the guest list from very far in advance.

He chose not to add that with a son close to becoming addicted to the gaming-tables, it was probably wise to keep him away from the biggest gaming event of the season.

In pursuit of a drink, Leah immediately discovered that Henry had abandoned the quest in favour of sitting once again with a jaded expression. She was sure that she had seen a tray of full glasses only a moment ago, and was about to rebuke him, until failing in the quest herself. Leaving the room, she crossed the hall, went down towards the kitchen, and there found Elizia with tray in hand.

'I was just bringing these up,' announced Bessie, which was a complete lie. She had already *brought* them up – on the orders of the other Driscoll sister – but upon seeing the Llewellyns, she had elected to walk straight back out again. To face not just one blast from the past, but two! What were the odds? She did try to tell herself that it could be worse – if Stewart Munroe were a family friend for instance, but nevertheless delivering refreshments to that room was far too risky. At dinner the guests would be occupied with Kerry and Abigail, and barely notice a third maid depositing items on the sideboard. But until then it was vital to keep her distance, which was why she felt truly grateful when Leah Driscoll offered to take up the tray herself. Now why was the other one not a bit more like that?

Half an hour later, that tray had been polished off, meaning that it was time to eat. The dining room table had been extended to accommodate everybody, and Millicent directed Gil and Ivy to sit on her right-hand side. Opposite them were Brigadier Trumble and his wife. A high-society couple, they were almost on a par with

Gil, and had only attended because of the suggestion that they might be privy to the hottest news Somerden had seen in years. Anthony was left with the Kendrick parents and O'Dwyers at his end, neither of whom he particularly liked, but he was on strict instructions to offer around informal wedding invitations if the occasion should call for it.

Everybody else was somewhere in the middle, and since it seemed necessary to pair off one with another, Nora was put next to Henry. A potentially perfect match for the future. With neither of them willing to speak, there would never be any friction or cause for complaint. Robbie was saddled with Melinda, but it was not too bad since Lester was on his other side, followed by Leah, keeping him close to the action.

On the surface there did not appear to be any action at all, but to a discerning eye the struggles were soon clear to see. Leah was trying everything in her power to avoid looking at Gil, but then the temptation became irresistible, and she would gaze at him – until Ivy did something to send her head back down again. It was almost like Gil and Ivy were the Roman deities, feasting, and Leah the poor mortal desperate to be thrown a crumb or two. "Or perhaps that's overly poetic", thought Robbie, before allowing himself to indulge in the imagery even further, in order to escape the stultifying boredom of Somerden conversation. If it were not the Brigadier regaling them with tales that focused intricately on the finer details of modern warfare, it was Mother recounting her year of affliction. An ankle injury which had spread right up to her hip – and beyond! Even when the topic turned to Robbie himself, it was still tedious in the extreme.

'So do you have any plans to follow in your father's footsteps?' enquired Mrs O'Dwyer.

'I have not yet decided upon my future,' he replied, trying to flash a cheeky glint at his father, but being ignored.

Anthony was well aware that his son could probably be brilliant at something if he put his mind to it, but that day did not appear to be in sight, and it was frankly rather depressing. Equally depressing was the concern he currently felt for his youngest daughter. He had known of her feelings for Gil for a long time now, and had tried to gently coax her away from them. See Gil as a friend – that had been the message, because as a friend he was second to none; but if you were a lady looking for commitment, it was a case of approach with extreme caution.

Despite Ivy being of a much tougher character, Anthony had given her precisely the same advice, but neither had obviously taken a blind bit of notice of him. Indeed some of Ivy's actions were now becoming uncomfortable to watch. Did she really have to cling to Gil in that manner? And go so far as to feed him!

Halfway through the main course, Ivy noticed that Gil had not touched his Sauce Soubise, so scooping some off her plate, she presented it to him.

'Here Gillie, try this. It's absolutely divine.'

He responded with an amused look, upon which she proceeded to spoon it in, and almost render Leah aghast. She could not believe what she was seeing. Not even married couples did things like that in public. It was . . . it was . . . well she was not quite sure of the adjective, but since Gil had no problem with it, she quickly tried to hide all notion of her feelings. "A saintly prude" – that was what Ivy had once called her, and it had stuck. So she turned away, trying to be casual, but then ended up facing her mother, and that was troubling in a very different sense.

'What's going on?' Leah whispered the words in Robbie's direction while dessert was being served.

'What do you mean?'

'Oh Robbie, tell me,' she pleaded, leaning back behind Lester, and although her brother was in two minds, he ultimately said it. The key words:

'Mother thinks Gil might be proposing to Ivy tonight.'

He had to do it. Ignorance irked him, so he could not inflict it upon anybody else, but he quickly began to regret that act of consideration when it looked like the world had just caved in around Leah's head.

Caved was the right word. She had loved Gil for so long, from before she had even really known what it meant, and at first it had been a joyous love. A secret which made her feel warm and full of hope, and that had persisted throughout the years of Sylvia. As time had passed with no developments, and with no sign of any to come, there had been nothing to fear. But recently all that had changed. Suddenly her love had become a nervous love which kept her awake at nights, and made her pensive. Panicky even. Yet even against that backdrop, there had still been some hope. Until now. Until Robbie's simple little statement had ripped it all away. Lost. Forever. To her very own sister.

'I only said *might*,' hissed Robbie, but Leah had descended into a world of her own, and he was planning on leaving there – until he saw her lip quivering, and tried to make the point again, before calling upon Lester for assistance.

Lester was of course more than happy to oblige, but instead of talking to Leah, he touched her – as he so often did. It was only on her hand this time, but from the faraway place that she had slipped to, it was startling, and she jerked.

'I'm sorry,' was her instinctive response, knowing that she had kicked somebody underneath the table.

'Oh was that your foot?' asked Gil.

'Yes, I'm very sorry.'

'No. It was probably my great boats getting in the way.'

The two of them locked eyes for a moment, Leah's desperate, Gil's gentle, but Ivy quickly intervened:

'Don't worry about her. Where there's no sense and all that.' She giggled, and Leah could take it. That cackle was a familiar weapon, but when Gil joined in, it was all too much. If only she had realised that his chuckle was a reflex reaction to Ivy placing her hand upon his lap.

'Make sure that he knows your answer will be yes,' had been Millicent's rasped instruction as they entered dinner, and Ivy was determined to do precisely that.

'Oh for pity's sake, why don't you just put us all out of our misery?' demanded Leah, loud enough for only half the table to hear, but the pricking of their ears was enough to silence the other half.

'What are you talking about?' Millicent shook her head in a flustered manner to convey that she did not actually want an answer.

'I'm talking about this sickening pretence. About the reason why you're sitting there like some expectant hen.'

'Really Leah! I don't know what's come over you. Do be quiet.'

'No I can't be quiet. I've had to sit here and watch those two fawning over each other for the best part of . . .' She checked the clock. '. . . two hours now, and I simply can't take it any more!'

'Leah!' urged Robbie, but she was utterly deaf to him.

'Ivy and Gil are merely enjoying each other's company,' explained Millicent, glancing at the Trumbles. 'And if you can't be more civil, I think you ought to leave the table.'

'You just can't stand to see anybody else being happy,' piped in Ivy, brushing the side of her hand against Gil's cheek as she spoke.

'Oh for God's sake, just leave him alone!' begged Leah, and since Gil was beginning to think exactly the same thing, he promptly removed Ivy's hand from his face, and pushed his chair back a bit.

'What I can't *stand* is to see my sister marrying the man that I love,' she continued, trying to swallow, but finding her mouth too dry. 'Yes, I said love Gil. I've loved you for years, and I don't know why I haven't done something about it before. I should have said something, or perhaps I shouldn't be saying this now, but I'm scared. Scared of living with no hope, of being left with nobody in this life except the likes of Lester.'

'*Excuse* me!' Lester threw down his napkin, and jumped up, waiting for somebody to issue a most profuse apology, but absolutely nothing was forthcoming, so he promptly stomped out.

'Why Mother? Why do you think that only men like him are good enough for me? I'm the one who wanted you back here, when Ivy preferred to keep you fifty miles away, and frankly wasn't afraid to say so. Why is she then so important? Why am I nothing more than a third-class citizen? I know I'm not as pretty as her, but there are other things that matter just as much.'

Millicent slapped both hands down onto the table, seemingly set to deal with this humiliation herself, but instead ordered her husband into action. He responded – eventually – preparing to guide Leah out of the room, except Leah was not about to go anywhere.

'I love you Gil, not for your money, or your land, but for who you are, and I need to know one thing. That's all. Was there ever any chance for me? Could I have done something different to change all this? Could I have ever made you love me?'

Gil pushed his chair back the required extra foot, and now stood up too. 'I'm not exactly sure what's been going on here tonight, but I think it's important to make it perfectly clear that I did not attend with the intention of proposing to anybody.'

'But . . .' Millicent was more shocked than at any point so far.

'But nothing Mrs Driscoll, you were misinformed.'

'So you don't love Ivy?' 'Yes you do, don't you?'

Leah asked the first question, Millicent the second, and Ivy's bottom lip tucked petulantly under her top to stress that she expected the right answer, but all Gil could think about in that instant was that Sylvia had never been as much trouble as this.

'You see – he does!' declared Ivy, interpreting the silence to suit herself, and thrusting it right back into Leah's face. 'So go upstairs like a good little girl, and leave us adults to enjoy the rest of dinner.'

Leah stared at Gil, tears welling up, searching for a reason to stay, but saw only emptiness staring back. There was nothing. Not for her. Seconds later, she ran from the room, but not upstairs like a naughty child. It was the front door which slammed shut.

'Good riddance,' declared Ivy, and Gil wondered how he could have been so blind to that level of spite.

'Don't you think somebody should go after her?' he demanded, really quite aggressively.

'No.'

'Yes,' snapped Robbie, and marched immediately over to the door.

'I'm coming with you,' announced Gil, 'and I won't be coming back.' He stared at Ivy to make his feelings perfectly clear, and then was soon out onto the street – where Bessie was hovering near the junction. Amidst all the tension, Robbie had not even noticed that his father had given her the nod to leave once dessert was served.

'Is everything alright?' she asked. 'I've just seen your sister running past me in tears.'

'Which way?'

'Down there.'

Gil followed the finger, setting off at speed, but Robbie held back. 'I think she might well need a female to talk to. I don't suppose you'd mind awfully . . . tagging along?'

Bessie hesitated. Clearly something major had just erupted, and although it was a bad thought, it would be nice to be diverted by somebody else's problems for a while. Either that or go home. There was no contest.

'Of course I don't mind,' she said, and Robbie literally rubbed his hands with glee.

CHAPTER TWENTY-TWO

By the time he had stopped rubbing, and Bessie had waited for him to retrieve a coat, Gil was long gone. It had not exactly been the warmest of days, and was turning cooler now, but nevertheless a coat was completely unnecessary – as an item of clothing that is. As a delaying tactic it had been absolutely perfect.

'Oh dear, now we have to search for them both,' lamented Robbie with only a moderate attempt at appearing genuine, before generously offering Elizia his coat, which was less than courteously refused.

She was here for one reason and one reason only – to assist somebody in their hour of distress – while also hopefully discovering the cause of that distress. It was tempting to ask outright, but that would be overly intrusive, and no doubt Robert Driscoll would seek to draw some advantage from it. Besides, if his sister were found, then the cause might become readily apparent, so Bessie focused upon searching high and low, in very nook and cranny of every alley off every sidestreet. Unfortunately Somerden had an awful lot of sidestreets, and of course there was always the possibility that Leah might be entering a street just as they were leaving.

As the half-hour mark approached, they were left wondering whether to go any further, or retrace their steps. The former seemed the most logical, but it would take them on towards the outskirts of town, where Robbie was sure that Leah had never been, and the fact that they had not yet encountered Gil suggested that it was easy to miss somebody.

'I know what we need,' declared Bessie suddenly. 'The town wall. It will give us a view of everything.'

Robbie twisted his neck round to have a look. 'But how do we get up there?'

'By taking the tump steps. It's quite straightforward.'

'You've done it before?'

'Yes.'

'Some childish prank?'

'Very childish indeed,' confirmed Bessie ruefully, before taking on the ninety-nine steps with gusto. They were steep, but without the heavy weight of sodden clothes, she was able to ascend easily – which was more than could be said for Robbie. He reached the top with legs aching, ribs hurting, and breathing at a decidedly shallow rate. Bessie did not pass comment, but her opinion was instantly obvious.

'Perhaps if I'd made one or two more beds in my time,' he translated regretfully, before finally summoning the puff to follow her onto the town wall itself.

There was indeed a magnificent view, but to their united disappointment, very little was *on* view. It was rapidly going dark now, and most of Somerden's residents were indoors. Of the few who remained abroad, none were wearing pink. In fact there were no unaccompanied females at all – and no sign of Gil.

'Oh Leah, where are you?' groaned Robbie, partly out of actual concern, but more importantly because women found male anguish rather attractive. Brought out their mothering instinct, although not with Elizia apparently. There was no crumb of comfort on offer, no warm hand of solace extended. She simply kept her back turned away from him, and avidly scanned the scene in front of her.

"I know what'll do it", he thought, and having moved a short distance away, he proceeded to fall off.

There was a ledge below, so he did not fall very far, but it did mean that Elizia's assistance was required in order for him to get back up.

'You should be more careful. You could have done yourself serious injury.'

'Or indeed killed myself,' pointed out Robbie.

'I wouldn't quite go that far.'

'On the contrary, I've just stared death in the face Elizia. You bought me back from the brink. You saved me.'

'You wouldn't have been up here at all if not for me, so if you think you've nearly died, then it's my fault.' She tried to draw her hand back, but he would not let go of it.

'What happened?' he asked. 'To the other one I mean.'

'That is not relevant to our present situation.'

'But it's relevant to you. You have to cope with it day after day, and you do brilliantly. I've watched you, and I just want to understand.'

'Understand what?'

'How it happened?'

'An accident.'

'What sort of an accident?'

'It really doesn't matter.' She managed to extract herself but in the process he caught hold of the other hand, gently cupping the injured palm. It was all designed to melt her in an instant – although much to Robbie's chagrin it had precisely the opposite effect. His soft touch reminded her so vividly of Drew, of how he had kissed that scar, and what she had then done in response. Her whole body literally recoiled.

'We should be looking for your sister.' She snatched her hand back, and promptly descended from the town wall with remarkable speed.

'Hold on a minute.' Robbie clambered down after her. 'Just because we're searching for Leah doesn't mean we can't talk. My sister's whole problem is that she's never talked enough.'

He dropped that last statement into the mix at the very moment of reaching Elizia's side, and then walked on, leaving *her* to do the chasing for a change. This particular maid might be causing him more bother than most, but he knew women, and he knew that she would not be able to resist.

Bessie similarly felt that by now she had a fair understanding of men – not that there was much to understand – and knew exactly what he was thinking. She was therefore determined to resist temptation, and completely ignored the bait for a full street and a half, before it all became too much.

'What do you mean?' she asked casually.

'What do I mean about what?'

'About your sister not talking enough.'

'Oh she bottles it all up, that's all. Until it becomes too big for her to handle, and then she explodes. Like tonight.'

'Explodes.'

'Yes.'

'As . . . in . . ?'

'You don't want to know, believe me.'

But she did want to know, she really did. It took her another street to decide how she could possibly convey that sentiment without showing herself up in a terrible light. Obviously "Please tell me, I'm desperate to know" was no good, so she went for: 'I'm a good listener.'

'Well it's to be hoped that you are,' he retorted gruffly, stopping with hands on his hips. 'Because you certainly aren't a very good talker.'

He now had the advantage, and was determined to make the most of it, but again he misjudged her. She retreated back into herself, muttered something about not meaning to pry, and walked on.

'Alright, alright!' conceded Robbie, bringing her swiftly to another stop. 'You might not want to talk to me, but I want to talk to you, so I'll tell you.' And he proceeded to do just that, hoping that the generosity of his gesture would thaw the ice a bit, but in fact it was the news itself which did that. Long before he had finished, the cold front had been fully swept aside by shock.

'So Mr Tremaine and . . . and Ivy?'

'Oh no, there's never been anything there. Never anything like a proposal anyway. It's all in Ivy's head, and my mother's of course. But Father seems to see it all pretty clearly. Reckons Gil isn't about to give in to any woman any time soon.'

"That's exactly what I think", pondered Bessie. Gil Tremaine ultimately never did anything unless it suited him, and she could not imagine a wife suiting him. 'How long do you think that Leah has felt this way?' she asked, completely abandoning her self-imposed rules, and embracing familiarity.

'Forever probably. Ever since they first met anyway. So I know what I'm talking about when I say that suppressed emotions are seriously bad for your health. She's now in a right state.'

Bessie felt sorry for her, very sorry indeed. Of all the men to fall for, Gil was not a good choice at all. While as for him? She felt no sympathy whatsoever. If at last he was being put on the spot, then it might teach him not to toy with people to such a degree in future.

'I just wish Leah would understand that nobody ever marries for love,' said Robbie. 'Love is always found in places where you never expect it.' Elizia was supposed to draw the relevant inferences, but she was still too preoccupied with Gil.

'What do you think Mr Tremaine is going to do now?'

'I have no idea,' came the dismissive reply, and after two more questions, Robbie decided that he had spent more than enough time on this, and got them moving again – down a street which ought to bring Elizia Scanlon much closer to his side.

'I'm not sure that your sister would have come down here,' she said after a little while.

'Why not?'

'Because it's . . . well . . . rather off the beaten track.' It was not in fact far from Holliston Road, nor of course the Nevin Street Slum, but mentioning either place would provoke far too many questions.

'But that's precisely what Leah will be looking for. Get out of the main squares, into a quieter area. Escape from the glare of society.'

Escape was one thing. This was very much another. 'I really think she would have turned back at this point.'

'Why? Because she'd be scared?'

'Yes.'

'Are *you* scared?'

'I'm not immune to the emotion.'

'Well there's no need. You have me,' declared Robbie reassuringly, and she managed to stop herself from saying that it was entirely because of his presence that she felt so scared.

'Right, I reckon it's about time we started asking if anybody's seen her. What about in here?' He indicated a public house up ahead, and now Bessie was adamant. No way was Leah Driscoll inside such an establishment.

'But she might have been dragged in,' argued Robbie. 'It might be down to us to save her. And anyway my feet are starting to hurt.' He pushed open the door without further ado, and Bessie's worst fears were immediately realised. The place was worse than The King George, and with less people, so it had an even more intimidating feel. Apart from four men playing cards in the corner, there was only the publican in attendance, and all five stared at the new arrivals.

"Take your life in your own hands all ye who enter here" would have been a good sign for the door.

'Ah good evening,' declared Robbie, advancing cheerfully. 'I was wondering whether you might have seen a man by the name of Wallace tonight?'

'Who's asking?'

'A friend.' Robbie turned to Elizia. 'Nothing happens in this town without Wallace knowing about it.'

'What kind of friend?' demanded the publican.

'A good one. I've known him for years.'

There was no response.

'Look – you don't have to be all testy, I'm not a threat. In fact I've been in here before. Lost a packet at that table over there.'

'What's your name?'

'Driscoll. Robbie Driscoll.'

'Never heard of you.'

'No, but Wallace has.'

'Wallace, you say?'

'Yes.' Robbie proceeded to spell out the letters in the hope that it might help.

'Don't know him either.'

'I'm sure that you do.'

'No.'

'Well can you tell me whether you've seen a girl this evening then?'

'Girl?'

'Yes. Average height, skinny, wearing pink.'

'Doesn't ring a bell,' came the reply in the sort of tone suggesting that it would have been the same answer if she had been sitting two feet away.

'Oh come *on* . . .' Robbie was poised to give a full physical description of Wallace, along with a background history if necessary, when one of the card-players stood up. 'Ah,' he declared, switching quickly from frustration to positivity. 'Have you seen her?'

'What did you say the name was again?'

'Robbie.'

'No. Surname.'

'Driscoll.'

'Irish name, isn't it?'

'Er . . . yes . . . originally.'

'Unusual around these parts.'

'I like to think that we're fairly unique.'

'I knew a Driscoll once.'

'Oh yes, Mr . . ?'

'Noolan. Scum he was. Murdering scum.'

'Murdering? Well I'm sure he can't have had anything to do with me.' Robbie suddenly realised that this was going in a decidedly unhealthy direction, and promptly backed towards the door, taking Elizia with him. 'Thank you anyway.'

Unfortunately "Thank you anyway" was not what Mr Noolan wished to hear as he blocked their path.

'Would you mind . . . possibly . . . stepping aside?' Robbie made the request in a perfectly pleasant manner, but it was not well-received.

'Killed my boy he did. Four bleeding girls, and then at last I get myself a boy, and he's dead within days.'

'I'm sorry, but as I say . . . wrong Driscolls.'

'Your father – what does he do?'

'Why does it matter?'

'Tell me.'

'He's a doctor. So you see – we're in the business of saving lives, not taking them.' Robbie accompanied that statement with the very slightest titter, largely because he had no desire to look timid in front of Elizia, but this man was not in the mood for any humour.

'You think it's funny, do you? My boy being dead.'

'No of course not.'

'Then why are you laughing?' Noolan pinned Robbie against the bar, and prepared to growl until he got an answer.

'It's just . . . you're obviously confusing your Driscolls,' explained Robbie, trying to appear in control despite his current position.

'I thought you said that you were unique.'

'I was wrong. We're probably crawling out of the woodwork all over the place.'

'And how many Doctor Driscolls do you think there can be in one town? Because it was a Doctor Driscoll who killed my boy. Bit of a fever, that was all he had, until your father got a hold of him.'

'I'm sure my father did his best.'

'Oh you're sure, are you?' Noolan did not appreciate a show of filial loyalty, and without warning dragged Robbie the entire length of the bar, sending glasses flying in all directions. Then he thrust him against the back wall, and put both hands around his throat. It was a very good fit since his hands were big, and Robbie's throat was quite small.

'What do you reckon eh lads? A son for a son. Sound fair to you?' Noolan turned to his friends, who duly gave their agreement by remaining silent, and then he began to twist.

It had fleetingly crossed Bessie's mind that this was all a ruse, manufactured by Robert in order to show himself up in some manly light. But now the bulging of his eyes put paid to that particular little theory.

'Do something,' she urged the publican, but all he was willing to do was repeat a long-held mantra:

'I don't interfere with my patrons. Never have. Never will.'

'Patrons? You probably don't even know what the word means.' Bessie tried to grab the bottle which he had managed to rescue from the bar, but she was not quick enough. It was behind his back in an instant, and that left her with only one option.

Years ago there might have been a second option of rushing forward unarmed as she had with Arnold on that hill, but it was a long time ago, and she was a very different person. Help was now required, so she picked up the only thing available – a bar-stool – and hit Noolan with it.

It was quite difficult to wield such a thing single-handedly, and at first she feared that she had not made good enough contact with the back of his head. Nothing happened. But then the man slowly crumpled to the floor – taking Robbie with him.

Darting forward, Bessie somehow managed to haul Doctor Driscoll's son out from underneath the substantial-sized aggressor, and practically dragged him towards the door, but before they could exit, Robbie stopped her.

'Choked, and then crushed – that must be some kind of record,' he gasped, before standing up relatively straight, and refusing to skulk out with his tail between his legs. 'I just want to thank you all for the utter generosity of your assistance. I don't think I've ever come across such a group of warm-spirited individuals in all my life, and you must let me know if I can ever return the favour. It's Robbie Driscoll as you know. At your service.' He gave a small bow, but as he did so it became visible through the corner of one eye that the men from the table were getting up – and that Elizia was also fleeing through the door. Those two factors combined were more than enough to send him on his way, and he scuttled off down the street, calling for her to stop. She was not running, but she was walking at a very fast pace, and when he finally caught up with her, he had to pull down on her arm to bring her to a halt.

'If you hadn't noticed, my windpipe is now half the size that it once was, and I haven't got the breath for all this running about.'

'You found plenty of breath for that parting shot though, didn't you?'

'Yes . . . well . . . I think they deserved it.'

He did not receive endorsement.

'Didn't they?'

'What I'm currently thinking is not something you probably wish to hear.'

'But I do. Go on.'

Bessie tried to move away, but he stopped her.

'I said go on.'

'Alright. With respect *sir*, I think that I would have done better to let him ring your neck.'

'*Why?*' Robbie's face held the perfect expression of injured indignation. 'I didn't do anything to his son, and neither did my father.'

'No, but you took us into an establishment which you knew was dangerous, and without any real cause.'

'I was looking for Wallace.'

'Oh yes, Wallace – who knows everybody and everything!'

'He does! And if he'd been in there, he would have helped us.'

'You took me in there because you wanted to frighten me, and got a little more than you bargained for.'

'Now why would I want to do that?'

'I don't know. You tell me.'

'Maybe it's because I wanted to see those eyes of yours wake up for a change.'

'Excuse me?'

'You know what I mean. Oh you work well enough, of course you do, and you're always polite – to a degree, but you're half-dead.'

'I'm . . .' Bessie had no idea what to say to that, except: 'I'm going home.'

'That's your little haven, isn't it? Scurrying off when anything gets interesting.'

'Tonight isn't interesting Mr Driscoll, it's distressing, on many a level, and you should be thinking about your sister.'

'I *am* thinking about her,' retorted Robbie, which was not strictly true. He had stopped thinking about Leah now, bored of all that, and had turned his attentions to Ivy. She deserved an apology. It had been wrong to side with Leah, and now the only thing which could possibly cheer up his big sister would be to partake in the ritual humiliation of maid number seven. Of course that entailed getting this particular maid back into the Driscoll house first – and into the annex – which meant that there was quite some work to do yet.

'It's because I'm thinking about Leah that I know exactly what I'm saying. I know how important it is that we stop talking in riddles, and are open with one another.'

'I came along to search for your sister. That's as open as I intend to be.'

'But you're just as lost. Can't you see that? Something . . . or someone . . . has made you shut down, and that's no way to live your life.'

It was the only way to live in her opinion. It felt like she had been swept along by a huge wave for so long, and the more she had tried to fight it, the bigger it had become. Now she simply wanted to exist, in calm, lifeless seas.

'What are you thinking about?'

'Nothing.'

'Yes you are. Tell me.'

'There's nothing to tell.'

'But there *is* Elizia. I know nothing about you. Your family. Where you're from. Where you worked before you came here.'

'I am here. Surely that is sufficient information.'

'No it isn't.' He stared imploringly, putting on his most perfect puppy-dog expression, and looking forward to the moment when she realised he was less puppy-dog, and more bloodhound.

'I do not wish to speak, and you should respect that,' she declared, as icy as ever.

'Perhaps I would if you hadn't just saved my life. Twice. But that elevates us to a slightly more friendly footing, doesn't it?'

'It means that I have the right to ask you to act more appropriately.'

'What on earth is inappropriate about talking? That's all I want to do, and we *have* to.' He gripped her by the shoulders. 'This is serious Elizia. You've stolen my heart.'

'I've stolen nothing,' she snapped, twisting her shoulders, and this time storming off.

'You have! You've robbed more Robbie of his senses, and I need to know when you're going to give them back!' He caught up with her again, walking alongside, and whichever way she turned, he refused to budge.

She just about tolerated it until they reached the junction, but then she was desperate to turn for home, and could not do it with him hanging about, so she had to declare as rudely as possible: 'I know you're my employer's son, and also somewhat older than me in years, but I really feel compelled to inform you that you very much need to grow up.'

'Now that's what I want to see. Fire!' Robbie's eyes sparkled with joy, and Bessie not only growled, but clenched her fists in irritation.

'Oh Mr Driscoll, will you please stop it?'

'Say it with more force, and I might just believe you.' He grinned, and as he did so, only a couple of streets away, a man was grimacing.

Having covered every place that he would think of, Gil was now devoid of ideas, and responsibility was weighing heavily upon his soul. Leah was a sweet-natured young thing. Not with an agenda like Sylvia or Ivy, but with genuine feelings, and she had genuinely fallen for him. He should have seen it, should have given more consideration towards his conduct. Instead he had been flippant, unthinking, and now that flippancy might have driven her to do something which they would both regret.

'Excuse me,' he said, pouncing forward as two men appeared. 'Have you seen a young woman out this evening? On her own, medium height, mousy-brown hair, probably crying.'

'Yes, like an angel she was. Flitting past. Flitter-flutter, flitter-flutter.'

The man was clearly as drunk as a sow, so Gil looked to the other one who was being leaned upon, and therefore presumably the more sober.

'Yes, we saw somebody a bit like that.'

'Are you sure?'

'Yes. Wearing pink.'

'That's it! Where did you see her?'

'Er . . . Cobb Street I think, heading for the canal.'

'The *old* canal?'

'Mm-hmm.'

'When?'

'Oh . . . about ten minutes ago.'

'Thank you. Thank you very much indeed.' Gil ran off in that direction, and almost called out her name, but then held back for fear that it might work to keep her away. He would no doubt be the last person she now wished to see. Embarrassment would have set in, and she would be wanting to hide. He just hoped to goodness that she had not chosen the canal as her place.

It was fully dark now, and the old canal was an isolated spot at the best of times. Cut off by development and a rerouting of the waterway many years ago, it had been left as something of an oxbow lake, stagnant, gloomy and frankly terrifying in the right light. He could see to the other side, and as he did so, awful questions began to consume him. Like: Would she float? Surely there would be some sign. A shoe left. An item of clothing. He hoped so, and began to convince himself more and more of it as he searched to the east, and then to the west, and saw absolutely nothing that belonged to Leah.

She was a sensible girl, and also a considerate one. Something like this was not in her nature. It would impact too much upon her family. She would not be able to go through with it. But then again, her actions tonight had caused an impact, and she had still gone through with them. Was it simply that he did not wish to plunge himself into the water and find out for sure?

Walking back to Erskine Avenue, he talked to Anthony's butler, but there was nothing to report. Nothing of note anyway. All the guests had gone, and Leah had not returned. He knew that he really ought to speak to Anthony himself, but could not face it at present, so retreated to Carrow Square. Not to give up, or to go to sleep, but to rouse his staff. Reeve would not particularly appreciate being stirred into service at this hour of the night, but together with the footmen, perhaps they could start to go about this in some sort of order.

Heading in through the back entrance, he went down to Reeve's room first of all, expecting to find him all tucked up in bed. Indeed his very last instruction before leaving had been about taking the rest of the evening off, and so it was a surprise to find the room empty. Where had his butler gone? The kitchen perhaps? Yes. Moving on into the cook's hallowed domain, Gil came upon him warming some soup.

'Didn't the cook feed you tonight?'

'Yes sir. She always feeds me well,' replied Reeve. He never reacted to his master's humour, especially when issued in such a weary tone. 'This is for the young lady upstairs.'

'Young lady?'

'Yes. She called a few minutes ago. *Un*accompanied. And asked to speak with you.' Reeve generally tried to keep disdain from his voice, but most often failed. Too many unaccompanied females called at this house, and it really ought to stop. 'I thought that she looked in need of nourishment,' he added.

'Did she give you a name?'

'Miss Driscoll.'

'Which one?'

'She did not provide clarification.'

'What was she wearing?'

'Er . . .' He was about to attempt a description of the style of dress, but Gil narrowed it down:

'What colour?'

'Light purple I would probably say.'

That was close enough.

'The soup is now ready sir. Shall I take it up to her?'

'No, no, I'll do that,' said Gil as Reeve ladled it out. 'You head off back to bed. Thank you for all you've done.'

'She is up in the drawing room.'

'Right.' Gil picked up the bowl, just about remembered a spoon, and approached his drawing room door with more trepidation than he had felt in a very long time. There were not many things which made him nervous, but this was one of them. He really ought to send word to Anthony first, but she must have come here for a reason, and he owed her the chance to speak before anybody else became involved. Yes, best to talk to her privately, although heaven knows what he was going to say.

'I will *not* discuss myself,' said Bessie for the third time as they neared Erskine Avenue. With the search having now become increasingly futile, and utterly unable to shake him off, there had been nothing else for it but to allow Robert Driscoll to escort her back to his home.

'It isn't fair Elizia. You know everything about me' he argued with a pained expression. 'Even down to my vagabond friends. At least that's what Father likes to call them. Just because somebody enjoys a game of cards every so often, it doesn't make them a vagabond, does it?'

Bessie did not answer. She had stopped answering questions like that about ten minutes ago.

'Come on. Let's find out if Leah is back,' he suggested, striding up towards the front door.

'I'll wait outside.'

'Why? You work here. Come on.'

She hovered for a moment, staring down the street in the direction of Arnold's address, and then again refused. 'There is nothing more that I can do anyway. I hope that your sister is well, and that everything turns out for the best.' She concluded matters quickly, and hurried away, while Robbie just as hurriedly sprang after her.

'Stop!' he ordered, barely keeping the anger in that word to an acceptable level, before trying to appear cheerful. But before he could embark on a fresh line of attack, events overtook them both as Luke ran up.

'Where have you been?' he demanded. 'I've been back and forth a dozen times, but nobody's seen you, and they won't let me in.'

'Who won't let you in?'

'That . . . that butler man, and . . . and some woman. You've got to fetch the doctor.'

'Why? What's happened?'

'It's Cynthie. She's having the baby, and Ma says it's not coming right. She's in trouble Bessie. In real trouble.'

'Wait here.' Bessie shot inside the Driscoll's house without hesitation, and found the doctor in his study, waiting for news of Leah. The only reason that he had not given chase himself was because he knew that if his youngest child returned, she would have to face her mother and sister alone, and he did not think that such a situation would be good for her. Not good at all.

'I'm sorry about your daughter,' said Bessie. 'We haven't found her yet, but I need your help with something else.'

'What sort of help?'

'My . . .' she began, but then paused. What term could possibly be used to describe Cynthia? For ease of explanation, she chose sister-in-law. 'My sister-in-law is giving birth, but there are problems. Quite serious problems by the sounds of it.'

'How long has she been in labour?'

'I don't know. It can't be long. She was fine when I left earlier this evening.'

'Is it her first child?'

'No, her second.'

'Is she due?'

Yes. In a matter of days anyway.'

'And have there been any difficulties with the pregnancy?'

'No. No, I don't think so.'

Anthony Driscoll was loading his bag all the time that he was talking, and then instructed Robbie to go around to the home of his assistant Mr Ulric.

'Mr Ulric? Is that really necessary?'

'Just do it Robert.'

'Alright, alright!' Robbie grudgingly moved off. Of all the nuisances. A baby! But it was only a postponement, he would see to that, and in fact it prompted him to make tracks at considerable speed. The sooner this baby was delivered, the sooner he might be able to pick up where things had left off, and at least the evening had provided him with one or two insights. Like the fact that she had a brother who called her Bessie. Presumably the rest of her family did so too, so why Elizia at work? And of course he also now knew where she lived. Eighteen, Nevin Street. That was the address where he and Mr Ulric arrived fifteen minutes later, and the groans of labour could be heard from outside the front door.

'I'll wait here,' said Robbie as the assistant went in. He did not like to witness pain. Not unless he was the one inflicting it of course.

As soon as Mr Ulric was inside, he immediately headed upstairs, where the woman in question was laid out on the bed, half-up, half-down, sweating, crying, and utterly unable to catch her breath. The doctor was trying to examine her, with a host of other people standing around watching.

'Make it stop. Oh God, please make it stop.'

'I need you to keep still, so that I can feel the baby.'

Doctor Driscoll gave his assistant the nod, who then pinned Cynthia to the bed in order for the position of her baby to be established.

'Yes, it's as I thought.' The doctor's sleeves were already pushed up, but now he rolled them up properly. 'I need to turn it.'

'Turn it?' demanded Luke, but instead of receiving more information, he was told to go.

'I must insist that you all leave.'

'No, I'm staying!'

'I need him,' groaned Cynthia, but Doctor Driscoll was not having any of it. He demanded boiling water, and once that was in place, he ordered everybody from the room. Marge, Bessie, Mrs Thorpe from next door, and Mr Prewitt from two doors down who had helped with quite a lot of calving in his day.

'This isn't a cow, it's a woman,' snapped the doctor. 'Now leave!'

He shut the door on them all, and soon afterwards the groans turned to screams. And then the screams became louder, and louder, and louder still.

Gil refused to let Leah utter a word, loud or otherwise, until she had warmed through and consumed some soup. She had no real need to do either, but upon his insistence both requirements had now been satisfied, and it was time for speech to enter the void.

'I had to come,' she explained breathlessly. 'To apologise. I've embarrassed you, and my family. I don't know what came over me.'

He did not say anything, but it was quite obvious what had come over her. The question was what to do about it.

'I have no interest whatsoever in your sister,' he volunteered, hoping that it might help the situation. But guilt had now firmly set in, and far from railing against Ivy, Leah suddenly felt very sad on her behalf.

'Why not? She's beautiful.'

'I suppose so, but I don't think I would make her a suitable husband.' The truth was that nobody amongst Somerden society had presented themselves as a remotely suitable wife, and many had tried over the years, but he did not vocalise that for fear of the effect it might have.

'Is there anybody else who . . . you think . . ?'

'No.'

'But . . . you will marry some day, won't you? I mean . . . everybody has to.'

'Convention would have it, yes, but it isn't actually the law.'

'Don't you *want* to be married?' Her look was so forlorn, and she realised that, so quickly added something else before he was obliged to answer. 'I don't think I'm particularly suitable either.'

'Why do you say that?'

'Because I don't seem to understand. I thought marriage was all about love, but my parents don't love each other, and I doubt they ever did. While as for Lester – he probably came to dinner with some sort of proposal in mind, but that *certainly* had nothing to do with love.'

'You're very young,' said Gil. 'I'm sure it will all make more sense at some point in the future.' The response was meant to be encouraging, but the lack of conviction actually had the opposite effect.

'Ivy will never forgive me. Nor Mother. They'll hate me forever.'

'I'll explain everything to them, don't worry.'

'And say what?'

'Well . . . that your actions had . . . no influence over my intentions.'

'But they won't believe you! They'll think I've ruined their future, and it won't alter the disgrace anyway. I've heaped disgrace upon my family.'

'Not disgrace. A little scandal perhaps. Keep the gossip-mongers busy, but they'll move onto something else in a week or two.'

Leah was not convinced, and even if it did blow over, she knew above all else that her heart would not repair in a week or two. It was selfish to still be thinking about herself, but her body felt like it was set to burst. Here she was, with Gil, all alone. Everything she had ever dreamt about, but yet he still remained a million miles away from her.

'You need a drink,' he announced when she began to look even more shaky. Pouring her a measure of Brandy, he placed it into her hand, and told her to knock it back in one go.

'Aren't you having one?'

'Not really thirsty.' He tapped her hand, encouraging her to tip it towards her mouth, but as soon as the liquid touched her lips, it made them sting, and she flinched.

'What is it?'

'My lips. I burnt them earlier.'

'Oh I'm sorry. Don't drink it if you don't want to.'

'It isn't you Gil. I burnt my lips deliberately when I was getting ready this evening, in the hope that you might notice me.'

The response which sprang to mind was: "Oh my God", but he managed to suppress it.

'You think that I'm a stupid child, don't you?'

'No, of course not.'

'Yes you do. And you should. I deserve the likes of Lester. He's all I'm fit for.'

'Don't say such a thing.'

'But it's true. Some self-inflated nincompoop who uses twenty words where one will do – he's perfect for me. That's what Mother thinks, and she's right.' Leah stood up, took a great swig, nearly choked, and then wobbled slightly on her feet.

'Everything will look a lot brighter in the morning,' assured Gil.

'How?'

'Because you'll have had a rest, and be able to appreciate that this evening might have been . . . a little different than usual, but really nothing much has changed.' He stood up too. 'Come on. I'll take you home.'

'But I don't want to go home. Mother and Ivy will be horrid to me.'

'I'm sure your father wouldn't allow anybody to be horrid to you.'

'He won't be able to stop it. He can never stop anything. It's like he isn't even master in his own house.' She put a hand to her mouth in horror. 'That's an awful thing to say, isn't it? I'm saying awful things about everybody, and I don't mean them.' She took another swig. 'It's just that I was trapped before, and I'll be even more trapped now. I've humiliated Mother in front of the Trumbles, and there's no greater sin than that.'

Gil tried not to grin, but simply could not help it.

'It isn't funny.'

'Isn't it?'

'No!'

'But your mother is one of those women to whom appearance is everything, and family means frankly very little. Isn't it right that such people should fall flat on their faces?'

Leah almost staggered backwards. 'I thought you liked her.'

'Not particularly, but she's Anthony's wife, so I tolerate her.'

'And what about me? Have you only been tolerating me?'

'No. I've very fond of you.'

'Really?'

'Why do you think I've spent half the night trying to find you?'

'You have?'

'Yes. Scouring the streets. Even went down to the old canal because I heard you might be there.'

'I was. I . . .' She crossed over to Gil's drinks' cabinet, and refilled herself. 'You don't mind, do you?'

'Not at all.' He raised his eyebrows in amusement.

'I thought about jumping in.'

'I'm glad you didn't.' He did not wish to have the chill of a second female on his conscience.

'Why are you glad?'

'Because I want you to be alive.' He was deliberately general – as if he wanted to see everybody alive, and well, and happy.

'But *why*? If you aren't interested in my sister, then Mother won't have you in the house ever again. You'll never come across me.'

'I'm sure she'll calm down eventually, and I'll see you around.'

'Where?'

Silence greeted the question.

'You see – you won't! So why does it matter whether I'm dead or alive?' She was trying to push him into saying something affectionate, but nothing was forthcoming. 'Please, tell me what you're thinking.'

'I haven't got a clue what I'm thinking.'

'Yes you do.' She took another swig, her biggest yet, and blurted it out. 'Marry me Gil.'

'What?'

'I want you to marry me.'

He winced. Perhaps a drink had not been such a good idea after all. 'I think maybe you've had enough.'

'This isn't the drink. It's me! I spoke this evening – really *spoke* – for the first time in my life, and then immediately regretted it, but why? I said only what was in my heart, and I might as well do it again. Be hung for a sheep as a lamb – isn't that the way? I'm lost without you Gil. I want to be with you every minute of every day. I can't sleep for thinking about you. I can't eat. I can't imagine a world if you're not in it. *Please* Gil. Please say you'll marry me.'

'But I think I've made it clear that I'm not the marrying kind.'

'Which is exactly why you should marry *me*. Everybody has to go through it eventually – you almost admitted as much yourself – and you've met nobody else that you want, so you'll have to settle for someone, and I'm happy to step into the breach. I really am.'

'Hardly a particularly nice life for you.'

'I don't care.'

'I'm nearly thirty-eight years old Leah. A poor match for a girl of your age, don't you think?'

'I'm older than I look.'

He did not like to comment, but her conduct seemed to suggest otherwise.

'I know that if we marry you'll receive all the criticism. Everybody will think you drove me to act in the way that I did, that you were . . . I don't know . . . playing off one sister against the other, and I was entitled to be upset. You'll be painted as some sort of . . .'

'Scoundrel?' finished Gil. 'Don't worry, I've been called worse today.'

'Really? By whom?'

'It doesn't matter.'

Leah frowned, and then shook her head, trying to get back on track. 'But in return I'll be the best wife that any man could ever ask for. You'll have saved my reputation, secured Mother's forgiveness, and I'll repay that debt every day of my life. I'll cook and clean and wash for you . . .'

'I have staff who do that.'

'Then I'll darn you socks, warm your bed, press your clothes. I'll do anything.'

'You really shouldn't say that to a man. It's most unwise.'

'But I mean it. I'll do whatever you want, whenever you want, and ask for nothing in return. Not even civility. I won't care if you don't even want to look at me. I'll just exist and serve. Your days will be exactly as they are now. I won't interfere with them at all . . .'

'Stop it,' said Gil. 'You're talking crazy now. That's no sort of a life.'

'Yes it is. As long as I can see you, it'll be the most wonderful life imaginable.'

'Please.' He removed the drink from her. 'Don't do this to yourself.'

'I have to. I'll get down on my knees if you want. I love you Gil. I can't live without you. I just can't. I can't!'

'Yes you can.' He eased her up from the low pleading position she had adopted, and then down onto the sofa. 'I'm really no great catch, and you'll see that very clearly in the morning. Come on, I'll take you home.'

'I'm not going home. Not ever!'

'But you can't stay here.'

'Why not? Because it would ruin my reputation? That hardly matters any more.'

'This evening really isn't as bad as you think. But it'll soon be very bad indeed if you don't stop this.'

'Stop? You mean no, don't you? You don't want me. Not on any terms. You can't bear the thought of being with me.'

'It isn't like that at all.'

'Then you *do* want me?'

'I . . .' Oh hell. Where was Sylvia Chaloner when you needed her? He was almost poised to say that he was privately engaged to the widow, but then would have to see it through, and she was the worst marital prospect of the lot.

'What?' pleaded Leah. 'What are you trying to tell me? Can you see how it might work, is that it? Are you willing to give us a chance?'

No, he was not, but how could he say that? How could he possibly crush what had obviously been a long-held dream? He had no idea, but he needed to get out.

'I have to get in there,' gasped Luke, having been up and down the stairs a hundred times, and now hovering halfway.

Mr and Mrs Prewitt were in the front room, taking care of Ella; Mrs Thorpe was in the hallway; Robbie was still outside the door; Bessie was just inside; and Luke and Marge had been at the bottom of the stairs, watching her son, but now moved up towards him.

'Something's wrong, I can feel it.'

The screaming had just stopped, and now there was silence, a dreadful, agonising silence which was too much for Luke to take. He charged in, immediately followed by Marge, but before anybody else could join them, the sound of a baby reached their ears. A baby crying.

'Oh Luke,' cried Cynthia, and Bessie could imagine him clinging to her embrace, but it was the shriek of Marge which stung the most.

'It's a boy. It's a boy!'

Bessie stared through into the front room. Ella was on Mrs Prewitt's lap, happy and contented, but in that moment her aunt felt like weeping for her. The little girl had no idea of it yet, and might not realise the significance of this day for many years, but she had just become utterly unimportant.

With no desire to witness the scene of joy just yet, Bessie was about to join Ella instead, shower her with as much love as possible, but Mr Ulric ran past before she could move. He was carrying something in a bloodied sheet, and for a second Bessie could see that it was a baby. Baby Tommy – with a small birthmark under his right eye.

'What are you doing? Where are you taking him?'

Mr Ulric opened the door and shot out.

'Hey, stop it!' She was about to give chase, but then the doctor appeared, carrying his bag, and himself in apparent pursuit. 'What is it? What's happening?'

'The boy isn't breathing as he should be.'

'What the hell's that supposed to mean? Why did he stop crying like that?' Luke shouted the questions desperately from the top of the stairs.

'I have resources at the surgery which might just be able to help him.'

'Help him with what?'

'Your son's breathing was impeded by the navel-string,' explained Doctor Driscoll quickly. 'I advise you to rejoin your wife at once.'

'No, that's my son, I'm coming.'

Marge was suddenly on the scene. 'Me too.'

'No, stay with Cynthie.' Luke's words were forceful, and then he ran down the stairs and out into the night. Catching up with the doctor's assistant almost immediately, he wanted to chase ahead, but knew that Mr Ulric had to be careful. Painfully careful, and the doctor was so slow too. Old, and ridiculously slow. But at least he kept on moving, which was more than could be said for Bessie.

'You go on, I'll catch up.' She flapped him ahead, and leaned against the wall that they were passing.

'What is it?' asked Robbie. 'Are you alright?'

'Yes, it's nothing. I just . . .'

He did not press her to finish, because frankly he did not care what was wrong with her. What mattered was being here for support. 'Let me help you.' He put an arm around her waist, and as much as she wanted to refuse him, she could not do it – because she really could not walk unaided. It was the nausea, so much nausea, and not for the first time either. Nor the second. It had been the same yesterday, and the day before, and the one before that. No fever, no rash, just an overwhelming sense of wanting to be sick.

Gil was feeling pretty sick himself. Having escaped into his study, he had chosen not to light a lamp, but simply sat down, his private thoughts shrouded by the night. This was the place in which to order them. It had always worked in the past. A cosy den in which clarity of mind came easily, and he certainly needed some clarity now.

Ever since leaving Leah, stupid thoughts had begun to creep forward. Was she actually right? Was she presenting him with an opportunity that he ought to consider on a serious level? He would indeed probably have to marry in the end, so why not now? Why not her? She would be inexpensive, unobtrusive. He would be freed from the attentions of Somerden's money-grubbing females, and their money-grubbing mothers. Free to focus on his other life. Indeed marriage could be something of a protection in that regard. Make him stand out a bit less. Appear more run-of-the-mill. But did he want all that, even if it was just on the surface? He had promised that he would not go down this route until well past the age of forty. Act in haste, repent at leisure – that was not the way in which he wished to live his life, and you had to be a husband to a wife, had to view them in a certain light. How on earth would that ever be possible with a wife like Leah?

And why exactly was he wasting his time with such questions anyway? She would sober up soon, retreat back into her shell, and no more would be said on the matter. He had given her no signals of intent. His only crime had been one of thoughtlessness, but that did not mean he owed her a wedding. If anything, he had given her sister a few hints which she might have been able to cling to, but not Leah, and commitment was simply not in his nature.

'Wedlock.'

He said the word out loud.

'Locks. Chains. Bonds.'

His body did not react well to being trapped, and although it was not something he had suffered for many a year, that physical response still scared him. Reminded him of his father, and the ever-present danger that he might one day turn into him. Although perhaps that was precisely why he should say yes. Because Leah was the one woman who would not suffocate him. Or at least not as long as he kept her away from the drink. She would not try to change him. This would not even really be a marriage at all, more of a simple exchange. She would get what she wanted, and in return he would secure something . . . convenient. Surely that was worthy of consideration?

Finally exiting the study, he crossed the hall, and re-entered his drawing room – not with any sort of resolution in mind, but thinking that perhaps clapping eyes on Leah again might help the cause. He could claim to be in need of a drink, and then retreat once more. A decision was not imminent, no way, but she thought otherwise as she sprang forth and ran up towards him.

'What is it? What are you going to say?' she implored, and he had never before witnessed desperation like it. Was there actually a risk that she might kill herself if he said no? View the canal as suddenly her only option? Or descend into a lifeless, pitiful state? Was this truly his responsibility, despite all those protestations to the contrary? Some sort of punishment for judging Bessie Cullen so harshly in her choice of spouse? And was that indeed the lesson to be learnt here? Walking down the aisle to Arnold had ultimately led to Thomas walking to the gallows. A sobering reflection if ever there was one.

'*Please*. Will you marry me Gil?' Tears were beginning to drop down her cheeks, and little did she realise that back at home there was a young man asking for exactly the same thing. Namely to be put out of his misery.

Luke Cullen was in the Driscolls' dining room, pacing back and forth. Bessie was there too, sitting, and Robbie was watching her from the fireplace.

'Leave the doctor to his work,' had been Mr Ulric's instruction, and so Luke had left it, and left it – until at last the door had opened, and Anthony Driscoll had appeared.

'My son – is he alive? Tell me! Is Tommy alive?'

Anthony swallowed, just as Gil was swallowing at Carrow Square, and almost together in time, they gave their answers. Yes or no. That was all it took. One word each, one syllable each, so quick, so impassive, and yet so palpably laden with ramifications that were now set to be resonating for the rest of their lives.